"You're nuts, Mr. Hammer ... You go blowing off your stack like you been doing and you'll be wearing a D.O.A. tag on your toe."

Women and the Web

Friends and enemies alike warned Mike Hammer to drop his feud with the dread Mafia, the sinister international crime network which spread its slimy web over a taxi dancer, a Central Park psychiatrist, a Yonkers millionaire and his impossibly beautiful sister, an ex-pug and a blonde with hair like snow.

But Mike was thirsting to revenge the murder of a satin-skinned Viking. So, single-handed, he defied police and F.B.I., determined to even his personal score with the head man of the Mafia. Deprived of his gun by the Feds, battling thugs from Manhattan penthouses to the Bowery, maddened by the evil around him, he pits himself against a notorious collection of organized criminals and pursues justice to a slam-bang finish.

SIGNET Thrillers by Mickey Spillane

Kiss Me, Deadly

by
MICKEY SPILLANE

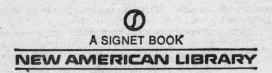

A SIGNET BOOK

NEW AMERICAN LIBRARY

SIGNET TRADEMARK REG. U.S. PAT. OFF. AND FOREIGN COUNTRIES
REGISTERED TRADEMARK—MARCA REGISTRADA
HECHO EN CHICAGO, U.S.A.

SIGNET, SIGNET CLASSIC, MENTOR, PLUME, MERIDIAN AND NAL
BOOKS *are published by New American Library,*
1633 Broadway, New York, New York 10019

36   37   38   39   40   41   42   43   44

PRINTED IN THE UNITED STATES OF AMERICA

Chapter One

ALL I SAW was the dame standing there in the glare of the headlights waving her arms like a huge puppet and the curse I spit out filled the car and my own ears. I wrenched the wheel over, felt the rear end start to slide, brought it out with a splash of power and almost ran up the side of the cliff as the car fishtailed. The brakes bit in, gouging a furrow in the shoulder, then jumped to the pavement and held.

Somehow I had managed a sweeping curve around the babe. For a few seconds she had been living on stolen time because instead of getting out of the way she had tried to stay in the beam of the headlights. I sat there and let myself shake. The butt that had fallen out of my mouth had burned a hole in the leg of my pants and I flipped it out the window. The stink of burned rubber and brake lining hung in the air like smoke and I was thinking of every damn thing I ever wanted to say to a harebrained woman so I could have it ready when I got my hands on her.

That was as far as I got. She was there in the car beside me, the door slammed shut and she said, "Thanks, mister."

Easy, feller, easy. She's a fruitcake. Don't plow her. Not yet. Hold your breath a minute, let it out easy, then maybe bend her over the fender and paddle her tail until she gets some sense in her head. Then boot her the hell out and make her walk the rest of the way home.

I fumbled out another cigarette, but she reached it before I did. For the first time I noticed her hands shaking as hard as mine were. I lit hers, got one out for me and lit that one too. "How stupid can you get?" I said.

She bit the words off. "Pretty stupid."

Behind me the lights of another car were reaching around a curve. Her eyes flicked back momentarily, fear pulling their corners tight. "You going to sit here all night, mister?"

"I don't know what I'm going to do. I'm thinking of throwing you over that cliff over there."

The headlights shone in the car through the rear window, bathed the roadway in light then swept on past. In the second that I had a good look at her she was rigid, her face froz-

7

en expressionlessly. When only the red dot of the taillight showed in front of us she let out her breath and leaned back against the seat.

In a way she was good-looking, but her face was more interesting than pretty. Wide-set eyes, large mouth, tawny hair that spilled onto her shoulders like melted butter. The rest of her was wrapped into a tailored trench coat that was belted around her waist and I remembered her standing there in the road like something conjured up too quickly in a dream. A Viking. A damn-fool crazy Viking dame with holes in her head.

I kicked the stalled engine over, crawled through the gears and held on tight to the wheel until my brain started working right. An accident you don't mind. Those you halfway expect when you're holding seventy on a mountain road. But you don't expect a Viking dame to jump out of the dark at you while you're coming around a turn. I opened the window all the way down and drank in some of the air. "How'd you get up here?"

"What does it look like?"

"Like you got dumped." I looked at her quickly and saw her tongue snake out over her lips. "You picked the wrong guy to go out with."

"I'll know better the next time."

"Pull a trick like that last one and there won't be any next time. You damn near became a painting on the face of that rockslide."

"Thanks for the advice," she said sarcastically, "I'll be more careful."

"I don't give a hoot what you do as long as you don't get strained through my radiator."

She plucked the cigarette from her lips and blew a stream of smoke at the windshield. "Look, I'm grateful for the ride. I'm sorry I scared hell out of you. But if you don't mind just shut up and take me somewhere or let me out."

My mouth pulled back in a grin. A dame with nerve like that sure could've made a mess out of a guy before he gave her the boot. "Okay, girl," I said, "now it's my turn to be sorry. It's a hell of a place for anybody to be stranded and I guess I would have done the same thing. Almost. Where do you want to go?"

"Where're you going?"

"New York."

"All right, I'll go there."

"It's a big city, kid. Name the spot and I'll take you there."

Her eyes got cold. The frozen expression came back in her face. "Make it a subway station. The first one you come to will do."

Her tone wiped my grin away. I eased the car around another turn and settled down to a straightway, jamming hard on the gas. "Damn rape-happy dame. You think all guys are the same?"

"I . . ."

"Shut up."

I could feel her watching me. I knew when she dropped her eyes in her lap and knew when she looked back at me again. She started to say something and closed her mouth over the words. She turned to stare out of the window into the blackness of the night and one hand wiped her eyes. Let her bawl. Maybe she'd learn how to be a little polite.

Another car was coming up behind us. She saw it first and pressed back into the seat until it was past. It went on down the long incline ahead of us until its taillight merged and disappeared into the maze of neons that were part of the town below.

The tires whined on a turn and the force of it made her lean across the seat until our shoulders touched. She pulled away at the contact, braced herself until the car rocked back to level and edged into the corner. I looked at her, but she was staring out of the window, her face still cold.

I slowed to fifty coming into the town, then to thirty-five and held it. The sign along the road said HANAFIELD, POP. 3600, SPEED LIMIT 25. A quarter mile up the highway a flashing red light winked in our direction and I got on the brakes. There was a police car in the middle of the road and two uniformed cops stood alongside it checking the cars as they came by. The car that had passed us further back was just getting the okay to go on through and the flashlight was waving at me to make a full stop.

Trouble. Like the smoke over a cake of dry ice. You can't smell it but you can see it and watch it boil and seep around things and know that soon something's going to crack and shatter under the force of the horrible contraction. I looked at the dame and she was stiffly immobile, her lips held so tight her teeth showed, a scream held in her throat ready to let go.

I leaned out the car before I reached the cop and took the

9

beam of his flash in the face before he lowered it. "Trouble, officer?"

His hat was pushed back on his head and a cigarette drooped from his mouth. The gun he wore hung cowboy style and for effect he draped his hand on its butt. "Where'd you come from, bud?"

A real cop, this guy. I wondered how much he paid for his appointment. "Coming down from Albany, officer. What's up?"

"See anybody along the road? Anybody hitchhiking?"

I felt her hand close over mine before I answered him. It closed and squeezed with a sudden warmth and urgency and in a quick movement she had taken my hand in hers and slid it under the trench coat and I felt the bare flesh of her thigh there, smooth and round, and when my fingers stiffened at the touch she thought I was hesitating and with a fluid motion moved her grip up my forearm and pulled my hand against her body where there was no doubting her meaning, then amplified it by squeezing her legs together gently to keep it there.

I said, "Not a thing, officer. My wife or me have been awake all the way and if anybody was there we sure would know about it. Maybe they came on ahead."

"Nobody came ahead, bud."

"Who were you looking for?"

"A dame. She escaped from some sanitarium upstate and hitched a ride down to a diner with a truck. When they started broadcasting a description she beat it outside and disappeared."

"Say, that's pretty serious. I wouldn't want to be the guy who picks her up. Is she dangerous?"

"All loonies are dangerous."

"What does she look like?"

"Tall blonde. That's about all we got on her. Nobody seems to remember what she was wearing."

"Oh. Well, okay for me to go?"

"Yeah, go on, beat it."

He walked back to the patrol car and I let out the clutch. I took my hand away slowly, keeping my eyes on the road. The town went by in a hurry, and on the other side I stepped on it again.

This time her hand crept up my arm and she slid across the seat until she was beside me. I said, "Get back where you came from sister. You didn't have to pull a stunt like that."

"I meant it."

"Thanks. It just wasn't necessary."

"You don't have to drop me at a subway station if you don't want to."

"I want to."

Her foot nudged mine off the gas pedal and the car lost headway. "Look," she said, and I turned my head. She had the coat wide open and was smiling at me. The coat, that's all, all the rest was sleekly naked. A Viking in satin skin. An invitation to explore the curves and valleys that lay nestled in the shadows and moved with her breathing. She squirmed in the seat and her legs made a beautifully obscene gesture and she smiled again.

She was familiar then. Not so much the person, but the smile. It was a forced, professional smile that looks warm as fire and really isn't anything at all. I reached over and flipped the coat closed. "You'll get cold," I said.

The smile twisted crookedly on her mouth. "Or is it that you're afraid because you think I'm not quite sane?"

"That doesn't bother me. Now shut up."

"No. Why didn't you tell him then?"

"Once when I was a kid I saw a dogcatcher about to net a dog. I kicked him in the shins, grabbed the pup and ran. The damn mutt bit me and got away, but I was still glad I did it."

"I see. But you believed what the man said."

"Anybody who jumps in front of a car isn't too bright. Now shut up."

The smile twisted a little more as if it weren't being forced. I looked at her, grinned at what had happened and shook my head. "I sure get some dillies," I said.

"What?"

"Nothing." I pulled the car off the road into the dull glare of the service-station sign and coasted up to the pumps. A guy came out of the building wiping his eyes and I told him to fill it up. I had to get out to unlock the gas cap and I heard the door open, then slam shut. The blonde went up to the building, walked inside and didn't come back until I was counting the money into the guy's hand.

When she got back in the car there was something there that hadn't been there before. Her face had softened and the frost had thawed until she seemed almost relaxed. Another car came by as we rolled off the gravel to the road only this time she didn't pay any attention to it at all. The coat was

11

belted again, the flicker of a smile she gave me was real, and she put her head back against the seat and closed her eyes.

I didn't get it at all. All I knew was that when I hit the city I was going to pull up to the first subway station I saw, open the door, say good-by, then check on the papers until I found where somebody had put her back on the shelf again. I thought that. I wished I could mean it. All I felt was the trouble like the smoke over dry ice and it was seeping all over me.

For five minutes she sat and watched the edge of the road, then said, "Cigarette?" I shook one into her hand and shoved the dashboard lighter in. When it was lit she dragged in deeply and watched the gray haze swirl off the windows. "Are you wondering what it's all about?" she asked me.

"Not particularly."

"I was . . ." she hesitated, "in a sanitarium." The second pull on the butt nearly dragged the lit end down to her fingers. "They forced me to go there. They took away my clothes to make me stay there."

I nodded as if I understood.

She shook her head slowly, getting the meaning of my gesture. "Maybe I'll find somebody who will understand. I thought maybe . . . you would."

I went to say something. It never came out. The moon that had been hidden behind the clouds came out long enough to bathe the earth in a quick shower of pale yellow light that threw startlingly long shadows across the road and among those dark fingers was one that seemed darker still and moved with a series of jerks and a roar of sound that evolved into a dark sedan cutting in front of us. For the second time I heard the scream of tires on pavement and with it another scream not from the tires as metal tore into metal with a nasty tearing sound as splintering glass made little incongruous musical high lights above it all.

I kicked the door open and came out of the car in time to see the men piling out of the sedan. The trouble was all around us and you couldn't walk away from it. But I didn't expect it to be as bad as that. The gun in the guy's hand spit out a tongue of flame that lanced into the night and the bullet's banshee scream matched the one that was still going on behind me.

He never got another shot out because my fist split his face open. I went into the one behind him as something hissed through the air behind my head then hissed again and

12

thudded against my shoulders. My arm went on that one and I spun around to get him with my foot. It was just a little too late. There was another hiss of something whipping through the air and whatever it was, it caught me across the forehead and for a second before all time and distance went I thought I was going to be sick and the hate for those bastards oozed out of my skin like sweat.

I didn't lie there for long. The pain that pounded across my head was too sharp, too damn deep. It was a hard, biting pain that burst in my ears with every heartbeat, sending a blinding white light flashing into my eyes even though they were squeezed shut.

In back of it all was the muffled screaming, the choked-off sobs, the cadence of harsh, angry voices biting out words that were indistinguishable at first. The motor of a car chewed into the sounds and there was more jangling of metal against metal. I tried to get up, but it was only my mind that could move. The rest of me was limp and dead. When the sense of movement did happen it wasn't by command but because arms had me around the waist and my feet and hands scraped cold concrete. Somewhere during those seconds the screaming had been chopped off, the voices had ceased and a certain pattern of action had begun to form.

You don't think at a time like that. You try to remember first, to collect events that led up to the end, to get things relatively assorted in their proper places so you can look at and study them with a bewildered sort of wonder that is saturated with pain, to find a beginning and an end. But nothing makes sense, all you feel is a madness and hate that rises and grows into a terrible frenzy that even wipes out the pain and you want to kill something so bad your brain is on fire. Then you realize that you can't even do that and the fire explodes into consciousness because of it and you can see once more.

They had left me on the floor. There were my feet and my hands, immobile lumps jutting in front of my body. The backs of the hands and the sleeves were red and sticky. The taste of the stickiness was in my mouth too. Something moved and a pair of shoes shuffled into sight so I knew I wasn't alone. The floor in front of my feet stretched out into other shoes and the lower halves of legs. Shiny shoes marred with a film of dust. One with a jagged scratch across the toe. Four separate pairs of feet all pointing toward the same

13

direction and when my eyes followed them I saw her in the chair and saw what they were doing to her.

She had no coat on now and her skin had an unholy whiteness about it, splotched with deeper colors. She was sprawled in the chair, her mouth making uncontrollable mewing sounds. The hand with the pliers did something horrible to her and the mouth opened without screaming.

A voice said, "Enough. That's enough."

"She can still talk," the other one answered.

"No, she's past it. I've seen it happen before. We were silly to go this far, but we had no choice."

"Listen . . ."

"I'll give the orders. You listen."

The feet moved back a little. "All right, go ahead. But so far we don't know any more than we did before."

"That's satisfactory. What we do know is still more than anyone else. There are other ways and at least she won't be talking to the wrong ones. She'll have to go now. Everything is ready?"

"Yeah." It was a disgusted acknowledgment. "The guy too?"

"Naturally. Take them out to the road."

"It's a shame to dress her."

"You pig. Do what you're told. You two, help carry them out. We've spent enough time on this operation."

I could feel my mouth working to get some words out. Every filthy name I could think of for them was stuck in my throat. I couldn't even raise my eyes above their knees to see their faces and all I could do was hear them, hear everything they said and keep the sound of their voices spilling over in my ears so that when I heard them again I wouldn't need to look at their faces to know I was killing the right ones. The bastards, the dirty lousy bastards!

Hands went under my knees and shoulders and for a second I thought I would see what I wanted to see, but the hate inside me sent the blood beating to my head bringing back the pain and it was like a black curtain being pulled closed across my mind. Once it drew back hesitatingly and I saw my car on the side of the road, the rear end lifted with a jack and red flares set in front and in back of it.

Clever, I thought. Very clever of them. If anybody passed they'd see a car in trouble with warning signals properly placed and the driver obviously gone into town for help. Nobody would stop to investigate. Then the thought passed into the darkness as quickly as it came.

It was like a sleep that you awaken from because you had been sleeping cramped up. It was a forced awakening that hurts and you hear yourself groan as you try to straighten out. *Then suddenly there's an immediate sharpness to the awakening as you realize that it hadn't been a bad dream after all, but something alive and terrifying instead.*

She was there beside me in the car, the open coat framing her nakedness. Her head lolled against the window, the eyes staring sightlessly at the ceiling. She jerked and fell against me.

But not because she was alive! The car was moving ahead as something rammed into the rear of it!

Somehow I got myself up, looked over the wheel into the splash of light ahead of me and saw the edge of the cliff short feet away and even as I reached for the door the wheels went over the edge through the ready-made gap in the retaining wall and the nose dipped down into an incredible void.

Chapter Two

"Mike . . ."

I turned my head toward the sound. The motion brought a wave of silent thunder with it like the surf crashing on a beach. I heard my name again, a little clearer this time.

"Mike . . ."

My eyes opened. The light hurt, but I kept them open. For a minute she was just a dark blur, then the fuzzy edges went away and the blue became beautiful. "Hello, kitten," I said.

Velda's mouth parted in a slow smile that had all the happiness in the world wrapped up in it. "Glad to see you back, Mike."

"It's . . . good to be back. I'm surprised . . . I got here."

"So are a lot of people."

"I . . ."

"Don't talk. The doctor said to keep you quiet if you woke up. Otherwise he'd chase me away."

I tried to grin at her and she dropped her hand over mine. It was warm and soft with a gentle pressure that said everything was okay. I held it for a long time and if she took it

15

away I never knew about it because when I awoke again it was still there.

The doctor was an efficient little man who poked and prodded with stiff fingers while he watched the expression on my face. He seemed to reel off yards of tape and gauze to dress me in and went away looking satisfied as though he had made me to start with.

Before he closed the door he turned around, glanced at his watch and said, "Thirty minutes, miss. I want him to sleep again."

Velda nodded and squeezed my hand. "Feel better?"

"Somewhat."

"Pat's outside. Shall I ask him to come in?"

". . . Yeah."

She got up and went to the door. I heard her speak to somebody, then there he was grinning at me foolishly, shaking his head while he looked me over.

"Like my outfit?" I said.

"Great. On you white looks good. Three days ago I was figuring I'd have to finance a new tux to bury the corpse in."

Nice guy, Pat. A swell cop, but he was getting one hell of a sense of humor. When his words sunk in I felt my forehead wrinkling under the turban. "Three days?"

He nodded and draped himself in the big chair beside the bed. "You got it Monday. This is Thursday."

"Brother!"

"I know what you mean."

He glanced at Velda. A quick look that had something behind it I didn't get. She bit her lip, her teeth glistening against the magenta ripeness of her mouth, then nodded in assent.

Pat said, "Can you remember what happened, Mike?"

I knew the tone. He tried to cover it but he didn't make out. It was the soft trouble tone, falsely light yet direct and insistent. He knew I had caught it and his eyes dropped while he fiddled with his coat. "I remember."

"Care to tell me about it?"

"Why?"

This time he tried to look surprised. That didn't work either. "No reason."

"I had an accident, that's all."

"That's all?"

I got the grin out again and turned it on Velda. She was

16

worried, but not too worried to smile back. "Maybe you can tell me what's cooking, kid. He won't."

"I'll let Pat tell you. He's been pretty obscure with me too."

"It's your ball, Pat," I said.

He stared at me a minute, then: "Right now I wish you weren't so sick. I'm the cop and you're the one who's supposed to answer questions."

"Sure, but I'm standing on my constitutional rights. It's very legal. Go ahead."

"All right, just keep your voice down or that medic will be hustling me out of here. If we weren't buddies I couldn't get within a mile of you with that watchdog around."

"What's the pitch?"

"You're not to be questioned . . . yet."

"Who wants to question me?"

"Among other law enforcement agencies, some government men. That accident of yours occurred in New York State, but right now you happen to be just over the state line in a Jersey hospital. The New York State Troopers will be looking forward to seeing you, plus some county cops from upstate a ways."

"I think I'll stay in Jersey a while."

"Those government men don't care what state you're in."

And there was that tone again.

"Suppose you explain," I said.

I watched the play of expression across his face to see what he was trying to hide. He looked down at his fingers and pared his nails absently. "You were lucky to get out of the car alive. The door sprung when it hit the side of the drop and you were thrown clear. They found you wrapped around some bushes. If the car hadn't sprayed the place with burning gas you might still be there. Fortunately, it attracted some motorists who went down to see what happened. Not much was left of the car at all."

"There was a dame in there," I told him.

"I'm coming to that." His head came up and his eyes searched my face. "She was dead. She's been identified."

"As an escapee from a sanitarium," I finished.

It didn't catch him a bit off base. "Those county cops were pretty sore about it when they found out. Why did you pass them up?"

"I didn't like their attitude."

He nodded as if that explained it. Hell, it did.

17

"You better start thinking before you pull stunts like that, Mike."

"Why?"

"The woman didn't die in the crash."

"I figured as much."

Maybe I shouldn't have been so calm about it. His lips got tight all of a sudden and the fingernails he had been tending disappeared into balled-up fists. "Damn it, Mike, what are you into? Do you realize what kind of a mess you've been fooling around with?"

"No. I'm waiting for you to tell me."

"That woman was under surveillance by the feds. She was part of something big that I don't know about myself and she was committed to the institution to recover so she could do some tall talking to a closed session of Congress. There was a police guard outside her door and on the grounds of the place. Right now the Washington boys are hopping and it looks like the finger is pointed at you. As far as they're concerned you got her out of there and knocked her off."

I lay there and looked at the ceiling. A crack in the plaster zigzagged across the room and disappeared under the molding. "What do *you* think, Pat?"

"I'm waiting to hear you say it."

"I already said it."

"An accident?" His smile was too damn sarcastic. "It was an accident to have a practically naked woman in your car? It was an accident to lie your way through a police roadblock? It was an accident to have her dead before your car went through the wall? You'll have to do better than that, pal. I know you too well. If accidents happen they go the way you want them to."

"It was an accident."

"Mike, look . . . you can call it what you like. I'm a cop and I'm in a position to help you out if there's trouble, but if you don't square away with me I'm not going to do a thing. When those Federal boys move in you're going to have to do better than that accident story."

Velda moved her hand up to my chin and turned my head so she could look at me. "It's big, Mike," she said. "Can you fill in the details?" She was so completely serious it was almost funny. I felt like kissing the tip of her nose and sending her out to play, but her eyes were pleading with me.

I said, "It was an accident. I picked her up on the way down from Albany. I don't know a thing about her, but she seemed like a nervy kid in a jam and I didn't like the snotty way that cop acted when he stopped the car. So I went on through. We got down maybe ten miles when a sedan pulled out from the side of the road and nudged me to a stop. Now here's the part you won't believe. I got out sore as hell and somebody took a shot at me. It missed, but I got sapped and sapped so beautifully I never came completely out of it. I don't know where the hell they took us, but wherever it was they tried to force something out of the dame. She never came across. Those lads were anxious to get rid of her and me too so they piled us in the car and gave it a shove over the cliff."

"Who are they?" Pat asked.

"Damned if I know. Five or six guys."

"Can you identify them?"

"Not by their faces. Maybe if I heard them speak."

I didn't mean maybe at all. I could still hear every syllable they spoke and those voices would talk in my mind until I died. Or they did.

The silence was pretty deep. The puzzle was on Velda's face. "Is that all?" she asked me.

Pat spoke out of the stillness, his voice soft again. "That's all he's going to tell anybody." He got up and stood by the bed. "If that's the way you want it, I'll play along. I hope like hell you're telling me the truth."

"But you're afraid I'm not, is that it?"

"Uh-huh. I'll check on it. I can still see some holes in it."

"For instance?"

"The gap in the guard rail. No slow-moving car did that. It was a fresh break, too."

"Then they did it with their car purposely."

"Maybe. Where was your heap while they were working the woman over?"

"Nicely parked off the road with a jack under it and flares set out."

"Clever thought."

"I thought so too," I said.

"Who could ever find anybody who noticed the flares? They'd just breeze right on by."

"That's right."

Pat hesitated, glanced at Velda, then back to me again. "You're going to stick with that story?"

"What else?"

"Okay, I'll check on it. I hope you aren't making any mistakes. Good night now. Take it easy." He started to the door.

I said, "I'll do my own checking when I'm up, Pat."

He stopped with his hand on the knob. "Don't keep asking for trouble, kid. You have enough right now."

"I don't like to get sapped and tossed over a cliff."

"Mike . . ."

"See you around, Pat." He shot me a wry grin and left. I picked up Velda's hand and looked at her watch. "You have five minutes left out of the thirty. How do you want to spend it?"

The seriousness washed away all at once. She was a big, luscious woman smiling at me with a mouth that was only inches away and coming closer each second. Velda. Tall, with hair like midnight. Beautiful, so it hurt to look at her.

Her hands were soft on my face and her mouth a hot, hungry thing that tried to drink me down. Even through the covers I could feel the firm pressure of her breasts, live things that caressed me of their own accord. She took her mouth away reluctantly so I could kiss her neck and run my lips across her shoulders.

"I love you, Mike," she said. "I love everything about you even when you're all fouled up with trouble." She traced a path down my cheek with her finger. "Now what do you want me to do?"

"Get your nose to the ground, kitten," I told her. "Find out what the hell this is all about. Take a check on that sanitarium and get a line into Washington if you can."

"That won't be easy."

"They can't keep secrets in the Capitol, baby. There will be rumors."

"And what will you do?"

"Try to make those feds believe that accident yarn."

Her eyes widened a little. "You mean . . . it didn't happen that way?"

"Uh-uh. I mean it did. It's just that nobody's going to believe it."

I patted her hand and she straightened up from the bed. I watched her walk toward the door, taking in every feline motion of her body. There was something lithe and animal-like in the way she swung her hips, a jungle tautness to her shoulders. Cleopatra might have had it. Josephine might have had it. But they never had it like she had it.

I said, "Velda . . ." and she turned around, knowing damn well what I was going to say. "Show me your legs."

20

She grinned impishly, her eyes dancing, standing in a pose no calendar artist could duplicate. She was a Circe, a lusty temptress, a piece of living staturary on display, that only one guy would be able to see. The hem of the dress came up quickly, letting the roundness under the nylon evolve into a magical symmetry, then the nylon ended in the quick whiteness of her thigh and I said, "Enough, kitten. Quit it."

Before I could say anything else she laughed down deep, threw me a kiss and grinned, "Now you know how Ulysses felt."

Now I knew. The guy was a sucker. He should have jumped ship.

Chapter Three

IT WAS MONDAY AGAIN, a rainy, dreary Monday that was a huge wet muffler draped over the land. I watched it through the window and felt the taste of it in my mouth. The door opened and the doctor said, "Ready?"

I turned away from the window and squashed out the cigarette. "Yeah. Are they waiting for me downstairs?"

His tongue showed pink through his lips for a moment and he nodded. "I'm afraid so."

I picked my hat up from the chair and walked across the room. "Thanks for keeping them off my back so long, doc."

"It was a necessary thing. You had quite a blow, young man. There still may be complications." He held the door open for me, waved toward the elevator down the hall and waited silently beside me for it to crawl up to the floor. He took his place beside me on the way down, once letting his eyes edge over so he could watch me.

We got out in the lobby, shook hands briefly and I went to the cashier's window. She checked my name, told me everything had been paid for by my secretary, then handed me a receipted bill.

When I turned around they were all standing there politely, hats in their hands. Young guys with old eyes. Sharp. Junior executive types. Maybe you could pick them out of a crowd but most likely you couldn't. No gun bulges under the suit jackets, no high-top shoes with arch supports. Not too fat, not too lean. Faces you wouldn't want to lie past. Junior executives all right, but in J. Edgar Hoover's organization.

The tall guy in the blue pin stripe said, "Our car is out front, Mr. Hammer." I fell in beside him with the others bringing up on the flank and went out to get driven home. We took the Lincoln Tunnel across into New York, cut east on Forty-first then took Ninth Avenue downtown to the modern gray building they used for operational headquarters.

They were real nice, those boys. They took my hat and coat, shoved up a chair for me to sit in, asked if I felt well enough to talk and when I told them sure, suggested that maybe I'd like a lawyer present.

I grinned at that one. "Nope, just ask questions and I'll do what I can to answer them. But thanks anyway."

The tall one nodded and looked over my head at someone else. "Bring in the file," he said. In back of me a door opened and closed. He leaned forward on the desk, his fingers laced together. "Now, Mr. Hammer, we'll get down to cases. You're completely aware of the situation?"

"I'm aware that no situation exists," I said bluntly.

"Really?"

I said, "Look, friend. You may be the F.B.I. and I may be up to my ears in something you're interested in, but let's get something straight. I don't get bluffed. Not even by the feds. I came here of my own free will. I'm fairly well acquainted with the law. The reason I didn't squawk about coming down here was because I wanted to get straightened out all the way around and quick because I have things to do when I leave and I don't want any cops tagging me around. That much understood?"

He didn't answer me right away. The door opened and closed again and a hand passed a folder over my shoulder. He took it, flipped it open and glanced through it. But he wasn't reading it. He knew the damn thing by heart. "It says here you're pretty tough, Mr. Hammer."

"Some people seem to think so."

"Several close brushes with the law, I notice."

"Notice the result."

"I have. I imagine your license can be waivered if we want to press the issue."

I dragged out my deck of Luckies and flipped one loose. "I said I'd cooperate. You can quit trying to bluff me."

His eyes came over the edge of the folder. "We're not bluffing. The police in upstate New York want you. Would you sooner talk to them?"

It was getting a little tiresome. "If you want. They can't do anything more than talk either."

"You ran a roadblock."

"Wrong, chum, I stopped for it."

"But you did lie to the officer who questioned you?"

"Certainly. Hell, I wasn't under oath. If he had any sense he would have looked at the dame and questioned her." I let the smoke drift out of my mouth toward the ceiling.

"The dead woman in your car . . ."

"You're getting lame," I said. "You know damn well I didn't kill her."

His smile was a lazy thing. "How do we know?"

"Because I didn't. I don't know how she died, but if she was shot you've already checked my apartment and found my gun there. You've already taken a paraffin test on me and it came out negative. If she was choked the marks on her neck didn't match the spread of my hands. If she was stabbed . . ."

"Her skull was crushed by a blunt instrument," he put in quietly.

And I said just as quietly, "It matched the indentation in my own skull then and you know it."

If I thought he was going to get sore I was wrong. He twisted his smile in a little deeper and leaned back in the chair with his head cradled in his hands. Behind me someone coughed to cover up a laugh.

"Okay, Mr. Hammer, you seem to know everything. Sometimes we can break even the tough ones down without much trouble. We did all the things you mentioned before you regained consciousness. Were you guessing?"

I shook my head. "Hell, no. I don't underestimate cops. I've made a pretty good living in the racket myself. Now if there's anything you'd really like to know I'd be glad to give it to you."

His mouth pursed in thought a minute. "Captain Chambers gave us a complete report on things. The details checked . . . and your part in it seems to fit your nature. Please understand something, Mr. Hammer. We're not after you. If your part was innocent enough that's as far as we need to go. It's just that we can't afford to pass up any angles."

"Good. Then I'm clear?"

"As far as we're concerned."

"I suppose they have a warrant out for me upstate."

"We'll take care of it."

23

"Thanks."

"There's just one thing . . ."

"Yeah?"

"From your record you seem to be a pretty astute sort of person. What's your opinion on this thing?"

"Since when do you guys deal in guesswork?"

"When that's all we have to go on."

I dropped the cigarette into the ash tray on the desk and looked at him. "The dame knew something she shouldn't have. Whoever pulled it were smart cookies. I think the sedan that waited for us was one that passed us up right after I took her aboard. It was a bad spot to try anything so they went ahead and picked the right one. She wouldn't talk so they bumped her. I imagine it was supposed to look like an accident."

"That's right, it was."

"Now do you mind if I ask one?"

"No. Go right ahead."

"Who was she?"

"Berga Torn." My eyes told him to finish it and he shrugged his shoulder. "She was a taxi dancer, night-club entertainer, friend of boys on the loose and anything else you can mention where sex is concerned."

A frown pulled at my forehead. "I don't get it."

"You're not supposed to, Mr. Hammer." A freeze clouded up his eyes. It told me that was as much as he was about to say and I was all through. I could go now and thanks. Thanks a lot.

I got up and pulled my hat on. One of the boys held the door open for me. I turned around and grinned at him. "I will, feller," I said.

"What?"

"Get it." My grin got bigger. "Then somebody else is going to get it."

I pulled the door closed and got out in the hall. I stood there a minute leaning up against the wall until the pounding in my forehead stopped and the lights left my eyes. There was a dry sour taste in my mouth that made me want to spit, a nasty hate buzzing around my head that pulled my lips tight across my teeth and brought the voices back in my ears and then I felt better because I knew that I'd never forget them and that some day I'd hear them again only this time they'd choke out the last sound they'd ever make.

I took the elevator downstairs, called a cab and gave him

Pat's office address. The cop on the desk told me to go ahead up and when I walked in Pat was sitting there waiting for me trying on a friendly smile for size.

He said, "How did it go, Mike?"

"It was a rotten pitch." I hooked a chair over with my foot and sat down. "I don't know what the act was for, but they sure wasted time."

"They *never* waste time."

"Then why the ride?"

"Checking. I gave them the facts they hadn't already picked up."

"They didn't seem to do anything about it."

"I didn't expect them to." He dropped the chair forward on all four legs. "I suppose you asked them some things too."

"Yeah, I know the kid's name. Berga Torn."

"That all?"

"Part of her history. What's the rest?"

Pat dropped his eyes and stared at his hands. When he was ready to speak he looked up at me, his face a study in caution. "Mike . . . I'm going to give you some information. The reason I'm doing it is because you're likely to fish around and find it yourself if I don't and interference is one thing we can't have."

"Go ahead."

"You've heard of Carl Evello?"

I nodded.

"Evello is the boy behind the powers. The last senatorial investigations turned up a lot of big names in the criminal world, but they never turned up his. That's how big he is. The others are pretty big too, but not like him."

I felt my eyebrows go up. "I didn't know he was that big. Where does it come from?"

"Nobody seems to know. A lot is suspected, but until there's plenty of concrete evidence, no charges are going to be passed around even by me. Just take my word for it that the guy is big. Now . . . they want him. They want him bad and when they get him all the other big boys are going to fall too."

"So what."

"Berga Torn was his mistress for a while."

It started to make sense now. I said, "So she had something on the guy?"

Pat shrugged disgustedly. "Who knows? She was supposed

to have had something. She can't talk. When they were giving her the business as you said they were trying to get it out of her."

"You figure they were Carl's men then."

"Evidently."

"What about the sanitarium she was in?"

"She was there under the advice of her doctor," Pat said. "She was going to testify to the committee and under the strain almost had a nervous breakdown. All the committee hearings were tied up until she was released."

I said, "That's a pretty picture, kid. Where do I come in?"

Little light lines seemed to grow around his eyes. "You don't. You stay out of it."

"Nuts."

"Okay, hero, then let's break it down. There's no reason for you to mess around. It was just an accident that got you into it anyway. There's nothing much you can do and anything you *try* to do is damn well going to be resented by all the agencies concerned."

I gave him my best big grin. All the teeth. Even the eyes. "You flatter me."

"Don't get smart, Mike."

"I'm not."

"All right, you're a bright boy and I know how you work. I'm just trying to stop any trouble before it starts."

"Pal, you got it wrong," I said, "it's already started, remember? I got patted between the eyes, a dame got bumped and my car is wrecked." I stood up and looked down at him feeling things changing in my smile. "Maybe I have too much pride, but I don't let anybody get away with that kind of stuff. I'm going to knock the crap out of somebody for all that and if it gets up to Evello it's okay with me."

"Pat's hand came down on the edge of the desk. "Damn it, Mike, why don't you get a little sense in your head? You . . ."

"Look . . . suppose somebody took you for a patsy. What would you do?"

"That didn't happen."

"No . . . but it happened to me. Those boys aren't that tough that they can get away with it. Damn it, Pat, you ought to know me better than that."

"I do, that's why I'm asking you to lay off. What do I have to do, appeal to your patriotism?"

"Patriotism, my back. I don't give a damn if Congress, the

26

President and the Supreme Court told me to lay off. They're only men and they didn't get sapped and dumped over a cliff. You don't play games with guys who pull that kind of stuff. The feds can be as cagey as they like, but when they wrap the bunch up what happens? So they testify. Great. Costello testified and I can show you where he committed perjury in the minutes of the hearing. What happened? Yeah . . . you know what happened as well as I do. They're too big to do anything with. They got too much dough and too much power and if they talk too many people are going to go under. Well, the hell with 'em. There are a bunch of guys who drove a sedan I want to see again. I don't know what they look like, but I'll know them when I see them. If the feds beat me to 'em it's okay by me, but I'll wait, pal. If I don't reach them first I'll wait until they get through testifying or serving that short sentence those babies seem to draw and when I do you won't be having much trouble from them again ever."

"You have it all figured?"

"Uh-huh. Right down to the self-defense plea."

"You won't get far."

I grinned at him again. "You know better than that, don't you?"

For a moment the seriousness left his face. His mouth cracked in a grin. "Yeah," he said, "that's what I'm afraid of."

"That wasn't any ordinary kill."

"No."

"They were a bunch of cold-blooded bastards. You should have seen what they did to that kid before they killed her."

"Nothing showed on her body . . . or what was left of it after the fire."

"It was there. It wasn't very pretty." I stared at him hard. "It changes something in the way you were thinking."

His eyes came up speculatively.

"They didn't give her the works to see how much she knew. They were after something she knew and they didn't. She was the key to something."

Pat's face was grave. "And you're going after it?"

"What did you expect?"

"I don't know, Mike." He wiped his hand across his eyes. "I guess I didn't expect you to take it lying down." He turned his head and glanced out of the window at the rain. "But since it's going to be that way you might as well know this much.

27

Those government boys are shrewd apples. They know your record and how you work. They even know how you think. Don't expect any help from this end. If you cross those boys you're going to wind up in the can."

"You have your orders?" I asked him.

"In writing. From pretty high authority." His eyes met mine. "I was told to pass the news on to you if you acted up."

I stood up and fiddled with my pack of butts. "Great guys. They want to do it all alone. They're too smart to need help."

"They have the equipment and manpower," Pat said defensively.

"Yeah, sure, but they don't have the attitude." A grimace pulled at my mouth. "They want to make a public example out of those big boys. They want to see them sweat it out behind bars. Nuts to that. Those lads in the sedan don't give a hoot for authority. They don't give a damn for you, me or anybody besides themselves. They only respect one thing."

"Say it."

"A gun in their bellies that's going off and splashing their guts around the room. That kind of attitude they respect." I stuck my hat on my head, keeping it back off the blue lump between my eyes. "See you around, Pat," I said.

"Maybe, maybe not," he said to my back.

I went downstairs into the rain and waited there until a cab came along.

Unless you knew they were there you'd never notice it. Just little things out of place here and there. A streak through the dust where a coat sleeve dragged, an ash tray not quite in place, the rubber seal around the refrigerator door hanging because they didn't know it was loose and had to be stuffed back by hand.

The .45 was still hanging in the closet, but this time there was a thumbprint on the side where I knew I had wiped it before I stuck it away. I picked the rig off the hook and laid it on the table. The Washington boys were pretty good at that sort of thing. I started to whistle a tuneless song as I climbed out of my jacket when I noticed the wastebasket beside the dresser. There was a cigarette butt in the bottom with the brand showing and it wasn't my brand. I picked it up, stared at it, threw it back and went on whistling. I stopped when the thought of it jelled, picked up the phone and dialed the super's number downstairs.

I said, "This is Mike Hammer, John. Did you let some men in up here?"

He hedged with, "Men? You know, Mr. Hammer, I . . ."

"It's okay, I had a talk with them. I just wanted to check on it."

"Well, in that case . . . they had a warrant. You know what they were? They were F.B.I. men."

"Yeah, I know."

"They said I shouldn't mention it."

"You're sure about it?"

"Sure as anything. They had a city cop along too."

"What about anybody else?"

"Nobody else, Mr. Hammer. I wouldn't let a soul in up there, you know that."

"Okay, John. Thanks." I hung up the phone and looked around again.

Somebody else had gone through the apartment. They had done a good job too. But not quite as good as the feds. They had left their trademark around.

The smoke that was trouble started to boil up around me again. You couldn't see it and you couldn't smell it, but it was there. I started whistling again and picked up the .45.

Chapter Four

SHE CAME IN at half-past eleven. She used the key I had given her a long time ago and walked into the living room bringing with her the warmth and love for life that was like turning on the light.

I said, "Hello, beautiful," and I didn't have to say anything more because there was more in the words than the sound of my voice and she knew it.

She started to smile slowly and her mouth made a kiss. Our lips didn't have to touch. She flung that warmth across the room and I caught it. Velda said, "Ugly face. You're uglier now than you were but I love you more than ever."

"So I'm ugly. Underneath I'm beautiful."

"Who can dig down that deep?" she grinned. Then added, "Except me, maybe."

"*Just* you, honey," I said.

The smile that played around her mouth softened a moment, then she slipped out of the coat and threw it across the back of a chair.

I could never get tired of looking at her, I thought. She was everything you needed just when you needed it, a bundle of woman whose emotions could be hard or soft or terrifying, but whatever they were it was what you wanted. She was the lush beauty of the jungle, the sleek sophisticate of the city. Like I said, to me she was everything, and the dull light of the room was reflected in the ring on her finger that I had given her.

I watched her go to the kitchen and open a pair of beer cans. I watched while she sat down, took the frosted can from her and watched while she sipped the top off hers and felt a sudden stirring when her tongue flicked the foam from her lips.

Then she said what I knew she was going to say. "This one's too big, Mike."

"It is?"

Her eyes drew a line across the floor and up my body until they were staring hard into mine. "I was busy while you were in the hospital, Mike. I didn't just let things wait until you got well. This isn't murder as you've known it before. It was planned, organizational killing and it's so big that even the city authorities are afraid of it. The thing has ballooned up to a point where it's Federal and even then it's touching such high places that the feds have to move carefully."

"So?" I let it hang there and pulled on the can of beer.

"It doesn't make any difference what I think?"

I set the can on the end table and made the three-ring pattern on the label. "What you think makes a lot of difference, kitten, but when it comes to making the decisions I'll make them on what I think. I'm a man. So I'm just one man, but as long as I have a brain of my own to use and experience and knowledge to draw on to form a decision I'll keep on making them myself."

"And you're going after them?"

"Would you like me better if I didn't?"

The grin crept back through the seriousness on her face. "No." Then her eyes laughed at me too. "Ten million dollars' worth of men and equipment bucking another multi-million outfit and you elect yourself to step in and clean up. But then, you're a man." She sipped from the beer can again, then said, "But what a man. I'll be glad when you step off that bachelorhood pedestal and move over to where I have a little control over you."

"Think you ever will?"

"No, but at least I'll have something to bargain with," she laughed. "I'd like to have you around for a long time without worrying about you."

"I feel the same way myself, Velda. It's just that some things come first."

"I know, but let me warn you. From now on you're going to be up against a scheming woman."

"That's been tried before."

"Not like this."

"Yeah," I said, and finished the beer. I waited until she put hers down too, then shook out a Lucky and tossed the pack over to her. "What did you pick up?"

"A few details. I found a trucker who passed your car where they had it parked with the flares fore and aft. The guy stopped, and when he saw nobody around he went on. The nearest phone was three miles down the road in a diner and he was surprised when nobody had shown up there because he hadn't seen anyone walking. The girl in the diner knew about an abandoned shack a few hundred yards from the spot and I went there. The place was alive with feds."

"Great."

"That's hardly the word for it." She squirmed in the chair and ran her fingers through her hair, the deep ebony of it rubbed to a soft glow in the pale lamplight. "They held me for a while, questioned me, and released me with a warning that had teeth in it."

"They find anything?"

"From what I could see, nothing. They backtracked the same way that I did and anything they found just supported what you had already told them.

"There's a catch in it though," she said. "The shack was a good fifty yards in from the highway and covered with brush. You could light the place up and it wouldn't be seen, and unless you knew where to look you'd never find it."

"It was too convenient to be coincidental, you mean?"

"Much too convenient."

I spit out a stream of smoke and watched it flow around the empty beer can. "That doesn't make sense. The kid was running away. How'd they know which direction she'd pick out?"

"They wouldn't, but how would they know where that shack was?"

"Who'd the shack belong to?"

A frown creased her forehead and she shook her head. "That's another catch. The place is on state property. It's been there for twenty years. One thing I did learn while I was being questioned was that aside from its recent use the place had no signs of occupancy at all. There were dates carved in the doorpost and the last one was 1937."

"Anything else?"

Velda shook her head slowly. "I saw your car. Or what's left of it."

"Poor old baby. The last of the original hot rods."

"Mike . . ."

I finished the beer and put the empty down on the table. "Yeah?"

"What are you going to do?"

"Guess."

"Tell me."

I had a long pull on the smoke and dropped the butt into the can. "They killed a dame and tried to frame me for it. They wrecked my heap and put me in the hospital. They're figuring us all for suckers and don't give a hang who gets hurt. The slobs, the miserable slobs." I rammed my fist against my palm until it stung. "I'm going to find out what the score is, kid. Then a lot of heads are going to roll."

"One of them might be yours, Mike."

"Yeah, one of 'em might, but it sure won't be the first to go. And you know something? They're worried, whoever they are. They read the papers and things didn't quite happen like they wanted them to. The law of averages bucked 'em for a change and instead of getting a sucker to frame they got me. Me. That they didn't like because I'm not just the average joe and they're smart enough to figure out an angle."

Her face pulled tight and the question was in her eyes. "They were up here looking around," I said.

"Mike!"

"Oh, I don't know what they were after, but I don't think they knew either. But you can bet on this, they went through this place because they thought I had something they wanted and just because they didn't find it doesn't mean they think I haven't got it. They'll be back. The next time I won't be in an emergency ward."

"But what could it be?"

"Beats me, but they tried to kill two people to find out. Whether I like it or not I'm in this thing as deep as that dame was." I grinned at Velda sitting there. "And I like it, too. I hate the guts of those people. I hate them so bad it's coming out of my skin. I'm going to find out who 'they' are and why and then they've had it."

A note of sarcasm crept into her voice. "Just like always, isn't that right?"

"No," I said, "Maybe not. Maybe this time I'll do it differently. Just for the fun of it."

Velda's hands were drawn tight on the arms of the chair. "I don't like you this way, Mike."

"Neither do a lot of people. They know something just like their own names. They know I'm not going to sit on my fanny and wait for something to happen. They know from now on they're going to have to be so careful they won't even be able to spit because I'm going to get closer and closer until I have them on the dirty end of a stick. They know it and I know it too."

"It makes you a target."

"Kitten, it sure does and that I go for. If that's one way of pulling 'em inside shooting range I'm plenty glad to be a target."

Her face relaxed and she sat back. For a long minute neither one of us spoke. She sat there with her head against the cushion staring at the ceiling, then, "Mike, I have news for you."

The way she said it made me look up. "Give."

"Any shooting that's to be done won't be done by you."

A muscle in my face twitched.

Velda reached in her jacket pocket and came out with an envelope. She flipped it across the room and I caught it. "Pat brought it in this morning. He couldn't do a thing about it, so don't get teed off at him."

I pulled the flap out and fingered the sheet loose. It was very brief and to the point. No quibbling. No doubting the source. The letterhead was all very official and I was willing to bet that for the one sheet they sent me a hundred more made up the details of why the thing should be sent.

It was a very simple order telling me I no longer had a license to carry a gun and temporarily my state-granted right to conduct private investigations was suspended. There was no mention of a full or partial refund of my two-hundred-buck fee for said license to said state.

33

So I laughed. I folded the sheet back into the envelope and laid it on the table. "They want me to do it the hard way," I said.

"They don't want you to do it at all. From now on you're a private citizen and nothing else and if they catch you with a gun you get it under the Sullivan law."

"This happened once before, remember?"

Velda nodded slowly. There was no expression at all on her face. "That's right, but they forgot about me. Then I had a P.I. ticket and a license for a gun too. This time they didn't forget."

"Smart boys."

"Very." She closed her eyes again and let her head drop back. "We're going to have it rough."

"Not we, girl. Me."

"We."

"Look . . ."

Only the slight reflection of the light from her pupils showed that her eyes were open and looking at me. "Who do you belong to, Mike?"

"You tell me."

She didn't answer. Her eyes opened halfway and there was something sad in the way her lips tried to curve into a smile. I said, "All right, kid, you know the answer. It's we and if I stick my neck out you can be there to help me get back in time." I picked the .45 up off the floor beside the chair, slid the clip out and thumbed the shells into my palm. "Your boy Mike is getting on in years, pal. Soft maybe?"

There was laughter in the sad smile now. "Not soft. Smarter. We're up against something that's so big pure muscle won't even dent it. We're up against a big brain and being smart is the only thing that's going to move it. At least you have the sense to change your style."

"Yeah."

"It won't be so easy."

"I know. I'm not built that way." I grinned at her. "Let's not worry about it. Everybody's trying to step on me because they don't want me around. Some of 'em got different reasons, but the big one is they're afraid I'll spoil their play. That happened before too. Let's make it happen again."

Velda said, "But let's not try so hard, huh? Seven years is a long time to wait for a guy." Her teeth were a white flash in the middle of her smile. "I'd like him in good shape when he gets ready to take the jump."

I said, "Yeah," but not so loud that she heard me.

"Where do we take it from here, Mike?"

I let the shells dribble from my fingers into the ash tray. They lay there, deadly and gleaming, but helpless without the mother that could give them birth.

"Berga Torn," I said. "We'll start with her. I want those sanitarium records. I want her life history and the history of anybody she was associated with. That's your job."

"And you?" she asked.

"Evello. Carl Evello. Someplace he comes into this thing and he's my job."

Velda nodded, drummed her fingernails against the arm of the chair and stared across the room. "He won't be easy."

"Nobody's easy."

"Especially Evello. He's organized. While you were under wraps in the hospital I saw a few people who had a little inside information on Evello. There wasn't much and what there was of it was mostly speculation, but it put the finger on a theme you might be interested in."

"Such as?"

She looked at me with a half smile, a beautiful jungle animal sizing up her mate before telling him what was outside the mouth of the den. "Mafia," she said.

I could feel it starting way down at my toes, a cold, burning flush that crept up my body and left in its wake a tingling sensation of rage and fear that was pure emotion and nothing else. It pounded in my ears and dried my throat until the words that came out were scratchy, raspy sounds that didn't seem to be part of me at all.

"How did they know?"

"They don't. They suspect, that's all. The Federal agencies are interested in the angle."

"Yeah," I said. "They *would* be interested. They'd go in on their toes, too. No wonder they don't want me fishing around."

"You make too much noise."

"Things happen, don't they?"

Velda didn't answer that one either.

"So now it makes sense," I told her. "They have the idea I'm in the deal someplace but they can't come out and say it. They play twenty questions hoping I do have a share of it so they'll have someplace to start. They won't give up until the day they die or I do because once the finger touches you it never comes away. There's no such thing as innocence, just innocence touched with guilt is as good a deal as you can get."

Velda's mouth moved slowly. "Maybe it's a good thing, Mike. It's a funny world. Pure innocence as such doesn't enter in much nowadays. There's always at least one thing people try to hide." She paused and ran her finger along the side of her cheek. "If a murderer is hung for the wrong killing, who is wrong?"

"That's a new twist for you, kid."

"I got it from you."

"Then finish it."

Her fingers reached out and plucked a cigarette from the pack. It was a graceful, feminine motion that spoke of soft girlishness, the texture of her skin satiny and amber in the light. You could follow the fingers into the hand and the hand into the arm, watching the curves melt into each other like a beautiful painting. Just watching like that and you could forget the two times that same hand held a snarling, spitting rod that chewed a guy's guts out. "Now innocence touched with guilt pays off," she said. "You'll be one of the baited hooks they'll use until something bites."

"And in the end the public will benefit."

"That's right." She grinned, the corner of her mouth twisting upward a little. "But don't feel badly about it, Mike. They're stealing your stuff. You taught them that trick a long time ago."

My fingers went out and began to play with the slugs that squatted in the bottom of the ash tray where I had dropped them. She watched me from across the room, her eyes half closed in speculation. Then she uncurled, tossed my deck of smokes into the chair beside me and reached for her coat.

I didn't watch her walk away. I sat there dreaming of the things I'd like to do and how maybe if nobody was there to see me I'd do anyway. I was dreaming of a lot of fat faces with jowls that got big and loose on other people's meat and how they'd look with that smashed, sticky expression that comes with catching the butt end of a .45 across their noses. I was dreaming of a slimy foreign secret army that held a parade of terror under the Mafia label and laughed at us with our laws and regulations and how fast their damned smug expressions would change when they saw the fresh corpses of their own kind day after day.

She didn't have to go far to read my mind. She had seen

me look like this before. She didn't have to go far to get me back on the track, either. "Isn't it about time you taught them some fresh tricks, Mike?" Velda said softly.

Then she left and the room got a little darker.

Chapter Five

I SAT THERE for a while, staring at the multicolored reflections of the city that made my window a living, moving kaleidoscope. The voice of the monster outside the glass was a constant drone, but when you listened long enough it became a flat, sarcastic sneer that pushed ten million people into bigger and better troubles, and then the sneer was heard for what it was, a derisive laugh that thought blood running from an open wound was funny, and death was the biggest joke of all.

Yeah, it laughed at people like me and you. It was the voice of the guy with the whip who laughed at each stroke to drown out the screams of the victim. A subtle voice that hid small cries, a louder voice that covered the anguished moans.

I sat and heard it and thought about it while the statistics ran through my head. So many a minute killed by cars, so many injured. So many dead an hour by out-and-out violence. So many this and so many that. It made a long impressive list that was recited at board meetings and assemblies.

There was only one thing left out. How many were scared stiff? How many lay awake nights worrying about things they shouldn't have to worry about at all? How many wondered where their kids were and what they were doing. *How many knew the army of silent men who made their whispered demands and either got them or extracted payment according to the code?*

Then I knew the voice outside for what it was. Not some intangible monster after all. Not some gigantic mechanical contrivance that could act of its own accord. Not a separate living being with its own rules and decrees. Not one of those things.

People, that's all.

Just soft, pulpy people, most of them nice. And some of them filthy and twisted who gorged themselves on flesh

37

and puffed up with the power they had so that when they got stuck they popped like ripe melons and splashed their guts all over the ground.

The Mafia. The stinking, slimy Mafia. An oversize mob of ignorant, lunkheaded jerks who ruled with fear and got away with it because they had money to back themselves up.

The Black Hand? You think you can laugh it off? You think all that stuff went out with prohibition? There's a lot of widows around who can tell you differently. Widowers, too.

Like Velda said, it wasn't going to be easy at all. You don't just ask around where you can find the top boy.

First you find somebody to ask and if you're not dead by then, or he's not dead, you ask. Then you ask and look some more, each time coming closer to the second when a bullet or a knife reaches across space and spears you.

There's a code they work by, a fixed unbreakable code. Once the Mafia touches you it never takes its hand away. And if you make one move, just one single, hesitant move to get out from under, it's all over. Sometimes it takes a day or two, even a year maybe, but it was all over from then.

You get dead.

In a sense though, it was funny. Someplace at the top of the heap was a person. From him the fear radiated like from the center of a spiderweb. He sat on his throne and made a motion of his hand and somebody died. He made another motion and somebody was twisted until they screamed. A nod of his head did something that sent a guy leaping from a roof because he couldn't take it any more.

Just one person did that. One soft, pulpy person.

I started to grin a little bit thinking how he'd act stripped of weapons and his power for a minute or so in a closed room with someone who didn't like him. I could almost see his face behind the glass and my grin got bigger because I was pretty sure of what I was going to do now.

It was late, but only by the clock. The city was yawning and stretching after its supper, waking up to start living. The rain had died, leaving a low grumble in the skies overhead to announce its passing. The air was fresher now, the light a little brighter, and the parade of cabs had slowed down enough so I could whistle one down and hop a ride over to Pat's apartment.

He let me in with a grin and muttered something between the folder of papers he had clamped in his teeth, waved me into the living room and took my coat. His eyes made a casual sweep over my chest and he didn't have to look a second time to tell I wasn't wearing a rig under my arm.

Pat said, "Drink?"

"Not now."

"It's only ginger ale."

I shook my head and sat down. He filled his glass, relaxed into a wing chair and shoved all the papers into an envelope. "Glad to see you traveling light."

"Didn't you expect me to?"

His mouth crooked up at the corner. "I figured you'd know better than not to. Just don't blame me for the deal, that's all."

"You're not too sorry about it, are you?"

"As a matter of fact, no." His fingers tapped the envelope, then his eyes came up to mine. "It puts you on the spot as far as business is concerned, but I don't imagine you'll starve."

"I don't imagine I will either," I grinned back at him. "How long am I supposed to be in solitary for?"

He didn't like the grin at all. He got those wrinkles around his eyes that showed when something was getting under his hide and took a long drag on the drink to muffle what he knew I saw. "When they're ready to lift it they'll lift it and not before."

"They won't have it that soft," I told him.

"No?"

I flicked a butt into my mouth and lit it. "Tomorrow you can remind 'em I'm an incorporated business, a taxpayer and a boy with connections. My lawyer has a judge probably getting up a show cause right now and until they settle the case in court they aren't pulling any bill-of-attainder stuff on me."

"You got a mouthful of words on that one, Mike."

"Uh-huh. And you know what I'm talking about. Nobody, not even a Federal agency is going to pull my tail and not get chewed a little bit."

His hands got too tight around the glass. "Mike . . . this isn't just murder."

"I know."

"How much?"

"No more than before. I've been thinking around it though."

"Any conclusions?"

"One." I looked at him, hard. "Mafia."

Nothing changed in his face. "So?"

"I can be useful if you'd quit booting me around." I took a drag on the smoke and let it curl out into the light. "I don't have to pull my record out. You know it as well as I do. Maybe I have shot up a few guys, but the public doesn't seem to miss them any. If your buddies think I'm stupid enough to go busting in on something over my head without knowing what I'm doing then it's time they took a refresher course. They haven't got one guy in Washington that's smarter than I am . . . not one guy. If they had they'd be making more moolah than I am and don't fool yourself thinking they're in there for love of the job. It's about the limit they can do."

"You sure think a lot of yourself."

"I have to, friend. Nobody else does. Besides, I'm still around when a lot of others have taken their last car ride."

Pat finished off the glass and swirled the last few drops around the bottom. "Mike," he said, "if I had my way I'd have you and ten thousand more in on this thing. That's about how many we'd need to fight it. As it is, I'm a city cop and I take orders. What do you want from me?"

"You say it, Pat."

He laughed this time. It was like the old days when neither one of us gave a damn about anything and if we had to hate it was the same thing. "Okay, you want me for your third arm. You're going to dive into this thing no matter who says what and as long as you are we'd might as well use your talents instead of tripping over them."

The grin was real. It was six years ago and not now any longer. The light was back in his eyes again and we were a team riding over anything that stood in our way. "Now I'll tell you something, Mike," he said, "I don't like the way the gold-badge boys do business either. I don't like political meddling in crime and I'm sick of the stuff that's been going on for so long. Everybody is afraid to move and it's about time something jolted them. For so damn long I've been listening to people say that this racket is over our heads that I almost began to believe it myself. Okay, I'll lay my job on the line. Let's give it a spin and see what happens. Tell me what you want and I'll feed it to you. Just don't hash up the play . . . at least not for a while yet. If something good comes of it I'll have a talking point and maybe I can keep my job."

"I can always use a partner."

"Thanks. Now let's hear your angle."

"Information. Detailed."

He didn't have to go far for it. The stuff was right there in his lap. He pulled it all out of the envelope and thumbed the sheets apart. The light behind his head made the sheets translucent enough so the lines of type stood out and there weren't very many lines.

"Known criminals with Mafia connections," he drawled. "Case histories of Mafia efficiency and police negligence. Twenty pages of arrests with hardly enough convictions to bother about. Twenty pages of murder, theft, dope pushing, and assorted felonies and all we're working with are the bottom rungs of the ladder. We can name some of the big ones but don't fool yourself and think they are the top joes. The boys up high don't have names we know about."

"Is Carl Evello there?"

Pat looked at the sheets again and threw them on the floor in disgust. "Evello isn't anywhere. He's got one of those investigatable incomes but it looks like he'll be able to talk his way out of it."

"Berga Torn?"

"Now we're back to murder. One of many."

"We don't think alike there, Pat."

"No?"

"Berga was special. She was so special they put a crew of boys on her who knew their business. They don't do that for everybody. Why did the committee want her?"

I could see him hesitate a moment, shrug and make up his mind. "There wasn't much to the Torn dame. She was a good-looking head with a respectable mind but engaged in a mucky racket, if you get what I mean."

"I know."

"There was a rumor that Evello was keeping her for a while. It was during the time he was raking in a pile. The same rumor had he gave her the boot and the committee figured she'd be mad enough to spill what she knew about him."

"Evello wouldn't be that dumb," I said.

"When it comes to dames, guys can be awfully dumb," he grinned at me knowingly.

"Finish it."

"The feds approached her. She was scared stiff, but she indicated that there was something she could give out, but she wanted time to collect her information and protection after she let it out."

"Great." I snuffed the butt out and leaned back in the

41

chair. "I can see Washington assigning her a permanent body-guard."

"She was going to appear before the committee masked."

"No good. Evello could still spot her from the info she handed them."

Pat confirmed the thought with a nod. "In the meantime," he went on, "she got the jitters. Twice she got away from the men assigned to cover her. Before the month was out she was practically hysterical and went to a doctor. He had her committed to a sanitarium and she was supposed to stay there for three weeks. The investigation was held up, there were agents assigned to guard the sanitarium, she got away and was killed."

"Just like that."

"Just like that only you were there when it happened."

"Nice of me."

"That's what those Washington boys thought."

"Coincidence is out," I said.

"Naturally." His mouth twitched again. "They don't know that you're the guy things happen to. Some people are ac-cident prone. You're coincidence prone."

"I've thought of it that way," I told him. "Now what about the details of her escape?"

He shrugged and shook his head slightly. "Utter sim-plicity. The kind of thing you can't beat. Precautions were taken for every inconceivable thing and she does the con-ceivable. She picked up a raincoat and shoes from the nurses' quarters and walked out the main entrance with two female attendants. It was raining at the time and one of them had an umbrella and they stayed together under it the way women will who try to keep their hair dry or something. They went as far as the corner together, the other two got in a bus while she kept on walking."

"Wasn't a pass required at the gate?"

He nodded deeply, a motion touched with sarcasm. "Sure, there was a pass all right, each of the two had a pass and showed it. Maybe the guy thought he saw the third one. At least he said he thought so."

"I suppose somebody was outside the gate too?"

"That's right. Two men, one on foot and one in a car. Neither had seen the Torn girl and were there to stop any-one making an unauthorized exit."

I let out a short grunt.

Pat said, "They thought it *was* authorized, Mike."

I laughed again. "That's what I mean. *They thought.* Those guys are supposed to think right or not at all. Those are the guys who had my ticket lifted. Those are the guys who want no interference. Nuts."

"Anyway, she got away. That's it."

"Okay, we'll leave it there. What attitude are the cops taking?"

"It's murder so they're working it from that end."

"And getting nowhere," I added.

"So far," Pat said belligerently. I grinned at him and the scowl that creased his forehead disappeared. "Lay off. How do you plan to work it?"

"Where's Evello?"

"Right here in the city."

"And the known Mafia connections?"

Pat looked thoughtful a moment. "Other big cities, but their operational center is here too." He bared his teeth in a tight grimace. His eyes went hard and nasty as he said, "Which brings us to the end of our informative little discussion about the Mafia. We know who some of them are and how they operate, but that's as far as it goes."

"Washington doesn't have anything?"

"Sure, but what good does it do. Nobody fingers the Mafia. There's that small but important little item known as evidence."

"We'll get it," I told him, ". . . one way or another. It's still a big organization. They need capital to operate."

Pat stared at me like he would a kid. "Sure, just like that. You know how they raise that capital? They squeeze it out of the little guy. It's an extra tax he has to pay. They put the bite on guys who are afraid to talk or who can't talk. They run an import business that drives the Narcotics Division nuts. They got their hand in every racket that exists with a political cover so heavy you can't bust through it with a sledge hammer."

He didn't have to remind me. I knew how they operated. I said, "Maybe, chum, maybe. Could be that nobody's really tried hard enough yet."

He grunted something under his breath, then, "You still didn't say how you were going to work it."

I pushed myself out of the chair, wiping my hand across my face. "First Berga Torn. I want to find out more about her."

Pat reached down and picked the top sheet off the pile he

had dropped on the floor beside him. "You might as well have this then. It's as much as anyone has to start with."

I folded it up and stuck it in my pocket without looking at it. "You'll let me know if anything comes up?"

"I'll let you know." I picked up my coat and started for the door.

"And Mike . . ."

"Yeah?"

"This is a two-way deal, remember?"

"Yeah, I remember."

Downstairs, I stood in front of the building a minute. I took the time to stick a Lucky in my mouth and even more time lighting it. I let the flare of the match bounce off my face for a good ten seconds, then dragged in deeply on the smoke and whipped it back into the night air. The guy in the doorway of the apartment across the street stirred and made a hesitant motion of having come out of the door and not knowing which way to walk. I turned east and he made up his mind. He turned east too.

Halfway down the block I crossed over to make it a little easier on him. Washington didn't discount shoe leather as expenses so there was no sense giving the boy a hard time. I went three more blocks closer to the subway station and pulled a few gimmicks that had him practically climbing up my back.

This time I had a good look at him and was going to say hello to add insult to injury when I caught the end of a gun muzzle in my ribs and knew he wasn't Washington at all.

He was young and good-looking until he smiled, then the crooked march of short, stained teeth across his mouth made him an expensively dressed punk on a high-class job. There was no hop behind his pupils so he was a classy workman being paid by an employer who knew what the score was. The teeth smiled bigger and he started to tell me something when I ripped his coat open and the gun in the pocket wasn't pointing at me any more. He was half spun around fighting to get the rod loose as the side of my hand caught him across the neck and he sat down on the sidewalk with his feet out in front of him, plenty alive, plenty awake, but not even a little bit active.

I picked the Banker's Special out of his hand, broke it, dumped the shells into the gutter and tossed the rod back into his lap. His eyes were hurting. They were all watered up like he was ashamed of himself.

"Tell your boss to send a man out on the job the next time," I said.

I walked on down the street and turned into the subway kiosk wondering what the deuce had happened to Washington. Little boy blue back on the sidewalk would have a good story to take home to papa this time. Most likely he wouldn't get his allowance. At least they'd know a pro was in the game for a change.

I shoved a dime in the turnstile, went through, pulled the sheet out of my pocket, glanced at it once and walked over to the downtown platform.

Chapter Six

SOMETHING HAPPENS to Brooklyn at night. It isn't a sister borough any more. She withdraws to herself and pulls the shades down, then begins a life that might seem foreign to an outsider. She's strange, exciting, tinted with bright lights, yet elusive somehow.

I got off the Brighton Line at De Kalb and went up to the street. A guy on the corner pointed the way to the address I wanted and I walked the few blocks to it.

What I was looking for was an old-fashioned brownstone, a hangover from a half-century past that had the number painted on the door and looked at the street with dull, blank eyes. I went up the four sandstone steps, held a match to the mailboxes and found what I wanted.

The names CARVER and TORN were there, but somebody had drawn a pencil through the two of them and had written in BERNSTEIN underneath. All I could do was mutter a little under my breath and punch the end button on the line, the one labeled SUPER. I leaned on it until the door started clicking then I opened it and went in.

He came to the door and I could almost see his face. Part of it stuck out behind the fleshy shoulder of a woman who towered all around him and glared at me as if I had crawled up out of a hole. Her hair was a gray mop gathered into tiny knots and clamped in place with metal curlers. She bulged through the bathrobe, trying to slow down her breathing enough so she could say something. Her hands were big and red, the knuckles showing as they bit into her hips.

Dames. The guy behind her looked scared to death. She said, "What the hell do you want! You know what time it is? You think . . ."

"Shut up." Her mouth stopped. I leaned against the door jamb. "I'm looking for the super."

"I'm the . . ."

"You're not anything to me, lady. Tell your boy to come out." I thought her face would fall apart. "Tell him," I repeated.

When men learn to be men maybe they can handle dames. There was something simpering in the way she forced a smile and stepped aside.

The boy didn't want to come out, but he did. He made himself as big as he could without it helping much. "Yes?"

I showed him the badge I still had. It didn't mean a thing any more, but it still shined in the light and wasn't something everybody carried. "Get your keys."

"Yessir, yessir." He reached up beside the door, unhooked a ring and stepped back into the hall.

The dame said. "You wait a minute, I'll be right . . ."

He seemed to stand on his toes. "*You* wait right there until I come *back*," he told her. "*I'm* the super." He turned and grinned at me. Behind him his wife's face puffed out and the door slammed.

"Yessir?" he said.

"Berga Torn's place. I want to go through it."

"But the police have already been through there."

"I know."

"Today I rented it already."

"Anybody there now?"

"Not yet. Tomorrow they're supposed to come."

"Then let's go."

First he hesitated, then he shrugged and started up the stairs. Two flights up he fitted a key into the lock of a door and threw it open. He felt around for the light switch, flipped it and stood aside for me.

I don't know what I expected to find. Maybe it was more curiosity than anything that dragged me up there. The place had been gone over by experts and if anything had been worth taking it was gone by now. It was what you might call a functional apartment and nothing more. The kitchen and living room were combined with a bathroom sand-

46

wiched between two bedrooms that jutted off the one wall.
There was enough furniture to be comfortable, nothing gaudy
and nothing out of place.

"Whose stuff is this?"

"We rent furnished. What you see belongs to the land-
lord."

I walked into the bedroom and opened the door of the
closet. A half dozen dresses and a suit hung there. The floor
was lined with shoes. The dresser was the same way, filled
to the brim. The clothes were good, fairly new, but not the
type that came out of exclusive shops.

Stockings were neatly rolled up and packed into a top
drawer. Beside them were four envelopes, two with paid-up
receipts, one a letter from the Millburn Steamship Line saying
that there were no available berths on the liner *Cedric*
and how sorry they were, and the other a heavier envelope
holding about a dozen Indianhead pennies.

The other small drawer was cluttered with half-used lip-
sticks and all the usual junk a dame can collect in hardly
any time at all.

It was the other bedroom that gave me the surprise. There
was nothing there at all. Just a made-up bed, a cleaned-out
closet and dresser drawers lined with old sheets of newspaper.

The super watched me until I backed out into the living
room, saying nothing.

"Whose room?" I jerked my thumb at the empty place.

"Miss Carver's."

"Where is she?"

"Two days ago . . . she moved out."

"The police see her?"

He nodded, a fast snap of the head. "Maybe that's why
she moved out."

"You going to empty this place out?"

"Guess I got to. The lease is up next month, but it was
paid in advance. Hope I don't get in trouble renting so soon."

"Who paid it?"

"Torn's name is on the lease." He looked at me pointedly.

"I didn't ask that."

"She handed me the dough." I stared at him hard and he
fumbled with his pajamas again. "How many times do I
have to tell you guys. I don't know where she got the dough.
Far as I know she didn't do any messing around. This place

47

sure wasn't no office or that nosy old lady of mine would've known about it."

"Did she have any men here to see her?"

"Mister," he said, "there's twelve apartments in this rat-trap and I can't keep track of who comes in and who goes out so long as they're paid up. If you ask me right off I'd say she wasn't no tramp. She was a dame splitting her quarters with another dame who paid her dough and didn't make trouble. If a guy was keeping her he sure didn't get his money's worth. If you want to know what I think then I'd say yes, she was being kept. Maybe the both of 'em. The old lady never thought so or she would've given them the boot, that's for sure."

"Okay then," I said, "that's it."

He held the door open for me. "You think anything's going to come of this?"

"Plenty."

The guy was another lip licker. "There won't be . . ."

"Don't worry about it. You know how I can reach the Carver girl?"

The look he gave me was quick and worried. "She didn't leave no address."

I made it sound very flat and businesslike. "You know . . . when you step in front of the law there's charges that can be pressed."

"Aw, look, mister, if I knew . . ." His tongue came out and passed over his mouth again. He thought about it, shrugged, then said, "Okay. Just don't let my wife know. She called today. She's expecting some mail from her boy friend and asked me to send it to her." He pulled in a deep breath and let it out in a sigh. "She don't want anybody to know where she is. Got a pencil?"

I handed him one with the remains of an envelope and he jotted it down.

"Wish I could do something right for a change. The kid sounded pretty worried."

"You don't want to buck the law, do you friend?"

"Guess not."

"Okay, then you did right. Tell you what though . . . don't bother giving it out to anyone else. I'll see her, but she won't know how I reached her. How's that?"

His face showed some relief. "Swell."

"By the way," I said, "what was she like?"

"Carver?"

"Yeah."

"Kind of a pretty blonde. Hair like snow."

"I'll find her," I said.

The number was on Atlantic Avenue. It was the third floor over a secondhand store and there was nothing to guide you in but the smell. All the doorbells had names that had been there long enough to get dirtied up, but the newest one said TRENTEN when it didn't mean that at all.

I punched the button three times while I stood there in the dark, heard nothing ringing so I eased myself into the smell. It wasn't just an odor. It was something that moved, something warm and fluid that came down the stairs, tumbling over slowly, merging with other smells until it leaked out into the street.

In each flight there were fourteen steps, a landing, a short corridor that took you to the next flight and at the top of the last one, a door. Up there the smell was different. It wasn't any fresher; it just smelled better. A pencil line of light marked the sill and for a change there was no bag of garbage to trip over.

I rapped on the door and waited. I did it again and springs creaked inside. A quiet little voice said, "Yes?"

"Carver?"

Again, "Yes." A bit tired-sounding this time.

"I'd like to speak to you. I'm pushing my card through under the door."

"Never mind. Just come right in."

I felt for the knob, twisted it and pushed the door open. She was sitting there swallowed up in a big chair facing me, the gun in her hand resting on her knee in a lazy fashion and there wasn't even the slightest bit of doubt that it would start going off the second I breathed too hard.

Carver wasn't pretty. She was small and full bodied, but she wasn't pretty. Maybe no dame can be pretty with a rod in her mitt, even one with bleached white hair and a scarlet mouth. A black velvet robe outlined her against the chair, seeming like the space of nighttime between the white of her hair and that of the fur-lined slippers she wore.

For a minute she looked at me, her eyes wandering over me slowly. I let her look and pushed the door shut. Maybe she was satisfied by what she saw, maybe not. She didn't say anything, but she didn't put the gun away either. I said, "Expecting someone else?"

What she did with her mouth didn't make up a smile. "I don't know. What have you to say?"

"I'll say what it takes to make you point that heater someplace else."

"You can't talk that loud or that long, friend."

"Do I reach in my pocket for a smoke?"

"There's some on the table beside you. Use those."

I picked one up, almost went for my lighter in my pocket, thought better of it and took the matches that went with the cigarettes. "You're sure not good company, kid." I blew a stream of smoke at the floor and rocked on my toes. That little round hole in the tip of the automatic never came off my stomach.

"The name is Mike Hammer," I told her. "I'm a private investigator. I was with Berga Torn when she got knocked off."

This time the rod moved. I was looking right down the barrel.

"More," her mouth said.

"She was trying to hitch a ride to the city. I picked her up, ran a roadblock that was checking for her, got edged off the road by a car and damn near brained by a pack of hoods who were playing for keeps. I was there with my head dented in when they worked her over and behind the wheel of the car they pushed over the cliff. To them I was a handy, class-A red herring that was supposed to cover the real cause of her death only it didn't quite happen that way."

"How did it happen?"

"I was thrown clear. If you want I'll show you my scars."

"Never mind."

So we stared at each other for a longer minute and I was still looking down the barrel and the hole kept getting bigger and bigger.

"You loaded?"

"The cops lifted my rod and P.I. ticket."

"Why?"

"Because they knew I'd bust into this thing and they wanted to keep me out."

"How did you find me?"

"It's not hard to find people when you know how. Anybody could do it." Her eyes widened momentarily, seemed to deepen, then narrowed sharply.

"Suppose I don't believe you," she said.

I sucked in a lungful of smoke and dropped the butt to the

floor. I didn't bother to squash it out. I let it lie there until you could smell the stink of burned wool in the room and felt my face start to tighten around the edges. I said, "Kid, I'm sick of answering questions. I'm sick of having guns pointed at me. You make the second tonight and if you don't stow that thing I'm going to beat the hell out of you. What'll it be?"

I didn't scare her. The gun came down until it rested in her lap and for the first time the stiffness left her face. Carver just looked tired. Tired and resigned. The scarlet slash of her mouth made a wry grimace of sadness. "All right," she said, "sit down."

So I sat down. No matter what else I could have done, nothing would have been more effective. The bewilderment showed on her face, the way her body arched before sinking back again. Her leg moved and the gun dropped to the floor and stayed there.

"Aren't you . . ."

"Who were you expecting, Carver?"

"The name is Lily." Her tongue was a lighter pink against the scarlet as it swept across her lips.

"Who, Lily?"

"Just . . . men." Her eyes were hopeful now. "You . . . told me the truth?"

"I'm not one of them if that's what you mean. Why did they come?"

The hardness left her face. It seemed to melt away like a film that should never have been there and now she was pretty. Her hair was a pile of snow that reflected the loveliness of her face. She breathed heavily, the robe drawing tight at regular intervals.

"They wanted Berga."

"Let's start at the beginning. With you and Berga. How's that?"

Lily paused and stared into the past. "Before the war, that's when we met. We were dance-hall hostesses. It was the first night for the both of us and we both sort of stuck together. A week later we found an apartment and shared it."

"How long?"

"About a year. When the war came I was pretty sick of things and went into a defense plant. Berga quit too . . . but what she did for a living was her business. She was a pretty good kid. When I was sick she moved back in and took care of me. After the war I lost my job when the plant

51

closed down and she got a friend of hers to get me a job in a night club in Jersey."

"Did she work there too?" I asked.

The white hair made a negative. "She was . . . doing a lot of things."

"Anybody special?"

"I don't know. I didn't ask. We went back living in the same apartment for a while, though she was paying most of the bills. She seemed to have a pretty good income."

Lily's eyes came off the wall behind my head and fastened on mine. "That's when I noticed her starting to change."

"How?"

"She was . . . scared."

"Did she say why?"

"No. She laughed it off. Twice she booked passage to Europe, but couldn't get the ship she wanted and didn't go."

"She was that scared."

Lily shrugged, saying nothing, saying much. "It seemed to grow on her. Finally she wouldn't even leave the house at all. She said she didn't feel well, but I knew she was lying."

"When was this?"

"Not so very long ago. I don't remember just when."

"It doesn't matter."

"She went out once in a while after that. Like to the movies or for groceries. Never very far. Then the police came around."

"What did they want?"

"Her."

"Questions or an arrest?"

"Questions, mostly. They asked me some things too. Nothing I knew about. That night I saw someone following me home." Her face had a curious strained look about it. "It's been that way every night since. I don't know if they've found me here yet or not."

"Cops?"

"Not cops." She said it very simply, very calmly, but couldn't quite hide the terror that tried to scream the answer out.

She begged me to say something, but I let her squeeze it out herself. "The police came again, but Berga wouldn't tell them anything." The tongue moistened the lips again. The scarlet was starting to wash away and I could see the natural tones of the wet flesh. "The other men came . . . they were different from the police. Federal men, I think. They took her away. Before she came back . . . *Those* men came."

She put something into the last three words that wasn't in the others, some breathless, nameless fear. Her hands were tight balls with the nails biting into the palms. A glassiness had passed over her eyes while she thought about it, then vanished as if afraid it had been seen.

"They said I'd die if I talked to anyone." Her hand moved up and covered her mouth. "I'm tired of being scared," she said. Her head drooped forward, nodding gently to the soft sobs that seemed to stick in her chest.

What's the answer? How do you tell them they won't die when they know you're lying about it because they're marked already?

I got up and walked to her chair, looked at her a second and sat down on the arm of it. I took her hand away from her face, tilted her chin up and ran my fingers through the snow piled on top of her head. It was as soft and as fine as it looked in the light and when my fingers touched her cheek she smiled, dropped her eyes and let that beauty come through all the way, every bit of it that she had kept hidden so long. There was a faint smell of rubbing alcohol about her, a clean, pungent odor that seemed to separate itself from the perfume she wore.

Her eyes were big and dark, soft ovals under the delicate brows, her mouth full and pink, parted in the beginning of a smile. My fingers squeezed her shoulder easily and her head went back, the mouth parting even further and I bent down slowly.

"You won't die," I said.

And it was the wrong thing to say because the mouth that was so close to mine pulled back and everything had changed. I just sat there next to her for a little while until the dry sobs had stopped. There were no tears to be wiped away. Terror doesn't leave any tears. Not that kind of terror.

"What did they want to know about Berga?"

"I don't know," she whispered. "They made me tell everything I knew about her. They made me sit there while they went through her things."

"Did they find anything?"

"No. I . . . I don't think so. They were horribly mad about it."

"Did they hurt you?" I asked.

An almost imperceptible shudder went through her whole body. "I've been hurt worse." Her eyes drifted up to mine.

"They were disgusting men. They'll kill me now, won't they?"

"If they do they've had it."

"But it would still be too late for me."

I nodded. It was all I could do. I got up, took the last smoke out of my old pack and tapped the butt against my knuckle. "Can't I take a look at that suitcase of hers?"

"It's in the bedroom." She pushed her hair back with a tired motion. "The closet."

I walked in, snapped on the light and found the closet. The suitcase was there where she said it was, a brown leather gladstone that had seen a lot of knocking around. I tossed it on the bed, unfastened the straps and opened it up.

But nothing was in there that could kill a person. Not unless a motive for murder was in a couple old picture albums, three yearbooks from high school, a collection of underwear, extra-short bathing suits, a stripper's outfit and a batch of old mail.

I thought maybe the mail would do it, but most of them were trivial answers from some friend to letters she had written and were postmarked from a hick town in Idaho. The rest were steamship folders and a tour guide of southern Europe. I shoved everything back in the suitcase, closed it up and dropped it in the closet.

When I turned around Lily was standing there in the doorway, a fresh cigarette in her mouth, one hand holding the robe closed around her waist, her hair a white cloud that seemed to hover above her. When she spoke the voice didn't sound as though it belonged to her at all.

"What am I to do now?"

I reached out and folded my hand over hers and drew her closer to me. The fingers were cold, her body was a warm thing that wanted to search for something.

"Got any place to go?"

"No," faintly.

"Money?"

"Just a little."

"Get dressed. How long will it take?"

"A . . . a few minutes."

For the briefest interval her face brightened with a new hope, then she smiled and shook her head. "It . . . won't do any good, I've seen men like that before. They're not like other people. They'd find me."

My laugh was short and hard. "We'll make it tough for them just the same. And don't kid yourself about them being

54

too different. They're just like anybody else in most ways. They're afraid of things too. I'm not kidding you or me. You know what the score is so all we can do is give it a try."

I stopped for a second and let a thought run through my head again. I grinned down at her and said, "You know . . . don't be a bit surprised if you live a lot longer than you think you should."

"Why?"

"I have an idea the outfit who worked you over don't really know what they're after and they're not going to kill any leads until they get it."

"But I . . . don't have any idea . . ."

"Let them find that out for themselves," I interrupted. "Let's get you out of here as fast as we can."

I dropped her hand and pushed her into the bedroom. She looked at me, her face happy, then her body went tight and it showed in the way her eyes lit up, that crazy desire to say thanks somehow; but I pulled the door shut before she could do what she wanted to do and went inside opening a fresh deck of Luckies.

The gun was still there on the floor, a metallic glitter asleep on a bed of faded green wool. The safety was off and the hammer was still back. All that time in the beginning I was about a literal ounce away from being nice and dead. Lily Carver hadn't been fooling a bit.

She took almost five minutes. I heard the door open and turned around. It wasn't the same Lily. It was a new woman, a fresh and lovely woman who was a taller, graceful woman. It was one for whom the green gabardine suit had been intended, exquisitely molding every feature of her body. Her legs were silken things, their curves flashing enough to take your eyes away from the luxury of her hair that poked out under the hat.

It wasn't a worried or a scared Lily this time. It was a Lily who took my arm and held it tightly, smiling a smile that was real. "Where are we going, Mike?"

It was the first time she had said my name and I liked the way she said it.

"To my place." I told her.

We went downstairs and out on Atlantic Avenue. We played a game of not being seen in case there were watchers and if there were they weren't good enough to keep up with us. We used the subway to go home and took a cab to the door. When I was sure nobody was in the lobby I took her in.

It was all very simple.

When we got upstairs I told her to hop into the sack and showed her the spare bedroom. She smiled, reached out and patted my cheek and said, "It's been a long time since I met a nice guy, Mike."

That strange excitement seemed to be inside her like a coiled spring. I squeezed her wrist and she knew what I was saying without having to use words and her mouth started to part.

I stopped it there.

Or maybe she stopped it.

The spring wound tighter and tighter, then I let her go and walked away.

Behind me the door closed softly and I thought I heard a whispered "Good night, Mike."

I started it that night. At three-thirty the word went out in the back room of a gin mill off Forty-second and Third. Before morning it would yell and before the night came again it would pay off. One way or another.

Wherever they were, whoever they were, they would hear about it. They'd know me and know what the word meant. They'd sit and think for a little while and if they knew me well enough maybe they'd feel a little bit sweaty and not so sure of themselves any more. They couldn't laugh it off. With anybody else, perhaps, but not with me.

Wise guys, A pack of conniving slobs with the world in their hands and the power and money to buck a government while they sat on their fat tails, yet before morning there wouldn't be one of them who didn't have a funny feeling around his gut.

This time they had to move.

The word was out.

I went back to the apartment and listened at the door of Lily's room. I could hear her regular, heavy breathing. I stood there a minute, took a final drag on the butt, put it out and headed for my sack.

Chapter Seven

SHE WAS UP when the phone rang in the morning. I heard the dishes rattling and smelt the coffee. She called out, "Any time you're ready, come eat."

I said okay and picked up the phone.

The voice was low and soft, the kind you'd never miss in a million years. It was the best way to wake up and it showed in my voice when I said, "Hi Velda, what's doing?"

"Plenty is doing, but nothing I want to talk about over the phone."

"Get something?"

"Yes."

"Where are you now?"

"Down at the office. A place you ought to try to get to once a week, at least."

"You know how things are, honey," I said.

Lily looked in the door, waved and pointed toward the kitchen. I nodded, glad that Velda didn't know how things were right then.

"Where were *you* last night? I called until I was too tired to stay awake and tried again this morning."

"I was busy."

"Oh, Pat called." She tried to keep her voice its natural huskiness but it wanted to get away.

"I suppose he said too much."

"He said enough." She stopped and I could hear her breathing into the phone. "Mike, I'm scared."

"Well don't be, kitten. I know what I'm doing. You ought to know that."

"I'm still scared. I think somebody tried to break into my apartment last night."

That one got a low whistle out of me. "What happened?"

"Nothing. I heard a noise in the lock for a while but whoever was trying it gave up. I'm glad I got that special job now. Are you coming over?"

"Not right away."

"You ought to. A lot of mail is piling up. I paid all the bills, but you have a sackful of personal stuff."

"I'll get to it later. Look, did you make out on that info?"

"Somewhat. Do you want it now?"

"*Right* now, kitten. I'll meet you in the Texan Bar in an hour."

"All right, Mike."

"And kitten . . . you got that little heater of yours handy?"

"Well . . ."

"Then keep it handy but don't let it show."

"It's handy."

"Good. Grab a cab and get over there."

"I'll be there in an hour."

I slapped the phone back, hopped up and took a fast shower. Lily had everything on the table when I got there, a hopeful smile on her face. The table was spread with enough for a couple of lumberjacks and I ate until I made a dent in the mess, then went for seconds on the coffee.

Lily handed me a fresh pack of Luckies, held out a match and smiled again when I slumped back in my chair. "Have enough?"

"Are you kidding? I'm a city boy, remember?"

"You don't look like a city boy."

"What do I look like?"

Her eyes did it slow. Up and down twice, then a steady scrutiny of my face. For a minute it was supposed to be funny, but the second time there was no humor in it. The eyes seemed to get bigger and deeper with some far-away hungry quality that was past defining. Then almost as quickly as it had come there was a crazy, fearful expression there in its place that lasted the blink of an eye and she forced a laugh out.

"You look like a nice guy, Mike. I haven't seen many nice guys. I'm afraid they make an impression."

"Don't get the wrong impression, Lily," I told her. "I used to think I wasn't much of a sentimentalist, but sometimes I wonder. Right now you're pretty important to me so I may look like a good egg to you. Just don't go walking off with anything while you're here or I'll look different to you."

Her smile got bigger. "You're not fooling me."

I tossed the butt in my empty cup and it fizzled out. "So I'm getting old. You don't stay young in this racket very long."

"Mike . . ."

I knew what she was going to say before she said it. "I'll be gone for awhile. I don't know how long. The chances are nobody will be up here, but just to keep from sticking our

58

necks out, don't answer that door. If a key goes in the lock it'll be me. Keep the chain on the door until I open it, look for yourself then to make sure and then open up."

"Supposing the phone rings?"

"Let it ring. If I want you I'll call the janitor, have him push the doorbell twice, then I'll call you. Got it?"

"I got it."

"Good. Now take it easy until I get back."

She gave me a slow, friendly wink and a grin, then followed it up with a soft kiss that formed on her lips and crossed the room to me. She was all dressed up with no place to go and didn't care, a beautiful white-headed doll with funny eyes that said she had been around too long and seen too many things. But now she looked happy.

I went downstairs, waited until a cab cruised by and grabbed it. We made the Texan Bar with ten minutes left out of the hour so I loafed around outside until a cab pulled into the curb and Velda got out.

Getting out of a cab is one of the things most women don't do right. But most women aren't Velda. Without half trying she made a production out of it. When you saw her do it you knew she wasn't getting out of a cab so much as making an entrance onto the street. Nothing showed, but there was so much to show that you had to watch to see if it would happen or not and even when it didn't you weren't a bit disappointed.

She turned around, gave me that impish grin and took my arm with a tight squeeze that said she was happy as all get out to see me and the guy with the packages beside me sighed and muttered something about some guys having all the luck.

Inside the Texan we picked a booth as far back as we could get, ordered up lunch for Velda, a beer for me and then she handed me the envelope from her handbag. "As much as I could get. It cost two hundred and a promise of favors to be repaid . . . if necessary.

"By you?"

Her face darkened, then twisted into a smile. "By you."

I slipped my finger under the flap and drew out the sheets. One was a handwritten copy of the sanitarium report with the rest filling in Berga Torn's life history. Velda had carried out instructions. At the bottom of the last page was a list of names.

Evello's was there. So was Congressman Geyfey's. At the tail end was Billy Mist and when I held my finger on it Velda said, "She went out with him periodically. She was seen with him, but whenever it was, the spotlight was on him . . . not her."

"No," I said softly, "the spotlight is always on Billy. The picture's starting to get dirty."

"Mike . . ." She was tapping her nails against the table. "Who is Billy Mist?"

I grunted, picked up a Lucky and lit it. "It's a picture that goes back pretty far. He used to be known as Billy the Kid and he had as many notches on his rod as the original, if they still notch rods. Just before the war he went legit. At least on the outside he looked clean. He's been tied into a lot of messy stuff but nothing's been proven against him."

"So?"

"He's a known Mafia connection," I said. "He sits pretty high, too."

Velda's face paled a little. "Brother!"

"Why?"

"Eddie Connely gave me the lead this morning in Toscio's Restaurant. He and another reporter seemed to have a pretty good inside track on the Torn gal, both of them being on the police beat. Trouble was, they had to suppress most of it and they were pretty disgusted. Anyway, Eddie mentioned Billy Mist and pointed him out. He was over at the bar and I turned around to look at him. About then he happened to turn around too, caught me watching him and got the wrong slant on things. He left his drink, came over and handed me the slimiest proposition I ever heard right out in the open. What I told him no lady should repeat, but Eddie and his pal got a little green and I thought the Mist character would pop his buttons. Eddie didn't say much after that. He finished his coffee, paid the check and out they went."

I could feel my teeth showing through the grin. My chest was tight and things were happening in my head. Velda said, "Easy, chum.

I spit the cigarette out and didn't say anything for a minute. Billy Mist, the jerk with the duck's-tail haircut held down with a pound of grease. The tough guy who took what he wanted whenever he wanted. The uptown kid with the big money and the heavy connections.

When I got rid of the things in my head I squinted at her across the table. "Kitten, don't every say I'm the guy who goes looking for trouble."

"Bad, Mike?"

"Bad enough. Mist isn't the type to forget. He can take anything except a slam at his manhood."

"I can take care of myself."

"Honey . . . *no* dame can take care of herself, including you. Be careful, will you?"

She seemed to smile all over. "Worried, Mike?"

"Certainly."

"Love me?"

"Yeah," I said, "I love you, but I go for the way you are and not the way you could look if Mist started working you over." I grinned at her and slapped my hand down over hers. "Okay, I'm not the romantic type this early and in this place."

"I don't care."

She sat there, tall and straight, the black page-boy hair swirling around her shoulders like a waterfall at night with the moon glinting on it. Broad-shouldered, smooth and soft-looking, but firm underneath. She always had that hungry animal quality about her, eyes that drank everything in and when they looked at me seemed to drain me dry. Her mouth was expressive, with full, ripe lips that shone wetly, a crimson blossom that hid even white teeth.

I said it again and this time it sounded different and her fingers curled up over mine and squeezed.

A guy like me doesn't take the kind of look she was giving me very long. I shook my head, got my hand loose and went back to the report she had compiled.

"Let's not get off the track." Her laugh was a silent thing, but I knew she felt the same way I did. "We have three names here. What about the other three?"

Velda leaned across the table to see where I was pointing and I had to keep my eyes down. "Nicholas Raymond was an old flame apparently. She went with him before the war. He was killed in an auto accident."

It wasn't much, but to pick up details like that takes time. "Who said?"

"Pat. The police know that much about her."

"He's really going all out, isn't he?"

"The next one came from him too. Walter McGrath seemed to be another steady she was heavy on. He kept her for about a year during the war. She had an apartment on Riverside Drive then."

"He local?"

"No, from out of state, but he was in the city often."

"Business?"

"Lumber. Gray-market operations on steel too. He has a police record." She saw my eyebrows go up. "One income-tax evasion, two arrests for disorderly conduct, one conviction and suspended sentence for carrying concealed weapons."

"Where is he now?"

"He's been in the city here for about a month taking orders for lumber."

"Nice." She nodded agreement.

"Who's this Leopold Kawolsky?"

Velda frowned, her eyes turning a little darker. "I can't figure that one out. Eddie tapped him for me. Right after the war Berga was doing a number in a night club and when the place closed down there was a street brawl that seemed to center around her. This guy knocked off a couple of men giving her a hard time and a photog happened along who grabbed a pic for the front page of his tabloid. It was pure sensationalism, but the picture and the name stuck in Eddie's mind. The same thing happened about a month later and one of those kids who snap photos in the night clubs caught the action and submitted it for the usual pay-on-acceptance deals. That's how Eddie remembered who the girl was so well."

"The guy, honey . . . what about him?"

"I'm coming to him. From the pictures he looked like an ex-fighter. I called the sports editor of a magazine and he picked the name out for me. Kawolsky fought under the name Lee Kawolsky for a year and was looking pretty good until he broke his hand in training. After that he dropped out of the picture. Now, about a month and a half after the last public brawl Lee was hit by a truck and killed. Since there were two deaths by cars in the picture I went into the insurance records and went over them carefully. As far as I could tell, or anybody else for that matter, they were accidents, pure and simple."

"Pure and simple," I repeated. "The way it would have to look."

"I don't think so, Mike."

"Positive."

"Good enough." I ran my eyes over the copy of the medical report, folded it before I finished it and tucked it back into the envelope. "Brief me on this thing," I said.

"There really isn't much. She appeared before Dr. Martin Soberin for an examination, he diagnosed her case as extreme nervousness and suggested a rest cure. They mutually agreed on the sanitarium she was admitted to, an examination there confirmed Dr. Soberin's diagnosis and that was that. She was to stay there approximately four weeks. She paid in advance for her treatment."

If ever there was a mess, this was it. Everything out of place and out of focus. The ends didn't even try to meet. Meet? Hell, they were snarled up so completely nothing made any sense.

"How about this Congressman Geyfey?"

"Nothing special. He was seen with her at a couple of political rallies. The man isn't married so he's clean that way. Frankly, I don't think he knew anything about her."

"This keeps getting worse."

"Don't get impatient. We're only getting started. What did Pat have to say about her?"

"It's all in writing. Probably the best parts they're not telling. Except for her connection with Evello she didn't seem to be out of the ordinary for a kid with her tastes. She was born in Pittsburgh in 1920. Her father was Swedish, her mother Italian. She made two trips to Europe, one when she was eight to Sweden, the next one in 1940 to Italy. The jobs she held didn't pay the kind of money she spent, but that's easy to arrange for a babe like that."

"Then Evello's the connection?"

"Evello's the one," I said. She looked at my face and her breathing seemed to get heavier. "He's here in New York. Pat'll give you the address."

"He's mine then?"

"Until I get around to him."

"What's the angle?"

"An approach. Better arrange for a regular introduction and let him do the rest. Find out who his friends are."

Only her eyes smiled. "Think I can pull it off?"

"You can't miss, baby, you can't miss."

The smile in her eyes got bigger.

"Where are you carrying the heater, kitten?"

The smile faded then. It got a little bit cold and deadly. "The shoulder rig. Left side and low down."

"Nobody'd ever notice, kitten."

"They're not supposed to," she said.

We finished eating and went back into the daylight. I watched her get into the cab the way she had got out and when the hack turned the corner I could feel the skin on my shoulder crawl thinking about where she was going. The next cab that came along I flagged down, gave him a Brooklyn address with instructions to stop by the Atlantic Avenue apartment first. The answer came fast enough when we reached the joint. The name was still on the wall but the neighbors said she had moved out during the night and the apartment was empty. A small truck with the trunks of a new customer started backing into the curb as we drove away.

The second Brooklyn address belonged to a newspaperman who had retired ten years ago. He was forty-nine years old but looked seventy. One side of his face had a scar that ran from the corner of his eye to his ear and down to his mouth. If he took off his shirt he could show you the three dimples in his stomach and the three larger angry pink scars in his back. One arm couldn't move at the elbow. He hadn't retired because he had wanted to. Seems like he had written an exposé about the Mafia one time.

When I came out it was two hours later and I had a folio of stuff under my arm that would have been worth ten grand to any good slick magazine. I got it free. I took another cab back uptown, sat in the back room of a drug store a buddy of mine ran, went through it twice, then wrapped it and mailed it back to the guy I got it from. I went into a bar and had a beer while the facts settled down in my mind. While I sat there I tried to keep from looking at myself in the mirror behind the back bar but it didn't work. My face wasn't pretty at all. Not at all. So I moved to a booth in the back that had no mirrors.

Evello's name was there. Billy Mist's name was there. In the very beginning. They were punks then but they showed promise. The guy in Brooklyn said you didn't pick up the connections any more because most likely the boys had new assignments. They had been promoted. That was a long time ago so by now they should be kings. There were other names that I didn't know, but before long I'd know. There were empty spaces where names should be but couldn't be supplied and those were in the throne room. Nobody knew who the royalty was. They couldn't even suspect.

Big? Sure, they were big. But then even the big ones would hear the word and their bigness would start to leak out all the holes. I was thinking about it and wondering if they had heard it yet when Mousie Basso came in.

Guys like Mousie you see around when there's not too much light and never see around when the heat's on. Guys like Mousie you see in the papers when the police pull in their dragnet at a time when there were no holes in the walls for them to duck into. In the faces of guys like Mousie you can tell the temperature of the underworld caldron or read your popularity with the wrong people by the way they shy away or hang on to you.

From Mousie's face I knew I was hot.

I knew, too, I wasn't very popular.

Mousie took one look at me sitting there, shot a quick look at the door and would have been out if I hadn't been reaching inside my coat for a smoke at the time. Mousie got white past the point of being pale when he saw where my hand was and when I gave him the nod to come over, he didn't walk, he slunk.

I said, "Hello, Mousie," and the corner of his mouth made a fast, fake smile and he slid into the booth hoping nobody had seen him.

He grabbed a nervous cigarette that didn't do him a bit of good, shook out the match and flicked it under the table. "Look, Mr. Hammer, you and me ain't got a thing to talk about. I . . ."

"Maybe I like your company, Mousie."

His lips got tight and he tried hard to keep from watching my hands. Half under his breath he said, "You ain't good company to be seen with."

"Who says?"

"Lots of people. You're nuts, Mr. Hammer . . ." He waited to see what would happen and when nothing did, said, "you go blowing off your stack like you been doing and you'll be wearing a D.O.A. tag on your toe."

"I though we were friends, kid." I bit into my sandwich and watched him squirm. Mousie wasn't happy. Not even a little bit.

"Okay, so you did me a favor. That doesn't make us that kind of buddies. If you want trouble you go find it by yourself. Me, I'm a peace-loving guy, I am."

"Yeah."

Mousie's face sagged under the sarcasm. "So I'm a chiseler. So what? I don't want shooting trouble. If I'm small potatoes that's all I want to be. Nobody gets bumped for being small potatoes."

"Unless somebody sees them talking to big potatoes," I grinned at him.

It scared him, right down to his shoes. "Don't . . . don't kid around with me, will you? You don't need me for nothing. Besides which if you do I ain't giving or selling. Lay off."

"What did you hear, Mousie?"

His eyes were quick things that swept the whole room twice before they came back to me. "You know."

"What?"

"You're going to scramble some people."

"What people." I didn't ask him. I told him to say it.

He whispered the word. "Mafia." Then as if it had been a key he swallowed he spilled over with the things he had been holding down while his eyes bulged in his head. His hands grabbed the edge of the table and hung on while the butt he had started to smoke burned through the tablecloth. "You're nuts. You went and got everybody hopped up. Wherever you go you'll be poison. Is it true you got something on the wheels? You better clam if you have. That kind of stuff is sure to lead to trouble. Charlie Max and Sugar . . ." The mouth stopped and stayed open.

"Say it, Mousie."

Maybe he didn't like the way I had edged forward. Maybe he saw the things that should have been written across my face.

The bulging eyes flattened out, sick. "They're spending advance money along the Stem."

"Moving fast?"

I could hardly hear his voice. "Covering the bars and making phone calls."

"Are they in a hurry?"

"Bonus, probably."

Mousie wasn't the same guy who came in. He was the mouse, but a mouse who didn't care any more. He was the mouse who spilled his guts to the cat about where the dog was and if the dog found out, he was dead. He reached for the remains of the cigarette, tried to drag some life into it and couldn't make it. I shook a new one out of my pack and handed it to him. The light I held out was steady, but he couldn't keep the tip of the butt in it. He got it going after a few seconds and stared into the flame of the lighter.

"You ain't scared a bit, are you?" He looked at his own hands, hating himself. "I wish I was that way. What makes a guy like me, Mr. Hammer?"

I could hate myself too. "Guys like me," I said.

The laugh came out his nose like he didn't believe me. "One guy," he said, "just one big guy and everybody gets hopped up. For anybody else, even the mayor, they wouldn't even blink, but for you they get hopped up. You say you're going to scramble and they make like a hillbilly feud. The word goes out and money starts passing hands. Two of the hottest rods in town combing the joints looking for you and you don't even get bothered enough to stop eating. They know you, Mr. Hammer. Guess maybe everybody knows something about you. That's why Charlie Max and Sugar Smallhouse got the job. They don't know nothing about you. They're Miami boys. You say you're going to do something, you do it and always there's somebody dead and it ain't you. Now the word has it you're going to scramble the top potatoes. Maybe you will and maybe you won't. With anybody else I'd take bets on your side, only this time it's different."

He stopped and waited to see what I'd say. "It's not so different."

"You'll find out."

He saw my teeth through the smile and shuddered. It does funny things to some people. "The world still goes," I said. "From now on to the end they'll have to stay away from windows and doors. They'll never be able to go out alone. Every one of the pack will have to keep a rod in his fist and wait. They'll have to double check everything to make sure I won't find out who they are and no matter how hard they try I'll reach them. Their office boys'll try to check me off but they're like flies on the wall. I'm going to the top. Straight up. I'm finding out who they are and when I do they're dead. I know how they operate . . . they're bad, but they know me and I'm worse. No mater where I find them, or when . . . any time, any place . . . that's it. The top dogs, those are the ones I want. The slime who pull the strings in the Mafia. The kings, you understand? I want them."

My grin got bigger all the time. "They've killed hundreds of people, see, but they finally killed the wrong dame. They tried to kill me and they wrecked my car. That last part I especially didn't like. That car was hand built and could do over a hundred. And for all of that a lot of those top dogs are paying through the kiester starting now. That's the word."

Mousie didn't say anything. He stood up slowly, his teeth holding his bottom lip to keep it up. He jerked his head in what was supposed to be a so-long and slid out from behind the table. I watched him walk to the door, forgetting the sandwich that lay on top of the counter. He opened the door slowly, walked out to the sidewalk and turned east, not looking to either side of himself. When he had gone I got up myself, paid my bill and took the change to a phone booth.

Pat was home and still up. I said, "It's me, pal. Velda told me you heard the news."

He sounded a little far away. "You don't have much sense, do you?"

"They're looking for me. Two boys by the name of Charlie Max and Sugar Smallhouse."

"They have reps."

"So I hear. What kind?"

"Teamwork. Max is the one to watch. They're killers, but Smallhouse likes to do it slow."

"I'll watch Max then. What else?"

"Charlie Max is an ex-cop. He'll probably have a preference for a hip holster."

"Thanks."

"Don't mention it."

I slapped the receiver back on the hook. The dime plinked into the box and the gaping mouth of the thing laughed at me silently. Well, in a way it was a pretty big joke. The army of silent men couldn't stay silent. I didn't know them but they knew me. They were just like the rest; crumbs who knew how to play a one-sided game, but when they were playing somebody who could be twice as silent, twice as dirty and twice as quick they broke in the middle and started begging. Someplace in the city were people with names and some without names. They were organized. They had big money in back of them. They had political connections. They had everything it took to stay where they were except one thing and that was me with my own slab in a morgue. They know what to expect from the cops and what to expect from the vast machine that squatted on the Potomac but they didn't know what to expect from me. Already one guy had told them, a punk with crooked yellow teeth who had had a gun on me and lost it. Then they'd ask around if they didn't already know and the stories they'd hear wouldn't be pretty. The fear they handed out so freely to others they'd taste themselves, knowing that before long, if I was still alive, they'd have to chew the whole lump and swallow it.

At the cigarette counter I picked up a fresh deck of Luckies, went out into the air and headed for the Stem. Out there were the hunters spending advance money. Cold boys with reps who didn't know the whole score. They knew the word was out and wanted to cut it off.

But they didn't hear the whole word. Before the night was over they'd hear a lot of things that might make them want to change their minds. One of the things was the rest of the word. They'd find out the hunters were being hunted.

Just for the fun of it.

Chapter Eight

THE *Globe* gave me the information on Nicholas Raymond. It was an old clipping that Ray Diker dragged out for me and which wouldn't have been printed at all if there hadn't been an editorial tie-up. The press was hot on hit-and-run drivers and used his case to point up their arguments about certain light conditions along the bridge approaches.

Nicholas Raymond got it as he stepped into the street as the light changed and his body was flung through a store window. Nobody saw the accident except a drunk halfway down the block and the car was never tracked down. The only details about him were that he was forty-two years old, a small-time importer and lived in an apartment hotel in the lower Fifties.

I told Ray Diker thanks and used his phone to call Raymond's old address. The manager told me in a thick accent that yes, he remembered Mr. Nick-o-las Raymondo, he was the fine man who always paid his bills and tipped like a gentleman extreme. It was too bad he should die. I agreed with him, poked around for some personal information and found that he was the kind nothing can be said about. Apparently he was clean.

Finding something on McGrath was easy. The papers carried the same stuff Velda had passed to me without adding anything to it. Ray made a couple calls downstairs and supplied the rest. Walter McGrath was a pretty frequent visitor to some of the gaudier night clubs around town and generally had a pretty chick in tow. A little persuasion and Ray managed to get his address. A big hotel on Madison Avenue. The guy was really living.

We sat there a few minutes and Ray asked, "Anything else?"

"Lee Kawolsky. Remember him?"

Ray didn't have to go to his files for that. "Good boy, Mike. It was a shame he couldn't follow through. Broke his hand in training and it never healed properly. He could have been a champ."

"What did he do for a living after that?"

"Let's see." Ray's face wrinkled in thought. "Seems like he bartended for Ed Rooney a bit, then he was doing a little training work with some of the other fighters. Wait a sec." He picked up the phone again, called Sports and listened for a minute to the droning voice on the other end. When he hung up he had a question in his eyes.

"What's the pitch, Mike?"

"Like what?"

His eyes sharpened a bit as they watched me. "Lee went to work for a private detective agency that specialized in supplying bodyguards for society brawls and stuff. One of his first assignments was sticking with a kid who was killed across the river a few days ago."

"Interesting," I said.

"Very. How about the story angle?"

"If I knew that I wouldn't be here now. How did he die?"

"It wasn't murder."

"Who says?"

He picked up a pipe, cradled it in his hand and began to scrape the bowl with a penknife. "Killers don't drive the same beer truck for ten years. They aren't married with five kids and don't break down and cry on the street when they've had their first accident."

"You got a good memory, kid."

"I was at the funeral, Mike. I was interested enough to find out what happened."

"Any witnesses?"

"Not a one."

I stood up and slapped my hat on. "Thanks for the stuff, Ray. If I get anything I'll let you know."

"Need any help?"

"Plenty. There's three names you can work on. Dig up anything good and I'll make it worth your while."

"All I want is an exclusive."

"Maybe you'll get one."

He grinned at me and stuck the pipe in his mouth. Ray wasn't much of a guy. He was little and skinny and tight as hell with a buck, but he could get places fast when he wanted to. I grinned back, waved and took the elevator to the street.

Dr. Martin Soberin had his office facing Central Park. It wasn't the world's best location, but it came close. It took in a corner, was blocked in white masonry with Venetian shuttered windows and a very discreet sign that announced his residency. The sign said he was in so I pushed open the door while the chimes inside toned my arrival.

Inside it was better than I thought it would be. There was a neat, precise air about the place that said here was a prominent medical man suited to the needs of the upper crust, yet certainly within the financial and confidential range of absolutely anybody. Books lined the walls, professional journals were neatly stacked on the table and the furniture had been chosen and arranged to put any patient at ease. I sat down, started to light a cigarette and stopped in the middle of it when the nurse walked in.

Some women are just pretty. Some are just beautiful. Some are just gorgeous. Some are like her. For a minute you think somebody slammed one to your belly then your breath comes back with a rush and you hope she doesn't move out of the light that makes a translucent screen out of the white nylon uniform.

But she does and she says hello and you feel all gone all over.

She's got light chestnut hair and her voice is just right. She's got eyes to go with the hair and they sweep over you and laugh because she knows how you feel. And only for a moment do the eyes show disappointment because somehow the cigarette gets lit as if she hadn't been there at all and the smoke from my mouth smooths out any expression I might have let show through.

"The doctor in?"

"Yes, but he's with a patient right now. He'll be finished shortly."

"I'll wait," I said.

"Would you care to step inside while I make out a card for you?"

I took a pull on the Lucky and let it out in a fast, steady stream. I stood up so I could look down at her, grinning a little bit. "Right now that would be the nicest thing I could think of, but I'm not exactly a patient."

She didn't change her expression. Her eyebrows went up slightly and she said, "Oh?"

"Let's say I'll pay the regular rates if it's necessary."

The eyebrows came down again. "I don't think that will be

71

necessary." Her smile was a quick, friendly one. "Is there any way I can help you?"

I grinned bigger and the smile changed to a short laugh.

"Please," she said.

"How long will the doctor be?"

"Another half hour perhaps."

"Okay, then maybe you can do it. I'm an investigator. The name is Michael Hammer, if it means anything to you. Right now I'd like to get some information on a girl named Berga Torn. A short while back Dr. Soberin okayed her for a rest cure at a sanitarium."

"Yes. Yes, I remember her. Perhaps you'd better come inside after all."

Her smile was a challenge no man could put up with. She opened the door, walked into the light again and over to a desk in the corner. She turned around, saw me standing there in the doorway and smoothed out her skirt with a motion of her hands. I could hear the static jump all the way across the room and the fabric clung even closer than it had.

"You'd be surprised how fast a person decides he really isn't sick after all," she said.

"What about the women patients?"

"They get sicker." Her mouth pursed in a repressed laugh. "What are you thinking?"

I walked over to the desk and pulled up the straight-backed chair. "Why a dish like you takes a job like this."

"If you must know, fame and fortune." She pulled out a file case and began to thumb through the cards.

"Try it again," I said.

She looked up quickly. "Truly interested?"

I nodded.

"I studied to be a nurse right after high school. I graduated, and quite unfortunately, won a beauty contest before I could start practicing. A week later I was in Hollywood sitting on my . . . . sitting around posing for stills and nothing more. Six months later I was car-hopping at a drive-in diner and it took me another year to get wise. So I came home and became a nurse."

"So you were a lousy actress?"

She smiled and shook her head.

"It couldn't have been that you didn't have a figure after all?"

Her cheeks sucked in poutingly and her eyes looked up at me with a you-should-know-better expression. "Funny

72

enough," she said, "I wasn't photogenic. Imagine that?"

"No, I can't."

She sat up with three typewritten cards in her hand. "Thank you, Mr. Hammer." Her voice was a song of some hidden forest bird that made you stop whatever you were doing to listen. She laid the cards out in front of her, the smile fading away. "I believe this is what you came for. Now can I see your insurance credentials, and if you have your forms I'll . . ."

"I'm not an insurance investigator."

She gave me a quizzical look and automatically gathered the cards together. "Oh . . . I'm sorry. You know, of course, that this information is always confidential and . . ."

"The girl is dead. She was murdered."

She went to say something and stopped short. Then: "Police?"

I nodded and hoped she didn't say anything more.

"I see." Her teeth pinched her lower lip and she looked sideways at the door to her left. "If I remember I believe the doctor had another policeman in to see him not long ago."

"That's right. I'm following up on the case. I'd like to go over everything personally instead of from reports. If you'd rather wait for the doctor . . ."

"Oh, no, I think it will be all right. Shall I read these off to you?"

"Shoot."

"To be brief, she was in an extremely nervous condition. Overwork, apparently. She was hysterical here in the office and the doctor had to administer a sedative. Complete rest was the answer and the doctor arranged for her to be admitted to the sanitarium." Her eyebrows pulled together slightly. "Frankly, I can't possibly see what there is here to interest the police. There was no physical disorder except symptoms brought on by her mental condition."

"Could I see the cards?"

"Certainly." She handed them to me and leaned forward on the desk, thought better of it when my head turned, smiled and sat back again.

I didn't bother with the card she had read from. The first gave the patient's name, address, previous medical history and down at the bottom along the left side was the notation *RECOMMENDED BY* and next to it was the name William Wieton. The other card gave the diagnosis, suggested treatment and corroboration from the sanitarium that the diagnosis was correct.

I looked at the cards again, made a face at the complete lack of information they gave me, then handed them back. "They help any?"

"Oh, you can never tell."

"Would you still like to see the doctor?"

"Not specially. Maybe I'll be back."

Something happened to her face. "Please do."

She didn't get up this time. I walked to the door, looked back and she was sitting there with her chin in her hands watching me. "You ought to give Hollywood another try," I said.

"I meet more interesting people here," she told me. Then added, "Though it's hard to tell on such short acquaintance."

I winked, she winked back and I went out on the street.

Broadway had bloomed again. It was there in all its colorful glory, stretching wide-open arms to the sucker, crying out with a voice that was never still. I walked toward the lights trying to think, trying to put bits together and add pieces where the holes were.

I found a delicatessen, went in and had a sandwich. I came out and headed up Broadway, making the stops as I came to them. Two hours went by in a hurry and nothing had happened. No, I didn't stay on the Stem because nobody would be looking for me on the Stem. Later maybe, but not now.

So I got off the Stem and went east where the people talked different and dressed different and were my kind of people. They didn't have dough and they didn't have flash, but behind their eyes was the knowledge of the city and the way it thought and ran. They were people who were afraid of the monster that grew up around them and showed it, yet they couldn't help liking it.

I made my stops and worked my way down to the Twenties.

I had caught the looks, seen the nods and heard the whispers.

At any time now I could have picked the boys out of a line-up by sight from the descriptions that came to me in an undertone.

In one place something else was added. There were others to watch for too.

74

Two-thirty and I had missed them by ten minutes.

The next half hour and they seemed to have lost themselves.

I got back to the Stem before all of the joints started closing down. The cabbie dropped me on a corner and I started the rounds on foot. In two places they were glad to see me and in the third the bartender who had pushed a lot of them my way tried to shut the door in my face, mumbling excuses that he was through for the night. I wedged it open, shoved him back inside and leaned against it until it clicked shut.

"The boys were here, Andy?"

"Mike, I don't like this."

"I don't either. When?"

"About an hour ago."

"You know them?"

His head bobbed and he glanced past me out the side window. "They were pointed out to me."

"Sober?"

"Two drinks. They barely touched 'em." I waited while he looked past me again. "The little guy was nervous. Edgy. He wanted a drink but the other one squashed it."

Andy ran his hands down under his fat waistband to keep them still. "Mike . . . nobody's to say a word to you. This is rough stuff. Do you . . . well, sort of stay clear of here until things blow over."

"Nothing's blowing over, friend. I want you to pass it around where it'll get heard. Tell the boys to stay put. I'll find them. They don't have to go looking for me any more."

"Jeepers, Mike."

"Tell it where it'll get heard."

My fingers found the door and pulled it open. The street outside was empty and a cop was standing on the corner. A squad car went by and he saluted it. Two drunks turned the corner behind his back and mimicked him with thumbs to their noses.

I turned my key in the lock. I knew the chain should be on so I opened the door a couple of inches and said, "It's me, Lily."

There was no sound at first, then only that of a deeply drawn breath being let out slowly. The light from the corner lamp was on, giving the room an empty appearance. She drifted into it silently and the glow from her hair seemed to brighten it a little.

Something was tight and strange in the smile she gave me through the opening in the door. Strange, faraway, curious. Something I couldn't put my finger on. It was there, then it was gone and she had the door unhooked and I stepped inside.

It was my turn to haul in my breath. She stood there almost breathlessly, looking up at me. "Her mouth was partly open and I could see her tongue working behind her teeth. For some reason her eyes seemed to float there, two separate dark wells that could knead your flesh until it crawled.

Then she smiled, and the light that gilded her hair made shadows across the flat of her stomach and I could see the lush contours harden with an eager anticipation that was like her first expression . . . there, then suddenly gone like a frightened bird.

I said, "You didn't have to wait up."

"I . . . couldn't sleep."

"Anybody call?"

"Two. I didn't answer." Her fingers felt for the buttons on the robe, satisfied themselves that they were all there from her chin down to her knees, an unconscious gesture that must have been a habit. "Someone was here." The thought of it widened her eyes.

"Who?"

"They knocked. They tried the door." Her voice was almost a whisper. I could see the tremor in her chin and from someplace in the past I could feel the hate pounding into my head and my fingers wanted to squeeze something bad.

Her eyes drifted away from mine slowly. "How scared can a person get, Mike?" she asked. "How . . . scared?"

I reached out for her, took her face in my hands and tilted it up. Her eyes were warm and misty and her mouth a hungry animal that wanted to bite or be bitten, a questioning thing waiting to be tasted and I wanted to tell her she never had to be scared again. Not ever.

But I couldn't because my own mouth was too close and she pulled away with a short, frenzied jerk that had a touch of horror in it and she was out of reach.

It didn't last long. She smiled and I remembered her telling me I was a nice guy and nice guys have to be careful even when the lady has been around. Especially a lady who has just stepped out of the tub to open the door for you and had nothing to put on but a very sheer silk robe and you know what happens when those things get wet. The smile

76

deepened and sparkled at me, then she drifted to the bedroom and the door closed.

I heard her moving around in there, heard her get into the bed, then I sat down in the chair facing the window and turned out the light. I switched the radio on to a late station, sitting there, seeing nothing at all, my mind miles away up in the mountains. I was coming around a curve and then there was that Viking girl standing there waving at me. She was in the beams of the lights, the tires shrieking to a stop, and she got closer and closer until there was no hope of stopping the car at all. She let out one final scream that had all the terror in the world in it and I could feel the sweat running down the back of my neck. Even when she was dead under the wheels the screaming didn't stop, then my eyes came open and my ears heard again and I picked up the phone and her cry stopped entirely.

I said a short hello into it, said it again and then a voice, a nice gentle voice asked me if this was Mike Hammer.

"That's right," I said. "Who's this?"

"It really doesn't matter, Mr. Hammer. I merely wanted to call your attention to the fact that as you go out today please notice the new car in front of your building. It belongs to you. The papers are on the seat and all you have to do is sign them and transfer your plates."

It was a long foul smell that seeped right through the receiver. "What's the rest of it, friend?"

The voice, the nice gentle voice, stopped purring and took on an insidious growl. "The rest of it is that we're sorry about your other car. Very sorry. It was too bad, but since things happened as they did, other things must change."

"Finish it."

"You can have the car, Mr. Hammer. I suggest that if you take it you use it to go on a long vacation. Say about three or four months?"

"If I don't?"

"Then leave it where it is. We'll see that it is returned to the buyer."

I laughed into the phone. I made it a mean, low kind of laugh that didn't need any words to go with it. I said. "Buddy . . . I'll take the car, but I won't take the vacation. Someday I'll take you too."

"However you wish."

I said. "That's the way it always is," but I was talking to a dead phone. The guy had hung up.

77

They were at me from both ends now. The boys walking around the Stem on a commission basis. One eye out for me, the other for the cops that Pat would have scouting. Now they were being generous.

Like Lily had said, how scared could a person get? They didn't like the way it was going at all. I sat there grinning at the darkness outside thinking about the big boys whose faces nobody knew. Maybe if I had boiled over like the old days they would have had me. The waiting they didn't go for.

I shook a Lucky out of the pack and lit it up. I smoked it down to the end, put it out, then went in and flopped down on the bed. The alarm was set for eight, too early even at that hour, but I set it back to seven and knew I'd be hating myself for it.

The heap was a beauty. It was a maroon Ford convertible with a black top and sat there gleaming in the early morning sunlight like a dew drop. Bob Gellie walked around it once, grinning into the chrome and came back and stood by me on the sidewalk.

"Some job, Mike. Got twin pipes in back." He wiped his hands on his cover-alls and waited to see what came next.

"She's gimmicked. Bob. Think you can reach it?"

"Come again?" He stared at me curiously.

"The job is a gift . . . from somebody who doesn't like me. They're hoping I step into it. Then goes the big boom. They're probably even smart enough to figure I'd put a mechanic on the job to find the gimmick so it'll be well hidden. Go ahead and dig it out."

He wiped the back of his hands across his mouth and shoved the hat back further on his head. "Best thing to do is run it in the river for a couple of hours."

"Hop to it, Bob, I need transportation."

"Look, for a hundred I can do a lot of things, but . . ."

"So I'll double it. Find the gimmick."

The two C's got him. For that many pieces of paper he could take his chances with a gallon of soup. He wiped his mouth clean again and nodded. The sun wasn't up over the apartments yet and it was still cool, but it didn't do much for the beads of sweat that started to shape up along Bob's forehead. I went down to a restaurant, filled up with breakfast, spent an hour looking in store windows and came back.

Bob was sitting behind the wheel looking thoughtful, the hood in front of him raised up like a kid with his thumb to his nose. He got out when he saw me, lit a cigarette and pointed to the engine. "She's hot, Mike. A real conversion."

I could see what he meant. The heads were finned aluminum jobs flanking dual carburetors and the headers that came off the manifold poked back in a graceful sweep.

"Wonder what she's like inside?"

"Probably complete. Think your old heap could take this baby?"

"I haven't even driven this one yet. Find the stuff?"

His mouth tightened and he looked around him once, fast. "Yeah. Six sticks wired to the ignition."

"It stinks."

"That's what I thought too," he told me. "Couldn't find a thing anyplace else though. Checked the whole assembly inside and out and if there's more of it the guy who placed it sure knew his business."

"He does, Bob. He's an expert at it."

I stood there while he finished his butt. He walked around the hood, got down under the car and poked around there, then came back and looked at the engine again.

Then his face changed, went back a half dozen years into the past, got tight, relaxed into a puzzled grin, then he looked at me and snorted. "Bet I got it, Mike."

"How much?"

"Another hundred?"

"You're on."

"I remember a booby trap they set on a Heinie general's car once. A real cutie." He grinned again. "Missed the general but got his driver a couple of days later."

He slid into the car, bent down under the dash and worked at something with his screwdriver. He got out looking satisfied, shoved his tools under the car and crawled in with them. The job took another twenty minutes and when he came out he was moving slowly, balancing something in his hand. It looked like a section of pipe cut lengthwise and from one end protruded a detonation cap.

"There she is," he said. "Nice, huh?"

"Yeah."

"Rigged to the speedometer. A few hundred miles from now a contact would have been made and you'd be dust. Had the thing wrapped around the top section of the muffler. What'll I do with it?"

"Drop it in the river, Bob. Keep the deal to yourself. Drop up to my place tonight and I'll write you a check."

He looked at the thing in his hand, shuddered and held it even tighter. "Er . . . if it doesn't mean anything to you, Mike . . . I'd like to have the dough now."

"I'm good for it. What're you worried . . ."

"I know, I know, but if anybody's after you this bad you might not live to tonight. Understand?"

I understood. I went up and wrote him out a check, gave him an extra buck for the cab fare to the river and got in the car. It wasn't a bad buy at all for three C's. And one buck. Then I started it up, felt good when I heard the low, throaty growl that poured out of the twin pipes and eased the shift into gear for the short haul north.

Pat had been wrong about Carl Evello being in the city. In one week he had gone through two addresses and the last was the best. Carl Evello lived in Yonkers, a very exclusive section of Yonkers.

At first the place seemed modest, then you noticed the meticulous care somebody gave the garden, and saw the Cadillac convertible and new Buick sedan that made love together in a garage that would have looked well as a wing on the Taj Mahal. The house must have gone to twenty rooms at the least and nothing was left out.

I rolled up the hard-topped driveway and stopped. From someplace behind the house I could hear the pleasant laughter of women and the faint strains of a radio. A man laughed and another joined him.

I cut the engine and climbed out, trying to decide whether I should crash the party or go through the regular channels. I started around the car when I heard tires turn into the driveway and while I stood there a light-green Merc drove up behind me, honked a short note of hello, revved up fast and stopped.

Beauty is a funny thing. Like all babies are beautiful no matter how they're shaped. Like how there are times when any woman is beautiful as long as she's the color you want. It's not something that only shows in a picture. It's a composite something that you can't quite describe, but can recognize the second you see it and that's the way this woman was.

Her hair was a pale brown ocean that swirled with motion and threw off the sunlight that bounced into it. She smiled at me, her mouth a gorgeous curve that had a peculiar attraction so that you almost missed the body that bore it. Her mouth was full and wet as if it had just been licked, a lush mouth with a will of its own and always hungry.

She walked up with a long stride, pressing against the breeze, smiling a little. And when she smiled her mouth twisted a bit in the corner with an even hungrier look and she said, "Hi. Going to the social?"

"I wasn't," I said. "Business, now I'm sorry."

Her teeth came out from under the soft curves and the laugh filled her throat. For the barest second she gave me a critical glance, frowned with a mixture of perplexed curiosity and the smile got a shade bigger. "You're a little different, anyway," she said.

I didn't answer and she stuck out her hand. "Michael Friday."

I grinned back and took it. "Mike Hammer."

"Two Mikes."

"Looks like it. You'll have to change your name."

"Uh-uh. You do it."

"You were right the first time . . . I'm different. I tell, not get told."

Her hand squeezed in mine and the laugh blotted out all the sounds that were around us. "Then I'll stay Michael . . . for a time, anyway." I dropped her hand and she said, "Looking for Carl?"

"That's right."

"Well, whatever your business is, maybe I can help you out. The butler will tell you he isn't in so let's not ask him, okay?"

"Okay," I said.

This, I thought, is the way they should be. Friendly and uncomplicated. Let the good breeding show. Let it stick out all over for anybody to see. That was beauty. The kind that took your hand as if you were lovers and had known each other a lifetime, picking up a conversation as if you had merely been interrupted in one already started.

We took the flagstone path that led around the house through the beds of flowers, not hurrying a bit, but taking in the fresh loveliness of the place.

I handed her a cigarette, lit it, then did mine.

As she let the smoke filter through her lips she said, "What *is* your business, by the way? Do I introduce you as a friend or what?"

Her mouth was too close and too hungry looking. It wasn't trying to be that way. It just was, like a steak being grilled

81

over an open fire when you're starved. I took a drag on my own butt and found her eyes. "I don't sell anything, Michael . . . not unless it's trouble. I could be wrong, but I doubt if I'll need much of an introduction to Carl."

"I don't understand."

"Sometime look up my history. Any paper will supply the dope."

I got looked at then like a prize specimen in a cage. "I think I will, Mike," she smiled, "but I don't think anything I find will surprise me." The smile went into that deep laugh again as we turned the corner of the building.

And there was Carl Evello.

He wasn't anything special. You could pass him on the street and figure him for a businessman, but nothing more. He was in his late forties, an average-looking joe starting to come out at the middle a bit but careful enough to dress right so it didn't show. He mixed drinks at a table shaded by a beach umbrella, laughing at the three girls who relaxed in steamer chairs around him.

The two men with him could have been other businessmen if you didn't know that one pulled the strings in a racket along the waterfront that made him a front-page item every few months.

The other one didn't peddle forced labor, hot merchandise or tailor-made misery, but his racket was just as dirty. He had an office in Washington somewhere and peddled influence. He shook hands with presidents and ex-cons alike and got rich on the proceeds of his introductions.

I would have felt better if the conversation had stopped when I walked over. Then I would have known. But nothing stopped. The girls smiled pleasantly and said hello. Carl studied me during the name swapping, his expression one of trying to recall an image of something that should have been familiar.

Then he said, "Hammer, Mike Hammer. Well, of course. Private detective, aren't you?"

"I was."

"Certainly. I've read about you quite often. Leave it to my sister to find someone unusual for an escort." He smiled broadly, his whole face beaming with pleasure. "I'd like you to meet Al Affia, Mr. Hammer. Mr. Affia is a business representative of a Brooklyn outfit."

The boy from the waterfront pulled his face into a crooked

smile and stuck out his hand. I felt like whacking him in the mouth.

I said, "Hello," instead and laughed into his eyes like he was laughing in mine because we had met a long time ago and both knew it.

Leo Harmody didn't seem to do anything. His hand was sticky with sweat and a little too limp. He repeated my name once, nodded and went back to his girl.

Carl said, "Drink?"

"No thanks. If you got a few minutes I'd like to speak to you."

"Sure, sure."

"This isn't a social visit."

"Hell, hardly anybody comes to see me socially. Don't feel out of place. This a private talk?"

"Yeah."

"Let's go inside." He didn't bother to excuse himself. He picked up a fresh drink, nodded to me and started across the lawn toward the house. The two goons sitting on the steps got up respectfully, held the door open and followed us in.

The house was just what I expected it to be. A million bucks properly framed and hung. A fortune in good taste that didn't come from the mouth of a guy who started life on the outer fringe of a mob. We went through a long hall, stepped into a study dominated by a grand piano at one end and Carl waved me to a chair.

The two goons closed the door and stood with their backs to it. I said, "This is a private talk."

Carl waved unconcernedly. "They don't hear anything," then sipped his drink. Only his eyes showed over the lip of the glass. They were almond shaped and beady. They were the kind of eyes I had seen too many times before, hard little diamonds nestling in their soft cushions of fat.

I looked at the goons and one grinned, rising on his toes and rocking back and forth. Both of them had a bulge on the right hip that meant just one thing. They were loaded. "They still have ears."

"They still don't hear anything. Only what I want them to hear." His face beamed into a smile. "They're necessary luxuries, you might say. There seem to be people who constantly make demands on me, if you know what I mean."

"I know what you mean." I pulled a cigarette out and tapped thoughtfully against the arm of the chair. Then I let him watch me make a smile, turning a little so the two goons could see it too. "But they're not worth a damn, Carl, not a damn. I could kill you and the both of them before any one of you could get a rod in his fist."

Carl half rose and the big goon stopped rocking. For a second he stood that way and it looked like he'd try it. I let my smile tighten up at the edges and he didn't try it after all. Carl said, "Outside, boys."

They went outside.

"Now we can talk," I said.

"I don't like that kind of stuff, Mr. Hammer."

"Yeah. It spoils 'em. They know they're not the hot rods they're paid off for being. It's kind of funny when you think of it. Put a guy real close to dying and he changes. I mean real close. They're only tough because they're different from ordinary people. They have little consciences and nothing bothers them. They can shoot a guy and laugh because they know they probably won't get shot back at, but like I said, let 'em get real close to dying and they change. They found out something right away. I got a little conscience too."

All the time I was speaking he was half out of his chair. Now he slid back into it again and picked up his drink. "Your business, Mr. Hammer."

"A girl. Her name was Berga Torn."

His nostrils seemed to flare out a little. "I understand she died."

"Was killed."

"And your interest in it?"

"Let's not waste time, you and me," I said. "You can talk to me now or I can do it the hard way. Take your pick."

"Listen, Mr. Hammer . . ."

"Shut up. You listen. I want to hear you tell me about your connection with the dame. Nothing else. No crap. You play games with somebody else, but not me. I'm not the law, but plenty of times there were guys who wished the law was around instead of me."

It was hard to tell what he was thinking. His eyes seemed to harden, then melted into the smile that creased his mouth. "All right, Mr. Hammer, there's no need to get nasty about anything. I've told the police exactly what the score was and it isn't important enough to keep back from you if you're genuinely interested. Berga Torn was a girl I liked. For a while back there I . . . well, kept her, you might say."

"Why?"

"Don't be ridiculous. If you knew her then you know why."

"She didn't have much to offer that you couldn't get someplace else."

"She had enough. Now, what else is there?"

"Why did you break it off?"

"Because I felt like it. She was getting in my hair. I thought you had a reputation with women. You should know what it's like."

"I didn't know you checked up on me that close, Carl." The eyes went hard again. "I thought we weren't playing games now."

I lit the cigarette I was fooling with, taking my time with that first drag. "How do you stand with the Mafia, Carl?"

He played it nice. Nothing showed at all, not even a little bit. "That's going pretty far."

"Yeah, I guess it is." I stuck the cigarette in my mouth and stood up. "But it's not nearly as far as it's going to go. I started for the door.

His glass hit the desk top and he came forward in his seat again. "You sure put up a big stink for a lot of small talk, Mr. Hammer."

I turned around and smiled at him, a nice dead kind of smile that had no laugh behind it and I could see him go tight from where I stood. I said, "I wasn't after talk, Carl. I wanted to see your face. I wanted to know it so I'd never forget it. Someday I'm going to watch it turn blue or maybe bleed to death. Your eyes'll get all wide and sticky and your tongue will hang out and I won't be making any mistake about it being the wrong joe. Think about it Carl, especially when you go to bed at night."

I turned the knob and opened the door.

The two boys were standing there. All they did was look at me and it wasn't with much affection. I was going to have to remember them too.

When I got back outside Michael Friday spotted me and waved. I didn't wave back so she came over, a mock frown across her face. I couldn't get my eyes off her mouth, even when she faked a pout. "Bum steer," she said, "no business?"

She looked like a kid, a very beautiful kid and all grown up where it counted, but with the grin and impishness of a kid nevertheless. And you don't get sore at kids. "I hear you're his sister."

"Not quite. We had the same mother but came from different hatches."

"Oh."

"Going to join the party?"

I looked over at the group still downing the drinks. "No thanks. I don't like the company."

"Neither do I for that matter. Let's both leave."

"Now you got something," I said.

We didn't even bother with good-byes. She just grabbed my arm and steered me around the building talking a blue streak about nothing at all. We made the front as a car was coming up the driveway and as I was opening the door of my new heap it stopped and a guy got out in a hurry, trotted around the side and opened the door.

I started wondering what the eminent Congressman Geyfey was doing up this way when he was supposed to be serving on a committee in Washington. Then I stopped wondering when he took the woman's arm and helped her out and Velda smiled politely in our direction a moment before going up the path.

Michael said, "Stunning, isn't she?"

"Very. Who is she?"

She stayed deadpan because she meant it. Her head moved slightly as she said, "I don't know. Most likely one of Bob's protégés. He seems to do very well for himself."

"He doesn't if he overlooked you."

Her laugh was quick and fresh. "Thank you, but he didn't overlook me, I overlooked him."

"Nice for me," I grinned. "What's a congressman doing with Carl? He may be your brother, but his reputation's got spots on it."

Her grin didn't fade a bit. "My brother certainly isn't the most ethical man I've known, but he is big business, and in case you haven't known about it, big business and government go hand in hand sometimes."

"Uh-uh. Not Carl's kind of business."

This time her frown wasn't put on. She studied me while she slid into the car and waited until I was behind the wheel. "Before Bob was elected he was Carl's lawyer. He handled some corporation account Carl had out West." She stopped and looked into my eyes. "It's wrong someplace, isn't it?"

"Frankly, Friday gal, it stinks."

I started the engine, sat and listened to it purr a minute then eased the gearshift in. All that power under the hood was dying to let go and I sat on it. I took the heap down the drive, rolled out to the street and swung toward the center of town. We didn't talk. We sat and rode for a while and watched the houses drift past. The sun was high overhead, a warm ball that smiled at the world, a big warm thing that made everything seem all right when everything was so damned wrong.

Pretty soon it would come. I thought about how she'd put it and how I'd answer it. It could come guarded, veiled or in a roundabout way, but it would come.

When it did come it was right out in the open and she asked, "What did you want with Carl?" Her voice sounded sleepy and relaxed. I glanced at her lying back there so lazily against the cushions, her hair spilling down the back of the seat. Her mouth was still a wet thing, deliciously red, firm, yet ready to vibrate like the strings on a fiddle the moment they were touched.

I answered her the same way she asked it; right out in the open. "He had a girl once. She's dead now and he may be involved in her murder. Your big-business brother may have a Mafia tie-up."

Her head rolled on the seat until she was looking at me. "And you?"

"When I get interested in people like your brother they usually wind up dead."

"Oh." That's all. Just "Oh" and she turned and looked out the window, staring straight ahead.

"You want me to take you back?"

"No."

"Want to talk about it?"

Her hand reached over and took the deck of Luckies from the seat beside me. She lit two at the same time and stuck one in my mouth. It tasted of lipstick, a nice taste. The kind that makes you want to taste it again, this time from the source.

"I'm surprised it took this long," she said. "He used to try to fool me, but now he doesn't bother. I've often wondered when it would happen." She breathed in deeply on the smoke, then watched it whip out the half-opened ventilator. "Do you mind if I cry a little bit?"

"Go ahead."

"Is it serious trouble?"

"You don't get more serious than killing somebody."

"But was it Carl?"

Her eyes were wet when they turned in my direction. "I don't know," I said.

"Then you're not sure?"

"That's right. But then again, I don't have to be sure."

"But . . . you're the police?"

"Nope. Not anybody. Just such an important nobody that a whole lot of people would like to see me knocked off. The only trouble is they can't make the grade."

I pulled the car to the curb, backed it into the slot in front of a gin mill and cut the engine. "You were talking about your brother."

She didn't look at me. She worked the cigarette down to a stub and flipped it into the gutter. "There isn't much to tell, really. I know what he's been and I know the people he's associated with. They aren't what you would call the best people, though he mixes with them too. Generally he has something they want."

"Ever hear of Berga Torn?"

"Yes, I remember her well. I thought Carl had quite a crush on her. He . . . kept her for a long time."

"Why did he dump her?"

"I . . . I don't know." There was a catch in her voice. "She was a peculiar sort of girl. All I remember is that they had an argument one night and Carl never bothered with her much after that. Somebody new came along."

"That all?"

Michael nodded.

"Ever hear of the Mafia?"

She nodded again. "Mike . . . Carl isn't . . . one of those people. I know he isn't."

"You wouldn't know about it if he was."

"And if he is?"

I shrugged. There was only one answer to a question like that.

Her fingers were a little unsteady when they picked up another cigarette. "Mike . . . I'd like to go back now."

I lit the butt for her and kicked the motor over. She sat there, smoked it out and had another. Never talking. Not seeming to do anything at all. Her bottom lip was puffed up from chewing on it and every few minutes her shoulders would twitch as she repressed a sob. I drove up to the gateway of the house, leaned across her and opened the door.

"Friday . . ."

"Yes, Mike?"

"If you think you know an answer to it . . . call me."

"All right, Mike." She started to get out, stopped and turned her head. "You looked like fun, Mike. For both of us, I'm honestly sorry."

Her mouth was too close and too soft to just look at. My fingers seemed to get caught in her hair and suddenly those lovely, wet lips were only inches away, and just as suddenly there was no distance at all.

The bubbling warmth was just what I expected. The fire and the cushiony softness and the vibrancy made a living bed of her mouth. I leaned into it, barely touched it and came away before there was too much hunger. The edges of her teeth showed in a faint smile and she touched my face with the tips of her fingers, then she climbed out of the car.

All the way back to Manhattan I could taste it. The warmth and the wetness and a tantalizing flavor.

The garage was filled so I parked at the curb, gassed up for an excuse to stay there and walked into the office. Bob Gellie was busy putting a distributor together, but he dropped it when I came in.

I said, "How did it go, kid?"

"Hi, Mike. You gave me a job, all right."

"Get it?"

"Yeah, I got it. I checked two dozen outlets before I found where those heads came from. A place out in Queens sold 'em. The rest of the stuff I couldn't get a line on at all. Most of it's done directly from California or Chicago."

"So?"

"They were ordered by phone and picked up and paid for by a messenger."

"Great."

"Want me to keep trying?"

"Never mind. Those boys have their own mechanics. What about the car?"

"Another cutie. It came out of the Bronx. The guy who bought it said it was a surprise for his partner. He paid cash. Like a jerk the dealer let him borrow his plates and it got driven down, the plates were taken off and handed back to the dealer again." He opened the drawer and slid an envelope across to me. "Here's your registration. I don't know how the hell they worked it but they did. Them guys left themselves wide open."

"Who bought the car?"

"Guess."

"Smith, Jones, Robinson. Who?"

"O'Brien. Clancy O'Brien. He was medium. Mr. Average Man. Nobody could describe him worth a hoot. You know the kind?"

"I know the kind. Okay, Bob, call it quits. It isn't worth pushing."

He nodded and squinted up his face at me. "Things pretty bad, Mike?"

"Not so bad they can't get worse."

"Gee."

I left him there fiddling with his distributor. Outside the traffic was thick and fast. Women with bundles were crowding the sidewalks and baby carriages were parked alongside the buildings.

Normal, I thought, a nice normal day. I hauled my heap away from the curb, cut back to Broadway and headed home. It took thirty minutes to get there, another thirty for a quick lunch at the corner and I went into the building fishing my keys out of my pocket.

Any other time I would have seen them. Any other time it would have been dark outside and light inside and my eyes wouldn't have been blanked out. Any other time I would have had a rod on me and it wouldn't have happened so easy. But this was now and not some other time.

They came out of the corners of the lobby, the two of them, each one with a long-nosed revolver in his fist and a yen to use it. They were bright boys who had been around a long time and who knew all the angles. I got in the elevator, leaned against the wall while they patted me down, turned around and faced the door as they pushed the LOBBY button instead of getting off, and walked out in front of them to my car.

Only the short one seemed surprised that I was clean. He didn't like it at all. He felt around the seat while his buddy kept his gun against my neck, then got in beside me.

You don't say much at a time like that. You wait and keep hoping for a break knowing that if it came at all it would be against you. You keep thinking that they wouldn't pop you out in broad daylight, but you don't move because you know they will. New York. This is New York. Something exciting happening every minute. After a while you get used to it and don't pay any attention to it. A gunshot, a backfire, who can tell the difference or who cares. A drunk and a dead man, they both look the same.

The boy next to me said, "Sit on your hands."

I sat on my hands. He reached over, found my keys in my pocket and started the car. "You're a sucker, mac," he said.

The one in the back said, "Shut up and drive." We pulled out into the street and his voice came again. This time it was closer to my ear. "I don't have to warn you about nothing, do I?"

The muzzle of the gun was a cold circle against my skin. "I know the score," I said.

"You only think you do," he told me.

Chapter Nine

I COULD FEEL THE SWEAT starting down the back of my neck. My insides were all bottled up tight. My hands got tired and I tried to slide them out and the side of the gun smashed into my head over my ear and I could feel the blood start its slow trickle downward to join the sweat.

The guy at the wheel threaded through Manhattan traffic, hit the Queens Midtown Tunnel and took the main drag out toward the airport. He did it all nice and easy so there wouldn't be any trouble along the way, deliberately driving slowly until I wanted to tell him to get it rolling and quit fooling around. They must have known how I felt because the guy in the back bored the rod into me every time I tightened up and laughed when he did it.

Overhead an occasional plane droned in for a landing and I thought we were going into the field. Instead he passed right by it, hit a stretch where no cars showed ahead and started to let the Ford out.

I said, "Where we going?"

"You'll find out."

The gun tapped my neck. "Too bad you took the car."

"You had a nice package under the hood for me."

The twitch on the wheel was so slight the car never moved, but I caught the motion. For a second even the pressure against my neck stopped.

"Like it?" the driver asked.

He shouldn't have licked his lips. They should have taught him better.

The pitch was right there in my lap and I swung on it hard. "It stunk. I figured the angle and had a mechanic pull it."

"Yeah?"

"So I punch the starter and blooie. It stunk."

This time his head came around and his eyes were little and black, eyes so packed with a crazy terror that they watered. His foot slammed into the brake and the tires screamed on the pavement.

It wasn't quite the way I wanted it but it was just as good. Buster in the back seat came pitching over my shoulder and I had his throat in my hands before he could do a thing about it. I saw the driver's gun come out as the car careened across the road and when it slapped the curbing the blast caught me in the face.

There wasn't any sense holding the guy's neck any more, not with the hole he had under his chin. I shoved as hard as I could, felt the driver trying to reach around the body to get at me while he spit out a string of curses that blended together in an incoherent babble.

I had to reach across the corpse to grab him and he slid down under the wheel still fighting, the rod in his hand. Then he had it out from the tangle of clothes and was getting up at me.

But by then it was too late. Much too late. I had my hand clamped over his, snapped it back and he screamed the same time the muzzle rocketed a bullet into his eyeball and in the second before he died the other eye that was still there glared at me balefully before it filmed over.

They happen fast, those things. They happen, yet time seems to drag by when there's only a matter of seconds and the first thing you wonder is why nobody has come up to see what was going on, then you look down the road and the car you saw in the distance when it all started still hasn't reached you yet, and although two kids across the street are pointing in your direction, nobody else is.

So I got in the driver's side, sat the two things next to me in an upright position and drove back the way we came. I found a cutoff near the airport, turned into it and followed the road until it became a one-lane drive and when I reached its limit there was a sign that read DEAD END.

I was real cute this time. I sat them both under the sign in a nice, natural position and drove back home. All the way back to the apartment I thought of the slobs who gave me credit for finding both gimmicks in the heap and then suddenly realized I was dumber than they figured and the big one was still there ready to go off any second.

Night had seeped in by the time I reached the apartment. I parked and went up to the apartment, opened the door enough to call in for her to take the chain off, but it wasn't necessary at all.

There was no chain.

There was no Lily either and I could feel that cold feeling crawl up my back again. I walked through the rooms to be sure, hoping I was wrong when I was right. She was gone and everything she owned was gone. There wasn't even a hairpin left to show that she had been there and I was so damned mad my eyes squinted almost shut and I was cursing them, the whole stinking pack of them under my breath, cursing the efficiency of their organization and the power they held in reserve, swearing at the way they were able to do things nobody else could do.

I grabbed the phone and dialed Pat's number. Headquarters told me he had left for the day and I put the call through to his apartment. He said hello and knew something was up the minute he heard my voice. "Lily Carver, Pat, you know her?"

"Carver? Damn, Mike . . ."

"I had her here at the apartment and she's gone."

"Where?"

"How am I supposed to know where! She didn't leave here by herself. Look . . ."

"Wait up, friend. You have some explaining to do. Did you know she had been investigated?"

"I know the whole story, that's why I pulled her out of Brooklyn. She had the city boys, the feds and another outfit on her back. The last bunch pulled a fast one today and got her out of here somehow."

"You stuck your neck out on that one."

"Ah, shut up," I said. "If you have a description, pass it around. She might know what it was the Torn kid was bumped for."

His breathing came in heavy over the receiver. "A pickup went out on her yesterday, Mike. As far as we knew she disappeared completely. I wish to hell you let me in on the deal."

"What have you got on her?" I asked him.

"Nothing. At least not now. A stoolie broke the news that she was to be fingered for a kill."

"Mafia?"

"It checks."

"Damn," I said.

"Yeah, I know how you feel." He paused, then, "I'll keep looking around. There's big trouble winding up, Mike."

"That's right."

"Stuff has been pouring in here."

"Like what?"

"Like more tough guys seen on the prowl. We picked up one on a Sullivan rap already."

I grunted. "That law finally did some good."

"The word is pretty strong. You know what?"

"What?"

"You keep getting mentioned in the wrong places."

"Yeah." I lit up a smoke and pulled in a deep drag. "This rumble strictly on the quiet between you and me?"

"I told you yes once."

"Good. Anybody find a pair of bodies propped up against a sign in Queens?"

He didn't say anything right away. Then he whispered huskily, "I should've figured it. I sure as blazes should've figured it."

"Well, just don't figure me for your boy. I checked my rod in a few days ago."

"How'd it happen?"

"It was real cute," I said. "Remind me to tell you someday."

"No wonder the boys are out for you."

"Yeah," I said, then I laughed and hung up.

Tonight there'd be more. Maybe a whole lot more.

I stood there and listened and outside the window there was another laugh. The city. The monster. It laughed back at me, but it was the kind of a laugh that didn't sound too sure of itself any more.

Then the phone jangled and the laugh became the muted hum once more as I said hello. The voice I half expected wasn't there. This one was low and soft and just a little bit sad. It said, "Mike?"

"Speaking."

"Michael Friday, Mike."

I could visualize her mouth making the words. A ripe, red mouth, moistly bright, close to the phone and close to mine. I didn't know what to answer her with, except, "Hi, where are you?"

"Downtown." She paused for a moment. "Mike . . . I'd like to see you again."

"Really?"

"Really."

"Why?"

"Maybe to talk, Mike. Would you mind?"

"At one time I would. Not any more."

Her smile must have had the same touch of sadness her voice had just then. "Perhaps I'm using that for an excuse."

"I'd like that better," I said.

"Will you see me then?"

"Just say where and when."

"Well . . . one of Carl's friends is giving a party this evening. I'm supposed to be there and if you don't mind . . . could we go together? We don't have to stay very long."

I thought about it a minute. I let a lot of things run through my mind, then I said, "Okay, I don't have anything else on the fire. I'll meet you in the Astor lobby at ten. How's that?"

"Fine, Mike. Shall I wear a red carnation or something so you'll know me?"

"No . . . just smile, kid. Your mouth is one thing I'll never forget."

"You've never really got close enough to tell."

"I can remember how I said good-bye the last time."

"That isn't *really* close," she said as she hung up.

I looked at the phone when I put it down. It was black, symmetrical and efficient. Just to talk to somebody put a thousand little things into operation and the final force of it all culminated in a minor miracle. You never knew or thought about how it happened until it was all over. Black, symmetrical, efficient. It could be a picture of a hand outlined in ink. Their organization was the same and you never knew the details until it was too late.

That's when they'd like me to see the picture.

When it was too late.

How many tries were there now? The first one they spilled me over the cliff. Then there was laughing boy who kept his gun in his pocket. And don't forget the dead-end sign. That one really must have scared them.

The jerks.

And someplace in the city were two others. Charlie Max and Sugar Smallhouse. For a couple of grand they'd fill a guy's belly with lead and laugh about it. They'd buck the biggest organization in the country because theirs was even bigger. They wouldn't give a damn where they scrammed to because wherever they went their protection went too. The name of the Mafia was magic. The color of cash was even bigger magic.

My lips peeled back over my teeth when I thought of them. Maybe now that they knew about the dead-end sign they'd do a little drinking to calm themselves down. Maybe they'd be thinking if they really were good enough after all. Then they'd decide that they were and wait around until it happened and if it came out right in a penthouse somewhere, or in a crummy dive someplace else one of the kings would swallow hard and make other plans and begin to get curious about footsteps behind him and the people around him. Curiosity that would put knots in their stomach first, tiny lumps that would harden into balls of terror before too long.

Ten o'clock. It was still a few hours off.

Ten o'clock, an exquisite, desirable mouth. Eyes that tried to eat you. Ten o'clock Michael Friday, but I had another appointment first.

I started in the low Forties and picked the spots. They were short stops because I wasn't after a good time. I could tell when I was getting ripe by the sidewise looks that came my way. In one place they started to move away from me so I knew I was nearing the end. A little pigeon I knew shook his head just enough so I knew they weren't there and when his mouth pulled down in a tight smile I could tell he wasn't giving me much of a chance.

Nine fifteen. I walked into Harvey Pullen's place in the Thirties. Harvey didn't want to serve me but I waited him out. He went for the tap and I shook my head and said, "Coke."

He poured it in a hurry, walked away and left me by the faded redhead to drink it. A plain-clothes man I recognized walked in, had a fast beer at the bar, took in the crowd through the back mirror, finished his butt and walked out. In a way I hoped he had spotted me, but if he did he was better at spotting than I was at keeping from being spotted.

She didn't move her mouth at all. Sometimes the things they pick up in stir pay off and this was one of them. She said, "Hammer, ain't 'cha?"

"Uh-huh."

"Long John's place. They're settin' you up."

I sipped my Coke. "Why you?"

"Take a look, buster. Them creeps gimme the business a long time ago. I coulda had a career."

"Who saw them?"

"I just came from there."

"What else?"

"The little guy's a snowbird and he's hopped."

"Coppers?"

"Nobody. Just them. The gang in the dump ain't wise yet."

I laid the Coke down, swirled the ice around in the glass and rubbed out my cigarette. The redhead had a sawbuck on her lap when I left.

Long John's. The name over the door didn't say so, but that's what everybody called it. The bartender had a patch over one eye and a peg leg. No parrot.

A drunk sat on the curb puking into the gutter between his legs. The door was open and you could smell the beer and hear a pair of shrill voices. Background music supplied by a jukebox. Maybe a dozen were lined up at the bar talking loud and fast. The curses and filth sifted out of the conversation like minor high lights and the women's voices shrilled again.

The boys were pros playing it cute.

Sugar Smallhouse was sitting at the corner of the bar, his back facing the door so anybody coming in wouldn't recognize him.

Charlie Max was in the back corner facing the door so anybody coming in he'd recognize.

They played it cute but they didn't play it right and Charlie Max took time out to bend his head into the match he held up to light his cigarette and that's when I came in and stood behind his partner.

I said, "Hello, Sugar," and thought the glass he held would crumple under his fingers. The little hairs on the back of his neck went up straight like happens to a dog when he meets another dog, only on this mutt the skin under the hair happened to be a pale, pale yellow.

Sugar had heard the word. He had heard other people talk. He knew about the sign marked DEAD END and about me and how things hadn't happened as they were planned. I could feel the things churning through his head as I reached under his arm for rod and all the while Sugar never moved a muscle. It was a little rod with a big bore. I flipped the shells out of the cylinder, dropped them in my pocket and put the gun back in its nest. Sugar didn't get it. He sweated until it soaked through the collar of his shirt but he still didn't get it.

Long John came up, saw me half hidden behind Sugar and said, "What'll it be, feller?" Then Sugar got it while Long John's eye got big and round. I had my hands around his middle in just the right spot, jerked hard and fast with my locked thumbs going into flesh under the breastbone like a kid snapping worms. Hard and fast . . . just once, and

Sugar Smallhouse was another drunk who was sleeping it off at the bar.

And Charlie Max was a guy suddenly alive and sober coming up out of his chair trying to clear a gun from a hip holster to collect his bonus. Eternity took place right then in the space of about five seconds of screaming confusion. Somebody saw the gun and the scream triggered the action. Charlie's gun never got quite cleared because the dame beside him pushed too hard getting away and his chair caught him behind the knees. They were all over the joint, cursing, pushing, falling out of the way and fighting to make the door. Then the noise stopped and it was just a tableau of silent panic because the crowd was behind me and there was nothing more to do except stand there with fascinated terror as Charlie Max scrambled for his rod and I closed in with a couple of quick steps.

The gun was there in his fist, coming up and around as I brought my foot up and the things that were in Charlie's face splashed all over the floor. His face looked soft and squashy a second, became something not at all human and he tried once more with the gun.

Nobody heard that kick because his arm made too much noise.

Somehow his eyes were still there, swelling fast, yet still bright. They were eyes that should have been filled with excruciating pain, but horror pushed it out as he saw what was going to happen to him.

"The job was too big, buddy. Somebody should have told you how many guys I put on their backs with skulls split apart because they were gunning for me." I said it real easy and reached for the gun.

The voice behind me said, "Don't touch it, Hammer."

I looked up at the tall guy in the blue pin-striped suit, straightened and grunted my surprise. His face stayed the way it was. There were two more of them standing in the back of the room. One was trying to wake up Sugar Smallhouse. The other came forward, ran his hands over me, looked at his partner with a startled expression that was almost funny before giving me a stare that you might see coming from a kid watching a ballplayer hit a homer.

There wasn't a damn thing they could do and they knew it, so I turned around, walked back outside and started crosstown to the Astor.

Washington had finally showed up.

She was waiting there in a corner of the lobby. There were others who were waiting too and used the time just to watch her. Some had even taken up positions where they could move in if the one she was waiting for didn't show up. She wasn't wearing a red carnation, but she did smile and I could almost feel that mouth on me across the room.

Her hair was the same swirly mass that was as buoyant as she was. There aren't many words to describe a woman like Michael Friday as she was just then. You have to look at the covers of books here and pick out the parts here and there that you like best, then put them all together and you have it. There was nothing slim about her. Maybe a sleekness like a well-fed, muscular cat, an athletic squareness to her shouldders, a sensual curve to her hips, and antagonizing play of motion across her stomach that seemed unconsciously deliberate. She stood there lazily, flexing one smoothly rounded leg that tightened the skirt across her thigh.

I grinned at her and she held out her hand. My own folded around it, stayed there and we walked out together. "Waiting long?" I asked her.

She squeezed my arm under hers. "Longer than I usually wait for anyone. Ten minutes."

"I hope I'm worth it."

"You aren't."

"But you can't help yourself," I finished.

Her elbow poked me. "How did you know?"

"I don't," I said. "I'm just bragging."

There wasn't any smile there now. "Damn you," she whispered. I could feel her go all tight against me, saw her do that trick with her tongue that left her mouth damp and waiting. I pulled my eyes away and opened the door of the cab that sat at the curb, helped her in and climbed in after her.

"Where to?"

She leaned forward, gave an address on Riverside Drive and eased back into the cushions.

It seemed to come slowly, the way sleep does when you're too tired, the gradual coming together of two people. Slow, then faster and all of a sudden her arms were around me and my hands were pressing into her back and my fingers curled in her hair. I looked at that mouth that wasn't just damp now, but wet and she said, "Mike, damn you," softly and I tasted the hunger in her until the fury of it was too much and I let her go.

Some shake and some cry, some even demand right then, but all she did was close her eyes, smile, open them again and relax beside me. I held out a cigarette, lit it for her, did mine and sat there without saying anything until the cab stopped by the building.

When we were in the lobby I said, "What are we supposed to be doing here, gal?"

"It's a party. Out-of-town friends of Carl and his business associates get together."

"I see. Where do you come in?"

"You might call me a greeter. I've always been the go-between for my big brother. You might say . . . he takes advantage of my good looks."

"It's an angle." I stopped her and nodded toward one of the love seats in the corner. She frowned, then went over and sat down. I parked next to her and turned out the light on the table beside me. "You said you wanted to talk. We'll never make it upstairs."

Her fingers made nervous little motions in her lap. "I know," she said softly. "It was about Carl."

"What about him?"

She looked at me appealingly. "Mike . . . I did what you told me to. I . . . found out all about you."

"So?"

"I . . . it's no use trying to be clever or anything. Carl is mixed up in something. I've always known that." She dropped her eyes to her hands, twining her fingers together. "A lot of people are . . . and it didn't seem to matter much, really. He has all sorts of important friends in government and business. They seem to know what he does so I never complained."

"You just took whatever he gave you without asking," I stated.

"That's right. Without asking."

"Sort of what you don't know won't hurt you."

Michael stared blankly at her lap for a few seconds. "Yes."

"Now you're worried."

"Yes."

"Why?"

The worry seemed to film her eyes over. "Because . . . before it was only legal things that gave him trouble. Carl . . . had lawyers for that. Good ones. They always took care of things." She laid her hand over mine. It shook a little. "You're different."

100

"Say it."

"I . . . can't."

"All right. You're a killer, Mike. You're dirty, nasty and you don't care how you do it as long as you do it. You've killed and you'll keep killing until you get killed yourself."

I said, "Just tell me one thing, kid. Are you afraid for me or Carl?"

"It isn't for you. Nothing will ever touch you." She said it with a touch of bitterness that was soft and sad at the same time.

I looked at her wonderingly. "You're not making sense now."

"Mike . . . look at me closely and you'll see. I . . . love Carl. He's always taken care of me. I love him, don't you see? If he's in trouble . . . there are other ways, but not you, Mike, not you. I . . . wouldn't want that."

I took my hand away gently, lit a cigarette and watched the smoke sift out into the room. Michael smiled crookedly as she watched me. "It happened fast, Mike," she said. "It sounds very bad and very inadequate. I'm a very lovely phony, you're thinking and I can't blame you a bit. No matter what I ever say, you'll never believe me. I could try to prove it but no matter how hard I tried or what I did, it would only make it look worse so I won't try any more at all. I'd just like to say this, Mike. I'm sorry it had to be this way. You . . . hit me awfully hard. It never happened to me before. Shall we go up now?"

I got up, let her take my arm and walked to the elevator. She hit the top button and stood there facing the door without speaking, but when I squeezed her arm her hand closed tighter around mine and she tossed her hair back to start the smile she'd have when we got out.

Carl's two boys were by the door in the foyer. They wore monkey suits and on them the term was absolutely descriptive. They started their smiling when they saw Michael and stopped when they saw me. You could see them exchange looks trying to figure the next move and they weren't up to it. We were through the door and a girl was taking my hat while they stood there watching us foolishly.

The place was packed. It was loud with laughs and conversation to the point where the music from the grand piano in the corner barely penetrated. Quiet little men with trays passed through the huddled groups handing out drinks and as heads turned to take them I could spot faces you see in

101

the paper often. Some you saw in the movies too, and there were a few you heard making political speeches over the air.

Important people. So damn important you wondered about the company they kept because in each group were one or two not so important unless you looked at police records or knew what they did for a living.

There were hellos from a dozen different directions. Michael smiled, waved back and started to steer me toward the closest group. Leo Harmody was there in all of his self-assuming importance ready to introduce her to the others. I took my arm away and said, "You go to it, baby. I'll find the bar and get a drink."

She nodded, a trace of a frown shadowing the corner of her mouth.

So I went to the bar.

Where Affia was holding Velda's hand and Billy Mist was giving her a snow job while Carl Evello watched cheerfully.

Velda was good. She showed pleasant curiosity and smiled. Carl wasn't so good. He got a little white.

Billy Mist was even worse. He got color in his greasy face but most of it was deep red and his lips tightened so much his teeth showed. I said, "If you're wondering, Carl, your little sister invited me along."

"Oh?"

"Charming girl," I said. "You'd never know she was your sister."

Then I looked at Billy. I was hating his guts inside and out so hard I could hardly stand still. I looked him over real slow like I was trying to find a spot in the garbage pail for the latest load and said, "Hello, stupid."

They can't take it. You can tear their heart out with one word and they can't take it. Billy's face was something ready to blow up like a landmine and he wasn't even thinking of the consequences. He was all alone in the room with me for that brief second and his hand tightened, got ready to grab something under his coat and right at the top of everything he felt I just stood there lazy-like and said, "Go ahead."

And he thought and thought about the dead men and watched his bubble bust wide open because his mind was telling him he'd never make it while he faced me and he got like Carl. White.

But I wasn't watching Billy Mist any more. I was watching Al Affia, plodding Al Affia who had the waterfront sewed up. Ignorant, thickheaded, slow Al who kept stroking Velda's hand all the while and who didn't turn color or go tight or do anything at all except say, "What's the matter with you guys?"

Velda repeated it. "What *is* the matter? After all . . ."

"Forget it, honey," Billy told her. "Just kidding around. You know how it is."

"Sure you know how it is," Al said.

I looked at the Brooklyn boy and watched him carve his face into a grin, muscle by muscle. Somebody should have mentioned Al's eyes to the boys. They weren't a bit stupid. They were small and close together, but they were bright with a lot of things nobody ever knew about. Someday they'd know.

"Nobody introduced me to the lady." I said.

Carl put his drink down on the bar, afraid to let go of it. "Hammer, I believe it is." He looked at me questioningly and I grinned. "Yes, Mike Hammer. This is Miss Lewis. Candy Lewis."

"Hello Candy," I said.

"Hello, Mike."

"Neat. Very neat. Model?"

"I do fashions for newspaper advertising."

Good mind, that secretary of mine. Nice and easy to explain to Billy how come she was shooting it with a couple of newshawks. I wondered how she had smoothed out his feelings.

She knew what I was thinking and went me one better. "What do you do, Mr. Hammer?"

They were watching me now. I said, "I hunt."

"Big game?"

"People," I said, and grinned at Billy Mist.

His nostrils seemed to flare out a little. "Interesting."

"You'll never know, chum. It gets to be real sport after a while." His mouth pressed together, a nasty smirk starting, "Like tonight. I got me two more. You ever hunt?"

His face wasn't red any more. It was calm and deadly. "Yeah, I hunt."

"We ought to try it together sometime. I'll show you a few tricks."

A low rumble came from Al's chest. "I'd like to see that," he laughed. "I sure would."

"Some people haven't got the guts for it," I told him. "It looks easy when you're always on the right side of a gun." I took them all in with one sweep of my eyes. "When you're on

103

the wrong end it gives you the squirms. You know what I mean?"

Carl was on the verge of saying something. I would like to have heard it, but Leo Harmody came up, bowed himself into our little clique with a deep laugh and spoke to Velda. "Could I borrow you long enough to meet a friend of mine, my dear?"

"No, certainly not. You don't care, do you, Billy?"

"Go ahead. Bring her back," he told Leo. "We was talking."

She smiled at the four of us, got down off the stool and walked away. Billy wasn't looking at me when he said, "You better stay home nights from now on, wise guy."

I didn't look at him either. I kept watching Velda passing through the crowd. I said, "Any time, any place," and left them there together. A waiter came by with a tray, offered me a drink and I picked one up. It was a lousy drink but I threw it down anyway.

People kept saying hello just to be polite and I said hello back. I picked Michael out of the crowd and saw that she was looking around for me too. Just as I started toward her I heard a whispered, "Mike!"

I stood there, took another drink from a passing waiter and sipped it. Velda said, "Meet me on the corner in an hour. The drug store."

It was enough. I walked off, waved to Michael and waited while she made excuses to her friends.

Her smile looked tired, her face worried, but she swung across the room and held her hands out to me. "Enjoying yourself?"

"Oh, somewhat."

"I saw you talking to my brother."

"And friends. He sure has great friends."

"Is everything . . . all right?"

"For now."

She sucked her lip between her teeth and frowned. "Take me home, Mike."

"Not tonight, kid." Her face came up, hurt. "I've been read off," I said. "I'm unhealthier than ever to be seen with. When it happens I don't want you around."

"Carl?"

"He's part of it."

"And you think I am too."

"Michael, you're a nice kid. You're lovely as hell and you

104

have everything to go with it. If you're trying to get something across to me I don't get it. Even if I did I wouldn't trust you a bit. I could go crazy nuts about you but I still wouldn't trust you. I told you a word the last time I saw you. It was Mafia. It's a word you don't speak right out because it means trouble. It's a word that has all the conniving and murder in the world behind it and as long as it touches you I'm not trusting you."

"You . . . didn't feel that way . . . when you kissed me."

There was no answer to it. I ran my hand along her cheek and squeezed her ear while I grinned at her. "A lot of things don't make much sense. They just happen."

"Will I see you again?"

"Maybe."

She walked to the door with me, said good-by and let her tongue run over her mouth slowly like she was enjoying the taste of something. I grabbed my hat and got out of there fast before she talked me into something I wasn't going to get talked into.

The two goons were still outside. There was something set in their faces and they didn't move when I went past them. When the elevator came up I stepped in, hit the button marked B and had a smoke on the way down. The door opened, I hit the main-floor buzzer as I got out and the elevator went back up a floor.

It wasn't hard to get out of there the back way. I went past the furnaces, angled around closed storerooms and found the door. There was a concrete yard in back bordered by a fence with a door that swung into the same arrangement on the other side. This time I met a young kid firing one of the furnaces, held out a bill as I went by and said, "Dames. You know how it is." He nodded wisely, speared the bill and went back to his work whistling.

I found the drug store and went in for a soda. They sold magazines up front so I brought one back with me while I waited. It was five minutes past the hour when Velda came in, saw me and slipped into the booth.

"You get around, Mike."

"I was thinking of saying the same to you. How come you tangled with Mist?"

"Later. Now listen, I haven't too much time. Earlier this evening two names came up. One of Carl's men turned in a report and I was close enough to hear it. The report was

105

that somebody had double checked on Nicholas Raymond and Walter McGrath. Carl got all excited about it.

"At the time I was talking to Al and Billy and had my back to Carl. He sent the guy off, called Billy off and I could tell from Billy's face that he passed the news on to him. He looked like a dead fish when he came back to the bar with us. He was so mad his hands were shaking."

I said, "Did Affia get the news?"

"Most likely. I excused myself for a few minutes to give him a chance to pass it politely."

"I wonder about something, Kitten."

"What?"

"I made a few phone calls."

"It sounded more important than that."

"Maybe Washington is getting hot."

"They'll have to get hotter," Velda grinned. "Billy said he had to talk a little business tonight." She reached in her handbag and brought out something. "He gave me a key to his apartment and told me to go ahead up and wait for him there."

I whistled between my teeth and picked the key out of her fingers. "Let's go then. This is hot."

"Not me, Mike. You go." There was a deadly seriousness about her face.

"What's the rest of it, Velda?"

"This is a duplicate key I dragged Carlo Barnes out of bed to make up for me. It took some fast and fancy working to get it so quickly."

"Yeah."

"Al Affia caught the pitch and invited me up to his place for awhile *before* I went to Billy's," Velda said softly.

"The lousy little . . ."

"Don't worry about it, Mike."

"I'm not. I'm just going to smash his face in for him, that's all." I sat there with my hands making fists and the hate pumping through my veins so hard it hurt.

Velda squeezed my hand and dumped a small aspirin bottle out of her bag and showed it to me. There weren't any pills in it, only a white powder. "Chloral," she said. "Don't worry."

I didn't like it. I knew what she figured to do and I didn't go for the play. "He's no tourist. The guy's been around."

"He's still a man."

My mouth felt dry. "He's a cagey guy."

106

Her elbow nudged her side meaningly. "I still have that, Mike."

You have to do things you don't want to do sometimes. You hate yourself for it but you still have to do it. I nodded, said, "Where's his place?"

"Not Brooklyn. He has a special little apartment under the name of Tony Todd on Forty-seventh between Eighth and Ninth Avenues." She pulled a note pad out, jotted down the number with the phone to go with it and handed it over. "Just in case, Mike."

I looked at it, memorized every detail there, then let the flame of my lighter wipe it out of existence. My beautiful, sleek animal was smiling at me, her eyes full of excitement and when you looked hard you could see the same thing there that you could see in mine. She stood up, winked and said, "Good hunting, Mike."

Then she was gone.

I gave her five minutes. I followed the shadows further uptown along the Drive to the building Billy Mist owned.

For the first time I was glad he was such a big man. He was so damn big he didn't have to stake anybody out around his place. He could relax in the luxury of security knowing that just one word could bring in an army if anybody tried to take the first step across the line.

It was another one of those things that came easy. You go in like you belonged there. You get on the elevator and nobody notices. You get off and go down the hall then stick the key in the lock and the door opens. You get treated to the best that money can buy even if the taste is crummy.

There were eight rooms in all. They were spotlessly clean and treated with all the care a well-paid maid could give them. I took forty-five minutes going through seven of them without finding one thing worth looking at until I came to the eighth.

It was a little room off the living room. At one time it must have been intended for a storeroom, but now it had a TV set, a tilt-back chair with an ottoman in place facing it, a desk and a bookcase loaded with pulps. Out of eight rooms here was the place where Billy Mist spent his solo time.

The desk was locked, but it didn't take more than a minute to get it open. Right in the middle section was a dimestore scrapbook fat with clippings and photos and he was in all of them. My greasy little friend was one hell of an egotist from the looks of the thumbmarks on the pages.

Another ten minutes went by going through the book and then I came to Berga's picture. There was no caption. It was just a rotogravure cutout and Billy was grinning at the camera. Berga was supposed to be background but she outsmiled Billy. Two pages later she came up again only this time she was with Carl Evello and it was Billy who was in the background talking to somebody hidden by Carl's back. I found two more like that, first with Billy, then with Carl, and topping it all was a close-up glossy of Berga at her best with *"love to my Handsome Man"* penned in white across the bottom.

Nothing else unless you wanted to count the medicine bottles in the pigeonholes. It looked like the cabinet in the bathroom. Billy must have had a pretty nervous stomach.

I closed the desk, locked it and wiped it clean. I went back to the living room, checked my watch and knew the time was getting close. I picked up the phone and dialed Pat's home number. Nobody answered so I called headquarters and that's where he was. It was a tired, disgusted Pat that said hello.

"Busy, Pat?"

"Yeah, up to my ears. Where have you been? I've been calling between your office and your house all night."

"If I told you you'd never believe it. What's up?"

"Plenty. Sugar Smallhouse talked."

I could feel the chills crawl up my legs until the hairs on the backs of my hands stood straight out.

"Give, Pat. What's the score?"

He lowered his voice deliberately and didn't sound like himself at all. "Sugar was on the deal when Berga got bumped. Charlie Max was called in on the job but didn't make it."

"Come on, come on. Who did he finger?"

"He didn't. The other faces were all new to him."

"Damn it," I exploded, "can't you get something out of him?"

"Not any more, pal. Nobody can. They were taking the two downtown to the D.A.'s and somebody chopped them."

"What're you talking about?"

"Sugar and Charlie are dead. One Federal man and one city cop are shot up pretty bad. They were sprayed by a tommy gun from the back seat of a passing car."

"Capone stuff. Hell, this isn't prohibition. For Pete's sake, Pat, how big are these guys? How far can they go?"

"Pretty far, it looks like. Sugar gave us one hot lead to a person with a Miami residence. He's big, too."

I could taste something sour in my mouth. "Yeah," I said, "so now he'll be asked polite questions and whatever answers he gives will satisfy them. I'd like to talk to the guy. Just him and me and a leather-covered sap. I'd love to hear his answers."

"It doesn't work that way, Mike."

"For me it does. Any trace of the car?"

"Sure, we found it." He sounded very tired. "A stolen job and the gun was still in it. We traced it to a group heisted from an armory in Illinois. No prints. Nothing. The lab is working on other things."

"Great. A year from now we'll get the report. I'd like to do it my way."

"That's why I was calling you."

"Now what."

"That screwball play of yours with Sugar and Max. The feds are pretty sore about it."

"You know what to tell them," I said.

"I did. They don't want to waste time pulling you out of jams."

"Why, those apple heads! Who are they supposed to be kidding? They must have had a tail on me all night to run me down in that joint and they sure waited until it was finished before they came in to get their suits dirty."

"Mike . . ."

"Nuts to them, brother. They can stick their heads . . ."

"Shut up for a minute, will you!" Pat's voice was a low growl. "You didn't have a tail . . . those two hoods did. They lost the boys and didn't get picked up again until they reached Long John's."

"So what?"

"So they needed a charge to drag them in on. The boys caught the tail, ditched their rods someplace and when one of our plain-clothes men braced them they were clean. They had a second tail and didn't know it, but they didn't take any chances and pulled some pretty fancy footwork just in case. If they could have been pulled in on a Sullivan rap we would have squeezed something out of them. You didn't leave them in condition to talk."

"Tell 'em thanks," I grunted. "I don't like to be gunned for. I'll try not to break up their next play."

"Yeah," Pat said sourly.

"Anything on Carver yet?" I asked him.

"Not a thing. We have two freshly killed blondes, more or less. One's been in the river at least three days and the other was shot by an irate lover just tonight. They interest you?"

"Quit being funny." I looked at my watch. Time was getting too damn short. I said, "I'll buzz you if anything turns up, otherwise I'll see you in the morning."

"Okay. Where are you now?"

"In the apartment of a guy named Billy Mist and he's due in any second."

His breath made a sharp hissing sound over the phone as I hung up.

I had almost timed it too close. The elevator marker was climbing toward the floor when I reached it and just in case I stepped around the corner of the stairs, went up to the first landing and waited.

Billy Mist and a heavyset muscleman came off the elevator, opened the apartment door and went in. There wasn't anything I wanted to talk to him about so I took the stairs back down instead of the elevator and got out the front door in one piece.

I got halfway down the block when some elusive little thing flashed across my mind and my eyes twisted into a squint as I tried to catch it. Something little. Something trivial. Something in the apartment I should have noticed and didn't. Something that screamed out to be seen and I had passed it by. I tried to bring it into focus and it wouldn't come and after a minute or so it passed out of sight altogether.

I stood there on the corner waiting for the light and a taxi swung by. I had the briefest glimpse inside the back and I saw Velda sitting there with somebody else. I couldn't stop it and I couldn't chase it. I had to stand there and think about it until I was all mixed up and I wasn't going to feel right until I knew the score. An empty cab came along and I told him to take me down to Forty-seventh Street.

The house was in the middle of the block. It was a beat-up affair fifty years old bearing the scars only a neighborhood like that can give it. The doorbell position said Todd lived on the ground floor in back. I didn't have to do any ringing because the front door was open. The hall was littered with junk I had to push aside until I came to the door that had *Todd* written on the card in the square metal holder.

I didn't have to ring any bells here either. This door was open too. I shoved it open and the light streamed out around me, light that glistened off the fetid pools of vomit on the floor, shining even more ominously from the drops of blood between the pools. The blood was in the hall too, and the light picked it up. It made sticky sounds on the soles of my shoes.

With a rod in my hand I would have felt better. It's company that can do your talking for you and a voice they listen to. I missed the rod, but I went in anyway but on my toes ready to move if I had to.

Nothing happened.

But I saw what had happened.

The glasses were there on the table with a half-empty bottle of mixer and an almost empty fifth of whisky. Ice had melted in the bowl with a few small pieces floating on top of the water.

On the floor was the remains of a milk bottle and there was blood all over one piece. Velda had given him the chloral treatment and he went out, but somehow he had spilled it out of his system and made a play for her. He would have killed her if he could have but she got him with the milk bottle.

Then it hit me all at once and I felt like adding to the pools on the floor. She had gone about in her search, left for Billy's and Al snapped out of it. He didn't stay cold as she had expected him to and Al would have got the news to him by now.

I made a grab for the phone in the corner, spun the dial to Pat's number again and sweated until he answered. I said, "Listen fast, Pat and no questions. They got Velda. She went up to Billy Mist's place and walked into a trap. Get a squad car up there as fast as you can. Got that? Get her the hell out of there no matter what happens and be damn fast about it because they may be working her over." I shot my number to him and told him to call back as soon as word came through.

When I hung up I was cold with sweat and tasting the cotton in my mouth. I closed the door and hoped Al would come back so I could do things to him myself. I didn't move out of the room until I got impatient waiting for the phone to ring, then I prowled through the place.

There was a full cabinet of liquor I was going to try but the smell of it sickened me when I got the bottle near my mouth so I shoved it back again. *Damn it, I thought, why doesn't he call!*

I started a butt going, spit it out after a second drag and went around the place some more. To keep my mind still and the buzzing out of my ears I used my eyes and saw why Al kept the place at all. For what he wanted it was a pretty good base of operation. There were souvenirs all over the place. It was a sloppy hovel, but sloppiness was part of the setup and probably nobody complained.

Al must have even done a little work there when he was finished with his parties. There were work sheets and union reports spread out on the table and a batch of company check stubs in the drawer held together by a rubber band. Like a sap he left a pair of empty checkbooks in the same drawer and the hundred and fifty he made a week from the company wouldn't have backed up the withdrawals shown in the books.

So he had a sideline. He cheated the government most likely. Try to find whose name the checking account was in and there'd be fun.

The phone still didn't ring so I rolled a stack of blueprints that showed dock layouts. At least two of them did. Nine of the others were ships' plans that were blown up in detail until they centered around one mass of lines I couldn't make out. I threw them all back on the table and started to walk away as the phone rang.

I caught it before the ring was finished and Pat said, "You Mike?"

"Speaking."

"What're you pulling, kid?"

"Cut the funny stuff, Pat, what happened?"

"Nothing, except a pair of my men are highly squiffed off. Mist was in bed alone. He let the cops in, let them look around, then chewed the hell out of them for pulling a search. He made one phone call and I've been catching it ever since."

I wasn't hearing him. I laid the phone back on its rack and stared at it dumbly. It started to ring again. It went through the motions four times, then stopped.

Outside it had started to rain. It tapped the windows in the back of the room, cutting streaks through the dust. When I looked again the dust was gone completely and the window seemed to have a live wavy motion about it. I pulled the Luckies out of my pocket, lit one and watched

112

the smoke. It floated lazily in the dead air, then slowly followed a draft that crossed the room.

I was thinking things that scared me.

My watch counted off the seconds and each tick was louder and more demanding, screaming not to be wasted.

I went back to the table, unfolded the blueprints, pushed the first two aside and looked at the legend on the bottom of the nine others.

The ship's name was there. Same ship. The name was *Cedric*.

It was starting to hang together now. When it was too late it was starting to hang together.

They wouldn't kill her yet, I thought. They'd do a lot of things, but they wouldn't kill her until they were sure. They couldn't afford the chance.

Then when they were sure they'd kill her.

Chapter Ten

I SLEPT HARD. The rain on the windows kept me asleep and I went through the morning and the rest of the day with all the things I pictured going through my mind and when they came together in one final, horrible ending I woke up. It was nearly six in the evening but I felt better. Time was too important to waste but I couldn't afford to let it pass while I was half out on my feet.

There was a box of frozen shrimp in the refrigerator I put on the fire and while it cooked up I put through a call. It took two more to locate Ray Diker and his voice sounded as sharp and pinched as his face. He said, "Glad you called, Mike. I was going to buzz you."

"Got something?"

"Maybe. I followed up on Kawolsky. The office he worked for pulled out the records and I got the details. He was hired to cover the Torn kid. She complained that someone was following her and she was a pretty scared baby. She paid the fee in cash and they put Lee on permanent duty. He picked her up in the morning and took her home at night."

"You told me that already, Ray."

"I know, but here's the good part. Lee Kawolsky quit reporting to the office in person after a week of it. He started checking in by phone. The office got ideas about it and put another man outside the apartment and found out Lee was pulling a voluntary twenty-four-hour duty. He was staying with the dame all the time."

"The office complain?"

"What for? It was his business and if she wanted it that way why sound off on it. Her checks still rolled in."

"Did they leave it that way?"

"There wasn't much they could do. The report the other investigator sent in said Lee was doing a fairly serious job of bodyguarding. He had already got into a couple of scrapes over her and she seemed to like it."

It was another thread being woven into place. The rope was getting longer and stronger.

Ray said, "You still there?"

"I'm still here."

"What did you call me for then?"

"The driver of the truck who killed Lee. Got that too?"

"Sure. Harvey Wallace. He lives upstairs over Pascale's saloon on Canal Street. You know where the place is."

"I know," I said.

"Might have something here on Nick Raymond."

"What?"

"He retailed imported tobacco through a concern in Italy. He had his name changed from Raymondo to Raymond before the war. Made a few trips back and forth every year. One of his old customers I ran down said he didn't look like much, but he spent the winters in Miami and dropped a wad of cabbage at the tables there. He was quite a ladies' man too."

"Okay, Ray. Thanks a lot."

"Got a story yet?"

"Not yet. I'll tell you when."

I hung up and turned the shrimp over in the pan. When they were done I ate, finished my coffee and got dressed.

Just as I was going out the front-door buzzer went off and when I opened it the super was standing there with his face twisted up into one big worry and he said, "You better come downstairs, Mr. Hammer."

Whatever it was he didn't want to speak about in the hall and I didn't ask him. I followed him down, got into his apartment and he motioned with his thumb and said, "In there."

She was sitting on the couch with the super's wife wiping

the tears away from her face, filthy dirty and her clothes torn and dust streaked.

I said, "Lily!" and she looked up. Her eyes were red things that stared back at me like a rabbit cornered in its hole.

"You know her, Mr. Hammer?"

"Hell yes, I know her." I sat on the couch beside her and felt her hair. It was greasy with dirt, its luster completely gone. "What happened, kid?"

The eyes filled with tears again and her breath came in short, jerky sobs.

"Let her alone a little bit, Mr. Hammer. She'll be all right."

"Where'd you find her?"

"In the cellar. She was holed up in one of the bins. I never would've seen her if I didn't see the milk bottles. First-floor tenants were squawking about somebody stealing their milk. I seen those two bottles and looked inside the bin and there she was. She said to call you."

I took her hand and squeezed it in mine. "You all right? You hurt or anything?"

She licked her lips, sobbed again and shook her head slowly.

The super's wife said, "She's just scared. Supposing I get her cleaned up and into some fresh clothes. She had a bag with her."

White outlined the red of Lily's eyes. She pulled back, her face tight. "No . . . I . . . I'm all right. Let me alone, please let me alone!" Then there was something fierce about the way she looked at me and bit out, "Mike . . . take me with you. Please. Take me with you!"

"She in trouble, Mr. Hammer?"

I looked at him steadily. "Not the kind of trouble you know about."

He saw what I meant, spoke rapidly to his wife in that language of his and her wise little eyes agreed.

"Help me get her upstairs."

The super took her bag, hooked one arm under hers and she came up from the couch. We used the service elevator in the rear, made my floor without meeting anybody and got her inside the apartment.

He said. "Anything I can do to help, just let me know."

"Right. Clam up about this. Tell your wife the same."

"Sure, Mr. Hammer."

"One other thing. Get me a damn big barrel bolt and slap it on my door."

"First thing tomorrow." He closed the door and I locked it after him.

She sat there in the chair like a kid waiting to be slapped. Her face was drawn and the eyes in it were as big as saucers. I fixed her a drink, made her take it all and filled it up again.

"Feel better?"

"A . . . little."

"Want to talk?"

Her teeth were a startling contrast to her skin when she bit her lip and nodded.

"From the beginning," I said.

"They came back," she said. Her voice was so low I could barely hear it. "They tried the door and one of them did something with the lock. It . . . opened. I sat there and I couldn't even scream. I couldn't move. The . . . the chain on the door stopped them." A shudder went through her whole body.

"They were arguing in whispers outside about the chain, then they closed the door and went away. One of them said they'd need a saw. I . . . couldn't stay here, Mike. I was terrified. I threw my clothes in the bag and ran out but when I got to the street I was afraid they might still be watching and I went down the cellar! Mike . . . I'm . . . I'm sorry."

"That's all right, Lily. I know how it is. Did you see them?"

"No. No, Mike."

The shudder racked her body again and she bit into her finger.

"When . . . that man found me . . . I thought he was . . . one of them."

"You don't have to worry any more, Lily. I'm not going to leave you here alone again. Look, go in and clean up. Take a nice hot bath and fix your hair. Then get something in your stomach."

"Mike . . . are you . . . going out?"

"For a little while. I'll have the super's wife stay with you until I get back. Would you mind that?"

"You'll hurry back?"

I nodded that I would and picked up the phone. The super's wife said she'd be more than glad to help out and would come right up.

From in back of me Lily said, "I'm so dirty. Ask her to bring some rubbing alcohol, Mike."

She said she'd do that too and hung up. Lily had finished her drink and lay with her head against the back of the chair watching me sleepily. The tautness had left her cheeks and color had come back to her mouth. She looked like a dog who had just been lost in the swamp then suddenly found his way home.

I started the water in the tub, filled it and lifted her out of the chair. She was light in my arms, completely relaxed, her breathing soft against my face. There was something too big in her eyes while she was so close to me and the strain of it showed in the corner of her mouth. She dug her fingers into my arms with a repressed hunger of a sort, sucked in her breath in a series of almost soundless staccato jerks and before I could kiss her she twisted her head and buried it against my shoulder.

The super's wife came in while she was still splashing around in the tub. She made clucking noises like a mother hen and wanted to go right to her, but the door was locked so she started scrounging some chow up in the kitchen. The bottle of alcohol was on the table and before I left I knocked on the door.

"You want a rub-down, Lily?"

The water stopped splashing.

"Glad to give you a hand if you want," I said.

She laughed from inside and I felt better. I left the bottle by the door, told the mother hen I was leaving and got.

Seven thirty-two. The gray overcast brought a premature dusk to the city, a gloomy wet shroud that came down and poured itself inside your clothes. It was the kind of night that made the city withdraw into itself, leaving the sidewalks empty and people inside the glass-fronted stores staring aimlessly into the wet.

I left my car where it was and hopped a cab down to Canal. He let me out at Pascale's and I went in the door on the right of the place. Here the hall was clean, clear and well lit. You could hear the hum of voices from the gin mill through the walls, but it diminished as I went up the stairs.

She was a short woman, her hair neatly in place with a ready smile that said hello.

"Mrs. Wallace?"

"Yes."

117

"My name is Hammer. I'd like to talk to your husband if he's home."

"Certainly. Won't you come in?"

She stepped aside, closed the door and called out, "Harv, there's a gentleman here to see you."

From inside a paper rustled and kids' voices piped up. He said something to them and they quieted down. He came out to the kitchen with that expression one stranger has for another stranger, nodded to his wife, then to me and stuck out his hand.

"Mr. Hammer," his wife said and smiled again. "I'll go in with the children if you'll excuse me."

"Sit down, Mr. Hammer." He pulled a chair out by the table, waved me into it and took one himself. He was one of those big guys with beefy shoulders and thinning hair. There was Irish in his face and a trace of Scandinavian.

"This'll be quick," I told him. "I'm an investigator. I'm not digging up anything unpleasant just for the fun of it and what you say won't go any further."

His tongue rolled around his cheek and he nodded.

"Sometime ago you drove the truck that killed a man named Lee Kawolsky."

The side of his face moved.

"I explained . . ."

"You don't get the angle yet," I said. "Wait. As far as you were concerned it was an out-and-out accident. Your first. It was one of those things that couldn't be helped so you weren't touched for it."

"That's right."

"Okay. Like I said, it's been a long time since it happened. Nobody else but you saw it. Tell me, have you ever gone over the thing in your mind since?"

Harvey said very quietly, "Mr. Hammer . . . there are some nights when I never get to sleep at all."

"You could see the thing happen. Sometimes the details would be sharp, then they'd fade?"

He squinted his eyes at me. "Something like that."

"What are you uncertain about?"

"You know something, Mr. Hammer?"

"Maybe."

This time he leaned forward, his face set in a puzzled grimace. "It's not clear. I see the guy coming out from behind the L pillar and I'm yelling at him while I slam on the brakes. The load in the truck lets go and rams the wall

118

back of the cab and I can feel the wheels . . ." He stopped and looked down at his hands. "He came out too fast. He didn't come out walking."

Harvey looked at me, his eyes beseeching. "You know what I mean? I'm not making up excuses."

"I know," I said.

"I came out of the cab fast and he was under the axle. I know I yelled for somebody to help me. Sometimes . . . I think I remember a guy running. Away, though. Sometimes I think I remember that and I can't be sure."

I stood up and put my hat on. "You can stop worrying then. It wasn't an accident." His eyes came wide open. "It was murder. Kawolsky was pushed. You were the sucker."

I opened a door, waved a finger at him. "Thanks for the help."

"Thank . . . you, Mr. Hammer."

"It's over with so there's no use fooling with the report," I said.

"No . . . but it's good to know. I won't be waking up in the middle of the night any more now."

Ten minutes after nine. In the lobby of the hotel a row of empty telephone booths gaped at me. Two people were sitting in the far corner holding hands. One other, not looking as though he belonged there was reading the paper and dripping water all over the floor.

The girl at the magazine counter changed a buck into dimes for me and I took the end booth on the row.

Thirty cents got me my party. His voice was deep and fat and it never sounded right coming out of the skinny little neck. He'd need a shave and his suit pressed but he didn't give a damn for either. He was strictly a nobody up until the squash was put on bookie operations then all of a sudden he was a somebody. He had a mind like a recording machine and was making hay in the new deal of black-market betting operations.

"I said, "Dave?"

"Right here."

"Mike Hammer."

The voice got closer to the phone and almost too casual. I could see him with his hand cupped around the mouthpiece and his eyes watching everybody in the place. "Sure, boy, what'cha doin'?"

"They're saying things along the row, Dave?"

"Piling up, big boy. Everybody got it."

"How do you feel about it?"

"Come on, mister, you know better'n that." The meaning sifted out of his words and I grinned. There was no humor in the grin.

I said, "I got what they want, kid. You tell it in the right places."

"You're killing me. Try again."

"So you saw me. I was in the bag and let it slip."

His voice dropped an octave. "Look, I'll do a lot of things, but you don't mess with them monkeys. They make a guy talk. Me, I got a big mouth when I get hurt up."

"It'll set, Dave. This is a big one. If it was a little one I'd ask somebody else. They got Velda. Understand that?"

He said three sharp, nasty curses at the same time. "You're trading."

"I'm willing. If it don't come off I'll blow the thing apart."

"Okay, Mike. I'll spin it. Don't bother calling me again, okay?"

"Okay," I said and hung up.

I walked over to the desk and the clerk smiled, "Room, sir?"

"Not now, thanks. I'd like to see the manager."

"I'm afraid you can't. He's gone for the evening. You see . . ."

"He live here?"

"Why, er . . . why, yes, but . . ."

I let a bill do the talking. The guy was well-dressed but underpaid and the ten looked big. "No trouble. I have to speak to him. He won't know."

The bill left my fingers magically. "Suite 101." He pointed a long forefinger across the room. "Take the stairs past the mezzanine. It's quicker."

There was a buzzer beside the door. I leaned on it until I heard the knob turn and a middle-aged, sensitive Latin face was peering out at me. The professional smile creased his lower jaw pulling the thin mustache tighter and he cocked his head in an attentive attitude ready to hear my complaint. His eyes were telling me that he trusted it would be a good one because Mr. Carmen Trivago was preparing to leave in a moment for a very important engagement.

I gave him a shove that wiped the smile clean off his face and he stumbled back inside while I closed the door. There was an instantaneous flash of mingled terror and hatred in his expression that dissolved into indignation as he drew

120

himself up stiffly and said, "What is the meaning of this?"

"Get back inside."

"I . . ."

My hand cracked him across the mouth so hard he hit the wall, flattened against it making unintelligible noises in his throat. He wasn't so stiff when I gave him a shove into the living room. He was all loose and jelly-like as if his bolts were ready to come apart.

I said, "Turn around and look at me." He did. "I'm going to ask you things and you answer them right. If you think you'd do better by lying look at my face and you won't lie. Let me catch you in one and I'll mangle you so damn bad you won't even crawl out of this dump for a month. Just for the hell of it I ought to do something to you now so you know I'm not kidding about it."

Carmen Trivago couldn't stand up any more. His knees went as watery as his eyes and he slumped crookedly on the edge of a chair.

"No . . . don't . . ."

"His right name was Nicholas Raymondo. With an 'O.' You were the only one who knew that. I thought it was your accent, but you knew his name, didn't you?"

His mouth opened to speak but the words wouldn't come out. He nodded dumbly.

"Where'd he get his dough?"

The spread of his hands said he didn't know and before he could shake his head to go with it I rocked him with another open-handed slap that left the prints of my fingers across his jaw.

He couldn't take anything at all and tried to burrow into the chair while he moaned, "Please. No . . . I tell you . . . anything. Please."

"When, then?"

"He had . . . the business. From abroad he . . ."

"I know about that. Business didn't give him the kind of money he spent."

"Yes, yes. It is true. But he never said. He spoke of big things but he never said . . ."

"He liked dames."

Carmen's eyes told me he didn't get what I was driving at.

I said slowly, "So do you. Two of a kind, you guys. Lady killers. You knew his right name. Those things only come when you know a person. You know that much and you

121

know a lot more. Think about it. I'll give you a minute. Just one."

His neck seemed to stretch out of shape as he held his head up. The longer he looked at me the more he curled up inside and his mouth started to move. "It is true . . . he had the money. It was enough. He was . . . satisfied to spend it all on much foolishness. There would be more soon, he told me, much more. At first . . . I thought he was making a boast. But no. He was serious. Never would he tell me more than that."

I took a slow step a little closer to him.

His hands went up to hold me off. "It is true, I swear it! This other money . . . several times when he was feeling, how you say it, high? he would ask me how I would like to have two million dollars. It was always the same. Two million dollars. I would ask how to get it and would smile. Raymondo . . . he had it, I know he had it. I tell you, this money was no good. I knew it would happen someday. I knew . . ."

"How?"

This time his eyes made passes around me, looking for something that wasn't there yet. "Before he . . . died . . . there were men. I knew of these men."

"Say the word."

It almost stuck in his throat, but he managed it. "Mafia," he said hoarsely.

"Did Raymondo know he was being followed?"

"I do not think so."

"You didn't tell him?"

He looked at me as if I was crazy.

"You never thought he was killed accidentally either, did you?" The fear showed in his face so plain it was a voice by itself. "You knew the score right along," I said.

"Please . . ."

"You're a crummy little bastard, Trivago. There's a lot of dead people lying around because you made them that way."

"No, I . . ."

"Shut up. You could have sounded off."

"No!" He stood up, his hands claws that dangled at his sides. "I know them! From Europe I know them and who am I to speak against them. You do not understand what they do to people. You . . ."

My knuckles cracked across his jaw so hard he went back over the arm of the chair and spilled in a heap on the floor.

He lay there with his eyes wide open and the spit dribbling out of his open mouth started to turn pink. He was the bug caught in the web trying to hide from the spider and he backed into the hornet's nest.

Carmen Trivago would never be the same again.

I used the phone in the lobby again. I buzzed my apartment and the super's wife answered it. I hadn't told her not to do so, she was doing me a favor. I told her it was me, asked if everything was okay and she said it was. Lily was asleep with the door locked but she could hear her breathing and talking in there. Her husband was making doubly sure things stayed quiet by pretending to do some work in the hall outside.

There were three other phone calls. A Captain Chambers had called and wanted to see me right away. I thanked her and hung up.

I turned up the collar of my trench coat and stepped out into the rain. The wind was lashing it up the street in waves now, pounding it against the buildings and as the cars went by you had a quick look at the drivers as the wipers ripped it aside before the faces muddled into a liquid haze.

The cab didn't wait to be called. He pulled into the curb and I hopped in, gave him the address and stuck a smoke in my mouth.

Someplace Velda was looking at the rain. It wouldn't be a pleasant sound, not this time. She'd be crazy with fear, scared so hard she wouldn't be able to think. They weren't the kind you could stall. She could only wait. And hope.

And someplace the people who had her were thinking too. They were thinking of a long string of kills and two fresh ones propped up against a dead-end sign. They were thinking of the word that went out and before they'd do anything at all they'd think harder still and it wouldn't be until I was dead that they'd feel right to do what they wanted to her.

I wasn't the cops and I wasn't the feds. I was one guy by himself but I was one who could add to the score without giving a damn at all. I was the one guy they were afraid of because the trail of dead men hadn't stopped yet. It was a trail that had to be walked and they were afraid of stepping on it.

Pat was in his office. You had to look twice to make sure he wasn't asleep, then you saw the light glinting off his almost-closed eyes and saw the movement of his mouth as he sucked on the dry pipe.

I threw my hat on the desk and sat down. He didn't say anything. I got out my next-to-last Lucky, held a light to it and let the smoke go. He still didn't say anything. I didn't have the time to trade thoughts. "Okay, chum, what is it?"

The pipe came out of his mouth slowly. "You conned me, Mike."

I started to get warm all over, an angry flush that burned into my chest. "Great. Just like that I gave you the business! You don't say anything . . . you sit there like a dummy then pull the cork. Say what's eating you or I'll get the hell out of here."

What distrust was in his face turned uncertain. "Mike, this thing is a bombshell. The biggest staff that ever operated on one case is out there working. They're going night and day looking for the answer then you come up with it ready to trade off for something."

I sat back in the chair. I took a deep, relieved pull on the smoke and grinned. "Thanks for the compliment. I didn't know it would get back so fast. Where'd you pick it up?"

"Every stoolie we know has his ears open. What are you trading for?"

My grin pulled tight at the edges, flattened across my teeth and stayed that way. "Velda. The bastards have Velda. She suckered Al Affia into a trap that didn't work and got caught in one herself. She played it too smart and now they have her."

It was quiet in the room. The clock on the wall hummed over the drone of the rain outside, but that was all.

"You don't look too worked up about it," Pat said. Then he saw my eyes and took it back without saying so out loud.

"They'll want to be sure. They'll want to know if I have it or not before they cut loose on her. They'll have to be sure. Right in the beginning they thought Berga Torn passed it on to me, went through my apartment. If it was anybody else they could have taken it easy, but not with me. They knew what was going to happen."

"Let's have it, Mike."

"The answer?" I said. I shook my head. "I don't have it. Not where I can reach out and touch it yet. I need more details."

"So do we. I thought we were sharing this thing."

"I didn't forget. What have you got?"

Pat stared at me a long time, reached out and fanned a few

papers across his desk. "Berga didn't escape from the sanitarium. She had it planned for her. She had a guest early that evening, a woman. The name and address were phony and we got no description except that she had brown hair. An attendant stated that she was pretty nervous after the guest left."

I cut in with, "How come you're just finding this stuff out?"

"It's a private sanitarium and they were afraid of ruining their reputation. They held off until we scared them. Anyway, we checked everybody in the place that night and came up with a spot from a couple of female visitors in the next room.

"When the closing bell ran they stood outside in the hall a few minutes talking. They were close to Berga's door and overheard a voice saying . . ." He glanced down at the sheet and read from it. ". . . 'they're after you. They were at the house today.'" The rest of it we had to put together and when we had it the dame was telling her something about the main gate, to be as casual as possible, and there would be a car waiting for her at the northwest corner."

Pat stopped and tapped the sheet. He tapped the stem of the pipe against his teeth and said, "On that corner was an F.B.I. wagon so whoever was waiting had to take up another spot. She got scared out of the deal and started hitchhiking when she didn't see the person she was expecting."

I said, "She saw the person, all right. He was in another car. She knew damn well she was being followed."

"There's something wrong," Pat said.

"Yeah. Like murders on the books as accidents."

Pat's jaw worked. "Proof?"

"No, but that's the way it happened." I couldn't see his face, but I knew what he was thinking. In his own way he had covered every detail I had. "The first one was Nicholas Raymond. That's where the answer is, Pat."

His eyes peered out at me. "Nicholas Raymond was a Mafia agent. He ran an import business as an excuse to make frequent overseas trips."

I didn't answer so he said, ". . . He was the guy who ran the stuff into this country that was turned into cash for Mafia operations."

He was watching me so closely that you couldn't see anything but the black pupils of his eyes. His face was all screwed up with the intensity of watching me and it was all I could do to hold still in the chair. I covered by dragging in another lungful of smoke and letting it go toward the ceiling so I could do something with my mouth except feel it try to stretch out of shape.

The picture was perfect now. It was the most beautiful piece of art work I had ever seen. The only trouble was I couldn't make out what it was all about nor who drew it.

I said, "How much would two million in narcotics before the war be worth now, Pat?"

"About double."

I got up and put on my hat. "That's what you're looking for, friend. A couple of shoe boxes that big. If I find them I'll tell you about it."

"Do *you* know where it is?"

"No. I have a great big fat idea, but if it's stayed buried this long it won't hurt anybody staying buried a while longer. All I want is the person who is after it because that person has Velda. If I have to I'll dig it up and trade for her."

"Where are you going now?"

"I think I'm going out and kill somebody, Pat," I said.

Chapter Eleven

THE COP AT THE SWITCHBOARD told me to go ahead and use the phone. He plugged in an outside line and I dialed the number that got me Michael Friday. I said, "Your line clear? This is Mike."

"Mike! Yes . . . There's no one here."

"Good. Now listen. There's a place called the Texan Bar on Fifty-sixth Street. Get down there as fast as you can. I'll be waiting. You got that?"

"Yes, but . . ."

I hung up on her. It was the best thing you could do with a woman when you wanted her to move fast. She'd be a good hour getting there which was just what I needed.

They were changing shifts outside the building and the flow of cops was getting thicker. I stepped outside, flagged down a cab and gave him the address of Al Affia's place. The rain had thinned traffic down to a minimum and he didn't take long getting there.

Nothing had changed. The blood was still there on the floor, dried into a crusty maroon. Close to the door the air was a little foul and inside it was worse. I shoved the door open, snapped on the light and there was Al grinning at me from

126

the corner of the room, but it was a horrible kind of grin because somebody had broken him into pieces with the whisky bottle. He wasn't killed plain. He was killed fancy as a person could be killed. He was killed so that he couldn't make any sound as he died and whoever did it must have had a great time laughing because Al died slow.

What I came for was gone. There were still two of the blueprints on the table but they showed the layout of the docks. The rest were missing. I picked the phone up, dialed the operator and said very quietly, "Operator . . . get me the local office of the F.B.I."

Somebody said briskly, "Federal Bureau of Investigation, Moffat speaking."

"You better get down here, Moffat," I said. I laid the phone down gently alongside the base and walked out.

They'd know. They were lads you never noticed in the crowd, but they were all eyes and ears and brains. They worked quietly and you never read about them in the papers, but they got things done and they'd know. Maybe they knew a lot more than I thought they'd know.

She was waiting for me at the bar. She was a lusty, beautiful woman with a mouth that made you hungry when she smiled at you as you came in. There was humor in her eyes, but the wonder and curiosity showed below in the little lines that radiated from the corners of her lips.

There was nothing in mine. I could feel them flat and dull in their sockets. I nudged my chin to the booths in the back and she followed me. We sat down and she waited for me to say something and all I could think of was the last time I had sat here it was with Velda and now time was getting short.

I took the cigarette she held out from the case, lit it and leaned on the table. "How much do you love your brother, kid?"

"Mike . . ."

"I'm asking the questions."

"He's my brother."

"Partially."

"That doesn't matter."

"He's mixed up in one of the dirtiest rackets you'll ever find. He has a part in it someplace and is paid off in the blood and terror you'll find wherever you find the Mafia operating. He's part of a chain of killers and thieves, yet you like what his money can buy. Your love doesn't stop anyplace, does it?"

She sat away from me as if I held a snake out at her.

"Stop, Mike, please stop!"

"You can stay on his side or mine, kid. The choice is up to you."

The hysteria was caught in her chest. Her mouth wasn't pretty any more. One little sob got loose and that was all. "Al Affia is dead. So far he's the latest. He isn't the last. Where do you stand?"

It came out slowly. She fought it all the way and won it. "With you, Mike."

"I need some information. About Berga Torn." She dropped her head and toyed with the ashtray. "Your brother played around with her some time ago. Why?"

"He . . . hated that woman. She was a tramp. He hated tramps."

"Did she know it?"

Michael shook her head. "In public he seemed fond of her. When we were alone . . . he said awful things about her."

"How far did he go?"

She looked up helplessly. "He kept her. I don't know why he did it . . . he didn't like her at all. The woman he did care for at the time left him because he spent all his time . . . nights . . . with Berga. Carl . . . was upset about it. One night he had an argument with someone about her in his study. He was so mad afterward he went out and got drunk, but he never saw Berga after that. He had an argument with her, too."

"You know about Carl's testifying before a congressional committee?"

"Yes. It . . . didn't seem to bother him. Not until . . . he heard that . . . she was going to speak against him."

"That was never made public."

"Carl has friends in Washington," she said simply.

"Yet he never worried about it?"

"No."

"Let's go back further, sugar. Let's go back before the war. Was there any time you can remember when something bothered Carl so much it damn near drove him nuts?"

The shadows around her eyes deepened, her hands pressed together tightly and she said, "How did you know? Yes, there was . . . a time."

"Now go over it slowly. Think about it. What did he do?"

Something panicky crossed her face. "I . . . nothing. He was hardly ever home. He wouldn't let me talk to him at all. When he was at home all he did was make long-distance calls. I remember because the phone bill was almost a thousand dollars for the month."

My breath was coming in hot. It hissed in between my teeth with a whisper and burned into my lungs. I said, "Can you get that bill? Can you get the itemized list that went with it?"

"I . . . might. Carl keeps everything . . . in the safe at home. Once I saw the combination on the back of the desk blotter."

I wrote down an address. Pat's. But all I gave her was the address and the apartment number. "Find it. When you do, bring it here." I folded the paper into her hand and she dropped it into her bag after looking at it long enough to etch it into her memory.

He'd get it. He'd pass it on and the boys in the blue suits would tie into it. They had the men and the time and the means. They'd do in a day what it would take me a year to do.

I snubbed out my butt, pulled the belt tight on the trench coat and stood up. "You'll spend the rest of your life hating yourself for doing this. Hating me too. If it gets too much I'll take you around and show you a lot of dirty little kids who are orphans and some widows your own age. I can show you pictures of bodies so cut up you'll get sick. I'll show you reports of kids who have killed and are condemned to death because they were sky-high on dope when they decided to see what it was like to burn a man down. You won't be stopping it all. You'll slow it down a little, maybe, but a few people who would have died will go on living because of you."

For a few seconds she seemed completely empty. If there was any emotion in her it had drained out and all she was left with were her thoughts. They showed on her face, every one of them. They showed when she looked back into the past and brought to life what she had known all along but had refused to acknowledge. They showed when the life came back to her eyes and her mouth. She tilted one eyebrow at me, did something to her head that shook her hair loose down her back.

"I won't hate you, Mike. Myself, perhaps, but not you."

I think she knew it then. The thought of it hung in the air like a charged cloud. Michael said, "They'll finally kill me, won't they, Mike." It wasn't a question.

"What's left of them . . . if they ever find out . . . would like to think they will. They'd like to kill me too. You can always remember one thing because they'll be remembering it too. They're not as big as they think they are."

She smiled, a wan, drawn smile. "Mike . . ."

I took the hand she held out to me.

"Kiss me again. Just in case."

The wetness glistened on her lips. They were firm lips, large, ripe, parted slightly over the even lines of her teeth. There was fire there that grew hotter as I came closer. I could see her mouth open even more, the tip of her tongue impatiently waiting, then the impatience broke and it met me before lips did.

I held her face in my hands, heard the soft moan she made, felt her nails biting into my arms through the coat, then I let her go. She trembled so violently she had to press her hands against the booth and the fiery liquid of her mouth passed on into her eyes.

"Please go, Mike," she said.

And I went. The rain took me back again, put its arms around me and held tight. I became part of the night, part of the wet, part of the noise and life that was the city. I could hear it laughing at me, a low, dull rumble with a sneer in it.

I walked down the side streets, crossed the avenues and got back to my kind of people again. I drifted through the night while my mind was days away and I was saying it off to myself and wondering how many other people were doing the same things. I was looking at a picture through the rain, knowing what was going on and not being able to make out the details.

It was a picture of a grim organization that stretched out its tentacles all over the world with the tips reaching into the highest places possible. It was an organization fed on the money of destruction and one tentacle was starving. The two million that was sent to feed it never arrived. No, that was wrong. It did arrive, but someplace it sat and was still there. In its sitting it had doubled its worth and the tentacle wanted it bad. It had to feast now to live. It was after the food with all the fury of its hunger, ready to do anything in the final, convulsive gesture of survival.

You could say it started with Berga. She wasn't the girl in the headlights any longer. She was younger now, a tall luscious Viking with eyes that could draw a man. She was a blonde snare with a body full of playful curves that held out triple challenges, a body full of dares waiting to be taken up. She was coming home from a visit to Italy and in the hidden hours on board that ship she had found a person who was ready to call the dare. He wasn't a special kind of a man. He was a guy with a small export business who could pass unnoticed in the crowd. He was a guy with a legitimate excuse to travel at certain times. He was a guy who was part of a great plan, a guy named Nicholas Raymond who really wasn't anything at all and because of it was the one they used as a messenger to bring in the vital food for the tentacle over here.

But he had a fault and because of it a lot of people died and the tentacle was starving. He liked the women. And Berga was special. He liked her so much he never followed the plan of delivery through and made plans to use the stuff himself. He and Berga. Two million bucks after conversion. Tax free. Someplace the stuff was still there. Maybe it took them a long time to find him again, or maybe they wanted the stuff first and were afraid the secret would die with him. However it was it took him a while to die. Maybe they thought Berga had it then. And she died. That put it on me.

I was thinking of something then. Horror, terror, fear . . . all of it that was there in her face for a little while, a confusion of emotions that stopped too suddenly.

I cursed to myself as the minute details started to fall into place, spun around and yelled at a cab. He jammed on the brakes, swerved slightly and was hardly stopped before I had the door opened. I told him where to take me and sat on the edge of the seat until we got there.

The elevator took me up to my office. I got out jangling my keys from my hand, stuck one in the lock and turned it. The outer office was empty, her typewriter a forlorn thing under its cover. Velda's desk was covered with mail separated into classified piles of bills, personals and miscellaneous. I went through them twice, didn't find what I was looking for, then spotted the pile that had come through the door slot I had pushed aside when I came in. There wasn't anything there, either. I went back to the desk, the curse still in my mouth when I saw it. The sheet lay under the stapler with the top under the flap of the envelope. I turned it over and saw the trade name of a gasoline company.

It was simple statement. One line. *"The way to a man's heart—"* and under it the initials, *"B.T."* Velda would have known, but Velda never saw it. Berga must have scribbled it at the service station after lifting the address from the registration tacked to the steering post of my heap, but it was the old

131

address. The new one was on the back out of sight and she hadn't seen the lines drawn through the words that voided it.

I looked at it, remembered her face again and knew what she was thinking when she wrote it. I felt the thing crumple in my hand as I squashed it in my fingers and never heard the door open behind me.

He stood in the doorway of my inner office and said, "I trust you can make something out of it. We couldn't."

I knew he had a gun without looking. I knew there were more of them without seeing them and I didn't give a damn in the world because I knew the voice. *I knew the voice and it was the one I said I'd never forget!* The last time it spoke I was supposed to die and before it could speak again I let out a crazy sound of hate that filled the room and was at them in a crouch with the bullets spitting over my head. I had the guy in my hands feeling my fingers tear his eyes loose while he screamed his lungs out and even the gun butt pounding on the back of my skull didn't stop me. I had enough left to lash out with my foot and hear it bite into flesh and bone and enough left to do something to one of them that turned his stomach inside out in my face. The horrible, choked scream of anguish one was letting out on the floor diminished to a whimper before disappearing altogether in the blackness that was closing in around me. Far in the distance I thought I heard sharp, flat sounds and a voice swearing hoarsely. Then I heard nothing at all.

It was a room. It had one window high off the floor and you could see the pinpoints that were stars through the film of dirt on the glass. I was spread-eagled on the bed with my hands and legs pulled tight to the frame and when I tried to twist the ropes bit into my skin and burned like acid. The muscles in my side had knotted in pain over ribs that were torturous hands gripping my chest.

There was a taste of blood in my mouth and as I came awake my stomach turned over and dragged long, agonized retches up my throat. I tried to breathe as deeply as I could, draw the air down to stop the retching. It seemed to take a long time before it stopped. I lifted my head and felt my hair stick to the bed. The back of it throbbed and felt like it was coming off so I let it ease back until the giddiness passed.

The room took shape, a square empty thing with a musty odor of disuse filling it. I could see the single chair in one corner, the door in the wall and the foot of the bed. I tried to move, but there wasn't an inch of play in the ropes and the knots that tied them only seemed to get tighter.

I wondered how long I had been there. I listened for sounds I could place but all I got was the steady drip of water outside the window. It was still raining. I listened even more intently, straining my ears into the silence and then I knew about how long I had been there.

My watch had stopped. I could see the luminous hands and number so it hadn't broken . . . it just stopped. This wasn't the same night it had happened. Everything I felt seemed to pour out of my mouth and I fought those damned ropes with every ounce of strength in me. They bit in, cut deeper and held like they were meant to and when I knew it wasn't any use fighting them I slumped back cursing myself for being so jackassed stupid as to walk into the deal without a rod and let them take me. I cursed myself for letting Velda do what she wanted to and cursed myself for not playing it right with Pat. No, I had to be a damned hero. I had to make it by myself. I had to take on the whole organization at once knowing what they were like and how they operated. I passed out advice all around then forgot to give some of it to myself.

There were footsteps in the other room that padded up to the door. It opened into an oblong of yellow light framing the man and the one behind him who stood there. They were opaque forms without faces but it didn't matter any more. One said, "He awake?"

"Yeah, he's out of it."

They came in and stood over me. Two of them and I could see the billies in their hands.

"Tough guy. You were hard to take, mister. You know what you did? You pulled the eyes right out of Foreman. He screamed so loud my friend here had to tap him one and he tapped too hard and now Foreman's lying in a Jersey swamp dead. They don't come like Foreman any more. You know something else? You ruptured Duke, you bastard. You fixed him good, you did."

"Go to hell," I said.

"Still tough. Sure, you got to keep up the act. You know it won't do any good even if you got down on your knees and begged." He grunted out a laugh. "Pretty soon the boss is coming in here. He's going to ask you some questions and to make sure you answer we're going to soften you up a little bit. Not much . . . just a little bit."

The billy went up slowly. I couldn't keep my eyes off it. The thing reached his shoulder then snapped down with a blur of motion and smashed into my ribs. They both did it then, a pair of sadistic bastards trying to kill me by inches, then one made the mistake of cutting for my neck and got the side of my head instead and that wonderful, sweet darkness came back again where there was no more pain or sound and I tumbled headlong into the pool.

But the same incredible pain that had brought the sleep brought the awakening. It was a pain that turned my whole body into a mass of broken nerve ends that shrieked their messages to my brain. I lay there with my mouth open sucking in air, wishing I could die, but knowing at the same time I couldn't yet.

The body doesn't stand for that kind of torture very long. It shocks itself into forgetting it and soon the pain goes away. It isn't gone for good, but the temporary relief is a kiss of love. It lies there in that state of extreme emergency, caring for its own, and when the realization of another emergency penetrates it readies itself to act again.

I had to think. There had to be a gimmick somewhere and I had to find it. I could see the outlines of the bed and feel the ropes that tied me to the steel frame. It was one of those fold-away things with a heavy innerspring mattress and I was laced down so tightly my hands dented the rolled edges of it. I looked down at my toes, over my head at my hands and took the only way out.

There was noise to it, time involved, and pressures that started the blood flowing down my wrists again. I rocked the bed sideways until it teetered on edge, then held my breath as it tipped. I hit the floor and the thing came halfway over on top of me before it slithered back on its side. The mattress had pulled out from under my feet and when I kicked around I got the lower half entirely free of the springs. I had to stop and get my breath, then when I tried the second time it came away from under my hands too and I had the play in the ropes that I needed. They were wet and slippery with my own blood. My fingernails broke tugging at them, but it was the blood that did it. I felt one come free, the next one and my hand was loose. It only took a few minutes longer to get the other one off and my feet off the end of the bed and I was standing up with my heart trying to pound the shock away and the pain back in place.

I didn't let it get that far. I was half drugged with exertion but I knew what I had to do. I put the bed back on its legs, spread the mattress out and got back the way I had been. I was able to dummy the ropes around both feet and one hand and hoped they wouldn't see the one I couldn't get to.

Time. Now I could use a little time. Every second of it put strength back in my body. I lay there completely relaxed, my eyes closed. I tried to bring the picture back in focus and got part of it. I got Berga and Nicholas Raymond and a guy pushing him into the path of a truck. I was thinking that if they had pulled an autopsy on the body they would have found a jugful of stuff in his veins that made him a walking automaton.

The picture got just a little bit clearer and I could see the work they did on Berga. Oh, it had to be easy. With two million bucks in the bag you don't barge around until you're sure what you're doing. First they tried to scare her, then came the big con job. Carl Evello, the man-about-town putting on the heavy rush act, trying to get close enough to the babe to see what she knew.

I thought about it while I lay there, trying to figure the mind of one little guy who thought he could beat the Mafia out of a fortune and pretty soon I was reading his thoughts as if they were my own. Raymond had planned pretty well. In some way he had planted the secret of his cache with Berga so that she'd have to do some tall thinking to get to it. It had taken her a long time, but she had finally caught on and the Mafia knew when she did. She had hired a body-guard that didn't work but she still wouldn't let go of what she knew because as soon as she did she'd take the long road too. Maybe she saw her way out of it when Uncle Sam put the squeeze on Evello. Maybe she thought with him away she'd have a chance. If she did she thought wrong. They still got to her.

My eyes opened and squinted at the ceiling. A couple more details were looking for a place to crawl into and I was just about to shove them there when I heard the voices outside.

They didn't try to be quiet. Two of them were bragging that I'd be ready to spill my guts and the other one said I had better be. It was a quiet voice that wasn't a bit new to me. It said, "Wait here and I'll see."

"You want us to come in, boss? He might need more softening."

"I'll call you if he does."

"Okay, boss."

Chairs rasped against the floor as the door opened. I could see the two of them there starting to open a bottle on the table, then the door closed and he was feeling for a light switch. He swore at the blackness, struck a match and held it out in front of him. There was no light, but a candle in a bottle was on the chair and he lit it. He put the bottle down beside me, drew up the chair and lit a cigarette.

The smoke tasted sweet in my nostrils. I licked my lips as I watched the butt glow a deep red and he grinned as he blew the cloud across my face.

I said, "Hello, Carl." I made it good and snotty, but he didn't lose the grin.

"The infamous Mike Hammer. I hope the boys did a good job. They can do a better one if I let them."

"They did a good job."

I rolled my head and took a good look at him. "So you're . . . the boss."

The grin changed shape this time. One side of it dropped caustically. "Not quite . . . yet." The evil in his eyes danced in the candlelight. "Perhaps by tomorrow I will be. I'm only the boss locally . . . now."

"You louse," I said. The words seemed to have an effort to them. My breathing was labored, coming through my teeth. I closed my eyes, stiffened and heard him laugh.

"You did a lot of legwork for us. I hear you blundered right on what we have been looking for."

I didn't say anything.

"You wanted to trade. Where is it?"

I let my eyes come open. "Let her go first."

He gave me that twisted grin again. "I'm not trading for her. Funny enough, I don't even know where she is. You see, she wasn't part of my department."

It took everything I could do to hold still. I could feel the nervous tremors creeping up my arms and I made fists of my hands to keep from shaking.

"It's you I'm trading for. You can tell me or I can walk out of here and say something to the boys. You'll want to talk then."

"The hell with you."

He leaned a little closer. "One of the boys is a knife man. He likes to do things with a knife. Maybe you can remember what he did to Berga Torn." I could see the smile on

136

his face get ugly. "That isn't even a little bit what he'll do to you."

The side of his hand traced horrible gestures across my body, meaningful, cutting gestures with the nastiest implications imaginable in them. Then the gestures ended as the side of his palm sliced into my groin for emphasis and the yell that started in my throat choked off in a welter of pain and I mumbled something Carl seemed to want to hear and he bent forward saying, "What? What?"

And that repeated question was the last Carl Evello ever spoke again because he got too close and there were my hands around his throat squeezing so hard his flesh buried my fingers while his eyes were hard little marbles trying to roll out of their sockets. I squeezed and pushed him on his knees and there wasn't even any sound at all. His fingernails bit into my wrists with an insane fury that lived only a few seconds, then relaxed as his head went back with his tongue swelling in the gaping opening that was his mouth. Things in his throat stretched and popped and when I let go there was only the slightest wheeze of air that trickled back into lungs that were almost at the bursting point.

I got him on the bed. I spread him out the way I had been and let him lie there. The joke was too good to pass up so Carl lived a minute longer than he should have. I tried to make my voice as close to his as I could and I called to the door, "He talked. Now put him away."

Outside a chair scraped back. There was a single spoken word, silence, and the slow shuffle of footsteps coming toward the door. He didn't even look at me. He walked up to the bed and I could hear the *snick* as the knife opened. The boy was good. He didn't drive it in. He put it in position and pushed. Carl's body ached, trembled and as I stepped away from the candle the boy saw the mistake and knew he had made his last one. I put everything I could find into the swing that caught the side of his neck and mashed his vertebrae into his spinal cord and he was dead before I eased him to the floor.

Cute. Getting cuter all the time.

I came out of the door with a yell I couldn't keep inside me and dived at the guy at the table. His frenzied stare of hesitation cost him the second he needed to clear his rod and while he was still digging for it my fingers were ripping into his face and my body smashed him right out of the chair. The gun hit the floor and bounced across the room.

137

My knees slammed into him, brought a scream bubbling out of his mouth that snapped off when my fist twisted his jaw out of shape. He didn't try for the gun any more. He just reached for his face and tried to cover it but I didn't let him have the pleasure out of not seeing what was happening. His eyes had to watch everything I did to him until they filmed over and blanked out when the back of his head cracked against the floor. The blood trickled out his nose and ears when I stood over him, a bright red that seemed to match the fire burning in my lungs. I pulled him inside to the other two, tangled his arms around the boy who still held the knife and left them that way.

Then I left. I got out on the street and let the rain wash me clean. I breathed the air until the fire went out, until some of the life I had left back inside crawled into my system again.

The guy sitting in the doorway ten feet away heard me laugh. His head jerked up out of the drunken stupor and he looked at me. Maybe he could see the way my face was and understand what was behind the laugh. The eyes bleary with cheap whisky lost their glassiness and he trembled a little bit, trying to draw back into his doorway. My laugh got louder and he couldn't stand it, so he stood up and lurched away, looking back twice to make sure I was still there.

I knew where I was. Once you put in time on Second Avenue you never forget it. The store front I came out of was dirty and deserted. At one time it had been a lunch counter, but now all that was left was the grease stains and the *FOR RENT* sign in the window. The gin mill on the corner was just closing up, the last of the human rubble that inhabited the place drifting across the street until he dissolved into the mist.

I walked slow and easy, another one of the dozens you could see sprawled out away from the rain. Another joe looking for a place to park, another joe who couldn't find one. I made the police call box on the second corner down, got it open and said hello when I heard the voice answer. I didn't have to try hard to put a rasp into my voice, I said, "Copper, you better get somebody down this way fast. Somebody screaming his head off in that empty dog wagon two blocks south."

Two minutes were all they took. The siren whined through the rain and the squad car passed me with its tires spitting spray. They'd find a nice little mess, all right. The one guy

138

left could talk his head off, but he was still going to cook in the hot squat up the river.

I pulled my wallet out and went through it. Everything was there except money. Even my change was gone. I needed a dime like I never needed one before and there wasn't even a character around to bum one from. Down the street lights of a diner threw a yellow blob on the sidewalks. I walked toward it, stood outside the door a second looking at the two drunks and the guy with the trombone case perched on the stools.

There wasn't any more I could lose so I walked in, called the counterman over and tossed my watch on the counter. "I need a dime. You can hold my watch."

"For a dime? Mac, you nuts? Look, if you need some coffee say so."

"I don't need coffee. I want to make a phone call."

His eyes went up and down me and his mouth rounded into a silent "oh." "You been rolled, huh?" He fished in his pocket, tossed a dime on the counter and pushed my watch back to me. "Go ahead, mac, I know how it is."

Pat wasn't at home. My dime clinked back and I tried his office. I asked for Captain Chambers and he wasn't there either. The cop on the board wanted to take a message and the captain would take care of it when he came in, I said, "Pal, this kind of message won't wait. It's something he's been working on and if I can't get word to him right away he's going to hit the roof."

The phone dimmed out as the operator spoke away from it. I could hear the hurried exchange of murmurs, then: "We'll try to contact the captain by radio. Can you leave your phone number?"

I read it off the dial, told him I'd wait and hung up. The counterman was still watching me. There was a steaming hot cup of coffee by an empty stool with a half pack of butts lying alongside it. The guy grinned, nodded to the coffee and made himself a friend. Coffee was about all my stomach would hold, but it sat there inside me like a million bucks in my hand. It took the shakes out of my legs and the ache from my body.

I lit a smoke, relaxed and watched the window. The wind in the street whipped the rain against the plate glass until it rattled. The door opened, a damp blast momentarily freshening the air. Another musician with a fiddle case under his coat sat down tiredly and ordered coffee. Someplace off in the distance a siren moaned, and a minute later another crossed its fading echo. Two more came on top of it, not close, but distant voices racing to a sore spot in the great sprawling sick body of the city.

Corpuscles, I thought. That's what they were like. White corpuscles getting to the site of the infection. They'd close in and wipe out the parasites and if they were too late they'd call for the carpenter corpuscles to come and rebuild broken tissue around the wound.

I was thinking about it when Pat walked in, tired lines around his eyes, his face set in a frozen expression. There was a twitch in the corner of his mouth he tried to wipe away with the back of his hand.

He came over and sat down. "Who kicked the crap out of you, Mike?"

"I look that bad?"

"You're a mess."

I could grin then. Tomorrow, the next day, the day after, maybe, I'd be too sore to move, but right then I could grin. "They reached me but they didn't hold on to me, chum."

His eyes got narrow and very, very bright. "There was a dirty little mess not too far from here. That wouldn't be it, would it?"

"How good is it like it stands?"

Pat's lips came apart over his teeth. "The one guy left is wanted for three different kills. This one finishes him."

"The coroner say that?"

"Yeah, the coroner says that. I say that. We have two experts on the spot who say that too but the guy doesn't say that. The guy doesn't know what to say. He's still half out and he says things about a girl named Berga Torn he worked over and when he knew what he did it woke him up and now he won't say anything. He's the scaredest clam you ever saw in your life."

"So it stands?"

"Nobody'll break it. Now what do you say about it?"

I took a big pull on the butt and stamped it out in the ash tray. "It's a detail. Right now it doesn't mean a damn one way or the other to you or me. Someday over a beer I'll make it into a good story."

"It better be good," Pat said, "I have all hell breaking loose around my ears. Evello's sister came to us with a list of phone calls yesterday and we tracked down the names into the damnedest places you ever saw. We have some of

140

the wheels in the Mafia dangling by their you-know-whats and they're scramming for cover. They're going nuts down in Florida and on the Coast the police have pulled in people big enough to make your hair stand on end. Some of 'em are talking and the thing's opening wider."

He passed his hand over his eyes and drew it away slowly. "Damn it, we're up as far as Washington itself. It makes me sick."

The shake was back in my legs again. "Talk names, Pat."

"Names you don't know and some you do. We have the connections down pat but the ones up top are sitting tight. The Miami police pulled a quick raid on a local big shot and turned up a filing case of information that gives us a line into half the narcotics outlets in the States. Right now the Federal boys have assigned extra men to pick up the stuff and they're coming home loaded."

"How about Billy Mist?" I asked him.

"Nothing doing. Not a word on him so far. He can't be located, anyway."

"Leo Harmody?"

"You got another case? He's howling police persecution and threatening to take things up with Congress. He can yell because there's nothing we can slap him with."

"And Al Affia's dead," I said.

Pat's head turned toward me, his eyes a sleepy gray. "You wouldn't know anything about that, would you?"

"It couldn't't've happened to a better guy."

"He was chopped up good. Somebody had a little fun."

I looked at him, lit another smoke and flipped the match in the ash tray where it turned into a charred arc. "How far did you get with him?"

"Not a thing. There wasn't a recognizable print on that bottle."

"What's the word on it, Pat?"

His eyes got sleepier. "His waterfront racket is going sky-high. There's been two killings down there already. The king is dead, but somebody is ready to take his place."

The rain had the sound of a rolling snare drum. It was working up in tempo, backed by the duller, more resonant peals of thunder that cracked the sky open. The three drunks stared at the window miserably, hugging their cups as an anchor to keep from drifting out into the night. The fiddle player shrugged, paid his bill and tucked the case back under his coat and left. At least he was lucky enough to grab an empty cab going by.

I said, "Do you have the picture yet, Pat?"

"Yeah, I have a picture," he said. "It's the biggest one I ever saw."

"You're lost, kid."

The sleepiness left his eyes. His fingers turned the ash tray around slowly, then he gave me that wry grin of his. "Play it out, Mike."

I shrugged. "Everything's coming your way. Now you're having fun. What started it?"

"Okay, so it began with Berga."

"Let's not forget it. Let's tie it all up together so when you're out there having fun you'll know why. I'll make it short and sweet and you can check on it. Ten, twelve, maybe fifteen years ago a guy was bringing a package of dope into the country for delivery to the Mafia. He tangled with a dame on board and fell for her. That's where Berga came into it. Instead of handing over the package he decided to keep it for his sweetie and himself even though he ran the risk of being knocked off."

"Nicholas Raymond," Pat said.

I knew the surprise showed on my face when I nodded. "Nicholas had them on the spot. They couldn't bump him until they located the stuff and he wasn't stupid enough to lead them to it. There was two million bucks' worth in that consignment and they needed it badly. So Nick goes on living with this gal and one day he dies accidentally. It's a tricky pitch but it isn't a hard one. They figured that by this time he would have passed the secret along to her or she would have found out herself somehow.

"But it didn't happen that way. Nick was trickier than they thought. He got the word to her in case something happened to him, but even she didn't know where it was or what it was that keyed it. I guess they must have tried to scare it out of her for a while because she hired herself a bodyguard. He played it too good and moved in. The Mafia didn't like that. If he came across the stuff they'd be out of luck, so he went too."

Pat was watching me closely. There was an expression on his face like I wasn't telling him anything new, but he wasn't saying a word.

"Now we come to Evello. He gets a proper knockdown to her somehow and off he goes on the big pitch. He gave her the whole treatment and probably winds it up with a proposal of marriage to make it sound good. Maybe he over-played his hand. Maybe he just wasn't smart enough to fool her. Something slipped and Berga got wise that he was one of the mob. But she got wise to something else too. *About then she suddenly discovered what it was they were all after and when she had the chance to get Evello creamed before that congressional committee she put in her bid figuring to get the stuff on her own hook later."*

Now Pat's face was showing that he didn't know it all. There were sharp lines streaking out from the corners of his eyes and he waited, his tongue wetting down his lips from time to time.

I said, "She pulled out all the stops and so did they. The boys with the black hands get around. They scared her silly and by that time it didn't take much. She went to pieces and tried to fight it out in that sanitarium."

"That was her biggest mistake," Pat said.

"You mentioned a woman who came to see her."

He gave a slow nod, his hands opening and closing slowly. "We still can't make her."

"Could it have been a man dressed like a dame?"

"It could have been anything. There was no accurate description and no record of it."

"It was somebody she knew."

"Great."

"Now the stuff is still missing."

"I know where it is."

Pat's head came around faster this time.

"The two million turned into four by just sitting there," I said. "Inflation."

"Damn it, Mike, where?" His voice was all tight.

"On the good ship *Cedric*. Our friend Al Affia was working on the deal. He had given all the plans to her in his dive back there and whoever killed him walked off with them."

"Now you tell me," he said hoarsely. "Now you spill it when somebody has had time to dig it loose."

I took a deep breath, grunted when the sting of pain stabbed across my chest and shook my head. "It's not that easy, Pat. Al had those plans a long time. I'm even beginning to think I know why he was bumped."

Pat waited me out.

"He tried to sucker Velda into his dump for a fast play at

143

her. She slipped him a dose of chloral and while he was out started turning the place upside down. Al didn't stay out very long. He got sick, his stomach dumped the stuff overboard and he saw what she was doing. Velda used the bottle on him then."

His eyes snapped wide open. "Velda!"

"She didn't kill him. She bopped him one and it cut his head open. He staggered out after her and got word to somebody. That somebody caught the deal in a hurry and someplace she's still sweating." All at once every bit of pain in my body flooded back and trapped me in its agony before fading away. I finished with, "I hope."

"Okay, Mike, let it loose! Damn it, what else have you got? So the kid's sweating, you hope . . . and I hope too. You know them well enough to realize what's liable to happen to her now."

"She was on her way to see Billy Mist." My grin turned sour and my teeth came out from under my lips again. "The cops didn't find her."

"Supposing she never reached there?"

"It's a possibility I've been considering, friend. I saw her pass in a cab and she wasn't alone."

I was going warm again. The coffee didn't sit so well in my gut any more. I thought about it as long as I could then shut out the picture when I buried my face in my hands.

Pat kept saying, "The bastards, the bastards!" His nails made a tattoo of sound on the counter and his breathing was almost as hard as mine was. "It's breaking fast, but it's not wide open yet, Mike. We'll get to Billy. One way or another."

I felt a little better. I took my hands away and reached for the last butt in the pack. "It won't break until you get the stuff. You and the whole staff up in Washington can work from now until ten years later and you won't make a hole in the organization big enough to stop it. You'll knock it kicking but you won't kill it. Slowing it down a little is all we can hope for. They're going to hang on to Velda until somebody has that four million bucks lined up.

"I'm the target, chum. Me personally. I've scared the crap out of those guys as individuals . . . not as an organization. They know I don't give a damn what happens to the outfit, the dough or anything that goes with it. All I want is a raft of hides nailed to the barn door. That's where I come in. I'm the little guy with a grudge. I'm the guy so damn burned

144

up he's after a man, not an organization. I'm the guy who wants to stand there and see him die and he knows it. He wants that consignment of narcotics in the worst way but before it does him any good I have to die first.

"So they're holding Velda. She's the bait and she's something else besides. I've been getting closer to this than anybody else and they've known something I never got wise to. Berga passed the clue to me before she died and I've been sitting on it all this time. For a little while they had it, but they couldn't make it out. They expect me to. When I do I'll have to use it to ransom Velda with it."

"They're not that dumb, Mike," Pat told me.

"Neither am I. Someplace the answer slapped me in the teeth and I was in such a hurry I missed it. I can feel the damn thing crawling around in my head and can't lay my finger on it. The damn arrogant bastards . . ."

Pat said, "The head is pretty far from the body."

"What?"

He looked out the window and watched the rain. "They can afford to be arrogant. The entire structure of the Mafia is built on arrogance. They flaunt the laws of every country in the world, they violate the integrity of the individual, they're a power in themselves backed by ruthlessness, violence and some of the shrewdest brains in existence."

"About the head and the body, I mean."

"We can smash the body of this thing, Mike, but in this country the head and the body aren't connected except by the very thin thread of a neck. The top man, men, or group is a separate caste. The organization is built so that the head can function without the body if it comes to it. The body parts can be assembled any time, but it's an assembly for the benefit of the head, never forget that. It's a government. The little people in it don't count. It's the rulers who are important and the government is run solely for their benefit and to satisfy their appetites. They're never known and they're not going to be known."

"Unless they make one stinking little mistake," I said.

Pat stopped looking at the rain.

I rubbed the ache out of my side. "The stuff is on the *Cedric*. All you have to do is find the ship. The records will carry the stateroom Raymond used. When you find it call Ray Diker at the *Globe* and give him first crack at the details of the yarn. Tell him to hold the story until I call you. By then I'll have Velda."

"Where are you going?"

"The last time you asked that I said I was going out to kill somebody." I held out my hand. "Gimmie a fin."

He looked puzzled, scowled, then pulled five ones out of his pocket. I laid two of them on the counter and nodded to the counterman to come get it. He was all smiles.

"Where's Michael Friday?"

"She said she was going to your place to see you."

"I wasn't home."

"Well, she's not reporting to me on the hour."

"No police guard?"

His frown got bigger this time. "I tried to but she said no. One of the feds pulled out after her anyway. He lost her when she got in a cab."

"Sloppy."

"Lay off. Everybody's up to their ears in this thing."

"Yeah. You going to trace the *Cedric?*"

"What do you think. Where are you going?"

I let a laugh out that sounded hollow as hell. "I'm going out in the rain and think some more. Then maybe I'll go kill somebody else."

I could see Pat remembering the other years. Younger years when the dirt seemed to be only on the surface. When being a cop looked good and the law was for protection and guidance. When there weren't so many strings and sticky red tape and corruption in high places.

His hand went into his pocket and brought out the blued .38. He handed it to me under the shelf of the hanger. "Here, use this for a change."

And I remembered what Velda had said and I shook my head. "Some other time. I like it better this way."

I went out and walked down the street and let the rain hit me in the face. Someplace there was a gimmick and that was what I had to find. I reached the subway kiosk, bought a pack of Luckies and dropped them in my pocket. I waited for the uptown local and got aboard when it came in.

With every jolt the train took I could feel the shock wear off a little bit more. It got worse and when it was too bad I stood up and leaned against the door watching the walls of the tunnel go by in a dirty blur.

A gimmick. One lousy little gimmick and I could have it. It was there trying to come out and whenever I thought I had it my stomach would retch and I'd lose it.

The train pulled into the station, opened its multitude of

mouths but I was the only one who stepped out. I had the platform all to myself then, so I let go and the coffee came up.

There weren't any cabs outside. I didn't waste time waiting for one. I walked toward my apartment not conscious of the rain any more, hardly conscious of the protest my body was setting up. I felt my legs starting to go when I reached the door and the super and his wife took a startled look at me and helped me inside.

Lily Carver came up out of the chair holding back the sharp intake of her breath with the back of her hand. Her eyes went soft, reflected the hurt mine were showing, then she had my hand and helped me into the bedroom.

I flopped on the bed and closed my eyes. Hands loosened my collar and pulled at my shoes. I could hear the super telling his wife to stay out, and hear her frightened sobs. I could hear Lily and feel her hands on my forehead. For a second I glimpsed the white halo of her hair and saw the sensuous curves of her body in hazy detail hovering over me.

The super said, "You want me to call a doctor, Mr. Hammer?"

I shook my head.

"I'll call a cop. Maybe . . ."

I shook my head again. "I'll be okay."

"You feel good enough to talk a minute?"

"What?" I could feel the sleep closing in as I said it.

"A woman was here. Friday, her name was. She left you a note in an envelope and said it was pretty important. She wanted you to see it as soon as you came in."

"What was in it?"

"I didn't look. Should I open it?"

"Go ahead."

The bed jounced as he got up. It left me rocking gently, a soothing motion of pure comfort and there was a heaviness under my closed eyes too great to fight. Then the bed jounced again as he sat down and I heard the tearing of paper.

"Here it is." His voice paused. "Not much in it though."

"Read it," I said.

"Sure. *'Dear Mike . . . I found the list. Your friend has it. I found something much more important too and must see you at once. Call me. Please call me at once. Love Michael.'* That's all there is to it, Mr. Hammer."

"Thanks," I said, "thanks a lot."

From the other room his wife set up a nervous twittering.

His fingers touched me. "Think it'll be all right if I go back?"

Before I could nod Lily said, "Go ahead. I'll take care of him. Thank you so much for everything."

"Well . . . if you need me, just call down."

"I'll do that."

I got my eyes open one last time. I saw the smooth beauty of her face unmarred by anything now. She was smiling, her hands doing things to my clothes. The strange softness was back in her eyes and she whispered, "Darling, darling . . ."

The sleep came. There was a face in it. The face had a rich, wet mouth, full and soft. It kept coming closer, opening slowly. It was Michael and in my dream I grinned at her, fascinated by her lips.

Chapter Twelve

YOU HURT too much to sleep. You wake up and it hurts more so you try to go back to sleep. There's a physical ache, a gnawing your body tries vainly to beat down and might have if the pain in your mind wasn't even worse. Processions of thoughts hammer at you, gouge and scrape until the brain is a wild thing seeking some kind of release. But there isn't any release. There's fire all around you, the tongues of it licking closer, needling the skin. The brain screams for you to awaken, but if you do you know the other things . . . the thoughts, will be a more searing pain so you fight and fight until the mind conquers and you feel the awakening coming on.

I thought I heard voices and one was Velda's. She kept calling to me and I couldn't answer back. Somebody was hurting her and I mouthed silent curses while I fought invisible bonds that held me tied to the ground. She was screaming, her voice tortured, screaming for me and I couldn't help her. I strained and kicked and fought but the ropes held until I was breathless and I had to lie there and listen to her die.

I opened my eyes and looked into the darkness, knowing it was only a dream but going nuts because I knew it could be real. My breathing was harsh, laboring, drying my mouth into leathery tissue.

The covers were pulled up to my neck, but under them there was nothing. The skin over my bruised muscles felt cool and pliable, then I found the answer with the tips of my

148

fingers as they slid along flesh that had been gently oiled with some aromatic unguent. From somewhere the faint clean odor of rubbing alcohol crossed my nostrils, disturbing because of its unusual pungent purity. It was the raw smell of fine chemistry, the sharp, natural smell you might expect, but don't find in fresh, virgin forests.

Slowly, waiting for the ache to begin, I pulled my arm free, laid it across the bed, felt the warmth of a body under the back of my hand, then jerked it away as she almost screamed and pulled out of reach to sit there bolt upright with eyes still dumb with sleep reflecting some emotion nobody in the world would be able to put his finger on.

"Easy, Lily . . . It's only me."

She let her breath out with more of a gasp than a sigh, trying to wipe the sleep from her eyes. "You . . . scared me, Mike. I'm sorry." She smiled, sat on the edge of the bed and put her shoes on.

Her dreams must have been pretty rough too. She had taken care of me, lay there while I slept until her eyes closed too. She was a good kid who had been through the mill and was scared to death of a return trip. She wasn't going to get it from me.

I said, "What time is it?"

Lily checked her watch. "A little after nine. Can I get you something to eat?"

"What happened to the day?"

"You slept through. You groaned and talked . . . I didn't want to wake you up, Mike. Can I get you some coffee?"

"I can eat. I need something in my gut."

"All right. I'll call you." Her mouth creased in a smile, one corner of it pulling up with an odd motion. I let my eyes drift over her slowly. As they moved her hands tightened at her throat and the strangeness came back in her face. The smile disappeared into a tight grimace and she twisted around to go out the door.

Some of them are funny, I thought. Beautiful kids who would do anything one minute and scared stiff of doing it the next.

I heard her in the kitchen, got up, showered, managed to get the brush off my face and climbed into some clean clothes. I could hear things frying when I got on the phone and dialed Michael Friday's number.

The voice that answered was deep and guarded. It said,

149

"Mr. Evello's residence," but the touch of Brooklyn in the tone was as plain as the badge it wore.

"Mike Hammer. I'm looking for Michael Friday, Carl's sister. She there?"

"I'm afraid . . ."

"Is Captain Chambers there?"

It caught the voice off base a second. "Who'd you say this was?"

"Hammer. Mike Hammer."

There was a muffled consultation, then: "This is the police, Hammer, what did you want?"

"I told you. I want Friday."

"So do we. She isn't around."

"Damn!" It exploded out of me. "You staked out there?"

"That's right. We're covering the place. You know where the girl is?"

"All I know is that she wants to see me bad, feller. How can I reach Chambers?"

"Wait a minute." The phone blanked out again and there was more talk behind a palm stretched over the mouthpiece. "You gonna be where you are a while?"

"I'll be here."

"Okay, the sergeant here says he'll try to get him for you. What's your number?"

"He knows it. Tell him to call me at home."

"Yeah. You get anything on that Friday dame, you pass it this way."

"No leads?"

"No nothing. She disappeared. She came back here after she left headquarters the other day, stayed a couple of hours and grabbed a cab into Manhattan."

"She was coming to see me," I said.

"She was what!"

"I was out. She left a note and took off again. That's why I called her place."

"I'll be damned. We checked all over the city to find out where she went to."

"If she's using cabs maybe you can pick her up from when she left here."

"Sure, sure. I'll pass it along."

The phone went dead and I socked it back in its hanger. Lily called me from the kitchen and I went out and sat down. She had it ready on the table, that same spread like she thought I was two more guys and instead of it looking good my stomach tried to sour at the sight of it. All I could think of was another one gone. Another kid cut down by a pack of scrimy hoods who wanted that two million bucks' worth of hell so bad they'd kill and kill and kill until they had every bit of it.

I smashed my fist into the table saying the same dirty words over and over until Lily's face went a pasty white and she backed against the wall. I was staring into space, but she was occupying the space ahead of me and whatever she saw going across my face made her shrink back even further.

How stupid were they? How far did they have to go? Wasn't their organization big enough to know every damn detail inside and out? They wouldn't be reaching the stuff now, not with the cops going over every inch of the *Cedric*. The whole shebang was coming apart at the edges and instead of piling up the counts against them they ought to be on the run.

Lily slid out of sight. She came up against me and reached out her hand until it was on my shoulder. "Mike . . ."

I looked at her without seeing her.

"What is it, Mike?"

The words started out of me. They came slow at first, then turned into a boiling current that was taking in the whole picture. I was almost finished with it when I could feel the sharp points of the gimmicks sticking out and ran my mind back to pick them up. Then I sat and cursed myself because I wasn't fast enough. They weren't there any more.

There was just one minor little detail. Just a little one I should have thought of long ago. I said to Lily, "Did you go to see Berga Torn in the sanitarium at all?"

Her eyebrows knit, puzzled. "No, I didn't." She pinched her lower lip between her teeth. "I called her twice and the second time she mentioned that someone had been to see her."

I was half out of my chair. "Who? Did she say who?"

She tried hard for it, reaching back through the days. "I think she did. I honestly didn't pay any attention at the time. I was so worried about what was happening it didn't register."

I had her by the shoulders, squeezing my fingers into her skin. "The name's important, kid. That somebody tipped the whole thing. Right then was the beginning of murder that hasn't ended yet. As long as you got that name in your head a killer is going to be prowling around loose and if he ever knows you might have it you're going the same way Berga did."

"Mike!"

"Don't worry about it. I'm not letting you out of my sight for a minute any more. Damn it, you got to dig that name out. You understand that?"

"I . . . think I do. Mike, please . . . you're hurting me."

I took my hands down and she rubbed the places where they had bitten in. There were tears in the corners of her eyes, little drops of crystal that swelled and I took a step closer to her. I reached out again, more gently this time, close enough for a second to taste the faint crispness of rubbing alcohol.

Lily smiled again. It was like the first time. The kind of smile you see on the face of a person waiting for death and ready to receive him almost gratefully. "Please eat something, Mike," she whispered.

"I can't, kid. Not now."

"You have to have something in your stomach."

Her words sent something racing up my back. It was a feeling you get when you know you have something and you can't wait to get it out of you. You stand there and wait for the final answer, waiting, waiting, waiting.

It was there in my hand when the phone set up a jangling that wouldn't stop. I grabbed the extension and Pat barked a short hello. I asked him, "Did you find Friday?"

He held his voice down. He sat on it all the way but the roughness showed through anyway. "We didn't find a damn thing. Nothing, got that? No Friday, no jug of hop, no nothing. This town's a madhouse. The feds are cutting a swath through the racket a mile wide and we still haven't come up with the stuff. Mike, if that stuff sits there . . ."

"I know what it means."

"Okay then, are you holding anything back?"

"You know better."

"Then what about Friday? If she was up there . . ."

"She wanted to see me. That's all I know."

"You know what I think?"

"I know what you think," I repeated softly. "Billy Mist . . . where's he?"

"You'd never guess."

"Tell me."

"Right now he's having supper at the Terrace. He's got an alibi for everything we can throw at him and nobody's going

152

to break it for a damn long while. He's got people in Washington batting for him and boys with influence pulling strings so hard they're knocking us silly . . . Mike . . ."

"Yeah?"

"Find Velda?"

"Not yet, Pat. Soon."

"You're not saying it right, friend."

"I know."

"In case it makes you feel better, I put men on it."

"Thanks."

"Figured it might not be holing out like you expected."

"Yeah."

"Something else you better know. Your joint's been covered. Three guys were stationed around waiting for you. The feds picked them up. One of the muscle lads is in the morgue."

"So?"

"There may be more. Keep your eyes open. You may have a tail or two if you leave. At least one'll be our man."

"They're sticking close to me." I said the words through my teeth.

"You're primed for the kill, Mike. You know why? I'll tell you. News has it you were part of the thing from the beginning. You've been fooling me and everybody else, but they got the pitch. Tell me one thing . . . *have* you been shoving it in me?"

"No."

"Good enough. We'll keep playing it this way then."

"What about the *Cedric?*"

He cursed under his breath. "It's screwballed, Mike. It's the whole, lousy, stinking reason behind all this. The ship is in a Jersey port right now undergoing repairs. She was a small liner before the war and was revamped to carry troops. All the staterooms were torn out of her and junked to make it over into a transport. The stuff might have been there once, but it's been gone a long time now. None of this should've happened at all."

I let a few seconds pass before I spoke. I was feeling cold and dead all over. "You got a lot of people you've been wanting to get."

"Yeah, a lot of them." His voice was caustic. "A lot of punks. A lot of middle-sized boys. A few big ones. Medusa even lost a few of her heads." He laughed sarcastically. "But Medusa is still alive, buddy. She's one big head who doesn't care how many of her little heads she loses. We can chop all

153

the little ones off and in a few months or years she'll grow a whole new crop as vicious as ever. Yeah, we're doing fine. I thought we did good when I had a look at the shiv hole in Carl. I felt great when I saw Affia's face. They were nothing, Mike. You know how I feel now?"

I didn't answer him. I put the phone back while he was still talking. I was thinking of Michael Friday's wet, wet mouth and the way Al Affia *had* looked and what Carl Evello had told me. I was thinking of undercurrents that could even work through an organization like the Mafia and I knew why Michael Friday had tried to see me.

Lily was a drawn figure slumped in the chair. Her fingers kept pushing the silken strands away from her eyes while she watched me. I said, "Get your coat."

"They'll be waiting for us outside?"

"That's right, they'll be waiting."

Even the last shred of hope she had nursed so long left her face. There was a dullness in her eyes and in the way she walked.

"We'll let them wait," I said, and she turned around and grinned with some of the life back in her.

While I waited for the life I turned out the light and stood in front of the window watching the city. The monster squirmed, its bright-colored lights marking the threshing of its limbs, a sprawling octopus whose mouth was hidden under a horribly carved beak. The mouth was open, the beak ready to rip and tear anything that stood in its way. It made sounds out there, incomprehensible sounds that were the muted whinings of deadly terror. There were no spoken words, but the sounds were enough. The meaning was clear.

"I'm ready, Mike."

She had on the green suit again, trimly beautiful, her hair gone now under a pert little hat with a feather in it. The expression on her face said that if she must die it would be quick and clean. And dressed. She was ready. We both were ready. Two very marked people stepping out to look for the mouth of the octopus.

We didn't go down the stairs. We went up to the roof and crossed the abutments between the apartments. We found the door we wanted through the roof of a building a hundred yards down and used that. We took the elevator to the basement and went out through the back. The yard there was an empty place, too steeped in darkness to reflect any of the window lights above. The wall was head-high brick, easy to get over. I pushed Lily up, got over myself and helped her down. We felt our way around the wall until we reached the other basement door but the luck we had had bent a little around a lock under the knob.

I was ready to start working on it when I heard the muffled talk inside and the luck unbent a little bit. I whispered to Lily to keep quiet and pushed her against the side of the building. The talk got louder, the lock clicked and somebody shoved the door open.

The stream of light that flooded the yard didn't catch us. We stayed behind the door and waited. The kid with the wispy mustache backed out swearing under his breath while he tugged at a leash and for a second I was ready to jump him before the racket started. Lily saw it too and grabbed my hand so hard her nails punched holes into my skin. Then the kid was out and walking toward the wall in back with so much to say about people who have cats taken for a walk on a leash that he never saw us go through the door at all.

We got out the other end of the building and circled around the block to the garage. Sammy was just coming on duty and waved my way when he saw us. It was a funny kind of a wave with a motion of the other hand under it. I pushed Lily in ahead of me and closed the door.

Sammy didn't know whether to laugh or not. He decided not to, wrinkled up his face in a serious expression and said, "You hot, Mike?"

"In a way I'm boiling. Why?"

"People been around asking about your new heap. One of the boys tipped me that there's eyes watching for it."

"I heard the story."

"Hear what happened to Bob Gellie?" His face grew pretty serious.

"No."

"He got worked over. Something to do with you."

"Bad?"

"He's in the hospital. Whatever it was he wouldn't talk."

The bastards knew everything. What they didn't know they could find out and when they did the blood ran. The organization. The syndicate. The Mafia. It was filthy, rotten right through but the iron glove it wore was so heavy and so sharp it could work with incredible, terrible efficiency. You worked as they'd tell you to work or draw the penalty. There was no in-between. There was only one penalty. It could be slow or fast, but the result was the same. You died. Until they died,

155

until every damn one of them was nothing but decaying flesh in a pile on the ground the killings would go on and on.

"I'll take care of him. You tell him that for me. How is he?"

"Bob'll come through it. He won't ever look the same, but he'll be okay."

"How do you feel, Sammy?"

"Lousy, if you gotta know. I got me a .32 in the drawer there that's gonna stay right handy all night and maybe afterward."

"Can you get me a car?"

"Take mine. I figured you'd be asking so I have it by the door nosing out. It's a good load and I like it, so bring it back in one piece."

He waved to the door, pulled down the blind over the window and followed us into the garage. He hauled the door up, grinned unhappily when we pulled out and let it slam back in place. I told Lily to get down until I was sure we were clear, made a few turns around one-way streets, parked for a few minutes watching for lights, then pulled out again and cut into traffic.

Lily said, "Where are we going, Mike?"

"You'll see."

"Mike . . . please. I'm awfully scared."

Her lower lip matched the flutter of her voice. She sat there pinching her hands together, her arms making jerky movements against her sides to control the shudder that was trying to take over her body.

"Sorry, kid," I told her. "You're as much a part of this as I am. You ought to know about it. We're going to see what made a woman want to see me pretty badly. We're going to find out what she knew that put her on the missing list. There isn't much you can do except sit tight, but while you're sitting there's plenty you can do. Remember that name. Dig up every detail of that talk you had with Berga and bring that name out."

She looked straight ahead, her face set, and nodded. "All right, Mike. I'll . . . try." Then her head came around and I could feel the challenge of her stare but couldn't match it while I was weaving through the traffic. "I'd do *anything* for you, Mike," she finished softly. There was a newness in her voice I'd never heard before. A controlled excitement that made me remember how I had awakened and what she was thinking of. Before I could answer she turned her head

156

with the same suddenness and stared straight ahead again, but this time with an excited expression of anticipation.

There were only two men assigned to the place when we got there. One sat in the car and the other was parked in a chair by the door looking like he wanted a cigarette pretty bad. He gave me that frozen look all cops keep in reserve and waited for me to speak my piece.

"I'm Mike Hammer. I've been cooperating with Captain Chambers on the deal here and would like to take a look around. Who do I see?"

The freeze melted loose and he nodded. "The boys were talking about you before. The captain say it's okay?"

"Not yet. He will if you want to go get a call in to him."

"Ah, guess it's okay. Don't touch anything, that's all."

"Anybody around inside?"

"Nope. Joint's empty. The butler took an inventory of liquor before he left though."

"Careful guy. I'll be right out."

"Take your time."

So I went in and stood in the long hallway. I held a light up to the Lucky between my lips and blew a thin overcast into the air. There were lights on along the walls, dim things that gave the place the atmosphere of a funeral parlor and hardly any light.

In the back of my mind I had an idea but I didn't know how to start it going. You don't walk in and pick up important things after the cops have been through a place. Not unless they don't want what you're looking for.

I made the rounds of the rooms downstairs, finished the butt and snubbed it, then tried upstairs. The layout was equally as elaborate, as well appointed as the other rooms, a chain of bedrooms, a study, a small music room and a miniature hobby shop on the south side. There was one room that smelled of life and living. It had that woman smell I couldn't miss. It had the jaunty, carefree quality that was Michael Friday and when I snapped the lights on I saw I was right.

There was an orderly disarray of things scattered around that said the woman who belonged to the room would be back. The creams, the perfumes, the open box of pins on the dresser. The bed was large with a fluffy-haired poodle doll propped against the pillows. There were pictures of men on the dresser and a couple of enlarged snapshots of Michael in a sailboat with a batch of college boys in attendance.

Scattered, but neat.

Other signs too, professional signs. A cigar ash in the tray. Indentations in the rolled stockings in the box where a thumb had squeezed them. I sat on the edge of the bed and smoked another cigarette. When I had it halfway down I reached over to the night table for an ash tray and laid it on the cover beside me. The tray made an oval in the center of the square there, a boxy outline in dust. I picked it up, looked at the smudge on the cover and wiped at it with my fingertip.

The other details were there too, the thin line of grit and tiny edges of brownish paper that marked the lip of a box somebody had spilled out in emptying it on the bed. With my fingers held together the flat of my hand filled the width of the square and two hands made the length. I finished the butt, put it out and went back downstairs.

The cop on the porch said, "Make out?"

"Nothing special. You find any safes around?"

"Three of 'em. One upstairs, two downstairs. Nothing there we could use. Maybe a few hundred in bills. Take a look yourself. There's a pair in his study."

They were a pair, all right. One was built into the wall behind a framed old map of New York harbor, but the other was a trick job in the window sill. Carl was kicking his psychology around when he had them built. Two safes in a house a person could expect, but rarely two in the same room. Anyone poking around couldn't miss the one behind the map, but it would take some inside dope to find the other. The dial was pretty badly beaten up and there were fresh scratches in the wood around the thing. I swung the door open, held my lighter in front of it and squinted around. The dust marked the outline of the box that had been there.

The cop had moved to the steps this time. He grinned and jerked his head at the house. "Not much to see."

"Who opened the safes?"

"The city boys brought Delaney in. He's the factory representative of the outfit who makes the safes. Good man. He could make a living working lofts."

"He's doing all right now," I said. I told him so-long and went back to the car. Lily was waiting, her face a pale glow behind the window.

I slid under the wheel, sat there fiddling with the gearshift letting the thought I had jell. Lily put her hand on my arm, held it still and waited. "I wonder if Pat found it," I muttered.

"What?"

"Michael Friday stooled on her brother. She went back home and found something else but this time she was afraid to give it to the police."

"Mike . . ."

"Let me talk, kid. You don't have to listen. I'm just getting it in order. There was trouble in the outfit. Carl was expecting to take over somehow. In that outfit you don't work your way up. Carl was expecting to move up a slot so somebody else had to go. That boy knew what he was doing. He spent some time getting something on the one he was after and was going to smear him with it."

I put it through my mind again, nodded, and said, "Carl was close enough to start the thing going so the other one knew about it. He went after what Carl had and found it gone. By that time the cops were having a field day with the labor department of the organization so he had a good idea who was responsible. He must have tailed her. He knew she had it and what she was going to do with it so he nailed her."

"But . . . who, Mike? Who?"

My teeth came apart in the kind of a smile nobody seemed to like. I was feeling good all over because I had my finger on it now and I wasn't letting go. "Friend Billy," I said. "Billy Mist. Now he sits quiet and enjoys his supper. Someplace he's got a dame on the hook and enjoying life because whatever it was Carl had isn't any more. Billy's free as a bird but he hasn't got two million in the bush to play with. He's got an ace in the hole with Velda in case the two million shows up and a deuce he can discard anytime if it doesn't. The greasy little punk is sitting pretty where he can't be touched."

The laugh started out of my chest and ripped through my throat. It was the biggest joke I ever laughed at because the whole play was made to block me out and I wasn't being mousetrapped. I was going back a couple of hours to the kitchen and what Lily had said and back even further to a note left in my office. Then, so I wouldn't forget how I felt right there at the beginning when I wanted to kill something with my hands, I went back to Berga and the way she had looked coming out of that gas station.

I kicked the engine over, pulled around the squad car and pointed the hood toward the bright eyes of Manhattan. I stayed with the lights watching the streets click by, cut over a few blocks to the building with the efficient look and antiseptic smell and pulled in behind the city hearse unloading a double cargo.

It was a little after one but you could still find dead people around.

The attendant in the morgue called me into his office and wanted to know if I wanted coffee. I shook my head. "It takes the smell away," he said. "What can I do for you?"

"You had a body here. Girl named Berga Torn."

"Still have it."

"Slated for autopsy?"

"Nope. At least I haven't heard about it. They don't usually in those cases."

"There will be one in this case. Can I use the phone?"

"Go ahead."

I picked it up and dialed headquarters. Pat wasn't around so I tried his apartment. He wasn't there, either. I buzzed a few of the places he spent time in but they hadn't seen him. I looked at my watch and the hand had spun another quarter. I swore at the phone and at myself and double cursed the red tape if I had to go through channels. I was thinking so hard I wasn't really thinking at all and while I was in the middle of it the door of the office opened and the little guy with the pot belly came in, dropped his bag on the floor and said, "Damn it, Charlie, why can't people wait until morning to die?"

I said, "Hi, doc," and the coroner gave me a surprised glance that wasn't any too pleased.

"Hello, Hammer, what are you doing here? Should I add 'again'?"

"Yeah, add it, doc. I always seem to come home, don't I?"

"I'd like it better if you stayed out of my sight."

He went to go past me. I grabbed his arm, turned him around and looked at a guy with a safe but disgusting job. He went up on his toes, tried to pull his arm away, but I held on. "Listen, doc. You and I can play games some other time. Right now I need you for a job that can't wait. I have to chop corners and it has to be quick."

"Let go of me!"

I let go of him. "Maybe you like to see those bodies stretched out in the gutter."

He turned around slowly. "What are you talking about?"

"Suppose you had a chance to do something except listen for a heartbeat that isn't there for a change. Supposing you had it in your hand to kick a few killers right into the chair.

· 160

Supposing you're the guy who stands between a few more people living or dying in the next few hours . . . how would you pitch it, doc?"

The puzzle twisted his nose into a ridge of wrinkles. "See here . . . you're talking like . . ."

"I'm talking plain. I've been trying to get some official backing for what I have in mind but nobody's home. Even then it might take up time we can't spare. That chance I was talking about is in your hand, doc."

"But . . ."

"I need a stomach autopsy on a corpse. Now. Can do?"

"I think you're serious," he said in a flat tone.

"You'll never know how serious. There may be trouble later. Trouble isn't as bad as somebody having to die."

I could see the protest coming out of the attendant. It started but never got there. The coroner squared his shoulders, let a little of the excitement that was in my voice trickle into his eyes and he nodded.

"Berga Torn," I told the attendant. "Let's go see her."

He did it the fast, easy way you do when you cut corners. He did it right there in the carrier she lay on and the light overhead winked on the steel in his hand. I didn't get past the first glimpse because fire does horrible things to a person and it was nicer to remember Berga in the headlights of the car.

I could hear him, though.

I could even tell when he found it.

He did me the favor of cleaning it before he handed it to me and I stood there looking at the dull glitter of the brass key wondering where the lock to it was. The coroner said, "Well?"

"Thanks."

"I don't mean that."

"I know . . . only where it goes nobody knows. I thought it would be something else."

He sensed the disappointment and held out his hand. I dropped the key in it and he held it up to the light, turning it over to see both sides. For a minute he concentrated on one side, held it closer to the bulb, then nodded for me to follow him across the room. From a closet he pulled out a bottle of some acrid liquid, poured it into a shallow glass container, then dropped the key in. He let it stay there about twenty seconds before dipping it out with a glass rod. This time the dullness was gone. It was a gleaming thing with a new look and no coating to dull the details. This time when he held it in the light you could see *City Athletic Club, 529* scratched into the surface and I squeezed his arm so hard he winced through his grin.

I said, "Listen, get on the phone out there and find Captain Chambers. Tell him I found what we were looking for and I'm going after it. I'm not going to take any chances on this getting away so he can hop up to my office for a print of this thing."

"He doesn't know?"

"Uh-uh. I'm afraid somebody else might find out the same way I did. I'll call you back to see how you made out. If there's any trouble about . . . back there . . . Chambers'll clear things. Someday I'll let you know just how much of a boost up you gave the department."

The excitement in his eyes sparkled brighter and he was holding his jaw like a guy who's just done the impossible. The morgue attendant was on his way over for an explanation and apparently he wanted it in writing. He tried to stop me for some talk on the way out but I was in too much of a rush.

Lily knew I had it when I came bouncing down the stairs, opened the door for me and said, "Mike?"

"I know almost all the answers now, chicken." I held up the key. "Here's the big baby. Look at it, a chunk of metal people have died for and all this time it was in the stomach of a girl who was ready to do anything to beat them out of it. The key to the deal. For the first time in my life a real one. I know who had it and what's behind the door it opens."

As if the words I had said were a formula that split open Valhalla to let a pack of vicious, false gods spill through, a jagged streak of lightning cut across the sky with the thunder rolling in its wake. The first crashing wave of it was so sudden Lily tightened against it, her eyes closed tight.

I said, "Relax."

"I . . . can't, Mike. I hate thunderstorms."

You could feel the dampness in the air, the fresh coolness of the new wind. She shuddered again and turned up the little collar of her jacket around her neck. "Close the window, Mike."

I rolled it up, got the heap going and turned into traffic heading east. The voice of the city was starting to go quiet now. The last few figures on the streets were starting

162

to run for cover and the cabs picked up their aimless cruising.

The first big drops of rain splattered on the hood and brought the scum flooding down the windshield. I started the wipers, but still had to hunch forward over the wheel to see where I was going. I could feel time going by. The race of the minutes. They never went any faster or any slower, but they always beat you. I turned south on Ninth Avenue, staying in tempo with the lights until I reached the gray-brick building with the small neon sign that read CITY ATHLETIC CLUB.

I cut the engine in front of the door and went to get out. Lily said, "Mike, will you be long?"

"Couple of minutes." Her face seemed to be all pinched up.

"What's the matter, kid?"

"Cold, I guess."

I pulled the blanket from the seat in the back and draped it over her shoulders. "You're catching something sure as hell. Keep it around you. I'll be right back."

She shivered and nodded, holding the edges of the blanket together under her chin.

The guy at the reception desk was a sleepy-eyed tall guy who sat there hating everybody who bothered him. He watched me cross the hall and didn't make any polite sounds until I got to him.

He asked one question. "You a member?"

"No, but ..."

"Then the place is closed. Scram."

I pulled a fin out of my wallet and laid it on the desk. He said, "Scram."

I took it back, stuffed it away and leaned across the chair and belted him right on his back. I picked him up by his skinny arms and popped him a little one in the gut before I threw him back in his chair again. "The next time be nice," I said. I held out the key and he looked at it with eyes that were wide awake now.

"You bastard."

"Shut up. What's the key for?"

"Locker room."

"See who has 529."

He curled his lip at me, ran his hand across his stomach under his belt and pulled a ledger out of the desk drawer. "Raymond. Ten-year membership."

"Let's go."

"You're nuts. I can't leave the desk. I . . ."

"Let's go."

"Lousy coppers," I heard him say. I grinned behind his back and followed him down the stairs. There was a sticky dampness in the air, an acrid smell of disinfectant. We passed a steam room and the entrance to the pool, then turned into the alcove that held the lockers.

They were tall affairs with hasps that allowed you to install your own lock. Raymondo had slapped on a beauty. It was an oversized brass padlock with a snap so big it barely passed through the hasp. I stuck the key in, turned it and the lock came apart.

Death, crime and corruption was lying on the floor in two metal containers the size of lunch pails. The seams were welded shut and the units painted a deep green. Attached to each was the cutest little rig you ever saw, a small CO_2 bottle with a heavy rubber ball attached to the nozzle. The rubber was rotted in the folds and the hose connection had cracked dry, but it didn't spoil the picture any. All you had to do was toss the unit out a porthole, the bottle stopper opened after a time interval and the stuff floated to the top where the rubber ball buoyed it until it was picked up.

The answer to the *Cedric* was there too, a short story composed of sales slips stapled together, a yarn that said Raymondo had taken good care of his investment and was on hand to pick up the junk when they stripped the ship. There was one special item marked *"wall ventilators— 12.50 ea. 25.00."*

I squatted down to pull them out and the guy down the end came away from the wall showing too much curiosity. The stuff had to be dumped someplace but I couldn't be carrying it to the dumping ground. Pat had to see it, the Washington boys would want a look at it. I couldn't take any kind of a chance at all on losing it. Not now.

So I shut the door and closed the lock through the hasp. It had been there a lot of years . . . a few more hours wouldn't hurt it any. But now I had something I could talk a trade with. I could describe the stuff so they'd be sure and it would be my way all the way.

The guy followed me back upstairs and got behind his desk again. He was snottier looking than ever but when I stood close the artificial toughness faded into blankness and he had to lick his lips.

I said, "Remember my face, buddy. Take a good look and keep it in your mind. If anybody who isn't a cop comes in here wanting to know about that locker and you kick through with the information I'm going to break your face into a dozen pieces. No matter what they do I'll do worse, so keep your trap shut." I turned to go, stopped a second and looked back over my shoulder. "The next time be polite. You could have made dough on the deal."

My watch read five minutes to three. Time, time, time. The rain was a solid sheet blasting the sidewalks and spraying back into the air again. I yelled for Lily to open the door, made a dash for it and slid aboard. She trembled under the gust of cold air that got in with me, her face set tighter than it was before.

I reached over and put my arm around her shoulders. She was pulled tight as a drumhead, a muscular stiffness that made her whole body almost immobile. "Cripes, Lily, I got to get you to a doctor."

"No . . . just get me where it's warm, Mike."

"I haven't got much sense."

She forced a smile. "I . . . really don't mind . . . as long as you . . ."

"No more chasing around, kid. I found it. I can take you back now."

There was a catch in the sob that came out of her. Her eyes glistened and the smile didn't have to be forced.

I sat there looking into the rain, pulling on a Lucky while I figured it out. I said, "You'll go back to my apartment, kid. Dry off and sit tight."

"Alone?"

"Don't worry about it. There are cops stationed around the building. I'll tip them to keep the place well covered. We have to move fast now and I can't waste time. I have a key to a couple of million bucks in my pocket and I can't put all my eggs in one basket. I'm getting a duplicate of that key made and you're hanging on to it until Captain Chambers picks it up. I don't want you to move out of that place until I get back and don't pull a stunt like you did before. Let's go, I still have a fast stop to make that won't take more than five minutes."

That was all it did take. My friend turned out the key while he swore at the world for getting him out of bed so I left him to buy a good night in a gin mill for his trouble.

We reached my block at a quarter to four with the rain

165

still lashing at the car in frenzied bursts. There was a patrol wagon at each end and two plain-clothes men were standing in the doorway. When they saw us they looked so mad they could bust and one spit disgustedly and shook his head.

I didn't give them a chance to ask questions. "Sorry you were standing guard over a hole, friend. One of those things. We got this business breaking over our heads and I can't go explaining every move I make. I've been putting in calls all over the lot for Pat Chambers and if one of you guys feels like expediting things you'll get on the line too."

I pointed to Lily. "This is Lily Carver. They're after her as bad as they are me. She's got a message for Pat that can't wait and if anything happens to her between now and when he sees her he'll have your hides. One of you better take her up and stick outside in the hall."

"Johnston'll go."

"Good. You'll call around for Pat."

"We'll locate the captain somehow."

I got Lily inside, saw her through the front door with the cop beside her and felt the load go lighter.

"You got something, Hammer?" The cop was watching me closely.

"Yeah. It's almost over."

His grunt was a sarcastic denial. "You know better, buddy. It never ends. This thing is stretched all over the states. Wait till you see the morning papers."

"Good?"

"Lovely. The voters'll go nuts when they see the score. This town is going to see a reform cleanup like it never happened before. We had to book four of our own boys this evening." His hand turned into a fist. "They were playing along with them."

"The little guys," I said. "They pay through the nose. The wheels keep rolling right along. They string the dead out and walk over them. The little guy pays the price."

"We got wheels too. Evello's dead."

"Yeah." I said.

"How far did they get with his step-sister?"

"As far as here, buddy. People are thinking about that."

I looked across the lobby at him. "They would. They'll try to put the finger anyplace."

Michael Friday and her wet, lovely mouth. The mouth that never did get close enough, really close. Michael Friday with the ready smile and the laugh in her walk, Michael

166

Friday who got tired of the dirt herself and put herself on my side of the fence. Coming to me with the thing I wanted even more than the stuff in the locker. She should have known. Damn it, those things had been happening under her nose. She should have known the kind of people she was messing around with. They're fast and smart and know the angles and they're ready to follow through. She should have thought it out and got herself a cordon of cops instead of cutting loose herself to get the stuff to me. Maybe she knew they'd be after her. Maybe she thought she was as smart as they were. Berga thought those things too.

Lovely Michael Friday. She steps outside and they have her. She could have been standing right where I was that minute. The door behind her locks shut. There's only one person outside and that's the one she's afraid of. Maybe she knew she only had a minute more to live and her insides must have been tumbling around loose.

Like Berga. But Berga did something in that minute.

I got that creepy feeling again, an indescribably tingling sensation that burned up my spine and touched my brain with thoughts that seemed improbable. I looked down at my feet, my teeth shut tight, squinting at the floor. The cop's breathing seemed the loudest thing in the room, even drowning out the thunder and the rain outside. I walked to the mailbox and opened it with my key.

Michael had thought too. She had left an empty envelope in there telling me exactly what she meant. It didn't have my name on it, but I read the message. It said, "William Mist," but it was enough.

It was more than enough. It was something else. The gimmick I was looking for, the one I knew I had come across someplace else but I couldn't put my finger on. But for a little while it was enough.

I crumpled the thing up into a little ball and dropped it. I could feel the hate welling up in me until I couldn't stand it any more. My head was filled with a crazy overture of sound that beat and beat and beat.

I ran out of the place. I left the cop standing there and ran out. I forgot everything I was doing except for one thing when I got in the car. Light, traffic? Hell, nothing mattered. There was only one thing. I was going to see that greaseball die between my fingers and he was going to talk before he did. The car screamed at the corners, the tail end whipping around violently. I could smell the rubber and brake lining and hear the whining protest of the engine and occasionally the hoarse curses that followed my path. The stops were all out this time and nothing else counted.

When I reached the apartment building I didn't push any bells to be let in. I kicked out a pane of glass on the inside door, reached through the hole and turned the knob. I went up the stairs to the same spot I had been before and this time I did hit the bell.

Billy Mist was expecting somebody, all right, but it wasn't me. He was all dressed except for his jacket and he had a gun slung in a harness under his shoulder. I rammed the door so hard it kicked him back in the room and while he was reaching for his rod I smashed his nose into a mess of bloody tissue. He made a second try while he was on the floor and this time I kicked the gun out of his hand under the table and picked him up to go over him good. I held him out where I wanted him and put one into his ribs that brought a scream choking up his throat and had the next one ready when Billy Mist died.

I didn't want to believe it. I wanted him alive so bad I shook him like a rag doll and when the mouth lolled open under those blank eyes I threw him away from me into the door and his head and shoulders slammed it shut. His broken face leered at me from the carpet, the eyes seeing nothing. They were filmy already. I let it go then. I let that raspy yell out of me and began to break things until I was out of breath.

But Billy still leered.

Billy Mist, who knew where Velda was. Billy Mist who was going to talk before he died. Billy Mist who was going to give me the pleasure of killing him slowly.

It was thinking of Velda that smoothed it. My hands stopped shaking and my mind started thinking again. I looked around the mess I had made of the place, avoiding the eyes on the floor.

Billy had been packing. He had been five minutes away from being killed and he was taking a quick-acting powder. The one suitcase had a week's supply of clothes in it but he could afford to buy more when he got there because the rest of the space was taken up by packets of new bills.

I was picking the stuff apart when I heard them at the door. They weren't cops. Not these boys. They wanted in because I was there and nothing was stopping them.

How long ago was it that I asked Berga how stupid could she get?

Now I was the one. Sammy had told me. They were waiting for me. Now in squad cars on the corner of my block. Not for the Ford because by now they'd have figured the switch. So I go busting loose with the pack on my back and now I was up the tree.

Shoulders slammed into the door and a vertical crack showed in it. I walked to the overturned chair, picked up Billy's rod and kicked the safety off. They were a little stupid too. They knew I was traveling clean but forgot Billy would be loaded. I pumped five fast ones through the wood belly-high and the screams outside made a deafening cacophony that brought more screams from others in the building.

The curses and screams didn't stop the others. The door cracked again, started to buckle and I turned and ran into the bathroom. There was a barrel bolt on the door made for decency purposes only and wouldn't hold anything longer than a minute or two. I slid it in place, took my time about opening the bathroom window and sighting along the ledge outside.

I got my feet on the sill, started to go through when my arm swept the bottles from the shelf. Dozens of bottles. A sick man's paradise and Billy had been a very sick man after all. There was one left my arm didn't touch and I picked it up. I stared at it, swore lightly and dropped it in my pocket.

The door inside let loose. There was more letting loose too. Shots and shrieks that didn't belong there and I crawled through the window before I could find out why. I felt along the ledge with my toes, leaning forward at an angle with my hands resting on the building on the other side of the airway. I made the end where the building joined, found handholds on the other sills and went up.

For a change I was glad of the rain. It covered the noises I made, washed clean places for my fingers and toes and when I reached the roof bathed me in its coolness. I lay there on the graveled top breathing the fire out of my lungs, barely conscious of the fury going on in the streets. When I could make it I got across the building, got on the fire escape and crawled down.

Somebody in a dark window was screaming her lungs out telling the world where I was. Shouts answered her from someplace else and two shots whined off into the night.

They never found me. I hit the yard and got out of there. Sirens were converging on the place and a hundred yards off the rapid belch of a tommy gun spit a skinful of sudden destruction into the airway.

I laughed my fool head off while I stood there on the sidewalk and felt good about it. In a way it paid to be stupid as long as you overdid it. I was too stupid to figure the boys planted around my apartment would follow me and too stupid to remember there were the Washington boys who would run behind them. It must have made a pretty picture when they joined forces. It was something that had to come. The Mafia wasn't a gang, it was a government. And governments have armies and armies fight.

The trouble was that while the war raged the leader got away and had time to cover his tracks. I pulled the bottle out of my pocket, looked at it and threw it away.

Not this leader. He wasn't going anywhere except a hole in the ground.

Chapter Thirteen

THE OFFICE was dark. Water leaked through the hole I had made in the glass and the pieces winked back at me. Nobody at the desk. No beautiful smile, challenging eyes. I knew where to look and pulled the file out. I held a match to it and the pieces clicked in place. I put the card back and went through the rooms.

Off the inner office a door led to stairs that ran up, thickly carpeted stairs that didn't betray the passage of a person. There was another door at the top and an apartment off it. I kicked my shoes off, laid the change in my pocket on the floor and walked away from the one that showed the light.

There was only one room that was locked, but those kind of locks never gave me any trouble at all. I stepped inside, eased the door shut and flicked my lighter.

She was laced into an easy chair with a strait jacket, her legs tied down. A strip of adhesive tape across her mouth and around it were red marks where other tapes had been ripped off to feed her or hear what she had to say. There was a sallowness about her face, a fearful, shrunken look, but the eyes were alive. They couldn't see me behind the lighter, but they cursed me just the same.

170

I said, "Hello, Velda," and the cursing stopped. The eyes didn't believe until I moved the lighter and the tears wiped out her vision. I took the ropes off, unlaced the jacket and lifted her up easily. The hurt sounds she wanted to make but couldn't came out in the convulsions of her body. She pressed against me, the tears wetting my face. I squeezed her, ran my hands across her back while I whispered things to her and told her not to be afraid any more. I found her mouth and tasted her, deeply, loving the way she held me and the things she said without really saying anything.

When I could I said, "You all right?"

"I was going to die tonight."

"Somebody'll take your place."

"Now?"

"You won't be here to see it." I found the key in my pocket and pressed it in her hand. I gave her my wallet to go with it and pulled her to the door. "Take a cab and find yourself a cop. Find Pat if you can. There's an address on that key. Go hold what's in the locker it opens. Can you do that much?"

"Can't I . . ."

"I said get a cop. The bastards know everything there is to know. We can't lose any time at all . . . and most of all I can't lose you at all. Tomorrow we'll talk."

"Tomorrow, Mike."

"It's crazy this way. Everything's crazy. I find you and I'm sending you off again. Damn it, move before I don't let you go."

"Tomorrow, Mike," she said and reached for me again. She wasn't tired now, she was brand-new again. She was a woman I was never going to let go again ever. She didn't know it yet, but tomorrow there would be more than talk. I wanted her since I had first seen her. Tomorrow I'd get her. The way she wanted it. Tomorrow she was going to belong to me all the way.

"Say it, Mike."

"I love you, kitten. I love you more than I've ever thought I could love anything."

"I love you too, Mike." I could feel her grin. "Tomorrow."

I nodded and opened the door. I waited until she had gone down the steps and this time walked the other way. To where the light showed.

I pushed it open, leaned against the sill and when the gray-

171

haired man writing at the table across the room spun around I said, "Doctor Soberin, I presume."

It caught him so far off base I had time to get halfway across to him before he dipped his hand in the drawer and I had his wrist before he could get the thing leveled. I let him keep the gun in his hand so I could bend it back and hear his fingers break and when he tried to yell I bottled the sound up by smashing my elbow into his mouth. The shattered teeth tore my arm and his mouth became a great hole welling blood. His fingers were broken stubs sticking at odd angles. I shoved him away from me, slashed the butt end of the rod across the side of his head and watched him drop into his chair.

"I got me a wheel," I said. "The boy at the top."

Dr. Soberin opened his mouth to speak and I shook my head.

"You're dead, mister. Starting from now you're dead. It took me a long time. It didn't really have to." I let out a dry laugh at myself. "I'm getting too old for the game. I'm not as fast as I used to be. One time I would have had it made as soon as I rolled it around a little bit.

"The gimmick, doc, there's always that damned gimmick. The kind you can't kick out of sight. This time the gimmick was on the bottom of that card your secretary made out on Berga Torn. She asked who sent her and she said William Mist. She signed the card, too. You pulled a cutie on that one. You couldn't afford to let a respectable dame know your business, and you knew she wouldn't put her name on a switch. You knew there might be an investigation and didn't want any suspicious erasures on the card so you simply dug up a name that you could type over Mist to make the letters fit. Wieton comes out pretty well. Unless you looked hard you'd never pick it up."

He had gone a deathly pale. His hand was up to his mouth trying to stop the blood. It was sickening him and he retched. All that came up was more blood. The hand with the broken fingers looked unreal on the end of his arm. Unreal and painful.

"You took a lot of trouble to get the information Berga had under her hat. A lot of clever thinking went into that deal at the sanitarium. You had it rigged pretty nicely, even to a spot where she could be worked over without anybody getting wise. Sorry I spoiled your plans. You shouldn't have wrecked my heap."

Something childish crept into his face. "You . . . got . . . another one."

"I'll keep it too. I didn't go for the booby trap, doc. That was kid stuff."

If his face screwed up any tighter he was going to cry. He sat there moaning softly, the complete uncertainty of it all making him rock in his chair.

I said, "This time I do it your way. I was the only one you were ever afraid of because I was like the men you give orders to. I'm not going to talk to you. Later I'll go over the details. Later I'll give my explanations and excuses to the police. Later I'll get raked over the coals for what I'm going to do now, but what the hell, doc. Like I said, I'm getting old in the game. I don't care any more."

He was quiet in his chair. The quiet that terror brings and for once he was knowing the hand of terror himself.

I said, "Doc . . ." and he looked at me. No, not me, the gun. The big hole in the end of the gun.

And while he was looking I let him see what came out of the gun.

Doctor Soberin only had one eye left.

I stepped across the body and picked up the phone. I called headquarters and tried to get Pat. He was still out. I had the call transferred to another department and the man I wanted said hello. I asked him for the identification on a dead blonde and he told me to wait.

A minute later he picked up the phone. "Think I got it. Death by drowning. Age, about . . ."

"Skip the details. Just the name."

"Sure, Lily Carver. Prints just came in from Washington. She had 'em taken while she worked at a war plant."

I said thanks, held the button down on the phone, let it go and when I heard the dial tone started working on my home number.

She said, "Don't bother, Mike. I'm right here."

And she was.

Beautiful Lily with hair as white as snow. Her mouth a scarlet curve that smiled. Differently, now, but still smiling. Her body a tight bundle of lush curves that swelled and moved under a light white terrycloth robe. Lovely Lily who brought the sharpness of an alcohol bath in with her so that it wet her robe until there was nothing there, no hill or valley, no shadow that didn't come out.

173

Gorgeous Lily with my .45 in her hand from where she had found it on the dresser.

"You forgot about me, Mike."

"I almost did, didn't I."

There was cold hate coming into her eyes now. Hate that grew as she looked again at the one eye in the body beside the table. "You shouldn't have done that, Mike."

"No?"

"He was the only one who knew about me." The smile left her mouth. "I loved him. He knew about me and didn't care. I loved him, you crumb you!" The words hissed out of her teeth.

I looked at her the way I did when she first held a gun on me. "Sure. You loved him so much you killed Lily Carver and took her place. You loved him so much you made sure there were no slips in his plan. You loved him so much you set Berga Torn up for the kill and damn near made sure Velda died. You loved him so much you never saw that all he loved was power and money and you were only something he could use.

"You fitted right into the racket. You were lucky once and smart the rest of the time. You reached Al after Velda left but you had time to catch up with her. By the way, did you ever find out why Al died? He was giving friend Billy Mist the needle. Billy knew what had happened when you called him down to tell him his girl friend wasn't what she was cracked up to be. With Billy that didn't go and he carved up his playmate. Nice people to have around."

"Shut up."

"Shut up hell. You stuck with me all the way. You ducked out because you thought the boys had me once, then came back when you found out I propped them up against a dead-end sign. You passed the word right under my nose and had Billy packing to blow town. What a deal that was. I even showed you how to get out of my apartment without a tail picking you up. That's why you're here now. So what was supposed to happen? You go back to your real identity? Nuts. You're part of it and you'll die with it. You played me for a sucker up and down Broadway but it's over. This isn't the first time you've pointed a rod at me, sugar. The last time was a game, but I didn't know it. I'm still going to take it away from you. What kind of a guy do you think I am anyway?"

Her face changed as if I had slapped her. For an instant

174

the strangeness was back again. "You're a deadly man, Mike."

Then I saw it in her face and she was faster than I was. The rod belched flame and the slug tore into my side and spun me around. There was a crazy spinning sensation, a feeling of tumbling end over end through space, an urge to vomit, but no strength left to vomit with.

My eyes cleared and I pushed myself up on an elbow. There was a loose, empty feeling in my joints. The end was right there ahead of me and nothing I could do about it.

Lily smiled again, the end of the .45 drifting down to my stomach. She laughed at me, knowing I could raise myself to reach for it. My mouth was dry. I wanted a cigarette. It was all I could think about. It was something a guy about to die always got. My fingers found the deck of Luckies, fumbled one loose and got it into my mouth. I could barely feel it laying there on my lips.

"You shouldn't have killed him," Lily said again.

I reached for the lighter. It wasn't going to be long now. I could feel things start to loosen up. My mind was having trouble hearing her. One more shot. It would be quick.

"Mike . . ."

I got my eyes open. She was a strong, pungent smell. Very strong. Still lovely though.

"I thought I almost loved you once. More than . . . him. But I didn't Mike. He would take me like I was. He was the one who gave me life, at least, after . . . it happened. He was the doctor. I was the patient. I loved him. You would have been disgusted with me. I can see your eyes now, Mike. They would have been revolted.

"He was deadly too, Mike . . . but not like you. You're even worse. You're the deadly one, but you would have been revolted. Look at me, Mike. How would you like to kiss me now? You wanted to before. Would you like to now? I wanted you to . . . you know that, don't you? I was afraid to even let you touch me. You wanted to kiss me . . . so kiss me."

Her fingers slipped through the belt of the robe, opened it. Her hands parted it slowly . . . until I could see what she was really like. I wanted to vomit worse than before. I wanted to let my guts come up and felt my belly retching.

She was a horrible caricature of a human! There was no skin, just a disgusting mass of twisted, puckered flesh from her knees to her neck making a picture of gruesome freakishness that made you want to shut your eyes against it.

The cigarette almost fell out of my mouth. The lighter shook in my hand, but I got it open.

"Fire did it, Mike. Do you think I'm pretty now?"

She laughed and I heard the insanity in it. The gun pressed into my belt as she kneeled forward, bringing the revulsion with her. "You're going to die now . . . but first you can do it. Deadly . . . deadly . . . kiss me."

The smile never left her mouth and before it was on me I thumbed the lighter and in the moment of time before the scream blossoms into the wild cry of terror she was a mass of flame tumbling on the floor with the blue flames of alcohol turning the white of her hair into black char and her body convulsing under the agony of it. The flames were teeth that ate, ripping and tearing, into scars of other flames and her voice the shrill sound of death on the loose.

I looked, looked away. The door was closed and maybe I had enough left to make it.

The End

SOLE
SURVIVOR

By Dean Koontz:

MR. MURDER
DRAGON TEARS
HIDEAWAY
COLD FIRE
THE BAD PLACE
MIDNIGHT
LIGHTNING
WATCHERS
STRANGERS
TWILIGHT EYES
DARKFALL
PHANTOMS
WHISPERS
THE MASK
THE VISION
THE FACE OF FEAR
NIGHT CHILLS
SHATTERED
THE VOICE OF THE NIGHT
THE SERVANTS OF TWILIGHT
THE HOUSE OF THUNDER
THE KEY TO MIDNIGHT
SHADOWFIRES
WINTER MOON*
THE DOOR TO DECEMBER
DARK RIVERS OF THE HEART*
ICEBOUND*
STRANGE HIGHWAYS
THE EYES OF DARKNESS*
INTENSITY*
TICKTOCK*
SOLE SURVIVOR*

*Published by Ballantine Books

SOLE
SURVIVOR

DEAN KOONTZ

BALLANTINE BOOKS • NEW YORK

Correspondence to the author should be addressed to:

Dean Koontz
P.O. Box 9529
Newport Beach, CA 92658

http://www.randomhouse.com

Library of Congress Catalog Card Number: 97-93636

ISBN 0-345-41294-X

This edition published by arrangement with Alfred A. Knopf, Inc.

Manufactured in the United States of America

First Ballantine Books International Edition: September 1997

10 9 8 7 6 5 4 3 2 1

ACKNOWLEDGMENT

The real Barbara Christman won a prize: the use of her name in this novel. Considering that she was one of a hundred booksellers involved in the lottery, I am surprised by the way in which her name resonates in this particular story. She was expecting to be portrayed as a psychotic killer; instead, she will have to settle for being a quiet heroine. Sorry, Barbara.

The sky is deep, the sky is dark.
The light of stars is so damn stark.
When I look up, I fill with fear.
If all we have is what lies here,
this lonely world, this troubled place,
then cold dead stars and empty space . . .
Well, I see no reason to persevere,
no reason to laugh or shed a tear,
no reason to sleep or ever to wake,
no promises to keep, and none to make.
And so at night I still raise my eyes
to study the clear but mysterious skies
that arch above us, as cold as stone.
Are you there, God? Are we alone?

—THE BOOK OF COUNTED SORROWS

ONE
LOST FOREVER

1

At two-thirty Saturday morning, in Los Angeles, Joe Carpenter woke, clutching a pillow to his chest, calling his lost wife's name in the darkness. The anguished and haunted quality of his own voice had shaken him from sleep. Dreams fell from him not all at once but in trembling veils, as attic dust falls off rafters when a house rolls with an earthquake.

When he realized that he did not have Michelle in his arms, he held fast to the pillow anyway. He had come out of the dream with the scent of her hair. Now he was afraid that any movement he made would cause that memory to fade and leave him with only the sour smell of his night sweat.

Inevitably, no weight of stillness could hold the memory in all its vividness. The scent of her hair receded like a balloon rising, and soon it was beyond his grasp.

Bereft, he got up and went to the nearest of two windows. His bed, which consisted of nothing but a mattress on the floor, was the only furniture, so he did not have to be concerned about stumbling over obstructions in the gloom.

The studio apartment consisted of one large room with a kitchenette, a closet, and a cramped bathroom, all over a two-car detached garage in upper Laurel Canyon. After selling the house in Studio City, he had brought no furniture

3

with him, because dead men needed no such comforts. He had come here to die.

For ten months he had been paying the rent, waiting for the morning when he would fail to wake.

The window faced the rising canyon wall, the ragged black shapes of evergreens and eucalyptuses. To the west was a fat moon glimpsed through the trees, a silvery promise beyond the bleak urban woods.

He was surprised that he was still not dead after all this time. He was not alive, either. Somewhere between. Halfway in the journey. He had to find an ending, because for him there could never be any going back.

After fetching an icy bottle of beer from the refrigerator in the kitchenette, Joe returned to the mattress. He sat with his back against the wall.

Beer at two-thirty in the morning. A sliding-down life.

He wished that he were capable of drinking himself to death. If he could drift out of this world in a numbing alcoholic haze, he might not care how long his departure required. Too much booze would irrevocably blur his memories, however, and his memories were sacred to him. He allowed himself only a few beers or glasses of wine at a time.

Other than the faint tree-filtered glimmer of moonlight on the window glass, the only light in the room came from the backlit buttons on the telephone keypad beside the mattress.

He knew only one person to whom he could talk frankly about his despair in the middle of the night—or in broad daylight. Though he was only thirty-seven, his mom and dad were long gone. He had no brothers or sisters. Friends had tried to comfort him after the catastrophe, but he had been too pained to talk about what had happened, and he had kept them at a distance so aggressively that he had offended most of them.

Now he picked up the phone, put it in his lap, and called Michelle's mother, Beth McKay.

In Virginia, nearly three thousand miles away, she picked up the phone on the first ring. "Joe?"

"Did I wake you?"

"You know me, dear—early to bed and up before dawn."

"Henry?" he asked, referring to Michelle's father.

"Oh, the old beast could sleep through Armageddon," she said affectionately.

She was a kind and gentle woman, full of compassion for Joe even as she coped with her own loss. She possessed an uncommon strength.

At the funeral, both Joe and Henry had needed to lean on Beth, and she had been a rock for them. Hours later, however, well after midnight, Joe had discovered her on the patio behind the Studio City house, sitting in a glider in her pajamas, hunched like an ancient crone, tortured by grief, muffling her sobs in a pillow that she had carried with her from the spare room, trying not to burden her husband or her son-in-law with her own pain. Joe sat beside her, but she didn't want her hand held or an arm around her shoulders. She flinched at his touch. Her anguish was so intense that it had scraped her nerves raw, until a murmur of commiseration was like a scream to her, until a loving hand scorched like a branding iron. Reluctant to leave her alone, he had picked up the long-handled net and skimmed the swimming pool: circling the water, scooping gnats and leaves off the black surface at two o'clock in the morning, not even able to see what he was doing, just grimly circling, circling, skimming, skimming, while Beth wept into the pillow, circling and circling until there was nothing to strain from the clear water except the reflections of cold uncaring stars. Eventually, having wrung all the tears from herself, Beth rose from the glider, came to him, and pried the net out of his hands. She had led him upstairs and tucked him in bed as though he were a child, and he had slept deeply for the first time in days.

Now, on the phone with her at a lamentable distance, Joe set aside his half-finished beer. "Is it dawn there yet, Beth?"

"Just a breath ago."

"Are you sitting at the kitchen table, watching it through the big window? Is the sky pretty?"

"Still black in the west, indigo overhead, and out to the east, a fan of pink and coral and sapphire like Japanese silk."

As strong as Beth was, Joe called her regularly not just for the strength she could offer but because he liked to listen to her talk. The particular timbre of her voice and her soft Virginia accent were the same as Michelle's had been.

He said, "You answered the phone with my name."

"Who else would it have been, dear?"

"Am I the only one who ever calls this early?"

"Rarely others. But this morning . . . it could only be you."

The worst had happened one year ago to the day, changing their lives forever. This was the first anniversary of their loss.

She said, "I hope you're eating better, Joe. Are you still losing weight?"

"No," he lied.

Gradually during the past year, he had become so indifferent to food that three months ago he began dropping weight. He had dropped twenty pounds to date.

"Is it going to be a hot day there?" he asked.

"Stifling hot and humid. There are some clouds, but we're not supposed to get rain, no relief. The clouds in the east are fringed with gold and full of pink. The sun's all the way out of bed now."

"It doesn't seem like a year already, does it, Beth?"

"Mostly not. But sometimes it seems ages ago."

"I miss them so much," he said. "I'm so lost without them."

"Oh, Joe. Honey, Henry and I love you. You're like a son to us. You *are* a son to us."

"I know, and I love you too, very much. But it's not enough, Beth, it's not enough." He took a deep breath. "This year, getting through, it's been hell. I can't handle another year like this."

"It'll get better with time."

"I'm afraid it won't. I'm scared. I'm no good alone, Beth."

"Have you thought some more about going back to work, Joe?"

Before the accident, he had been a crime reporter at the *Los Angeles Post*. His days as a journalist were over.

"I can't bear the sight of the bodies, Beth."

He was unable to look upon a victim of a drive-by shooting or a car-jacking, regardless of age or sex, without seeing Michelle or Chrissie or Nina lying bloody and battered before him.

"You could do other kinds of reporting. You're a good writer, Joe. Write some human interest stories. You need to be working, doing something that'll make you feel useful again."

Instead of answering her, he said, "I don't *function* alone. I just want to be with Michelle. I want to be with Chrissie and Nina."

"Someday you will be," she said, for in spite of everything, she remained a woman of faith.

"I want to be with them now." His voice broke, and he paused to put it back together. "I'm finished here, but I don't have the guts to move on."

"Don't talk like that, Joe."

He didn't have the courage to end his life, because he

had no convictions about what came after this world. He did not truly believe that he would find his wife and daughters again in a realm of light and loving spirits. Lately, when he gazed at a night sky, he saw only distant suns in a meaningless void, but he couldn't bear to voice his doubt, because to do so would be to imply that Michelle's and the girls' lives had been meaningless as well.

Beth said, "We're all here for a purpose."

"They were my purpose. They're gone."

"Then there's another purpose you're meant for. It's your job now to find it. There's a reason you're still here."

"No reason," he disagreed. "Tell me about the sky, Beth."

After a hesitation, she said, "The clouds to the east aren't gilded anymore. The pink is gone too. They're white clouds, no rain in them, and not dense but like a filigree against the blue."

He listened to her describe the morning at the other end of the continent. Then they talked about fireflies, which she and Henry had enjoyed watching from their back porch the previous night. Southern California had no fireflies, but Joe remembered them from his boyhood in Pennsylvania. They talked about Henry's garden too, in which strawberries were ripening, and in time Joe grew sleepy.

Beth's last words to him were: "It's full daylight here now. Morning's going past us and heading your way, Joey. You give it a chance, morning's going to bring you the reason you need, some purpose, because that's what the morning does."

After he hung up, Joe lay on his side, staring at the window from which the silvery lunar light had faded. The moon had set. He was in the blackest depths of the night.

When he returned to sleep, he dreamed not of any glorious approaching purpose but of an unseen, indefinable, looming menace. Like a great weight falling through the sky above him.

2

Later Saturday morning, driving to Santa Monica, Joe Carpenter suffered an anxiety attack. His chest tightened, and he was able to draw breath only with effort. When he lifted one hand from the wheel, his fingers quivered like those of a palsied old man.

He was overcome by a sense of falling, as from a great height, as though his Honda had driven off the freeway into an inexplicable and bottomless abyss. The pavement stretched unbroken ahead of him, and the tires sang against the blacktop, but he could not reason himself back to a perception of stability.

Indeed, the plummeting sensation grew so severe and terrifying that he took his foot off the accelerator and tapped the brake pedal.

Horns blared and skidding tires squealed as traffic adjusted to his sudden deceleration. As cars and trucks swept past the Honda, the drivers glared murderously at Joe or mouthed offensive words or made obscene gestures. This was Greater Los Angeles in an age of change, crackling with the energy of doom, yearning for the Apocalypse, where an unintended slight or an inadvertent trespass on someone else's turf might result in a thermonuclear response.

His sense of falling did not abate. His stomach turned over as if he were aboard a roller coaster, plunging along a precipitous length of track. Although he was alone in the car, he heard the screams of passengers, faint at first and then louder, not the good-humored shrieks of thrill seekers at an amusement park, but cries of genuine anguish.

As though from a distance, he listened to himself whispering, *"No, no, no, no."*

A brief gap in traffic allowed him to angle the Honda off the pavement. The shoulder of the freeway was narrow. He stopped as close as possible to the guardrail, over which lush oleander bushes loomed like a great cresting green tide.

He put the car in Park but didn't switch off the engine. Even though he was sheathed in cold sweat, he needed the chill blasts of air conditioning to be able to breathe. The pressure on his chest increased. Each stuttering inhalation was a struggle, and each hot exhalation burst from him with an explosive wheeze.

Although the air in the Honda was clear, Joe smelled smoke. He tasted it too: the acrid mélange of burning oil, melting plastic, smoldering vinyl, scorched metal.

When he glanced at the dense clusters of leaves and the deep-red flowers of the oleander pressing against the windows on the passenger side, his imagination morphed them into billowing clouds of greasy smoke. The window became a rectangular porthole with rounded corners and thick dual-pane glass.

Joe might have thought he was losing his mind—if he hadn't suffered similar anxiety attacks during the past year. Although sometimes as much as two weeks passed between episodes, he often endured as many as three in one day, each lasting between ten minutes and half an hour.

He had seen a therapist. The counseling had not helped.

His doctor recommended anti-anxiety medication. He rejected the prescription. He wanted to feel the pain. It was all he had.

Closing his eyes, covering his face with his icy hands, he strove to regain control of himself, but the catastrophe continued to unfold around him. The sense of falling intensified. The smell of smoke thickened. The screams of phantom passengers grew louder.

Everything shook. The floor beneath his feet. The cabin walls. The ceiling. Horrendous rattling and twanging and banging and gong-like clanging accompanied the shaking, shaking, shaking.

"Please," he pleaded.

Without opening his eyes, he lowered his hands from his face. They lay fisted at his sides.

After a moment, the small hands of frightened children clutched at his hands, and he held them tightly.

The children were not in the car, of course, but in their seats in the doomed airliner. Joe was flashing back to the crash of Flight 353. For the duration of this seizure, he would be in two places at once: in the real world of the Honda and in the Nationwide Air 747 as it found its way down from the serenity of the stratosphere, through an overcast night sky, into a meadow as unforgiving as iron.

Michelle had been sitting between the kids. Her hands, not Joe's, were those that Chrissie and Nina gripped in their last long minutes of unimaginable dread.

As the shaking grew worse, the air was filled with projectiles. Paperback books, laptop computers, pocket calculators, flatware and dishes—because a few passengers had not yet finished dinner when disaster struck—plastic drinking glasses, single-serving bottles of liquor, pencils, and pens ricocheted through the cabin.

Coughing because of the smoke, Michelle would have urged the girls to keep their heads down. *Heads down. Protect your faces.*

Such faces. Beloved faces. Seven-year-old Chrissie had

her mother's high cheekbones and clear green eyes. Joe would never forget the flush of joy that suffused Chrissie's face when she was taking a ballet lesson, or the squint-eyed concentration with which she approached home plate to take her turn at bat in Little League baseball games. Nina, only four, the pug-nosed munchkin with gray-violet eyes, had a way of crinkling her sweet face in pure delight at the sight of a dog or cat. Animals were drawn to her—and she to them—as though she were the reincarnation of St. Francis of Assisi, which was not a far-fetched idea when one saw her gazing with wonder and love upon even an ugly garden lizard cupped in her small, careful hands.

Heads down. Protect your faces.

In that advice was hope, the implication that they would all survive and that the worst thing that might happen to them would be a face-disfiguring encounter with a hurtling laptop or broken glass.

The fearsome turbulence increased. The angle of descent grew more severe, pinning Joe to his seat, so that he couldn't easily bend forward and protect his face.

Maybe the oxygen masks dropped from overhead, or maybe damage to the craft had resulted in a systems failure, with the consequence that masks had not been deployed at every seat. He didn't know if Michelle, Chrissie, and Nina had been able to breathe or if, choking on the billowing soot, they had struggled futilely to find fresh air.

Smoke surged more thickly through the passenger compartment. The cabin became as claustrophobic as any coal mine deep beneath the surface of the earth.

In the blinding blackdamp, hidden sinuosities of fire uncoiled like snakes. The wrenching terror of the aircraft's uncontrolled descent was equaled by the terror of not knowing where those flames were or when they might flash with greater vigor through the 747.

As the stress on the airliner increased to all but intolerable levels, thunderous vibrations shuddered through the fuselage. The giant wings thrummed as though they would tear loose. The steel frame groaned like a living beast in mortal agony, and perhaps minor welds broke with sounds as loud and sharp as gunshots. A few rivets sheered off, each with a piercing *screeeeek.*

To Michelle and Chrissie and little Nina, perhaps it seemed that the plane would disintegrate in flight and that they would be cast into the black sky, be spun away from one another, plummeting in their separate seats to three separate deaths, each abjectly alone at the instant of impact.

The huge 747-400, however, was a marvel of design and a triumph of engineering, brilliantly conceived and soundly constructed. In spite of the mysterious hydraulics failure that rendered the aircraft uncontrollable, the wings did not tear loose, and the fuselage did not disintegrate. Its powerful Pratt and Whitney engines screaming as if in defiance of gravity, Nationwide Flight 353 held together throughout its final descent.

At some point Michelle would have realized that all hope was lost, that they were in a dying plunge. With characteristic courage and selflessness, she would have thought only of the children then, would have concentrated on comforting them, distracting them as much as possible from thoughts of death. No doubt she leaned toward Nina, pulled her close, and in spite of the breath-stealing fumes, spoke into the girl's ear to be heard above the clamor: *It's okay, baby, we're together, I love you, hold on to Mommy, I love you, you're the best little girl who ever was.* Shaking down, down, down through the Colorado night, her voice full of emotion but devoid of panic, she had surely sought out Chrissie too: *It's all right, I'm with you, honey, hold my hand, I love you so much, I'm so very proud of you, we're together, it's all right, we'll always be together.*

In the Honda alongside the freeway, Joe could hear Michelle's voice almost as if from memory, as though he had been with her as she had comforted the children. He wanted desperately to believe that his daughters had been able to draw upon the strength of the exceptional woman who had been their mother. He needed to know that the last thing the girls heard in this world was Michelle telling them how very precious they were, how cherished.

The airliner met the meadow with such devastating impact that the sound was heard more than twenty miles away in the rural Colorado vastness, stirring hawks and owls and eagles out of trees and into flight, startling weary ranchers from their armchairs and early beds.

In the Honda, Joe Carpenter let out a muffled cry. He doubled over as if he had been struck hard in the chest.

The crash was catastrophic. Flight 353 exploded on impact and tumbled across the meadow, disintegrating into thousands of scorched and twisted fragments, spewing orange gouts of burning jet fuel that set fire to evergreens at the edge of the field. Three hundred and thirty people, including passengers and crew, perished instantly.

Michelle, who had taught Joe Carpenter most of what he knew about love and compassion, was snuffed out in that merciless moment. Chrissie, seven-year-old ballerina and baseball player, would never again pirouette on point or run the bases. And if animals felt the same psychic connection with Nina that she felt with them, then in that chilly Colorado night, the meadows and the wooded hills had been filled with small creatures that cowered miserably in their burrows.

Of his family, Joe Carpenter was the sole survivor.

He had not been with them on Flight 353. Every soul aboard had been hammered into ruin against the anvil of the earth. If he had been with them, then he too would have been identifiable only by his dental records and a printable finger or two.

His flashbacks to the crash were not memories but exhausting fevers of imagination, frequently expressed in dreams and sometimes in anxiety attacks like this one. Racked by guilt because he had not perished with his wife and daughters, Joe tortured himself with these attempts to share the horror that they must have experienced.

Inevitably, his imaginary journeys on the earthbound airplane failed to bring him the healing acceptance for which he longed. Instead, each nightmare and each waking seizure salted his wounds.

He opened his eyes and stared at the traffic speeding past him. If he chose the right moment, he could open the door, step out of the car, walk onto the freeway, and be struck dead by a truck.

He remained safely in the Honda, not because he was afraid to die, but for reasons unclear even to him. Perhaps, for the time being at least, he felt the need to punish himself with more life.

Against the passenger-side windows, the overgrown oleander bushes stirred ceaselessly in the wind from the passing traffic. The friction of the greenery against the glass raised an eerie whispering like lost and forlorn voices.

He was not shaking anymore.

The sweat on his face began to dry in the cold air gushing from the dashboard vents.

He was no longer plagued by a sensation of falling. He had reached bottom.

Through the August heat and a thin haze of smog, passing cars and trucks shimmered like mirages, trembling westward toward cleaner air and the cooling sea. Joe waited for a break in traffic and then headed once more for the edge of the continent.

3

The sand was bone white in the glare of the August sun. Cool and green and rolling came the sea, scattering the tiny shells of dead and dying creatures on the shore.

The beach at Santa Monica was crowded with people tanning, playing games, and eating picnic lunches on blankets and big towels. Although the day was a scorcher farther inland, here it was merely pleasantly warm, with a breeze coming off the Pacific.

A few sunbathers glanced curiously at Joe as he walked north through the coconut-oiled throng, because he was not dressed for the beach. He wore a white T-shirt, tan chinos, and running shoes without socks. He had not come to swim or sunbathe.

As lifeguards watched the swimmers, strolling young women in bikinis watched the lifeguards. Their rhythmic rituals distracted them entirely from the architects of shells cast on the foaming shore near their feet.

Children played in the surf, but Joe could not bear to watch them. Their laughter, shouts, and squeals of delight abraded his nerves and sparked in him an irrational anger.

Carrying a Styrofoam cooler and a towel, he continued north, gazing at the seared hills of Malibu beyond the curve of Santa Monica Bay. At last he found a less populated stretch of sand. He unrolled the towel, sat facing the sea, and took a bottle of beer from its bed of ice in the cooler.

If ocean-view property had been within his means, he would have finished out his life at the water's edge. The ceaseless susurration of surf, the sun-gilded and moon-silvered relentlessness of incoming breakers, and the smooth liquid curve to the far horizon brought him not any sense of peace, not serenity, but a welcome numbness.

The rhythms of the sea were all he ever expected to know of eternity and of God.

If he drank a few beers and let the therapeutic vistas of the Pacific wash through him, he might then be calm enough to go to the cemetery. To stand upon the earth that blanketed his wife and his daughters. To touch the stone that bore their names.

This day, of all days, he had an obligation to the dead.

Two teenage boys, improbably thin, wearing baggy swim trunks slung low on their narrow hips, ambled along the beach from the north and stopped near Joe's towel. One wore his long hair in a ponytail, the other in a buzz cut. Both were deeply browned by the sun. They turned to gaze at the ocean, their backs to him, blocking his view.

As Joe was about to ask them to move out of his way, the kid with the ponytail said, "You holding anything, man?"

Joe didn't answer because he thought, at first, that the boy was talking to his buzz-cut friend.

"You holding anything?" the kid asked again, still staring at the ocean. "Looking to make a score or move some merchandise?"

"I've got nothing but beer," Joe said impatiently, tipping up his sunglasses to get a better look at them, "and it's not for sale."

"Well," said the kid with the buzz cut, "if you ain't a

candy store, there's a couple guys watching sure think you are."

"Where?"

"Don't look now," said the boy with the ponytail. "Wait till we get some distance. We been watching them watch you. They stink of cop so bad, I'm surprised you can't smell 'em."

The other said, "Fifty feet south, near the lifeguard tower. Two dinks in Hawaiian shirts, look like preachers on vacation."

"One's got binoculars. One's got a walkie-talkie."

Bewildered, Joe lowered his sunglasses and said, "Thanks."

"Hey," said the boy with the ponytail, "just doing the friendly thing, man. We hate those self-righteous assholes."

With nihilistic bitterness that sounded absurd coming from anyone so young, the kid with the buzz cut said, "Screw the system."

As arrogant as young male tigers, the boys continued south along the beach, checking out the girls. Joe had never gotten a good look at their faces.

A few minutes later, when he finished his first beer, he turned, opened the lid of the cooler, put away the empty can, and looked nonchalantly back along the strand. Two men in Hawaiian shirts were standing in the shadow of the lifeguard tower.

The taller of the two, in a predominantly green shirt and white cotton slacks, was studying Joe through a pair of binoculars. Alert to the possibility that he'd been spotted, he calmly turned with the binoculars to the south, as if interested not in Joe but in a group of bikini-clad teenagers.

The shorter man wore a shirt that was mostly red and orange. His tan slacks were rolled at the cuffs. He was barefoot in the sand, holding his shoes and socks in his left hand.

In his right hand, held down at his side, was another object, which might have been a small radio or a CD player. It might also have been a walkie-talkie.

The tall guy was cancerously tanned, with sun-bleached blond hair, but the smaller man was pale, a stranger to beaches.

Popping the tab on another beer and inhaling the fragrant foamy mist that sprayed from the can, Joe turned to the sea once more.

Although neither of the men looked as if he'd left home this morning with the intention of going to the shore, they appeared no more out of place than Joe did. The kids had said that the watchers stank of cop, but even though he'd been a crime reporter for fourteen years, Joe couldn't catch the scent.

Anyway, there was no reason for the police to be interested in him. With the murder rate soaring, rape almost as common as romance, and robbery so prevalent that half the populace seemed to be stealing from the other half, the cops would not waste time harassing him for drinking an alcoholic beverage on a public beach.

High on silent pinions, shining white, three sea gulls flew northward from the distant pier, at first paralleling the shoreline. Then they soared over the shimmering bay and wheeled across the sky.

Eventually Joe glanced back toward the lifeguard tower. The two men were no longer there.

He faced the sea again.

Incoming breakers broke, spilling shatters of foam on the sand. He watched the waves as a willing subject might watch a hypnotist's pendant swinging on a silver chain.

This time, however, the tides did not mesmerize, and

he was unable to guide his troubled mind into calmer currents. Like the effect of a planet on its moon, the calendar pulled Joe into its orbit, and he couldn't stop his thoughts from revolving around the date: August 15, August 15, August 15. This first anniversary of the crash had an overwhelming gravity that crushed him down into memories of his loss.

When the remains of his wife and children had been conveyed to him, after the investigation of the crash and the meticulous cataloguing of both the organic and the inorganic debris, Joe was given only fragments of their bodies. The sealed caskets were the size usually reserved for the burial of infants. He received them as if he were taking possession of the sacred bones of saints nestled in reliquaries.

Although he understood the devastating effects of the airliner's impact, and though he knew that an unsparing fire had flashed through the debris, how strange it had seemed to Joe that Michelle's and the girls' physical remains should be so small. They had been such enormous presences in his life.

Without them, the world seemed to be an alien place. He didn't feel as if he belonged here until he was at least two hours out of bed. Some days the planet turned twenty-four hours without rotating Joe into an accommodation with life. Clearly this was one of them.

After he finished the second Coors, he put the empty can in the cooler. He wasn't ready to drive to the cemetery yet, but he needed to visit the nearest public rest room.

Joe rose to his feet, turned, and glimpsed the tall blond guy in the green Hawaiian shirt. The man, without binoculars for the moment, was not south near the lifeguard tower but north, about sixty feet away, sitting alone in the sand. To screen himself from Joe, he had taken a position beyond two young couples on blankets and a Mexican family that had staked their territory with folding chairs and two big yellow-striped beach umbrellas.

Casually Joe scanned the surrounding beach. The shorter of the two possible cops, the one wearing the predominantly red shirt, was not in sight.

The guy in the green shirt studiously avoided looking directly at Joe. He cupped one hand to his right ear, as if he were wearing a bad hearing aid and needed to block the music from the sunbathers' radios in order to focus on something else that he wanted to hear.

At this distance, Joe could not be certain, but he thought the man's lips were moving. He appeared to be engaged in a conversation with his missing companion.

Leaving his towel and cooler, Joe walked south toward the public rest rooms. He didn't need to glance back to know that the guy in the green Hawaiian shirt was watching him.

On reconsideration, he decided that getting soused on the sand probably *was* still against the law, even these days. After all, a society with such an enlightened tolerance of corruption and savagery needed to bear down hard on minor offenses to convince itself that it still had standards.

■

Nearer the pier, the crowds had grown since Joe's arrival. In the amusement center, the roller coaster clattered. Riders squealed.

He took off his sunglasses as he entered the busy public rest rooms.

The men's lavatory stank of urine and disinfectant. In the middle of the floor between the toilet stalls and the sinks, a large cockroach, half crushed but still alive, hitched around and around in a circle, having lost all sense of direction and purpose. Everyone avoided it— some with amusement, some with disgust or indifference.

After he had used a urinal, as he washed his hands, Joe studied the other men in the mirror, seeking a conspirator. He settled on a long-haired fourteen-year-old in swim trunks and sandals.

When the boy went to the paper-towel dispenser, Joe followed, took a few towels immediately after him, and said, "Outside, there might be a couple of cop types hanging out, waiting for me."

The boy met his eyes but didn't say anything, just kept drying his hands on the paper towels.

Joe said, "I'll give you twenty bucks to reconnoiter for me, then come back and tell me where they are."

The kid's eyes were the purple-blue shade of a fresh bruise, and his stare was as direct as a punch. "Thirty bucks."

Joe could not remember having been able to look so boldly and challengingly into an adult's eyes when he himself had been fourteen. Approached by a stranger with an offer like this, he would have shaken his head and left quickly.

"Fifteen now and fifteen when I come back," said the kid.

Wadding his paper towels and tossing them in the trash can, Joe said, "Ten now, twenty when you come back."

"Deal."

As he took his wallet from his pocket, Joe said, "One is about six two, tan, blond, in a green Hawaiian shirt. The other is maybe five ten, brown hair, balding, pale, in a red and orange Hawaiian."

The kid took the ten-dollar bill without breaking eye

contact. "Maybe this is jive, there's nobody like that outside, and when I come back, you want me to go into one of those stalls with you to get the other twenty."

Joe was embarrassed not for being suspected of pedophilia but for the kid, who had grown up in a time and a place that required him to be so knowledgeable and street smart at such a young age. "No jive."

"'Cause I don't jump that way."

"Understood."

At least a few of the men present must have heard the exchange, but none appeared to be interested. This was a live-and-let-live age.

As the kid turned to leave, Joe said, "They won't be waiting right outside, easy to spot. They'll be at a distance, where they can see the place but aren't easily seen themselves."

Without responding, the boy went to the door, sandals clacking against the floor tiles.

"You take my ten bucks and don't come back," Joe warned, "I'll find you and kick your ass."

"Yeah, right," the kid said scornfully, and then he was gone.

Returning to one of the rust-stained sinks, Joe washed his hands again so he wouldn't appear to be loitering.

Three men in their twenties had gathered to watch the crippled cockroach, which was still chasing itself around one small portion of the lavatory floor. The bug's track was a circle twelve inches in diameter. It twitched brokenly along that circumference with such insectile single-mindedness that the men, hands full of dollar bills, were placing bets on how fast it would complete each lap.

Bending over the sink, Joe splashed handfuls of cold water on his face. The astringent taste and smell of chlorine was in the water, but any sense of cleanliness that it

provided was more than countered by a stale, briny stink
wafting out of the open drain.

The building wasn't well ventilated. The still air was
hotter than the day outside, reeking of urine and sweat
and disinfectant, so noxiously thick that breathing it was
beginning to sicken him.

The kid seemed to be taking a long time.

Joe splashed more water in his face and then studied
his beaded, dripping reflection in the streaked mirror. In
spite of his tan and the new pinkness from the sun that he
had absorbed in the past hour, he didn't look healthy. His
eyes were gray, as they had been all his life. Once, however, it had been the bright gray of polished iron or wet
induline; now it was the soft dead gray of ashes, and the
whites were bloodshot.

A fourth man had joined the cockroach handicappers.
He was in his mid-fifties, thirty years older than the other
three but trying to be one of them by matching their enthusiasm for pointless cruelty. The gamblers had become an
obstruction to the rest room traffic. They were getting
rowdy, laughing at the spasmodic progress of the insect,
urging it on as though it were a thoroughbred pounding
across turf toward a finish line. *"Go, go, go, go, go!"* They
noisily debated whether its pair of quivering antennae
were part of its guidance system or the instruments with
which it detected the scents of food and other roaches
eager to copulate.

Striving to block out the voices of the raucous group,
Joe searched his ashen eyes in the mirror, wondering what
his motives had been when he sent the boy to scope out
the men in the Hawaiian shirts. If they were conducting a
surveillance, they must have mistaken him for someone
else. They would realize their error soon, and he would
never see them again. There was no good reason to con-
front them or to gather intelligence about them.

He had come to the beach to prepare himself for the visit to the graveyard. He needed to submit himself to the ancient rhythms of the eternal sea, which wore at him as waves wore at rock, smoothing the sharp edges of anxiety in his mind, polishing away the splinters in his heart. The sea delivered the message that life was nothing more than meaningless mechanics and cold tidal forces, a bleak message of hopelessness that was tranquilizing precisely because it was brutally humbling. He also needed another beer or even two to further numb his senses, so the lesson of the sea would remain with him as he crossed the city to the cemetery.

He *didn't* need distractions. He didn't need action. He didn't need mystery. For him, life had lost all mystery the same night that it had lost all meaning, in a silent Colorado meadow blasted with sudden thunder and fire.

Sandals slapping on the tiles, the boy returned to collect the remaining twenty of his thirty dollars. "Didn't see any big guy in a green shirt, but the other one's out there, sure enough, getting a sunburn on his bald spot."

Behind Joe, some of the gamblers whooped in triumph. Others groaned as the dying cockroach completed another circuit either a few seconds quicker or a few slower than its time for the previous lap.

Curious, the boy craned his neck to see what was happening.

"Where?" Joe asked, withdrawing a twenty from his wallet.

Still trying to see between the bodies of the circled gamblers, the boy said, "There's a palm tree, a couple of folding tables in the sand where this geeky bunch of Korean guys are playing chess, maybe sixty, eighty feet down the beach from here."

Although high frosted windows let in hard white

sunshine and grimy fluorescent tubes shed bluish light overhead, the air seemed yellow, like an acidic mist.

"Look at me," Joe said.

Distracted by the cockroach race, the boy said, "Huh?"

"Look at me."

Surprised by the quiet fury in Joe's voice, the kid briefly met his gaze. Then those troubling eyes, the color of contusions, refocused on the twenty-dollar bill.

"The guy you saw was wearing a red Hawaiian shirt?" Joe asked.

"Other colors in it, but mostly red and orange, yeah."

"What pants was he wearing?"

"Pants?"

"To keep you honest, I didn't tell you what else he was wearing. So if you saw him, now you tell me."

"Hey, man, I don't know. Was he wearing shorts or trunks or pants—how am I supposed to know?"

"You tell me."

"White? Tan? I'm not sure. Didn't know I was supposed to do a damn fashion report. He was just standing there, you know, looking out of place, holding his shoes in one hand, socks rolled up in them."

It was the same man whom Joe had seen with the walkie-talkie near the lifeguard station.

From the gamblers came noisy encouragements to the cockroach, laughter, curses, shouted offers of odds, the making of bets. They were so loud now that their voices echoed harshly off the concrete-block walls and seemed to reverberate in the mirrors with such force that Joe half expected those silvery surfaces to disintegrate.

"Was he actually watching the Koreans play chess or pretending?" Joe asked.

"He was watching this place and talking to the cream pies."

"Cream pies?"

"Couple of stone-gorgeous bitches in thong bikinis. Man, you should see the redhead bitch in the green thong. On a scale of one to ten, she's a twelve. Bring you all the way to attention, man."

"He was coming on to them?"

"Don't know what he thinks he's doing," said the kid. "Loser like him, neither of those bitches will give him a shot."

"Don't call them bitches," Joe said.

"What?"

"They're women."

In the kid's angry eyes, something flickered like visions of switchblades. "Hey, who the hell are you—the pope?"

The acidic yellow air seemed to thicken, and Joe imagined that he could feel it eating away his skin.

The swirling sound of flushing toilets inspired a spiraling sensation in his stomach. He struggled to repress sudden nausea.

To the boy, he said, "Describe the women."

With more challenge in his stare than ever, the kid said, "Totally stacked. Especially the redhead. But the brunette is just about as nice. I'd crawl on broken glass to get a whack at her, even if she is deaf."

"Deaf?"

"Must be deaf or something," said the boy. "She was putting a hearing aid kind of thing in her ear, taking it out and putting it in like she couldn't get it to fit right. Real sweet-looking bitch."

Even though he was six inches taller and forty pounds heavier than the boy, Joe wanted to seize the kid by the throat and choke him. Choke him until he promised never to use that word again without thinking. Until he understood how hateful it was and how it soiled him when he used it as casually as a conjunction.

Joe was frightened by the barely throttled violence of

his reaction: teeth clenched, arteries throbbing in neck and temples, field of vision abruptly constricted by a blood-dark pressure at the periphery. His nausea grew worse, and he took a deep breath, another, calming himself.

Evidently the boy saw something in Joe's eyes that gave him pause. He became less confrontational, turning his gaze once more to the shouting gamblers. "Give me the twenty. I earned it."

Joe didn't relinquish the bill. "Where's your dad?"

"Say what?"

"Where's your mother?"

"What's it to you?"

"Where are they?"

"They got their own lives."

Joe's anger sagged into despair. "What's your name, kid?"

"What do you need to know for? You think I'm a baby, can't come to the beach alone? Screw you, I go where I want."

"You go where you want, but you don't have any-where to be."

The kid made eye contact again. In his bruised stare was a glimpse of hurt and loneliness so deep Joe was shocked that anyone should have descended to it by the tender age of fourteen. "Anywhere to be? What's that supposed to mean?"

Joe sensed that they had made a connection on a profound level, that a door had opened unexpectedly for him and for this troubled boy, and that both of their futures could be changed for the better if he could just under-stand where they might be able to go after they crossed that threshold. But his own life was as hollow—his store of philosophy as empty—as any abandoned shell washed up on the nearby shore. He had no belief to share, no wisdom to impart, no hope to offer, insufficient substance to sustain himself, let alone another.

He was one of the lost, and the lost cannot lead.

The moment passed, and the kid plucked the twenty-dollar bill out of Joe's hand. His expression was more of a sneer than a smile when he mockingly repeated Joe's words, "'They're women.'" Backing away, he said, "You get them hot, they're all just bitches."

"And are we all just dogs?" Joe asked, but the kid slipped out of the lavatory before he could hear the question.

Although Joe had washed his hands twice, he felt dirty.

He turned to the sinks again, but he could not easily reach them. Six men were now gathered immediately around the cockroach, and a few others were hanging back, watching.

The crowded lavatory was sweltering, Joe was streaming sweat, and the yellow air burned in his nostrils, corroded his lungs with each inhalation, stung his eyes. It was condensing on the mirrors, blurring the reflections of the agitated men until they seemed not to be creatures of flesh and blood but tortured spirits glimpsed through an abattoir window, wet with sulfurous steam, in the deepest kingdom of the damned. The fevered gamblers shouted at the roach, shaking fistfuls of dollars at it. Their voices blended into a single shrill ululation, seemingly senseless, a mad gibbering that rose in intensity and pitch until it sounded, to Joe, like a crystal-shattering squeal, piercing to the center of his brain and setting off dangerous vibrations in the core of him.

He pushed between two of the men and stamped on the crippled cockroach, killing it.

In the instant of stunned silence that followed his

intrusion, Joe turned away from the men, shaking, shaking, the shattering sound still tremulant in his memory, still vibrating in his bones. He headed toward the exit, eager to get out of there before he exploded.

As one, the gamblers broke the paralytic grip of their surprise. They shouted angrily, as righteous in their outrage as churchgoers might be outraged at a filthy and drunken denizen of the streets who staggered into their service to sag against the chancel rail and vomit on the sanctuary floor.

One of the men, with a face as sun red as a slab of greasy ham, heat-cracked lips peeled back from snuff-stained teeth, seized Joe by one arm and spun him around. "What the shit you think you're doing, pal?"

"Let go of me."

"I was winning money here, pal."

The stranger's hand was damp on Joe's arm, dirty fingernails blunt but digging in to secure the slippery grip.

"Let go."

"I was winning money here," the guy repeated. His mouth twisted into such a wrathful grimace that his chapped lips split, and threads of blood unraveled from the cracks.

Grabbing the angry gambler by the wrist, Joe bent one of the dirty fingers back to break the bastard's grip. Even as the guy's eyes widened with surprise and alarm, even as he started to cry out in pain, Joe wrenched his arm up behind his back, twisted him around, and ran him forward, giving him the bum's rush, facefirst into the closed door of a toilet stall.

Joe had thought his strange rage had been vented earlier, as he had talked to the teenage boy, leaving only despair, but here it was again, disproportionate to the offense that seemed to have caused it, as hot and explosive as ever. He wasn't sure why he was doing this, why these men's callousness mattered to him, but before he quite realized the enormity of his overreaction, he battered the door with the guy's face, battered it again, and then a third time.

The rage didn't dissipate, but with the blood-dark pressure constricting his field of vision, filled with a primitive frenzy that leaped through him like a thousand monkeys skirling through a jungle of trees and vines, Joe was nevertheless able to recognize that he was out of control. He let go of the gambler, and the man fell to the floor in front of the toilet stall.

Shuddering with anger and with fear of his anger, Joe moved backward until the sinks prevented him from going any farther.

The other men in the lavatory had eased away from him. All were silent.

On the floor, the gambler lay on his back in scattered one- and five-dollar bills, his winnings. His chin was bearded with blood from his cracked lips. He pressed one hand to the left side of his face, which had taken the impact with the door. "It was just a cockroach, Christ's sake, just a lousy cockroach."

Joe tried to say that he was sorry. He couldn't speak.

"You almost broke my nose. You could've broke my nose. For a cockroach? Broke my nose for a cockroach?"

Sorry not for what he had done to this man, who had no doubt done worse to others, but sorry for himself, sorry for the miserable walking wreckage that he had become and for the dishonor that his inexcusable behavior brought to the memory of his wife and daughters, Joe nonetheless remained unable to express any regret. Choking on self-loathing as much as on the fetid air, he walked out of the reeking building into an ocean breeze that didn't refresh, a world as foul as the lavatory behind him.

In spite of the sun, he was shivering, because a cold coil of remorse was unwinding in his chest.

Halfway back to his beach towel and his cooler of beer, all but oblivious of the sunning multitudes through which he weaved, he remembered the pale-faced man in the red and orange Hawaiian shirt. He didn't halt, didn't even look back, but slogged onward through the sand.

He was no longer interested in learning who was conducting a surveillance of him—if that was what they were doing. He couldn't imagine why he had *ever* been intrigued by them. If they were police, they were bumblers, having mistaken him for someone else. They were not genuinely part of his life. He wouldn't even have noticed them if the kid with the ponytail hadn't drawn his attention to them. Soon they would realize their mistake and find their real quarry. In the meantime, to hell with them.

More people were gravitating to the portion of the beach where Joe had established camp. He considered packing and leaving, but he wasn't ready to go to the cemetery. The incident in the lavatory had opened the stopcock on his supply of adrenaline, canceling the effects of the lulling surf and the two beers that he had drunk.

Therefore, onto the beach towel again, one hand into the cooler, extracting not a beer but a half-moon of ice, pressing the ice to his forehead, he gazed out to sea. The gray-green chop seemed to be an infinite array of turning gears in a vast mechanism, and across it, bright silver flickers of sunlight jittered like electric current across a power grid. Waves approached and receded as monotonously as connecting rods pumping back and forth in an engine. The sea was a perpetually laboring machine with no purpose but the continuation of its own existence, romanticized and cherished by countless poets but incapable of knowing human passion, pain, and promise.

He believed that he must learn to accept the cold mechanics of Creation, because it made no sense to rail at a mindless machine. After all, a clock could not be held responsible for the too-swift passage of time. A loom could not be blamed for weaving the cloth that later was sewn into an executioner's hood. He hoped that if he came to terms with the mechanistic indifference of the universe, with the meaningless nature of life and death, he would find peace.

Such acceptance would be cold comfort, indeed, and deadening to the heart. But all he wanted now was an end to anguish, nights without nightmares, and release from the need to care.

Two newcomers arrived and spread a white beach blanket on the sand about twenty feet north of him. One was a stunning redhead in a green thong bikini skimpy enough to make a stripper blush. The other was a brunette, nearly as attractive as her friend.

The redhead wore her hair in a short, pixie cut. The brunette's hair was long, the better to conceal the communications device that she was no doubt wearing in one ear.

For women in their twenties, they were too giggly and girlish, high-spirited enough to call attention to themselves even if they had not been stunning. They lazily oiled themselves with tanning lotion, took turns greasing each other's back, touching with languorous pleasure, as if they were in the opening scene of an adult video, drawing the interest of every heterosexual male on the beach.

The strategy was clear. No one would suspect that he was under surveillance by operatives who concealed so little of themselves and concealed themselves so poorly. They were meant to be as unlikely as the men in the Hawaiian shirts had been obvious. But for thirty dollars' worth of reconnaissance and the libidinous observations of a horny fourteen-year-old, their strategy would have been effective.

With long tan legs and deep cleavage and tight round rumps, maybe they were also meant to engage Joe's interest and seduce him into conversation with them. If this was part of their assignment, they failed. Their charms didn't affect him.

During the past year, any erotic image or thought had the power to stir him only for a moment, whereupon he was overcome by poignant memories of Michelle, her precious body and her wholesome enthusiasm for pleasure. Inevitably, he thought also of the terrible long fall from stars to Colorado, the smoke, the fire, then death. Desire dissolved quickly in the solvent of loss.

These two women distracted Joe only to the extent that he was annoyed about their incompetent misidentification of him. He considered approaching them to inform them of their mistake, just to be rid of them. After the violence in the lavatory, however, the prospect of confrontation made him uneasy. He was drained of anger now, but he no longer trusted his self-control.

One year to the day.

Memories and gravestones.

He would get through it.

Surf broke, gathered the foamy fragments of itself, stole away, and broke again. In the patient study of that endless breaking, Joe Carpenter gradually grew calm.

Half an hour later, without the benefit of another beer, he was ready to visit the cemetery.

He shook the sand out of his towel. He folded the towel in half lengthwise, rolled it tight, and picked up the cooler.

As silken as the sea breeze, as buttery as sunlight, the lithe young women in the thong bikinis pretended to be enthralled by the monosyllabic repartee of two steroid-thickened suitors, the latest in a string of beach-boy Casanovas to take their shot.

The direction of his gaze masked by his sunglasses, Joe could see that the beauties' interest in the beefcake was pretense. They were *not* wearing sunglasses, and while they chattered and laughed and encouraged their admirers, they glanced surreptitiously at Joe.

He walked away and did not look back.

As he took some of the beach with him in his shoes, so he strove to take the indifference of the ocean with him in his heart.

Nevertheless, he could not help but wonder what police agency could boast such astonishingly beautiful women on its force. He had known some female cops who were as lovely and sexy as any movie star, but the redhead and her friend exceeded even celluloid standards.

In the parking lot, he half expected the men in the Hawaiian shirts to be watching his Honda. If they had it staked out, their surveillance post was well concealed.

Joe drove out of the lot and turned right on Pacific Coast Highway, checking his rearview mirror. He was not being followed.

Perhaps they had realized their error and were frantically looking for the right man.

From Wilshire Boulevard to the San Diego Freeway, north to the Ventura Freeway and then east, he drove out of the cooling influence of the sea breezes into the furnace heat of the San Fernando Valley. In the August glare, these suburbs looked as hot and hard-baked as kiln-fired pottery.

Three hundred acres of low rolling hills and shallow vales and broad lawns comprised the memorial park, a city of the deceased, Los Angeles of the dead, divided into neighborhoods by gracefully winding service roads. Famous actors and ordinary salesmen were buried here, rock-'n'-roll stars and reporters' families, side by side in the intimate democracy of death.

Joe drove past two small burial services in progress: cars parked along the curb, ranks of folding chairs set up on the grass, mounds of grave earth covered with soft green tarps. At each site, the mourners sat hunched, stifled in their black dresses and black suits, oppressed by heat as well as by grief and by a sense of their own mortality.

The cemetery included a few elaborate crypts and low-walled family garden plots, but there were no granite forests of vertical monuments and headstones. Some had chosen to entomb the remains of their loved ones in niches in the walls of communal mausoleums. Others preferred the bosom of the earth, where graves were marked only with bronze plaques in flat stone tablets flush with the ground, so as not to disturb the park-like setting.

Joe had put Michelle and the girls to rest on a gently rising hillside shaded by a scattering of stone pines and Indian laurels. Squirrels scampered across the grass on milder days than this, and rabbits came out at twilight. He believed that his three treasured women would have preferred this to the hardscape of a mausoleum, where there would not be the sound of wind-stirred trees on breezy evenings.

Far beyond the second of the two burial services, he parked at the curb, switched off the engine, and got out of the Honda. He stood beside the car in the hundred-degree heat, gathering his courage.

When he started up the gentle slope, he didn't look toward their graves. If he were to see the site from a distance, the approach to it would be daunting, and he would turn back. Even after an entire year, each visit was as disturbing to him as if he had come here to view not their burial plots but their battered bodies in a morgue. Wondering how many years would pass before his pain diminished, he ascended the rise with his head down, eyes on the ground, slump-shouldered in the heat, like an old dray horse following a long-familiar route, going home.

Consequently, he didn't see the woman at the graves until he was only ten or fifteen feet from her. Surprised, he halted.

She stood just out of the sun, in pine shadows. Her back was half to him. With a Polaroid camera, she was snapping photographs of the flush-set markers.

"Who are you?" he asked.

She didn't hear him, perhaps because he had spoken softly, perhaps because she was so intent upon her photography.

Stepping closer, he said, "What are you doing?"

Startled, she turned to face him.

Petite but athletic-looking, about five feet two, she had an immediate impact far greater than her size or her appearance could explain, as though she were clothed not merely in blue jeans and a yellow cotton blouse but in some powerful magnetic field that bent the world to her. Skin the shade of milk chocolate. Huge eyes as dark as the silt at the bottom of a cup of Armenian espresso, harder to read than the portents in tea leaves, with a distinct almond shape suggesting a touch of Asian blood in the family line. Hair not Afro-kinky or in cornrows but feather-cut, thick and naturally straight and so glossy black that it almost looked blue, which seemed Asian too. Her bone structure was all out of Africa: smooth broad brow, high cheekbones, finely carved but powerful, proud but beautiful. She was maybe five years older than Joe, in her early forties, but a quality of innocence in her knowing eyes and a faint aspect of child-like vulnerability in her otherwise strong face made her seem younger than he was.

"Who are you, what're you doing?" he repeated.

Lips parted as if to speak, speechless with surprise, she gazed at him as though he were an apparition. She raised one hand to his face and touched his cheek, and Joe did not flinch from her.

At first he thought he saw amazement in her eyes. The extreme tenderness of her touch caused him to look again, and he realized that what he saw was not wonderment but sadness and pity.

"I'm not ready to talk to you yet." Her soft voice was musical.

"Why're you taking pictures . . . why pictures of their graves?"

Clutching the camera with two hands, she said, "Soon. I'll be back when it's time. Don't despair. You'll see, like the others."

An almost supernatural quality to the moment half convinced Joe that *she* was an apparition, that her touch had been so achingly gentle precisely because it was barely real, an ectoplasmic caress.

The woman herself, however, was too powerfully present to be a ghost or a heatstroke illusion. Diminutive but dynamic. More real than anything in the day. More real than sky and trees and August sun, than granite and bronze. She had such a compelling presence that she seemed to be coming at him though she was standing still, to loom over him though she was ten inches shorter than he. She was more brightly lighted in the pine shadows than he was in the direct glare of the sun.

"How are you coping?" she asked.

Disoriented, he answered only by shaking his head.

"Not well," she whispered.

Joe looked past her, down at the granite and bronze markers. As if from very far away, he heard himself say, "Lost forever," speaking as much about himself as about his wife and daughters.

When he returned his attention to the woman, she was gazing past him, into the distance. As the sound of a racing engine rose, concern crinkled the corners of her eyes and creased her forehead.

Joe turned to see what was troubling her. Along the road that he had traveled, a white Ford van was approaching at a far higher speed than the posted limit.

"Bastards," she said.

When Joe turned to the woman again, she was already running from him, angling across the slope toward the brow of the low hill.

"Hey, wait," he said.

She didn't pause or look back.

He started after her, but his physical condition wasn't as good as hers. She seemed to be an experienced runner. After a few steps, Joe halted. Defeated by the suffocating heat, he wouldn't be able to catch up with her.

Sunlight mirroring the windshield and flaring off the headlight lenses, the white van shot past Joe. It paralleled the woman as she sprinted across the grave rows.

Joe started back down the hill toward his car, not sure

what he was going to do. Maybe he should give chase.
What the hell was going on here?

Fifty or sixty yards beyond the parked Honda, brakes
shrieking, leaving twin smears of rubber on the pavement
behind it, the van slid to a stop at the curb. Both front
doors flew open, and the men in Hawaiian shirts leaped
out. They bolted after the woman.

Surprise halted Joe. He hadn't been followed from
Santa Monica, not by the white van, not by any vehicle.
He was sure of that.

Somehow they had known that he would come to the
cemetery. And since neither of the men showed any
interest in Joe, but went after the woman as if they were
attack dogs, they must have been watching him at the
beach not because they were interested in him, per se, but
because they hoped that she would make contact with
him at some point during the day.

The woman was their only quarry.

Hell, they must have been watching his apartment too,
must have followed him from there to the beach.

As far as he knew, they had been keeping him under
surveillance for days. Maybe weeks. He had been in such
a daze of desolation for so long, walking through life like
a sleeper drifting through a dream, that he would not
have noticed these people slinking at the periphery of his
vision.

*Who is she, who are they, why was she photographing
the graves?*

Uphill and at least a hundred yards to the east, the
woman fled under the generously spreading boughs of
stone pines clustered along the perimeter of the burial
grounds, across shaded grass only lightly dappled with
sunshine. Her dusky skin blended with the shadows, but
her yellow blouse betrayed her.

She was heading toward a particular point on the crest,

as if familiar with the terrain. Considering that no cars were parked along this section of the cemetery road, except for Joe's Honda and the white van, she might have entered the memorial park by that route, on foot.

The men from the van had a lot of ground to make up if they were going to catch her. The tall one in the green shirt seemed in better shape than his partner, and his legs were considerably longer than the woman's, so he was gaining on her. Nevertheless, the smaller guy didn't relent even as he fell steadily behind. Sprinting frantically up the long sun-seared slope, stumbling over a grave marker, then over another, regaining his balance, he charged on, as though in an animal frenzy, in a blood fever, gripped by the *need* to be there when the woman was brought down.

Beyond the manicured hills of the cemetery were other hills in a natural condition: pale sandy soil, banks of shale, brown grass, stinkweed, mesquite, stunted manzanita, tumbleweed, scattered and gnarled dwarf oaks. Arid ravines led down into the undeveloped land above Griffith Observatory and east of the Los Angeles Zoo, a rattlesnake-infested plot of desert scrub in the heart of the urban sprawl.

If the woman got into the scrub before being caught, and if she knew her way, she could lose her pursuers by zigging and zagging from one narrow declivity to another.

Joe headed toward the abandoned white van. He might be able to learn something from it.

He wanted the woman to escape, though he wasn't entirely sure why his sympathies were with her.

As far as he knew, she might be a felon with a list of heinous crimes on her rap sheet. She hadn't looked like a criminal, hadn't sounded like one. This was Los Angeles, however, where clean-cut young men brutally shotgunned their parents and then, as orphans, tearfully begged the jury to pity them and show mercy. No one was what he seemed.

Yet . . . the gentleness of her fingertips against his cheek, the sorrow in her eyes, the tenderness in her voice, all marked her as a woman of compassion, whether she was a fugitive from the law or not. He could not wish her ill.

A vicious sound, hard and flat, cracked across the cemetery, leaving a brief throbbing wound in the hot stillness. Another crack followed.

The woman had nearly reached the brow of the hill. Visible between the last two bristling pines. Blue jeans. Yellow blouse. Stretching her legs with each stride. Brown arms pumping close to her sides.

The smaller man, in the red and orange Hawaiian shirt, had run wide of his companion, whom he was still trailing, to get a clear line of sight on the woman. He had stopped and raised his arms, holding something in both hands. A handgun. The son of a bitch was *shooting* at her.

Cops didn't try to shoot unarmed fugitives in the back. Not righteous cops.

Joe wanted to help her. He couldn't think of anything to do. If they were cops, he had no right to second-guess them. If they *weren't* cops, and even if he could catch up with them, they would probably shoot him down rather than let him interfere.

Crack.

The woman reached the crest.

"Go," Joe urged her in a hoarse whisper. "Go."

He didn't have a cellular phone in his own car, so he couldn't call 911. He had carried a mobile unit as a reporter, but these days he seldom called anyone even from his home phone.

The keening crack of another shot pierced the leaden heat.

If these men weren't police officers, they were desperate or crazy, or both, resorting to gunplay in such a public place, even though this part of the cemetery was currently deserted. The sound of the shots would travel, drawing the attention of the maintenance personnel who, merely by closing the formidable iron gate at the entrance to the park, could prevent the gunmen from driving out.

Apparently unhit, the woman disappeared over the top of the hill, into the scrub beyond.

Both of the men in Hawaiian shirts went after her.

4

Heart knocking so fiercely that his vision blurred with each hard-driven surge of blood, Joe Carpenter sprinted to the white van.

The Ford was not a recreational vehicle but a paneled van of the type commonly used by businesses to make small deliveries. Neither the back nor the side of the vehicle featured the name or logo of any enterprise.

The engine was running. Both front doors stood open.

He ran to the passenger side, skidded in a soggy patch of grass around a leaking sprinkler head, and leaned into the cab, hoping to find a cellular phone. If there was one, it wasn't in plain sight.

Maybe in the glove box. He popped it open.

Someone in the cargo hold behind the front seats, mistaking Joe for one of the men in the Hawaiian shirts, said, "Did you get Rose?"

Damn.

The glove box contained a few rolls of Life Savers that spilled onto the floor—and a window envelope from the Department of Motor Vehicles.

By law, every vehicle in California was required to carry a valid registration and proof of insurance.

"Hey, who the hell are you?" the guy in the cargo hold demanded.

Clutching the envelope, Joe turned away from the van.

He saw no point in trying to run. This man might be as quick to shoot people in the back as were the other two.

With a clatter and a *skreeeek* of hinges, the single door at the rear of the vehicle was flung open.

Joe walked directly toward the sound. A sledge-faced specimen with Popeye forearms, neck sufficiently thick to support a small car, came around the side of the van, and Joe opted for the surprise of instant and unreasonable aggression, driving one knee hard into his crotch.

Retching, wheezing for air, the guy started to bend forward, and Joe head-butted him in the face. He hit the ground unconscious, breathing noisily through his open mouth because his broken nose was streaming blood.

Although, as a kid, Joe had been a fighter and something of a troublemaker, he had not raised a fist against anyone since he met and married Michelle. Until today. Now, twice in the past two hours, he had resorted to violence, astonishing himself.

More than astonished, he was sickened by this primitive rage. He had never known such wrath before, not even during his troubled youth, yet here he was struggling to control it again as he had struggled in the public lavatory in Santa Monica. For the past year, the fall of Flight 353 had filled him with terrible despondency and grief, but he was beginning to realize that those feelings were like layers of oil atop another—darker—emotion that he had been denying; what filled the chambers of his heart to the brim was anger.

If the universe was a cold mechanism, if life was a journey from one empty blackness to another, he could not rant at God, because to do so was no more effective than screaming for help in the vacuum of deep space, where sound could not travel, or like trying to draw breath underwater. But now, given any excuse to vent his fury on *people*, he had seized the opportunity with disturbing enthusiasm.

Rubbing the top of his head, which hurt from butting the guy in the face, looking down at the unconscious hulk with the bleeding nose, Joe felt a satisfaction that he did not want to feel. A wild glee simultaneously thrilled and repulsed him.

Dressed in a T-shirt promoting the videogame Quake, baggy black pants, and red sneakers, the fallen man appeared to be in his late twenties, at least a decade younger than his two associates. His hands were massive enough to juggle cantaloupes, and a single letter was tattooed on the base phalange of each finger, thumbs excluded, to spell out ANABOLIC, as in anabolic steroid.

This was no stranger to violence.

Nevertheless, although self-defense justified a preemptive strike, Joe was disturbed by the savage pleasure he took from such swift brutality.

The guy sure didn't look like an officer of the law. Regardless of his appearance, he might be a cop, in which case assaulting him ensured serious consequences.

To Joe's surprise, even the prospect of jail didn't diminish his twisted satisfaction in the ferocity with which he had acted. He felt half nauseated, half out of his mind—but more alive than he had been in a year.

Exhilarated yet fearful of the moral depths into which this new empowering anger might take him, he glanced in both directions along the cemetery road. There was no oncoming traffic. He knelt beside his victim.

Breath whistled wetly through the man's throat, and he issued a soft childlike sigh. His eyelids fluttered, but he did not regain consciousness while his pockets were searched.

Joe found nothing but a few coins, a nail clipper, a set of house keys, and a wallet that contained the standard

ID and credit cards. The guy's name was Wallace Morton Blick. He was carrying no police-agency badge or identification. Joe kept only the driver's license and returned the wallet to the pocket from which he had extracted it.

The two gunmen had not reappeared from the rugged scrub land beyond the cemetery hill. They had scrambled over the crest, after the woman, little more than a minute ago; even if she quickly slipped away from them, they weren't likely to give up on her and return after only a brief search.

Wondering at his boldness, Joe quickly dragged Wallace Blick away from the rear corner of the white van. He tucked him close to the flank of the vehicle, where he was less likely to be seen by anyone who came along the roadway. He rolled him onto his side so he would not choke on the blood that might be draining from his nasal passages down the back of his throat.

Joe went to the open rear door. He climbed into the back of the van. The low rumble of the idling engine vibrated in the floorboard.

The cramped cargo hold was lined on both sides with electronic communications, eavesdropping, and tracking equipment. A pair of compact command chairs, bolted to the floor, could be swiveled to face the arrayed devices on each side.

Squeezing past the first chair, Joe settled into the second, in front of an active computer. The interior of the van was air-conditioned, but the seat was still warm because Blick had vacated it less than a minute ago.

On the computer screen was a map. The streets had names meant to evoke feelings of peace and tranquillity, and Joe recognized them as the service roads through the cemetery.

A small blinking light on the map drew his attention. It

was green, stationary, and located approximately where the van itself was parked.

A second blinking light, this one red and also stationary, was on the same road but some distance behind the van. He was sure that it represented his Honda.

The tracking system no doubt utilized a CD-ROM with exhaustive maps of Los Angeles County and environs, maybe of the entire state of California or of the country coast to coast. A single compact disc had sufficient capacity to contain detailed street maps for all of the contiguous states and Canada.

Someone had fixed a powerful transponder to his car. It emitted a microwave signal that could be followed from quite a distance. The computer utilized surveillance-satellite uplinks to triangulate the signal, then placed the Honda on the map relative to the position of the van, so they could track him without maintaining visual contact.

Leaving Santa Monica, all the way into the San Fernando Valley, Joe had seen no suspicious vehicle in his rearview mirror. This van had been able to stalk him while streets away or miles behind, out of sight.

As a reporter, he had once gone on a mobile surveillance with federal agents, a group of high-spirited cowboys from the Bureau of Alcohol, Tobacco and Firearms, who had used a similar but less sophisticated system than this.

Acutely aware that the battered Blick or one of the other two men might trap him here if he delayed too long, Joe swiveled in his chair, surveying the back of the van for some indication of the agency involved in this operation. They were tidy. He couldn't spot a single clue.

Two publications lay beside the computer station at which Blick had been working: one issue each of *Wired*, featuring yet another major article about the visionary splendiferousness of Bill Gates, and a magazine aimed at former Special Forces officers who wished to make horizontal career moves from military service into jobs as paid mercenaries. The latter was folded open to an article about belt-buckle knives sharp enough to eviscerate an adversary or cut through bone. Evidently this was Blick's reading matter during lulls in the surveillance operation, as when he had been waiting for Joe to grow weary of contemplating the sea from Santa Monica Beach.

Mr. Wallace Blick, of the ANABOLIC tattoo, was a techno geek with an edge.

When Joe climbed out of the van, Blick was groaning but not yet conscious. His legs pumped, a flurry of kicks, as if he were a dog dreaming of chasing rabbits, and his cool red sneakers tore divots from the grass.

Neither of the men in Hawaiian shirts had returned from the desert scrub beyond the hill.

Joe hadn't heard any more gunshots, although the terrain might have muffled them.

He hurried to his car. The door handle was bright with the kiss of the sun, and he hissed with pain when he touched it.

The interior of the car was so hot that it seemed on the verge of spontaneous combustion. He cranked down the window.

As he started the Honda, he glanced at the rearview mirror and saw a flatbed truck with board sides approaching from farther east in the cemetery. It was probably a groundskeeper's vehicle, either coming to investigate the gunfire or engaged in routine maintenance.

Joe could have followed the road to the west end of the memorial park and then looped all the way around to the entrance at the east perimeter, but he was in a hurry and wanted to go directly back the way he had come. Over-whelmed by a feeling that he had stretched his luck too far, he could almost hear a ticking like a time-bomb clock. Pulling away from the curb, he tried to hang a U-turn but couldn't quite manage it in one clean sweep.

He shifted into Reverse and tramped on the accelerator hard enough to make the tires squeal against the hot pavement. The Honda shot backward. He braked and shifted into Drive again.

Tick, tick, tick.

Instinct proved reliable. Just as he accelerated toward the approaching groundskeeper's truck, the rear window on the driver's side of the car, immediately behind his head, exploded, spraying glass across the backseat.

He didn't have to hear the shot to know what had happened.

Glancing to the left, he saw the man in the red Hawaiian shirt, stopped halfway down the hillside, in a shooter's stance. The guy, pale as a risen corpse, was dressed for a margarita party.

Someone shouted hoarse, slurred curses. Blick. Crawl-ing away from the van on his hands and knees, dazedly shaking his blocky head, like a pit bull wounded in a dogfight, spraying bloody foam from his mouth: Blick.

Another round slammed into the body of the car with a hard thud, followed by a brief trailing twang.

With a rush of hot gibbering wind at the open and the shattered windows, the Honda spirited Joe out of range. He rocketed past the groundskeeper's truck at such high speed that it swerved to avoid him, though he was not in the least danger of colliding with it.

Past one burial service, where black-garbed mourners drifted like forlorn spirits away from the open grave, past another burial service, where the grieving huddled on chairs as if prepared to stay forever with whomever they had lost, past an Asian family putting a plate of fruit and cake on a fresh grave, Joe fled. He passed an unusual white church—a steeple atop a Palladian-arch cupola on columns atop a clock tower—which cast a stunted shadow in the early-afternoon sun. Past a white Southern Colonial mortuary that blazed like alabaster in the California aridity but begged for bayous. He drove recklessly, with the expectation of relentless pursuit, which didn't occur. He was also certain that his way would be blocked by the sudden arrival of swarms of police cars, but they still were not in sight when he raced between the open gates and out of the memorial park.

He drove under the Ventura Freeway, escaping into the suburban hive of the San Fernando Valley.

At a stoplight, quaking with tension, he watched a procession of a dozen street rods pass through the intersection, driven by the members of a car club on a Saturday outing: an era-perfect '41 Buick Roadmaster, a '47 Ford Sportsman Woodie with honey-maple paneling and black-cherry maroon paint, a '32 Ford Roadster in Art Deco style with full road pants and chrome speed lines. Each of the twelve was a testament to the car as art: chopped, channeled, sectioned, grafted, some on dropped spindles, with custom grilles, reconfigured hoods, frenched headlights, raised and flared wheel wells, hand-formed fender skirts. Painted, pinstriped, polished passion rolling on rubber.

Watching the street rods, he felt a curious sensation in his chest, a loosening, a stretching, both painful and exhilarating.

A block later he passed a park where, in spite of the heat, a young family—with three laughing children—was playing Frisbee with an exuberant Golden Retriever.

Heart pounding, Joe slowed the Honda. He almost pulled to the curb to watch.

At a corner, two lovely blond college girls, apparently twins, in white shorts and crisp white blouses, waited to cross the street, holding hands, as cool as spring water in the furnace heat. Mirage girls. Ethereal in the smog-stained concrete landscape. As clean and smooth and radiant as angels.

Past the girls was a massive display of zauschneria alongside a Spanish-style apartment building, laden with gorgeous clusters of tubular scarlet flowers. Michelle had loved zauschneria. She had planted it in the backyard of their Studio City house.

The day had changed. Indefinably but unquestionably changed.

No. No, not the day, not the city. Joe himself had changed, was changing, felt change rolling through him, as irresistible as an ocean tide.

His grief was as great as it had been in the awful lone-liness of the night, his despair as deep as he had ever known it, but though he had begun the day sunk in mel-ancholy, yearning for death, he now wanted desperately to live. He *needed* to live.

The engine that drove this change wasn't his close brush with death. Being shot at and nearly hit had not opened his eyes to the wonder and beauty of life. Nothing as simple as that.

Anger was the engine of change for him. He was bit-terly angry not so much for what he had lost but angry for Michelle's sake, angry that Michelle had not been able to see the parade of street rods with him, or the masses of red flowers on the zauschneria, or, now, here, this colorful riot of purple and red bougainvillea cas-cading across the roof of a Craftsman-style bungalow. He was furiously, wrenchingly angry that Chrissie and

Nina would never play Frisbee with a dog of their own, would never grow up to grace the world with their beauty, would never know the thrill of accomplishment in whatever careers they might have chosen or the joy of a good marriage—or the love of their own children. Rage changed Joe, gnashed at him, bit deep enough to wake him from his long trance of self-pity and despair.

How are you coping? asked the woman photographing the graves.

I'm not ready to talk to you yet, she said.

Soon. I'll be back when it's time, she promised, as though she had revelations to make, truths to reveal.

The men in Hawaiian shirts. The computer-nerd thug in the Quake T-shirt. The redhead and the brunette in the thong bikinis. *Teams* of operatives keeping Joe under surveillance, evidently waiting for the woman to contact him. A van packed solid with satellite-assisted tracking gear, directional microphones, computers, high-resolution cameras. Gunmen willing to shoot him in cold blood because . . .

Why?

Because they thought the black woman at the graves had told him something he wasn't supposed to know? Because even being aware of her existence made him dangerous to them? Because they thought he might have come out of their van with enough information to learn their identities and intentions?

Of course he knew almost nothing about them, not who they were or what they wanted with the woman. Nevertheless, he could reach one inescapable conclusion: What he thought he knew about the deaths of his wife and daughters was either wrong or incomplete. Something wasn't kosher about the story of Nationwide Flight 353.

He didn't even need journalistic instinct to arrive at this chilling insight. On one level, he had known it from the moment that he saw the woman at the graves. Watching her snap photographs of the plot markers, meeting her compelling eyes, hearing the compassion in her soft voice, racked by the mystery of her words—*I'm not ready to talk to you yet*—he had known, by virtue of sheer common sense, that something was rotten.

Now, driving through placid Burbank, he seethed with a sense of injustice, treachery. There was a hateful wrongness with the world beyond the mere mechanical cruelty of it. Deception. Deceit. Lies. Conspiracy.

He had argued with himself that being angry with Creation was pointless, that only resignation and indifference offered him relief from his anguish. And he had been right. Raging at the imagined occupant of some celestial throne was wasted effort, as ineffective as throwing stones to extinguish the light of a star.

People, however, were a worthy target of his rage. The people who had concealed or distorted the exact circumstances of the crash of Flight 353.

Michelle, Chrissie, and Nina could never be brought back. Joe's life could never be made whole again. The wounds in his heart could not be healed. Whatever hidden truth waited to be uncovered, learning it would not give him a future. His life was over, and nothing could ever change that, nothing, but he had a right to know precisely how and exactly why Michelle and Chrissie and Nina had died. He had a sacred *obligation* to them to learn what had really happened to that doomed 747.

His bitterness was a fulcrum and his rage was a long lever with which he would move the world, the whole damn world, to learn the truth, no matter what damage he caused or whom he destroyed in the process.

On a tree-lined residential street, he pulled to the curb. He switched off the engine and got out of the car. He might not have much time before Blick and the others caught up with him.

The queen palms hung dead-limp and whisperless in the heat, which currently seemed to be as effective an embalming medium as a block of fly-trapping amber.

Joe looked under the hood first, but the transponder wasn't there. He squatted in front of the car and felt along the underside of the bumper. Nothing.

The clatter of a helicopter swelled in the distance, rapidly growing louder.

Groping blindly inside the front wheel well on the passenger side and then along the rocker panel, Joe found only road dirt and grease. Nothing was concealed inside the rear wheel well, either.

The chopper shot out of the north, passing directly overhead at extremely low altitude, no more than fifty feet above the houses. The long graceful fronds of the queen palms shook and whipped in the downdraft.

Joe looked up, alarmed, wondering if the crew of the chopper was looking for him, but his fear was pure paranoia and unjustified. Southbound, the aircraft roared away across the neighborhood without a pause.

He hadn't seen any police seal, any lettering or insignia.

The palms shuddered, shivered, then trembled into stillness once more.

Groping again, Joe found the transponder expansion-clamped to the energy absorber behind the Honda's rear bumper. With batteries, the entire package was the size of a pack of cigarettes. The signal that it sent was inaudible.

It looked harmless.

He placed the device on the pavement, intending to hammer it to pieces with his tire iron. When a gardener's truck approached along the street, hauling a fragrant load of shrub prunings and burlap-bundled grass, he decided to toss the still-functioning transponder among the clippings.

Maybe the bastards would waste some time and man-power following the truck to the dump.

In the car again, on the move, he spotted the helicopter a few miles to the south. It was flying in tight circles. Then hovering. Then flying in circles again.

His fear of it had not been groundless. The craft was either over the cemetery or, more likely, above the desert scrub north of the Griffith Observatory, searching for the fugitive woman.

Their resources were impressive.

TWO

SEARCHING BEHAVIOR

5

The *Los Angeles Times* booked more advertising than any newspaper in the United States, churning out fortunes for its owners even in an age when most print media were in decline. It was quartered downtown, in an entire high-rise, which it owned and which covered one city block.

Strictly speaking, the *Los Angeles Post* was not even in Los Angeles. It occupied an aging four-story building in Sun Valley, near the Burbank Airport, within the metroplex but not within the L.A. city limits.

Instead of a multiple-level underground garage, the *Post* provided an open lot surrounded by a chain-link fence topped with spirals of razor wire. Rather than a uniformed attendant with a name tag and a welcoming smile, a sullen young man, about nineteen, watched over the ungated entrance from a folding chair under a dirty café umbrella emblazoned with the Cinzano logo. He was listening to rap music on a radio. Head shaved, left nostril pierced by a gold ring, fingernails painted black, dressed in baggy black jeans with one carefully torn knee and a loose black T-shirt with the words FEAR NADA in red across his chest, he looked as if he were assessing the parts value of each arriving car to determine which would bring the most cash if stolen and delivered to a chop shop. In fact, he was checking for an employee

sticker on the windshield, ready to direct visitors to on-
street parking.

The stickers were replaced every two years, and Joe's
was still valid. Two months after the fall of Flight 353,
he had tendered his resignation, but his editor, Caesar
Santos, had refused to accept it and had put him on an
unpaid leave of absence, guaranteeing him a job when he
was ready to return.

He was not ready. He would never be ready. But right
now he needed to use the newspaper's computers and
connections.

No money had been spent on the reception lounge:
institutional-beige paint, steel chairs with blue vinyl pads,
a steel-legged coffee table with a faux-granite Formica
top, and two copies of that day's edition of the *Post*.

On the walls were simple framed black-and-white
photographs by Bill Hannett, the paper's legendary prize-
winning press photographer. Shots of riots, a city in
flames, grinning looters running in the streets. Earthquake-
cracked avenues, buildings in rubble. A young Hispanic
woman jumping to her death from the sixth floor of a
burning building. A brooding sky and a Pacific-facing
mansion teetering on the edge of ruin on a rain-soaked,
sliding hillside. In general, no journalistic enterprise,
whether electronic or print, built its reputation or revenues
on good news.

Behind the reception counter was Dewey Beemis, the
combination receptionist and security guard, who had
worked at the *Post* for over twenty years, since an insanely
egotistical billionaire had founded it with the naive and
hopeless intention of toppling the politically connected
Times from its perch of power and prestige. Originally the
paper had been quartered in a new building in Century
City, with its public spaces conceived and furnished by the
*uber*designer Steven Chase, at which time Dewey had been

only one of several guards and not a receptionist. Even a megalomaniacal billionaire, determined to prevent the dehydration of his pride, grows weary of pouring away money with the tap open wide. Thus the grand offices were traded for more humble space in the valley. The staff had been pared down, and Dewey had hung on by virtue of being the only six-feet-four, bull-necked, plank-shouldered security guard who could type eighty words a minute and claim awesome computer skills.

With the passage of time, the *Post* had begun to break even. The brilliant and visionary Mr. Chase subsequently designed numerous striking interiors, which were celebrated in *Architectural Digest* and elsewhere, and then died in spite of his genius and talent, just as the billionaire would one day die in spite of his vast fortune, just as Dewey Beemis would die in spite of his commendable variety of skills and his infectious smile.

"Joe!" Dewey said, grinning, rising from his chair, a bearish presence, extending his big hand across the counter.

Joe shook hands. "How're you doing, Dewey?"

"Carver and Martin both graduated *summa cum laude* from UCLA in June, one going to law school now, the other medical," Dewey gushed, as if this news were only hours old and about to hit the front page of the next day's *Post*. Unlike the billionaire who employed him, Dewey's pride was not in his own accomplishments but in those of his children. "My Julie, she finished her second year on scholarship at Yale with a three-point-eight average, and this fall she takes over as editor of the student literary magazine, wants to be a novelist like this Annie Proulx she's always reading over and over again—"

With the sudden memory of Flight 353 passing through his eyes as obviously as a dimming cloud across a bright moon, Dewey silenced himself, ashamed to have been boasting about his sons and daughter to a man whose children were lost forever.

"How's Lena?" Joe asked, inquiring about Dewey's wife.

"She's good . . . she's okay, yeah, doing okay." Dewey smiled and nodded to cover his uneasiness, editing his natural enthusiasm for his family.

Joe hated this awkwardness in his friends, their pity. Even after an entire year, here it was. This was one reason he avoided everyone from his old life. The pity in their eyes was genuine compassion, but to Joe, although he knew that he was being unfair, they also seemed to be passing a sad judgment on him for being unable to put his life back together.

"I need to go upstairs, Dewey, put in a little time, do some research, if that's okay."

Dewey's expression brightened. "You coming back, Joe?"

"Maybe," Joe lied.

"Back on staff?"

"Thinking about it."

"Mr. Santos would love to hear that."

"Is he here today?"

"No. On vacation, actually, fishing up in Vancouver."

Relieved that he wouldn't have to lie to Caesar about his true motives, Joe said, "There's just something I've gotten interested in, a quirky human interest story, not my usual thing. Thought I'd come do some background."

"Mr. Santos would want you to feel like you're home. You go on up."

"Thanks, Dewey."

Joe pushed through a swinging door into a long hallway with a worn and stained green carpet, age-mottled paint, and a discolored acoustic-tile ceiling. Following the abandonment of the fat-city trappings that had characterized the *Post*'s years in Century City, the preferred image was guerrilla journalism, hardscrabble but righteous.

To the left was an elevator alcove. The doors at both shafts were scraped and dented.

The ground floor—largely given over to file rooms, clerical offices, classified ad sales, and the circulation department—was full of Saturday silence. In the quiet, Joe felt like an intruder. He imagined that anyone he encountered would perceive at once that he had returned under false pretenses.

While he was waiting for an elevator to open, he was surprised by Dewey, who had hurried from the reception lounge to give him a sealed white envelope. "Almost forgot this. Lady came by few days ago, said she had some information on a story just right for you."

"What story?"

"She didn't say. Just that you'd understand this."

Joe accepted the envelope as the elevator doors opened.

Dewey said, "Told her you hadn't worked here ten months, and she wanted your phone number. Of course I said I couldn't give it out. Or your address."

Stepping into the elevator, Joe said, "Thanks, Dewey."

"Told her I'd send it on or call you about it. Then I discovered you moved and got a new phone, unlisted, and we didn't have it."

"Can't be important," Joe assured him, indicating the envelope. After all, he was not actually returning to journalism.

As the elevator doors started to close, Dewey blocked them. Frowning, he said, "Wasn't just personnel records not up to speed with you, Joe. Nobody here, none of your friends, knew how to reach you."

"I know."

Dewey hesitated before he said, "You've been way down, huh?"

"Pretty far," Joe acknowledged. "But I'm climbing back up."

"Friends can hold the ladder steady, make it easier."

Touched, Joe nodded.

"Just remember," Dewey said.

"Thanks."

Dewey stepped back, and the doors closed.

The elevator rose, taking Joe with it.

The third floor was largely devoted to the newsroom, which had been subdivided into a maze of somewhat claustrophobic modular workstations, so that the entire space could not be seen at once. Every workstation had a computer, telephone, ergonomic chair, and other fundamentals of the trade.

This was very similar to the much larger newsroom at the *Times*. The only differences were that the furniture and the reconfigurable walls at the *Times* were newer and more stylish than those at the *Post*, the environment there was no doubt purged of the asbestos and formaldehyde that lent the air here its special astringent quality, and even on a Saturday afternoon the *Times* would be busier per square foot of floor space than the *Post* was now.

Twice over the years, Joe had been offered a job at the *Times*, but he had declined. Although the Gray Lady, as the competition was known in some circles, was a great newspaper, it was also the ad-fat voice of the status quo. He believed he'd be allowed and encouraged to do better and more aggressive reporting at the *Post*, which was like an asylum at times, but also heavy on ballsy attitude and gonzo style, with a reputation for never treating a politician's handout as real news and for assuming that every public official was either corrupt or incompetent, sex crazed or power mad.

A few years ago, after the Northridge earthquake, seismologists had discovered unsuspected links between a fault that ran under the heart of L.A. and one that lay beneath a series of communities in the San Fernando Valley. A joke swept the newsroom regarding what losses the city would suffer if one temblor destroyed the *Times* downtown and the *Post* in Sun Valley. Without the *Post*, according to the joke, Angelenos wouldn't know which politicians and other public servants were stealing them blind, accepting bribes from known drug dealers, and having sex with animals. The greater tragedy, however, would be the loss of the six-pound Sunday edition of the *Times*, without which no one would know what stores were conducting sales.

If the *Post* was as obstinate and relentless as a rat terrier crazed by the scent of rodents—which it was—it was redeemed, for Joe, by the nonpartisan nature of its fury. Furthermore, a high percentage of its targets were at least as corrupt as it wanted to believe they were.

Also, Michelle had been a featured columnist and editorial writer for the *Post*. He met her here, courted her here, and enjoyed their shared sense of being part of an underdog enterprise. She had carried their two babies in her belly through so many days of work in this place.

Now he found this building haunted by memories of her. In the unlikely event that he could eventually regain emotional stability and con himself into believing life had a purpose worth the struggle, the face of that one dear ghost would rock him every time he saw it. He would never be able to work at the *Post* again.

He went directly to his former workstation in the Metro section, grateful that no old friends saw him. His place had been assigned to Randy Colway, a good man, who wouldn't feel invaded if he found Joe in his chair.

Tacked to the noteboard were photographs of Randy's wife, their nine-year-old son, Ben, and six-year-old Lisbeth. Joe looked at them for a long moment—and then not again.

After switching on the computer, he reached into his pocket and withdrew the Department of Motor Vehicles envelope that he'd filched from the glove box of the white van at the cemetery. It contained the validated registration card. To his surprise, the registered owner wasn't a government body or a law-enforcement agency; it was something called Medsped, Inc.

He had not been expecting a corporate operation, for God's sake. Wallace Blick and his trigger-happy associates in the Hawaiian shirts didn't seem entirely like cops or federal agents, but they smelled a lot more like the law than they did like any corporate executives Joe had ever encountered.

Next he accessed the *Post*'s vast file of digitized back issues. Included was every word of every edition the newspaper had published since its inception—minus only the cartoons, horoscopes, crossword puzzles, and the like. Photographs were included.

He initiated a search for *Medsped* and found six mentions. They were small items from the business pages. He read them complete.

Medsped, a New Jersey corporation, had begun as an air ambulance service in several major cities. Later, it had expanded to specialize in the nationwide express delivery of emergency medical supplies, refrigerated or otherwise delicately preserved blood and tissue samples, as well as expensive and frangible scientific instruments. The company even undertook to carry samples of highly contagious bacteria and viruses between cooperating research laboratories in both the public and the military sectors. For these tasks, it maintained a modest fleet of aircraft and helicopters.

Helicopters.

And unmarked white vans?

Eight years ago, Medsped had been bought by Teknologik, Inc., a Delaware corporation with a score of wholly owned subsidiaries in the medical and computer industry. Its computer-related holdings were all companies developing products, mostly software, for the medical and medical-research communities.

When Joe ran a search on Teknologik, he was rewarded with forty-one stories, mostly from the business pages. The first two articles were so dry, however, so full of investment and accounting jargon, that the reward quickly began to seem like punishment.

He ordered copies of the four longest articles for review later.

While those were sliding into the printer tray, he asked for a list of stories the *Post* had published about the crash of Nationwide Flight 353. A series of headlines, with accompanying dates, appeared on the screen.

Joe had to steel himself to scan this story file. He sat for a minute or two with his eyes closed, breathing deeply, trying to conjure, in his mind's eye, an image of surf breaking on the beach at Santa Monica.

Finally, with teeth clenched so tightly that his jaw muscles twitched continuously, he called up story after story, scanning the contents. He wanted the one that, as a sidebar, would provide him with a complete passenger manifest.

He skipped quickly past photographs of the crash scene, which revealed debris chopped into such small chunks and tangled in such surreal shapes that the baffled eye could not begin to reconstruct the aircraft from its ruins. In the bleak dawn caught by these pictures, through the gray drizzle that had begun to fall about two hours after the disaster, National Transportation Safety Board investigators in biologically secure bodysuits with visored hoods prowled the blasted meadow. Looming in the background were scorched trees, gnarled black limbs clawing at the low sky.

He searched for and found the name of the NTSB Go-Team leader in charge of the investigation— Barbara Christman—and the fourteen specialists working under her.

A couple of the articles included photos of some of the crew and passengers. Not all of the three hundred and thirty souls aboard were pictured. The tendency was to focus on those victims who were Southern Californians returning home rather than on Easterners who had been coming to visit. Being part of the *Post* family, Michelle and the girls were prominently featured.

Eight months ago, upon moving into the apartment, in reaction to a morbid and obsessive preoccupation with family albums and loose snapshots, Joe had packed all the photos in a large cardboard box, reasoning that rubbing a wound retarded healing. He had taped the box shut and put it at the back of his only closet.

Now, in the course of his scanning, when their faces appeared on the screen, he was unable to breathe, though he had thought he would be prepared. Michelle's publicity shot, taken by one of the *Post*'s staff photographers, captured her beauty but not her tenderness, not her intelligence, not her charm, not her laughter. A mere picture was so inadequate, but still it was Michelle. Still. Chrissie's photo had been snapped at a *Post* Christmas party for children of the paper's employees. She was caught in a grin, eyes shining. How they shone. And little Nina, who sometimes wanted it pronounced *neen-ah* and other times *nine-ah*, was smiling that slightly lopsided smile that seemed to say she knew magical secrets.

Her smile reminded Joe of a silly song he sometimes sang to her when he put her to bed. Before he realized what he was doing, he found his breath again and heard himself whispering the words: *"Nine-ah, neen-ah, have you seen her? Neen-ah, nine-ah, no one finah."*

A breaking inside him threatened his self-control.

He clicked the mouse to get their images off the screen. But that didn't take their faces out of his mind, clearer than he had seen them since packing their photos away.

Bending forward in the chair, covering his face, shuddering, he muffled his voice in his cold hands. "Oh, shit. Oh, shit."

Surf breaking on a beach, now as before, tomorrow as today. Clocks and looms. Sunrises, sunsets, phases of the moon. Machines clicking, ticking. Eternal rhythms, meaningless motions.

The only sane response is indifference.

He lowered his hands from his face. Sat up straight again. Tried to focus on the computer screen.

He was concerned that he would draw attention to himself. If an old acquaintance looked into this three-walled cubicle to see what was wrong, Joe might have to explain what he was doing here, might even have to summon the strength to be sociable.

He found the passenger manifest for which he had been searching. The *Post* had saved him time and effort by listing separately those among the dead who had lived in Southern California. He printed out all their names, each of which was followed by the name of the town in which the deceased resided.

I'm not ready to talk to you yet, the photographer of graves had said to him, from which he had inferred that she would have things to tell him later.

Don't despair. You'll see, like the others.

See what? He had no idea.

What could she possibly tell him that would alleviate his despair? Nothing. Nothing.

. . . like the others. You'll see, like the others.

What others?

Only one answer satisfied him: other people who had lost loved ones on Flight 353, who had been as desolate as he was, people to whom she had already spoken.

He wasn't going to wait for her to return to him. With Wallace Blick and associates after her, she might not live long enough to pay him a visit and quench his curiosity.

■

When Joe finished sorting and stapling the printouts, he noticed the white envelope that Dewey Beemis had given him at the elevator downstairs. Joe had propped it against a box of Kleenex to the right of the computer and promptly forgotten about it.

As a crime reporter with a frequently seen byline, he had from time to time received story tips from newspaper readers who, to put it charitably, were not well glued together. They earnestly claimed to be the terrified victims of vicious harassment by a secret cult of Satanists operating in the city's parks department, or to know of sinister tobacco-industry executives who were plotting to lace baby formula with nicotine, or to be living across the street from a nest of spider-like extraterrestrials trying to pass as a nice family of Korean immigrants.

Once, when cornered by a pinwheel-eyed man who insisted that the mayor of Los Angeles was not human but a robot controlled by the audioanimatronics department at Disneyland, Joe had lowered his voice and said, with nervous sincerity, "Yes, we've known about that for years. But if we print a word of it, the people at Disney will kill us all." He had spoken with such conviction that the nutball had exploded backward and fled.

Consequently, he was expecting a crayon-scrawled message about evil psychic Martians living among us as Mormons—or the equivalent. He tore open the envelope. It contained a single sheet of white paper folded in thirds.

The three neatly typed sentences initially impressed him as a singularly cruel variation on the usual paranoid shriek: *I have been trying to reach you, Joe. My life depends on your discretion. I was aboard Flight 353.*

Everyone aboard the airliner had perished. He didn't believe in ghost mail from the Other Side, which probably made him unique among his contemporaries in this New Age City of Angels.

At the bottom of the page was a name: Rose Tucker. Under the name was a phone number with a Los Angeles area code. No address was provided.

Lightly flushed by the same anger that had burned so hotly in him earlier, and which could easily become a blaze again, Joe almost snatched up the phone to call Ms. Tucker. He wanted to tell her what a disturbed and vicious piece of garbage she was, wallowing in her schizophrenic fantasies, psychic vampire sucking on the misery of others to feed some sick need of her own—

And then he heard, in memory, the words that Wallace Blick first said to him in the cemetery. Unaware that anyone was in the white van, Joe had leaned through the open passenger door and popped the glove box in search of a cellular phone. Blick, briefly mistaking him for one of the men in the Hawaiian shirts, had said, *Did you get Rose?*

Rose.

Because Joe had been frightened by the gunmen, afraid for the woman they were pursuing, and startled to discover someone in the van, the importance of what

Blick said had failed to register with him. Everything happened so fast after that. He had forgotten Blick's words until now.

Rose Tucker must have been the woman with the Polaroid camera, photographing the graves.

If she was nothing more than a whacked-out loser living in some schizophrenic fantasy, Medsped or Teknologik— or whoever the hell they were—wouldn't be throwing so much manpower and money into a search for her.

He remembered the exceptional presence of the woman in the cemetery. Her directness. Her self-possession and preternatural calm. The power of her unwavering stare.

She hadn't seemed like a flake. Quite the opposite.

I have been trying to reach you, Joe. My life depends on your discretion. I was aboard Flight 353.

Without realizing that he had gotten off the chair, Joe was standing, heart pounding, electrified. The sheet of paper rattled in his hands.

He stepped into the aisle behind the modular workstation and surveyed what he could see of the subdivided newsroom, seeking someone with whom he could share this development.

Look here. Read this, read it. Something's terribly wrong, Jesus, all wrong, not what we were told. Somebody walked away from the crash, lived through it. We have to do something about this, find the truth. No survivors, they said, no survivors, catastrophic crash, total wipeout catastrophic crash. What else have they told us that isn't true? How did the people on that plane really die? Why did they die? Why did they die?

Before anyone saw him standing there in furious distress, before he went in search of a familiar face, Joe had second thoughts about sharing anything he had learned. Rose Tucker's note said that her life depended on his discretion.

Besides, he had the crazy notion, somehow more powerfully convincing *because* of its irrationality, that if he shared the note with others, it would prove to be blank, that if he pressed Blick's driver's license into their hands, it would turn out to be his own license, that if he took someone with him to the cemetery, there would be no spent cartridges in the grass and no skid marks from the tires of the white van and no one there who had ever seen the vehicle or heard the gunshots.

This was a mystery delivered to him, to no one else but him, and he suddenly perceived that pursuing answers was not merely his duty but his *sacred* duty. In the resolution of this mystery was his mission, his purpose, and perhaps an unknowable redemption.

He didn't even understand precisely what he meant by any of that. He simply felt the truth of it bone-deep.

Trembling, he returned to the chair.

He wondered if he was entirely sane.

6

Joe called downstairs to the reception desk and asked Dewey Beemis about the woman who had left the envelope.

"Little bit of a lady," said Dewey.

He was a giant, however, and even a six-foot-tall Amazon might seem petite to him.

"Would you say five six, shorter?" Joe asked.

"Maybe five one, five two. But mighty. One of those ladies looks like a girl all her life but been a mountain-mover since she graduated grade school."

"Black woman?" Joe asked.

"Yeah, she was a sister."

"How old?"

"Maybe early forties. Pretty. Hair like raven wings. You upset about something, Joe?"

"No. No, I'm okay."

"You sound upset. This lady some kind of trouble?"

"No, she's okay, she's legit. Thanks, Dewey."

Joe put down the phone.

The nape of his neck was acrawl with gooseflesh. He rubbed it with one hand.

His palms were clammy. He blotted them on his jeans.

Nervously, he picked up the printout of the passenger manifest from Flight 353. Using a ruler to keep his place, he went down the list of the deceased, line by line, until he came to *Dr. Rose Marie Tucker*.

Doctor.

She might be a doctor of medicine or of literature, biologist or sociologist, musicologist or dentist, but in Joe's eyes, her credibility was enhanced by the mere fact that she had earned the honorific. The troubled people who believed the mayor to be a robot were more likely to be patients than doctors of any kind.

According to the manifest, Rose Tucker was forty-three years old, and her home was in Manassas, Virginia. Joe had never been in Manassas, but he had driven past it a few times, because it was an outer suburb of Washington, near the town where Michelle's parents lived.

Swiveling to the computer once more, he scrolled through the crash stories, seeking the thirty or more photographs of passengers, hoping hers would be among them. It was not.

Judging by Dewey's description, the woman who had written this note and the woman in the cemetery—whom Blick had called *Rose*—were the same person. If this Rose was truly Dr. Rose Marie Tucker of Manassas, Virginia—which couldn't be confirmed without a photo—then she had indeed been aboard Flight 353.

And had survived.

Reluctantly, Joe returned to the two largest accident-scene photographs. The first was the eerie shot with the stormy sky, the scorched-black trees, the debris pulverized and twisted into surreal sculpture, where the NTSB investigators, faceless in biohazard suits and hoods, seemed to drift like praying monks or like ominous spirits in a cold and flameless chamber in some forgotten level of Hell. The second was an aerial shot revealing wreckage so shattered and so widely strewn that the term "catastrophic accident" was a woefully inadequate description.

No one could have survived this disaster.

Yet Rose Tucker, if she was the *same* Rose Tucker who had boarded the plane that night, had evidently not only survived but walked away under her own power. Without serious injury. She had not been scarred or crippled.

Impossible. Dropping four miles in the clutch of planetary gravity, four long *miles*, accelerating unchecked into hard earth and rock, the 747 had not just smashed but splattered like an egg thrown at a brick wall, and then exploded, and then tumbled in seething furies of flame. To escape unmarked from the God-rattled ruins of Gomorrah, to step as unburnt as Shadrach from the fiery furnace of Nebuchadnezzar, to arise like Lazarus after four days in the grave, would have been less miraculous than to walk away untouched from the fall of Flight 353.

If he genuinely believed it was impossible, however, his mind would not have been roiled with anger and anxiety, with a strange awe, and with urgent curiosity. In him was a crazy yearning to embrace incredibilities, walk with wonder.

■

He called directory assistance in Manassas, seeking a telephone number for Dr. Rose Marie Tucker. He expected to be told that there was no such listing or that her service had been disconnected. After all, officially she was dead.

Instead, he was given a number.

She could not have walked away from the crash and gone home and picked up her life without causing a sensation. Besides, dangerous people were hunting her. They would have found her if she had ever returned to Manassas.

Perhaps family still lived in the house. For whatever reasons, they might have kept the phone in her name.

Joe punched in the number.

The call was answered on the second ring. "Yes?"

"Is this the Tucker residence?" Joe asked.

The voice was that of a man, crisp and without a regional accent: "Yes, it is."

"Could I speak to Dr. Tucker, please?"

"Who's calling?"

Intuition advised Joe to guard his own name. "Wally Blick."

"Excuse me. Who?"

"Wallace Blick."

The man at the other end of the line was silent. Then: "What is this in regard to?" His voice had barely changed, but a new alertness colored it, a shade of wariness.

Sensing that he had been too clever for his own good, Joe put down the phone.

He blotted his palms on his jeans again.

A reporter, passing behind Joe, reviewing the scribblings on a note pad as he went, greeted him without looking up: "Yo, Randy."

Consulting the typewritten message from Rose, Joe called the Los Angeles number that she had provided.

On the fifth ring, a woman answered. "Hello?"

"Could I speak to Rose Tucker, please?"

"Nobody here by that name," she said in an accent out of the deep South. "You got yourself a wrong number."

In spite of what she'd said, she didn't hang up.

"She gave me this number herself," Joe persisted.

"Sugar, let me guess—this was a lady you met at a party. She was just makin' nice to get you out of her hair."

"I don't think she'd do that."

"Oh, don't mean you're ugly, honey," she said in a voice that brought to mind magnolia blossoms and mint juleps and humid nights heavy with the scent of jasmine.

"Just means you weren't the lady's type. Happens to the best."

"My name's Joe Carpenter."

"Nice name. Good solid name."

"What's *your* name?"

Teasingly, she said, "What kind of name do I sound like?"

"Sound like?"

"Maybe an Octavia or a Juliette?"

"More like a Demi."

"Like in Demi Moore the movie star?" she said disbelievingly.

"You have that sexy, smoky quality in your voice."

"Honey, my voice is pure grits and collard greens."

"Under the grits and collard greens, there's smoke."

She had a wonderful fulsome laugh. "Mister Joe Carpenter, middle name 'Slick.' Okay, I like Demi."

"Listen, Demi, I'd sure like to talk to Rose."

"Forget this old Rose person. Don't you pine away for her, Joe, not after she gives you a fake number. Big sea, lots of fish."

Joe was certain that this woman knew Rose and that she had been expecting him to call. Considering the viciousness of the enemies pursuing the enigmatic Dr. Tucker, however, Demi's circumspection was understandable.

She said, "What do you look like when you're bein' honest with yourself, sugar?"

"Six feet tall, brown hair, gray eyes."

"Handsome?"

"Just presentable."

"How old are you, Presentable Joe?"

"Older than you. Thirty-seven."

"You have a sweet voice. You ever go on blind dates?"

Demi was going to set up a meeting, after all.

He said, "Blind dates? Nothing against them."

"So how about with sexy-smoky little me?" she suggested with a laugh.

"Sure. When?"

"You free tomorrow evenin'?"

"I was hoping sooner."

"Don't be so eager, Presentable Joe. Takes time to set these things up right, so there's a chance it'll work, so no one gets hurt, so there's no broken hearts."

By Joe's interpretation, Demi was telling him that she was going to make damned sure the meeting was put together carefully, that the site needed to be scouted and secured in order for Rose's safety to be guaranteed. And maybe she couldn't get in touch with Rose with less than a twenty-four-hour notice.

"Besides, sugar, a girl starts to wonder why you're so pitiful desperate if you're really presentable."

"All right. Where tomorrow evening?"

"I'm goin' to give you the address of a gourmet coffee shop in Westwood. We'll meet out front at six, go in and have a cup, see do we like each other. If I think you really are presentable and you think I'm as sexy-smoky as my voice . . . why, then it could be a shinin' night of golden memories. You have a pen and paper?"

"Yes," he said, and he wrote down the name and address of the coffee shop as she gave it to him.

"Now do me one favor, sugar. You have a paper there with this phone number on. Tear it to bitty pieces and flush it down a john." When Joe hesitated, Demi said, "Won't be no good ever again, anyway," and she hung up.

The three typed sentences would not prove that Dr. Tucker had survived Flight 353 or that something about the crash was not kosher. He could have composed them himself. Dr. Tucker's name was typed as well, so there was no evidentiary signature.

Nevertheless, he was loath to dispose of the message.

Although it would never prove anything to anyone else, it made these fantastic events seem more real to *him*.

He called Demi's number again to see if she would answer it in spite of what she had said.

To his surprise, he got a recorded message from the telephone company informing him that the number he had called was no longer in service. He was advised to make sure that he had entered the number correctly and then to call 411 for directory assistance. He tried the number again, with the same result.

Neat trick. He wondered how it had been done. Demi clearly was more sophisticated than her grits-and-collard-greens voice.

As Joe returned the handset to the cradle, the telephone rang, startling him so much that he let go of it as if he had burned his fingers. Embarrassed by his edginess, he picked it up on the third ring. "Hello?"

"Los Angeles Post?" a man asked.

"Yes."

"Is this Randy Colway's direct line?"

"That's right."

"Are you Mr. Colway?"

Startlement and the interlude with Demi had left Joe slow on the uptake. Now he recognized the uninflected voice as that of the man who had answered the phone at Rose Marie Tucker's house in Manassas, Virginia.

"Are you Mr. Colway?" the caller asked again.

"I'm Wallace Blick," Joe said.

"Mr. Carpenter?"

Chills climbed the ladder of his spine, vertebra to vertebra, and Joe slammed down the phone.

They knew where he was.

The dozens of modular workstations no longer seemed like a series of comfortably anonymous nooks. They were a maze with too many blind corners.

Quickly he gathered the printouts and the message that Rose Tucker had left for him.

As he was getting up from the chair, the phone rang again. He didn't answer it.

∎

On his way out of the newsroom, he encountered Dan Shavers, who was returning from the photocopying center with a sheaf of papers in his left hand and his unlit pipe in the right. Shavers, utterly bald, with a luxuriant black beard, wore pleated black dress slacks, red-and-black checkered suspenders over a gray-and-white pin-striped shirt, and a yellow bow tie. His half-lens reading glasses dangled from his neck on a loop of black ribbon.

A reporter and columnist on the business desk, Shavers was as pompous and as awkward at small talk as he thought he was charming; however, he was benign in his self-delusion and touching in his mistaken conviction that he was a spellbinding raconteur. He said without pre-amble, "Joseph, dear boy, opened a case of '74 Mondavi Cabernet last week, one of twenty I bought as an invest-ment when it was first released, even though at the time I was in Napa not to scout the vintners but to shop for an antique clock, and let me tell you, this wine has matured so well that—" He broke off, realizing that Joe had not worked at the newspaper for the better part of a year. Fum-blingly, he tried to offer his condolences regarding "that terrible thing, that awful thing, all those poor people, your wife and the children."

Aware that Randy Colway's telephone was ringing again farther back in the newsroom, Joe interrupted Shavers, intending to brush him off, but then he said, "Listen, Dan, do you know a company called Teknologik?"

"Do I know them?" Shavers wiggled his eyebrows. "Very amusing, Joseph."

"You do know them? What's the story, Dan? Are they a pretty large conglomerate? I mean, are they powerful?"

"Oh, very profitable, Joseph, absolutely uncanny at recognizing cutting-edge technology in start-up companies and then acquiring them—or backing entrepreneurs who need cash to develop their ideas. Generally medically related technology but not always. Their top executives are infamous self-aggrandizers, think of themselves as some kind of business royalty, but they are no better than us. They, too, answer to He Who Must Be Obeyed."

Confused, Joe said, "He Who Must Be Obeyed?"

"As do we all, as do we all," said Shavers, smiling and nodding, raising his pipe to bite the stem.

Colway's phone stopped ringing. The silence made Joe more nervous than the insistent trilling tone had done.

They knew where he was.

"Got to go," he said, walking away as Shavers began to tell him about the advantages of owning Teknologik corporate bonds.

He proceeded directly to the nearest men's room. Fortunately, no one else was in the lavatory, no old acquaintances to delay him.

In one of the stalls, Joe tore Rose's message into small pieces. He flushed it down the toilet, as Demi had requested, waiting to confirm that every scrap vanished, flushing a second time to be sure that nothing was caught in the drain.

Medsped. Teknologik. Corporations conducting what appeared to be a police operation. Their long reach, from Los Angeles to Manassas, and their unnerving omniscience, argued that these were corporations with powerful connections beyond the business world, perhaps to the military.

Nevertheless, regardless of the stakes, it made no sense for a corporation to protect its interests with hit men brazen enough to shoot at people in public places—or anywhere else, for that matter. Regardless of how profitable Teknologik might be, big black numbers at the bottom of the balance sheet did not exempt corporate officers and executives from the law, not even here in Los Angeles, where the *lack* of money was known to be the root of all evil.

Considering the impunity with which they seemed to think they could use guns, the men whom he had encountered *must* be military personnel or federal agents. Joe had too little information to allow him even to conjecture what role Medsped and Teknologik played in the operation.

All the way along the third-floor hall to the elevators, he expected someone to call his name and order him to stop. Perhaps one of the men in Hawaiian shirts. Or Wallace Blick. Or a police officer.

If the people seeking Rose Tucker were federal agents, they would be able to obtain help from local police. For the time being, Joe would have to regard every man in uniform as a potential enemy.

As the elevator doors opened, he tensed, half expecting to be apprehended here in the alcove. The cab was empty.

On the way down to the first floor, he waited for the power to be cut off. When the doors opened on the lower alcove, he was surprised to find it deserted.

In all his life, he had never previously been in the grip of paranoia such as this. He was overreacting to the events of the early afternoon and to what he had learned since arriving at the offices of the *Post*.

He wondered if his exaggerated reactions—spells of extreme rage, spiraling fear—were a response to the past year of emotional deprivation. He had allowed himself to feel nothing whatsoever but grief, self-pity, and the terrible hollowness of incomprehensible loss. In fact, he'd striven hard not to feel even that much. He had tried to shed his pain, to rise from the ashes like a drab phoenix with no hope except the cold peace of indifference. Now that events forced him to open himself to the world again, he was swamped by emotion as a novice surfer was overwhelmed by each cresting wave.

In the reception lounge, as Joe entered, Dewey Beemis was on the telephone. He was listening so intently that his usually smooth dark face was furrowed. He murmured, "Yes, uh-huh, uh-huh, yes."

Heading toward the outer door, Joe waved good-bye.

Dewey said, "Joe, wait, wait a second."

Joe stopped and turned.

Though Dewey was listening to the caller again, his eyes were on Joe.

To indicate that he was in a hurry, Joe tapped one finger against his wristwatch.

"Hold on," Dewey said into the phone, and then to Joe, he said, "There's a man here calling about you."

Joe shook his head adamantly.

"Wants to talk to you," Dewey said.

Joe started toward the door again.

"Wait, Joe, man says he's FBI."

At the door, Joe hesitated and looked back at Dewey. The FBI couldn't be associated with the men in the Hawaiian shirts, not with men who shot at innocent people without bothering to ask questions, not with men like Wallace Blick. Could they? Wasn't he letting his fear run away with him again, succumbing to paranoia? He might get answers and protection from the FBI.

Of course, the man on the phone could be lying. He might not be with the Bureau. Possibly he was hoping to delay Joe until Blick and his friends—or others aligned with them—could get here.

With a shake of his head, Joe turned away from Dewey. He pushed through the door and into the August heat.

Behind him, Dewey said, "Joe?"

Joe walked toward his car. He resisted the urge to break into a run.

At the far end of the parking lot, by the open gate, the young attendant with the shaved head and the gold nose ring was watching. In this city where sometimes money mattered more than fidelity or honor or merit, style mattered more than money; fashions came and went even more frequently than principles and convictions, leaving only the unchanging signal colors of youth gangs as a sartorial tradition. This kid's look, punk-grunge-neopunk-whatever, was already as dated as spats, making him look less threatening than he thought and more pathetic than he would ever be able to comprehend. Yet under these circumstances, his interest in Joe seemed ominous.

Even at low volume, the hard beat of rap music thumped through the blistering air.

The interior of the Honda was hot but not intolerable. The side window, shattered by a bullet at the cemetery, provided just enough ventilation to prevent suffocation.

The attendant had probably noticed the broken-out window when Joe had driven in. Maybe he'd been thinking about it.

What does it matter if he has been thinking? It's only a broken window.

He was certain the engine wouldn't start, but it did.

As Joe backed out of the parking slot, Dewey Beemis opened the reception-lounge door and stepped outside onto the small concrete stoop under the awning that bore the logo of the *Post*. The big man looked not alarmed but puzzled.

Dewey wouldn't try to stop him. They were friends, after all, or had once been friends, and the man on the phone was just a voice.

Joe shifted the Honda into Drive.

Coming down the steps, Dewey shouted something. He didn't sound alarmed. He sounded confused, concerned.

Ignoring him nonetheless, Joe drove toward the exit.

Under the dirty Cinzano umbrella, the attendant rose from the folding chair. He was only two steps from the rolling gate that would close off the lot.

Atop the chain-link fence, the coils of razor wire flared with silver reflections of late-afternoon sunlight.

Joe glanced at the rearview mirror. Back there, Dewey was standing with his hands on his hips.

As Joe went past the Cinzano umbrella, the attendant didn't even come forth out of the shade. Watching with heavy-lidded eyes, as expressionless as an iguana, he wiped sweat off his brow with one hand, black finger-nails glistening.

Through the open gate and turning right into the street, Joe was driving too fast. The tires squealed and sucked wetly at the sun-softened blacktop, but he didn't slow down.

He went west on Strathern Street and heard sirens by the time that he turned south on Lankershim Boulevard. Sirens were part of the music of the city, day and night; they didn't necessarily have anything to do with him.

Nevertheless, all the way to the Ventura Freeway, under it, and then west on Moorpark, he repeatedly checked the rearview mirror for pursuing vehicles, either marked or unmarked.

He was not a criminal. He should have felt safe going to the authorities to report the men in the cemetery, to tell them about the message from Rose Marie Tucker, and to report his suspicions about Flight 353.

On the other hand, in spite of being on the run for her life, Rose apparently hadn't sought protection from the cops, perhaps because there was no protection to be had. *My life depends on your discretion.*

He had been a crime reporter long enough to have seen more than a few cases in which the victim had been targeted not because of anything he had done, not because of money or other possessions that his assailant desired, but merely because of what he had known. A man with too much knowledge could be more dangerous than a man with a gun.

What knowledge Joe had about Flight 353 seemed, however, to be pathetically inadequate. If he was a target merely because he knew that Rose Tucker existed and that she claimed to have survived the crash, then the secrets *she* possessed must be so explosive that the power of them could be measured only in megatonnage.

As he drove west toward Studio City, he thought of the red letters emblazoned on the black T-shirt worn by the attendant at the *Post* parking lot: FEAR NADA. "Fear nothing" was a philosophy Joe could never embrace. He feared so much.

More than anything, he was tormented by the possibility that the crash had not been an accident, that Michelle and Chrissie and Nina died not at the whim of fate but by the hand of man. Although the National Transportation Safety Board hadn't been able to settle on a probable cause, hydraulic control systems failure complicated by human error was one possible scenario—and one with which he had been able to live because it was so impersonal, as mechanical and cold as the universe itself. He would find it intolerable, however, if they had perished from a cowardly act of terrorism or because of some more personal crime, their lives sacrificed to human greed or envy or hatred.

He feared what such a discovery would do to him. He feared what he might become, his potential for savagery, the hideous ease with which he might embrace vengeance and call it justice.

name. They glanced at her until her choline was inch to service.

California money banks were like undertakers, scum chasers, thriving it out, looking are charged fanges.

Heather pursued, with graded exhaustion, and the ment that they were made to accommodate him, though there were, it can be, professional that must be followed. If it baked under the safe, the assistant manager was intent on his professional suspicion had no longer about the subject of the conversation, Joe knew he was the

7

In the current atmosphere of fierce competitiveness that marked their industry, California bankers were keeping their offices open on Saturdays, some as late as five o'clock. Joe arrived at the Studio City branch of his bank twenty minutes before the doors closed.

When he sold the house here, he had not bothered to switch his account to a branch nearer his one-room apartment in Laurel Canyon. Convenience wasn't a consideration when time no longer mattered.

He went to a window where a woman named Heather was tending to paperwork as she waited for last-minute business. She had worked at this bank since Joe had first opened an account a decade ago.

"I need to make a cash withdrawal," he said, after the requisite small talk, "but I don't have my checkbook with me."

"That's no problem," she assured him.

It became a small problem, however, when Joe asked for twenty thousand dollars in hundred-dollar bills. Heather went to the other end of the bank and huddled in conversation with the head teller, who then consulted the assistant manager. This was a young man no less handsome than the current hottest movie hero; perhaps he was one of the legion of would-be stars who labored in the real world to survive while waiting for the fantasy of fame. They glanced at Joe as if his identity was now in doubt.

Taking in money, banks were like industrial vacuum cleaners. Giving it out, they were clogged faucets.

Heather returned with a guarded expression and the news that they were happy to accommodate him, though there were, of course, procedures that must be followed.

At the other end of the bank, the assistant manager was talking on his phone, and Joe suspected that he himself was the subject of the conversation. He knew he was letting his paranoia get the better of him again, but his mouth went dry, and his heartbeat increased.

The money was his. He needed it.

That Heather had known Joe for years—in fact, attended the same Lutheran church where Michelle had taken Chrissie and Nina to Sunday school and services—did not obviate her need to see his driver's license. The days of common trust and common sense were so far in America's past that they seemed not merely to be ancient history but to be part of the history of another country altogether.

He remained patient. Everything he owned was on deposit here, including nearly sixty thousand dollars in equity from the sale of the house, so he could not be denied the money, which he would need for living expenses. With the same people seeking him who were searching for Rose Tucker, he could not go back to the apartment and would have to live out of motels for the duration.

The assistant manager had concluded his call. He was staring at a note pad on his desk, tapping it with a pencil.

Joe had considered using his few credit cards to pay for things, supplemented by small sums withdrawn as needed from automated teller machines. But authorities could track a suspect through credit-card use and ATM activity—and be ever on his heels. They could even have his plastic seized by any merchant at the point of purchase.

A phone rang on the assistant manager's desk. He snatched it up, glanced at Joe, and turned away in his swivel chair, as if he worried that his lips might be read.

After procedures were followed and everyone was satisfied that Joe was neither his own evil twin nor a bold impersonator in a clever rubber mask, the assistant manager, his phone conversation concluded, slowly gathered the hundred-dollar bills from other tellers' drawers and from the vault. He brought the required sum to Heather and, with a fixed and uneasy smile, watched as she counted it for Joe.

Perhaps it was imagination, but Joe felt they disapproved of his carrying so much money, not because it put him in danger but because these days people who dealt in cash were stigmatized. The government required banks to report cash transactions of five thousand dollars or more, ostensibly to hamper attempts by drug lords to launder funds through legitimate financial institutions. In reality, no drug lord was ever inconvenienced by this law, but the financial activities of average citizens were now more easily monitored.

Throughout history, cash or the equivalent—diamonds, gold coins—had been the best guarantor of freedom and mobility. Cash meant the same things to Joe and nothing more. Yet from Heather and her bosses, he continued to endure a surreptitious scrutiny that seemed to be based on the assumption that he was engaged in some criminal enterprise or, at best, was on his way for a few days of unspeakable debauchery in Las Vegas.

As Heather put the twenty thousand in a manila envelope, the phone rang on the assistant manager's desk.

Murmuring into the mouthpiece, he continued to find Joe of interest.

By the time Joe left the bank, five minutes past closing time, the last customer to depart, he was weak-kneed with apprehension.

The heat remained oppressive, and the five-o'clock sky was still cloudless and blue, although not the profound blue that it had been earlier. Now it was curiously depthless, a flat blue that reminded him of something he had seen before. The reference remained elusive until he had gotten into the car and started the engine—and then he recalled the dead-blue eyes of the last corpse that he had seen on a morgue gurney, the night he walked away from crime reporting forever.

When he drove out of the bank lot, he saw that the assistant manager was standing beyond the glass doors, all but hidden by the reflected bronze glare of the westering sun. Maybe he was storing away a description of the Honda and memorizing the license-plate number. Or maybe he was just locking the doors.

The metropolis shimmered under the blind blue stare of the dead sky.

■

Passing a small neighborhood shopping center, from across three lanes of traffic, Joe saw a woman with long auburn hair stepping out of a Ford Explorer. She was parked in front of a convenience store. From the passenger side jumped a little girl with a cap of tousled blond hair. Their faces were hidden from him.

Joe angled recklessly across traffic, nearly colliding with an elderly man in a gray Mercedes. At the intersection, as the light turned from yellow to red, he made an illegal U-turn.

He already regretted what he was about to do. But he could no more stop himself than he could hasten the day's end by commanding the sun to set. He was in the grip of a bizarre compulsion.

Shaken by his lack of self-control, he parked near the woman's Ford Explorer. He got out of the Honda. His legs were weak.

He stood staring at the convenience store. The woman and the child were in there, but he couldn't see them for the posters and merchandise displays in the big windows.

He turned away from the store and leaned against the Honda, trying to compose himself.

After the crash in Colorado, Beth McKay had referred him to a group called The Compassionate Friends, a nationwide organization for people who had lost children. Beth was slowly finding her way to acceptance through Compassionate Friends in Virginia, so Joe went to a few meetings of a local chapter, but he soon stopped attending. In that regard, he was like most other men in his situation; bereaved mothers went to the meetings faithfully and found comfort in talking with others whose children had been taken, but nearly all the fathers turned inward and held their pain close. Joe wanted to be one of the few who could find salvation by reaching out, but male biology or psychology—or pure stubbornness or self-pity—kept him aloof, alone.

At least, from The Compassionate Friends, he had discovered that this bizarre compulsion, by which he was now seized, was not unique to him. It was so common they had a name for it: *searching behavior.*

Everybody who lost a loved one engaged in a degree of searching behavior, although it was more intense for those who lost children. Some grievers suffered it worse than others. Joe had it bad.

Intellectually, he could accept that the dead were gone

forever. Emotionally, on a primal level, he remained convinced that he would see them again. At times he expected his wife and daughters to walk through a door or to be on the phone when it rang. Driving, he was occasionally overcome by the certainty that Chrissie and Nina were behind him in the car, and he turned, breathless with excitement, more shocked by the emptiness of the backseat than he would have been to find that the girls were indeed alive again and with him.

Sometimes he saw them on a street. On a playground. In a park. On the beach. They were always at a distance, walking away from him. Sometimes he let them go, but sometimes he was compelled to follow, to see their faces, to say, "Wait for me, wait, I'm coming with you."

Now he turned away from the Honda. He went to the entrance of the convenience store.

Opening the door, he hesitated. He was torturing himself. The inevitable emotional implosion that would ensue when this woman and child proved not to be Michelle and Nina would be like taking a hammer to his own heart.

The events of the day—the encounter with Rose Tucker at the cemetery, her words to him, the shocking message waiting for him at the *Post*—had been so extraordinary that he discovered a gut-deep faith in uncanny possibilities that surprised him. If Rose could fall more than four miles, smash unchecked into Colorado rock, and walk away . . . Unreason overruled facts and logic. A brief, sweet madness stripped off the armor of indifference in which he'd clothed himself with so much struggle and determination, and into his heart surged something like hope.

He went into the store.

The cashier's counter was to his left. A pretty Korean woman in her thirties was clipping packages of Slim Jim sausages to a wire display rack. She smiled and nodded.

A Korean man, perhaps her husband, was at the cash register. He greeted Joe with a comment about the heat.

Ignoring them, Joe passed the first of four aisles, then the second. He saw the auburn-haired woman and the child at the end of the third aisle.

They were standing at a cooler full of soft drinks, their backs to him. He stood for a moment at the head of the aisle, waiting for them to turn toward him.

The woman was in white ankle-tie sandals, white cotton slacks, and a lime-green blouse. Michelle had owned similar sandals, similar slacks. Not the blouse. Not the blouse, that he could recall.

The little girl, Nina's age, Nina's size, was in white sandals like her mother's, pink shorts, and a white T-shirt. She stood with her head cocked to one side, swinging her slender arms, the way Nina sometimes stood.

Nine-ah, neen-ah, have you seen her?

Joe was halfway down the aisle before he realized that he was on the move.

He heard the little girl say, "Please, root beer, please?"

Then he heard himself say, "Nina," because Nina's favorite drink had been root beer. "Nina? Michelle?"

The woman and the child turned to him. They were not Nina and Michelle.

He had known they would not be the woman and the girl whom he had loved. He was operating not on reason but on a demented impulse of the heart. He had known, had *known*. Yet when he saw they were strangers, he felt as though he had been punched in the chest.

Stupidly, he said, "You . . . I thought . . . standing there . . ."

"Yes?" the woman said, puzzled and wary.

"Don't . . . don't let her go," he told the mother, surprised by the hoarseness of his own voice. "Don't let her go, out of your sight, on her own, they vanish, they're gone, unless you keep them close."

Alarm flickered across the woman's face.

With the innocent honesty of a four-year-old, piping up in a concerned and helpful tone, the little girl said, "Mister, you need to buy some soap. You sure smell. The soap's over that way, I'll show you."

The mother quickly took her daughter's hand, pulled her close.

Joe realized that he must, indeed, smell. He had been on the beach in the sun for a couple of hours, and later in the cemetery, and more than once he'd broken into a sweat of fear. He'd had nothing to eat during the day, so his breath must be sour with the beer that he had drunk at the shore.

"Thank you, sweetheart," he said. "You're right. I smell. I better get some soap."

Behind him, someone said, "Everything all right?"

Joe turned and saw the Korean proprietor. The man's previously placid face was now carved by worry.

"I thought they were people I knew," Joe explained. "People I knew . . . once."

He realized that he had left the apartment this morning without shaving. Stubbled, greasy with stale sweat, rumpled, breath sour and beery, eyes wild with blasted hope, he must be a daunting sight. Now he better understood the attitude of the people at the bank.

"Everything all right?" the proprietor asked the woman.

She was uncertain. "I guess so."

"I'm going," Joe said. He felt as if his internal organs were slip-sliding into new positions, his stomach rising and his heart dropping down into the pit of him. "It's okay, okay, just a mistake, I'm going."

He stepped past the owner and went quickly to the front of the store.

As he headed past the cashier's counter toward the door, the Korean woman worriedly said, "Everything all right?"

"Nothing, nothing," Joe said, and he hurried outside into the sedimentary heat of the settling day.

When he got into the Honda, he saw the manila envelope on the passenger's seat. He had left twenty thousand dollars unattended in an unlocked car. Although there had been no miracle in the convenience store, it was a miracle that the money was still here.

Tortured by severe stomach cramps, with a tightness in his chest that restricted his breathing, Joe wasn't confident of his ability to drive with adequate attention to traffic. But he didn't want the woman to think that he was waiting for her, stalking her. He started the Honda and left the shopping center.

Switching on the air conditioning, tilting the vents toward his face, he struggled for breath, as if his lungs had collapsed and he was striving to reinflate them with sheer willpower. What air he was able to inhale was heavy inside him, like a scalding liquid.

This was something else that he had learned from Compassionate Friends meetings: For most of those who lost children, not just for him, the pain was at times physical, stunning.

Wounded, he drove half hunched over the steering wheel, wheezing like an asthmatic.

He thought of the angry vow that he had made to destroy those who might be to blame for the fate of Flight 353, and he laughed briefly, sourly, at his foolishness, at the unlikely image of himself as an unstoppable engine of vengeance. He was walking wreckage. Dangerous to no one.

If he learned what had really happened to that 747, if treachery was indeed involved, and if he discovered who was responsible, the perpetrators would kill him before he could lift a hand against them. They were powerful, with apparently vast resources. He had no chance of bringing them to justice.

Nevertheless, he'd keep trying. The choice to turn away from the hunt was not his to make. Compulsion drove him. Searching behavior.

∎

At a Kmart, Joe purchased an electric razor and a bottle of aftershave. He bought a toothbrush, toothpaste, and toiletries.

The glare of the fluorescent lights cut at his eyes. One wheel on his shopping cart wobbled noisily, louder in his imagination than in reality, exacerbating his headache.

Shopping quickly, he bought a suitcase, two pairs of blue jeans, a gray sports jacket—corduroy, because the fall lines were already on display in August—underwear, T-shirts, athletic socks, and a new pair of Nikes. He went strictly by the stated size, trying on nothing.

After leaving Kmart, he found a modest, clean motel in Malibu, on the ocean, where later he might be able to sleep to the rumble of the surf. He shaved, showered, and changed into clean clothes.

By seven-thirty, with an hour of sunlight left, he drove east to Culver City, where Thomas Lee Vadance's widow lived. Thomas had been listed on the passenger manifest for Flight 353, and his wife, Nora, had been quoted by the *Post*.

At a McDonald's, Joe bought two cheeseburgers and a cola. In the steel-tethered book at the restaurant's public phone, he found a number and an address for Nora Vadance.

From his previous life as a reporter, he had a *Thomas*

Brothers Guide, the indispensable book of Los Angeles County street maps, but he thought he knew Mrs. Vadance's neighborhood.

While he drove, he ate both of the burgers and washed them down with the cola. He was surprised by his own sudden hunger.

The single-story house had a cedar-shingle roof, shingled walls, white trim, and white shutters. It was an odd mix of California ranch house and New England coastal cottage, but with its flagstone walkway and neatly tended beds of impatiens and agapanthus, it was charming.

The day was still warm. Heat shimmered off the flagstones.

With an orange-pink glow growing in the western sky and purple twilight just sliding into view in the east, Joe climbed two steps onto the porch and rang the bell.

The woman who answered the door was about thirty years old and pretty in a fresh-faced way. Although she was a brunette, she had the fair complexion of a redhead, with freckles and green eyes. She was in khaki shorts and a man's threadbare white shirt with the sleeves rolled up. Her hair was in disarray and damp with sweat, and on her left cheek was a smudge of dirt.

She looked as if she had been doing housework. And crying.

"Mrs. Vadance?" Joe asked.

"Yes."

Although he had always been smooth about ingratiating himself with an interviewee when he had been a reporter, he was awkward now. He felt too casually dressed for the serious questions that he had come to ask. His jeans were loose, the waistband gathered and cinched with a belt, and because the air was hot, he'd left the sports jacket in the Honda. He wished he'd bought a shirt instead of just T-shirts.

"Mrs. Vadance, I was wondering if I could speak with you—"

"I'm very busy right now—"

"My name's Joe Carpenter. My wife died on the plane. And my two little girls."

Her breath caught in her throat. Then: "One year ago."

"Yes. Tonight."

She stepped back from the door. "Come in."

He followed her into a cheery, predominantly white and yellow living room with chintz drapes and pillows. A dozen Lladró porcelains stood in a lighted corner display case.

She asked Joe to have a seat. As he settled in an armchair, she went to a doorway and called, "Bob? Bob, we have a visitor."

"I'm sorry to bother you on a Saturday night," Joe said.

Returning from the doorway and perching on the sofa, the woman said, "Not at all. But I'm afraid I'm not the Mrs. Vadance you came to see. I'm not Nora. My name's Clarise. It was my mother-in-law who lost her husband in the . . . in the accident."

From the back of the house, a man entered the living room, and Clarise introduced him as her husband. He was perhaps two years older than his wife, tall, lanky, crew-cut, with a pleasant and self-confident manner. His handshake was firm and his smile easy, but under his tan was a paleness, in his blue eyes a sorrow.

As Bob Vadance sat on the sofa beside his wife, Clarise explained that Joe's family had perished in the crash. To Joe, she said, "It was Bob's dad we lost, coming back from a business trip."

Of all the things that they might have said to one another, they established their bond by talking about how they had first heard the dreadful news out of Colorado.

Clarise and Bob, a fighter pilot assigned to Miramar

Naval Air Station north of San Diego, had been out to
dinner with two other pilots and their wives. They were
at a cozy Italian restaurant and, after dinner, moved into
the bar, where there was a television set. The baseball
game was interrupted for a bulletin about Nationwide
Flight 353. Bob had known his dad was flying that night
from New York to L.A. and that he often traveled
Nationwide, but he hadn't known the flight number.
Using a bar phone to call Nationwide at LAX, he was
quickly connected with a public-relations officer who
confirmed that Thomas Lee Vadance was on the passenger manifest. Bob and Clarise had driven from
Miramar to Culver City in record time, arriving shortly
after eleven o'clock. They didn't call Nora, Bob's
mother, because they didn't know if she had heard. If she
was still unaware of the news, they wanted to tell her in
person rather than over the phone. When they arrived just
after midnight, the house was brightly lighted, the front
door unlocked. Nora was in the kitchen, making corn
chowder, a big pot of corn chowder, because Tom loved
her corn chowder, and she was baking chocolate-chip
cookies with pecans because Bob loved those cookies
too. She knew about the crash, knew that he was dead out
there just east of the Rockies, but she needed to be doing
something for him. They had been married when Nora
was eighteen and Tom was twenty, had been married for
thirty-five years, and she had needed to be doing something for him.

"In my case, I didn't know until I got to the airport to
pick them up," Joe said. "They'd been to Virginia to visit
Michelle's folks, and then three days in New York so the
girls could meet their aunt Delia for the first time. I
arrived early, of course, and first thing when I went into
the terminal, I checked the monitors to see if their flight
was on time. It was still shown as on time, but when I

went up to the gate where it was supposed to arrive, air-line personnel were greeting people as they approached the area, talking to them in low voices, leading some of them away to a private lounge. This young man came up to me, and before he opened his mouth, I knew what he was going to say. I wouldn't let him talk. I said, 'No, don't say it, don't you dare say it.' When he tried to speak anyway, I turned away from him, and when he put a hand on my arm, I knocked it off. I might have punched him to keep him from talking, except by then there were three of them, him and two women, around me, close around me. It was as if I didn't want to be told because being told was what made it real, that it wouldn't be real, you know, wouldn't actually have happened, if they didn't *say* it."

They were all silent, listening to the remembered voices of last year, the voices of strangers with terrible news.

"Mom took it so hard for a long time," Clarise said at last, speaking of her mother-in-law as fondly as if Nora had been her own mother. "She was only fifty-three, but she really didn't want to go on without Tom. They were—"

"—so close," Bob finished. "But then last week when we came to visit, she was way up, so much better. She'd been so bitter, depressed and bitter, but now she was full of life again. She'd always been cheerful before the crash, a real—"

"—people person, so outgoing," Clarise continued for him, as if their thoughts ran always on precisely the same track. "And suddenly here again last week was the woman we'd always known . . . and missed for the past year."

Dread washed through Joe when he realized they were speaking of Nora Vadance as one speaks of the dead. "What's happened?"

From a pocket of her khaki shorts, Clarise had taken a

Kleenex. She was blotting her eyes. "Last week she said she knew now that Tom wasn't gone forever, that no one was ever gone forever. She seemed so *happy*. She was—"

"—radiant," Bob said, taking his wife's hand in his. "Joe, we don't know why really, with the depression gone and her being so full of plans for the first time in a year . . . but four days ago, my mom . . . she committed suicide."

The funeral had been held the previous day. Bob and Clarise didn't live here. They were staying only through Tuesday, packing Nora's clothes and personal effects for distribution to relatives and the Salvation Army Thrift Shop.

"It's so hard," Clarise said, unrolling and then rerolling the right sleeve on her white shirt as she talked. "She was such a sweet person."

"I shouldn't be here right now," Joe said, getting up from the armchair. "This isn't a good time."

Rising quickly, extending one hand almost pleadingly, Bob Vadance said, "No, please, sit down. Please. We need a break from the sorting . . . the packing. Talking to you . . . well . . ." He shrugged. He was all long arms and legs, graceful before but not now. "We all know what it's like. It's easier because—"

"—because we all know what it's like," Clarise finished.

After a hesitation, Joe sat in the armchair again. "I only have a few questions . . . and maybe only your mother could've answered them."

Having readjusted her right sleeve, Clarise unrolled and then rerolled the left. She needed to be doing something while she talked. Maybe she was afraid that her unoccupied hands would encourage her to express the grief that she was striving to control—perhaps by covering her face, by twisting and pulling her hair, or by curling into fists and striking something. "Joe . . . this heat . . . would you like something cold to drink?"

"No, thanks. Quick is better, and I'll go. What I wanted to ask your mother was if she'd been visited by anyone recently. By a woman who calls herself Rose."

Bob and Clarise exchanged a glance, and Bob said, "Would this be a black woman?"

A quiver passed through Joe. "Yes. Small, about five two, but with . . . real presence."

"Mom wouldn't say much about her," Clarise said, "but this Rose came once, and they talked, and it seemed as if something she told Mom was what made all the difference. We got the idea she was some sort of—"

"—spiritual adviser or something," Bob finished. "At first we didn't like the sound of it, thought it might be someone taking advantage of Mom, her being so down and vulnerable. We thought maybe this was some New Age crazy or—"

"—a con artist," Clarise continued, now leaning forward from the sofa to straighten the silk flowers in an arrangement on the coffee table. "Someone trying to rip her off or just mess with her mind."

"But when she talked about Rose, she was so—"

"—full of peace. It didn't seem this could be bad, not when it made Mom feel so much better. Anyway—"

"—she said this woman wasn't coming back," Bob finished. "Mom said, thanks to Rose, she knew Dad was somewhere safe. He hadn't just died and that was the end. He was somewhere safe and fine."

"She wouldn't tell us how she'd come around to this faith, when she'd never even been a churchgoer before," Clarise added. "Wouldn't say who Rose was or what Rose had told her."

"Wouldn't tell us much at all about the woman," Bob confirmed. "Just that it had to be a secret now, for a little while, but that eventually—"

"—everyone would know."

"Eventually everyone would know what?" Joe asked.

"That Dad was somewhere safe, I guess, somewhere safe and fine."

"No," Clarise said, finishing with the silk flowers, sitting back on the sofa, clasping her hands in her lap. "I think she meant more than that. I think she meant eventually everyone would know that none of us ever just dies, that we . . . go on somewhere safe."

Bob sighed. "I'll be frank with you, Joe. It made us a little nervous, hearing this superstitious stuff coming from my mother, who was always so down-to-earth. But it made her happy, and after the awfulness of the past year—"

"—we didn't see what harm it could do."

Spiritualism was not what Joe had expected. He was uneasy if not downright disappointed. He had thought that Dr. Rose Tucker knew what had really happened to Flight 353 and was prepared to finger those responsible. He had never imagined that what she had to offer was merely mysticism, spiritual counseling.

"Do you think she had an address for this Rose, a telephone number?"

Clarise said, "No. I don't think so. Mom was . . . mysterious about it." To her husband, she said, "Show him the picture."

"It's still in her bedroom," Bob said, rising from the sofa. "I'll get it."

"What picture?" Joe asked Clarise as Bob left the living room.

"Strange. It's one this Rose brought to Nora. It's kind

of creepy, but Mom took comfort from it. It's a photo of Tom's grave."

■

The photograph was a standard color print taken with a Polaroid camera. The shot showed the headstone at Thomas Lee Vadance's grave: his name, the dates of his birth and death, the words "cherished husband and beloved father."

In memory, Joe could see Rose Marie Tucker in the cemetery: *I'm not ready to talk to you yet.*

Clarise said, "Mom went out and bought the frame. She wanted to keep the picture behind glass. It was important to her that it not get damaged."

"While we were staying here last week, three full days, she carried it with her everywhere," Bob said. "Cooking in the kitchen, sitting in the family room watching TV, outside on the patio when we were barbecuing, always with her."

"Even when we went out to dinner," Clarise said. "She put it in her purse."

"It's just a photograph," Joe said, puzzled.

"Just a photograph," Bob Vadance agreed. "She could've taken it herself—but for some reason it meant more to her because this Rose woman had taken it."

Joe slid a finger down the smooth silver-plated frame and across the glass, as if he were clairvoyant and able to read the meaning of the photograph by absorbing a lingering psychic energy from it.

"When she first showed it to us," said Clarise, "she watched us with such . . . expectation. As if she thought—"

"—we would have a bigger reaction to it," Bob concluded.

Putting the photograph on the coffee table, Joe frowned. "Bigger reaction? Like how?"

"We couldn't understand," Clarise said. She picked up the photo and began to polish the frame and glass on her shirttail. "When we didn't respond to it the way she hoped, then she asked us what we saw when we looked at it."

"A gravestone," Joe said.

"Dad's grave," Bob agreed.

Clarise shook her head. "Mom seemed to see more."

"More? Like what?"

"She wouldn't say, but she—"

"—told us the day would come when we would see it different," Bob finished.

In memory, Rose in the graveyard, clutching the camera in two hands, looking up at Joe: *You'll see, like the others.*

■

"Do you know who this Rose is? Why did you ask us about her?" Clarise wondered.

Joe told them about meeting the woman at the cemetery, but he said nothing about the men in the white van. In his edited version, Rose had left in a car, and he had been unable to detain her.

"But from what she said to me . . . I thought she might have visited the families of some other crash victims. She told me not to despair, told me that I'd see, like the others had seen, but she wasn't ready to talk yet. The trouble is, I couldn't wait for her to be ready. If she's talked to others, I want to know what she told them, what she helped them to see."

"Whatever it was," Clarise said, "it made Mom feel better."

"Or did it?" Bob wondered.

"For a week, it did," Clarise said. "For a week she was happy."

"But it led to this," Bob said.

If Joe hadn't been a reporter with so many years of experience asking hard questions of victims and their families, he might have found it difficult to push Bob and Clarise to contemplate another grim possibility that would expose them to fresh anguish. But when the events of this extraordinary day were considered, the question had to be asked: "Are you absolutely sure that it was suicide?"

Bob started to speak, faltered, and turned his head away to blink back tears.

Taking her husband's hand, Clarise said to Joe, "There's no question. Nora killed herself."

"Did she leave a note?"

"No," Clarise said. "Nothing to help us understand."

"She was so happy, you said. Radiant. If—"

"She left a videotape," Clarise said.

"You mean, saying good-bye?"

"No. It's this strange . . . this terrible . . ." She shook her head, face twisting with distaste, at a loss for words to describe the video. Then: "It's this *thing*."

Bob let go of his wife's hand and got to his feet. "I'm not much of a drinking man, Joe, but I need a drink for this."

Dismayed, Joe said, "I don't want to add to your suffering—"

"No, it's all right," Bob assured him. "We're all of us out of that crash together, survivors together, family of a sort, and there shouldn't be anything you can't talk about with family. You want a drink?"

"Sure."

"Clarise, don't tell him about the video until I'm back. I know you think it'll be easier on me if you talk about it when I'm not in the room, but it won't."

Bob Vadance regarded his wife with great tenderness, and when she replied, "I'll wait," her love for him was so evident that Joe had to look away. He was too sharply reminded of what he had lost.

When Bob was out of the room, Clarise started to adjust the arrangement of silk flowers again. Then she sat with her elbows on her bare knees, her face buried in her hands.

When finally she looked up at Joe, she said, "He's a good man."

"I like him."

"Good husband, good son. People don't know him— they see the fighter pilot, served in the Gulf War, tough guy. But he's gentle too. Sentimental streak a mile wide, like his dad."

Joe waited for what she really wanted to tell him.

After a pause, she said, "We've been slow to have children. I'm thirty, Bob's thirty-two. There seemed to be so much time, so much to do first. But now our kids will grow up without ever knowing Bob's dad or mom, and they were such *good* people."

"It's not your fault," Joe said. "It's all out of our hands. We're just passengers on this train, we don't drive it, no matter how much we like to think we do."

"Have you really reached that level of acceptance?"

"Trying."

"Are you even close?"

"Shit, no."

She laughed softly.

Joe hadn't made anyone laugh in a year—except Rose's friend on the phone earlier. Although pain and irony colored Clarise's brief laughter, there was also relief in it. Having affected her this way, Joe felt a connection with life that had eluded him for so long.

After a silence, Clarise said, "Joe, could this Rose be an evil person?"

"No. Just the opposite."

Her freckled face, so open and trusting by nature, now clouded with doubt. "You sound so sure."

"You would be too, if you met her."

Bob Vadance returned with three glasses, a bowl of cracked ice, a liter of 7UP, and a bottle of Seagram's 7 Crown. "I'm afraid there's no real choice to offer," he apologized. "Nobody in this family's much of a drinker—but when we do take a touch, we like it simple."

"This is fine," Joe said, and accepted his 7-and-7 when it was ready.

They tasted their drinks—Bob had mixed them strong—and for a moment the only sound was the clinking of ice.

Clarise said, "We know it was suicide, because she taped it."

Certain that he had misunderstood, Joe said, "Who taped it?"

"Nora, Bob's mother," Clarise said. "She videotaped her own suicide."

■

Twilight evaporated in a steam of crimson and purple light, and out of that neon vapor, night coalesced against the windows of the yellow and white living room.

Quickly and succinctly, with commendable self-control, Clarise revealed what she knew of her mother-in-law's horrible death. She spoke in a low voice, yet every word was bell-note clear and seemed to reverberate through Joe until he gradually began to tremble with the cumulative vibrations.

Bob Vadance finished none of his wife's sentences. He remained silent throughout, looking at neither Clarise nor Joe. He stared at his drink, to which he resorted frequently.

The compact Sanyo 8mm camcorder that had captured the death was Tom Vadance's toy. It had been stored in the closet in his study since before his death aboard Flight 353.

The camera was easy to use. Fuzzy-logic technology automatically adjusted the shutter speed and white balance. Though Nora had never had much experience with it, she could have learned the essentials of its operation in a few minutes.

The nicad battery had not contained much juice after a year in the closet. Therefore, Nora Vadance had taken time to recharge it, indicating a chilling degree of premeditation. The police found the AC adaptor and the battery charger plugged into an outlet on the kitchen counter.

Tuesday morning of this week, Nora went outside to the back of the house and set the camcorder on a patio table. She used two paperback books as shims to tilt the camera to the desired angle, and then she switched it on.

With the videotape rolling, she positioned a vinyl-strap patio chair ten feet from the lens. She revisited the camcorder to peer through the viewfinder, to be sure that the chair was in the center of the frame.

After returning to the chair and slightly repositioning it, she completely disrobed in view of the camcorder, neither in the manner of a performer nor with any hesitancy but simply as though she were getting ready for a bath. She neatly folded her blouse, her slacks, and her underwear, and she put them aside on the flagstone floor of the patio.

Naked, she walked out of camera range, apparently going into the house, to the kitchen. In forty seconds, when she returned, she was carrying a butcher knife. She sat in the chair, facing the camcorder.

According to the medical examiner's preliminary report, at approximately ten minutes past eight o'clock, Tuesday morning, Nora Vadance, in good health and previously thought to be of sound mind, having recently rebounded from depression over her husband's death, took her own life. Gripping the handle of the butcher knife in both hands, with savage force, she drove the blade deep into her abdomen. She extracted it and stabbed herself again. The third time, she pulled the blade left to right, eviscerating herself. Dropping the knife, she slumped in the chair, where she bled to death in less than one minute.

The camcorder continued to record the corpse to the end of the twenty-minute 8mm cassette.

Two hours later, at ten-thirty, Takashi Mishima, a sixty-six-year-old gardener on his scheduled rounds, discovered the body and immediately called the police.

■

When Clarise finished, Joe could say only, "Jesus."

Bob added whiskey to their drinks. His hands were shaking, and the bottle rattled against each glass.

Finally Joe said, "I gather the police have the tape."

"Yeah," Bob said. "Until the hearing or inquest or whatever it is they have to hold."

"So I hope this video is secondhand knowledge to you. I hope neither of you had to see it."

"I haven't," Bob said. "But Clarise did."

She was staring into her drink. "They told us what was

in it . . . but neither Bob nor I could believe it, even though they were the police, even though they had no reason to lie to us. So I went into the station on Friday morning, before the funeral, and watched it. We had to know. And now we do. When they give us the tape back, I'll destroy it. Bob should never see it. Never."

Though Joe's respect for this woman was already high, she rose dramatically in his esteem.

"There are some things I'm wondering about," he said. "If you don't mind some questions."

"Go ahead," Bob said. "We have a lot of questions about it too, a thousand damn questions."

"First . . . it doesn't sound like there could be any possibility of duress."

Clarise shook her head. "It's not something you could force anyone to do to herself, is it? Not just with psychological pressure or threats. Besides, there wasn't anyone else in camera range—and no shadows of anyone. Her eyes didn't focus on anyone off camera. She was alone."

"When you described the tape, Clarise, it sounded as if Nora was going through this like a machine."

"That was the way she looked during most of it. No expression, her face just . . . slack."

"During *most* of it? So there was a moment she showed emotion?"

"Twice. After she'd almost completely undressed, she hesitated before taking off . . . her panties. She was a modest woman, Joe. That's one more weird thing about all of this."

Eyes closed, holding his cold glass of 7-and-7 against his forehead, Bob said, "Even if . . . even if we accept that she was so mentally disturbed she could do this to herself, it's hard to picture her videotaping herself naked . . . or wanting to be found that way."

Clarise said, "There's a high fence around the back-yard. Thick bougainvillea on it. The neighbors couldn't have seen her. But Bob's right . . . she wouldn't want to be found like that. Anyway, as she was about to take off the panties, she hesitated. Finally that dead, slack look dissolved. Just for an instant, this terrible expression came across her face."

"Terrible how?" Joe asked.

Grimacing as she conjured the grisly video in her mind, Clarise described the moment as if she were seeing it again: "Her eyes are flat, blank, the lids a little heavy . . . then all of a sudden they go wide and there's depth to them, like normal eyes. Her face *wrenches*. First so expressionless but now *torn* with emotion. Shock. She looks so shocked, terrified. A lost expression that breaks your heart. But it lasts only a second or two, maybe three seconds, and now she shudders, and the look is gone, gone, and she's as calm as a machine again. She takes off her panties, folds them, and puts them aside."

"Was she on any medication?" Joe asked. "Any reason to believe she might have overdosed on something that induced a fugue state or a severe personality change?"

Clarise said, "Her doctor tells us he hadn't prescribed any medication for her. But because of her demeanor on the video, the police suspect drugs. The medical examiner is running toxicological tests."

"Which is ridiculous," Bob said forcefully. "My mother would never take illegal drugs. She didn't even like to take aspirin. She was such an *innocent* person, Joe, as if she wasn't even aware of all the changes for the worse in the world over the last thirty years, as if she was living decades behind the rest of us and happy to be there."

"There was an autopsy," Clarise said. "No brain tumor,

brain lesions, no medical condition that might explain what she did."

"You mentioned a second time when she showed some emotion."

"Just before she . . . before she stabbed herself. It was just a flicker, even briefer than the first. Like a spasm. Her whole face wrenched as if she were going to scream. Then it was gone, and she remained expressionless to the end."

Jolted by a realization he had failed to reach when Clarise had first described the video, Joe said, "You mean she *never* screamed, cried out?"

"No. Never."

"But that's impossible."

"Right at the end, when she drops the knife . . . there's a soft sound that may be from her, hardly more than a sigh."

"The pain . . ." Joe couldn't bring himself to say that Nora Vadance's pain must have been excruciating.

"But she never screamed," Clarise insisted.

"Even involuntary response would have—"

"Silent. She was silent."

"The microphone was working?"

"Built-in, omnidirectional mike," Bob said.

"On the video," Clarise said, "you can hear other sounds. The scrape of the patio chair on the concrete when she repositions it. Bird songs. One sad-sounding dog barking in the distance. But nothing from her."

■

Stepping out of the front door, Joe searched the night, half expecting to see a white van or another suspicious-looking vehicle parked on the street in front of the Vadance place. From the house next door came the faint strains of Beethoven. The air was warm, but a soft breeze had sprung up from the west, bringing with it the fragrance of night-blooming jasmine. As far as Joe could discern, there was nothing menacing in this gracious night.

As Clarise and Bob followed him onto the porch, Joe said, "When they found Nora, was the photograph of Tom's grave with her?"

Bob said, "No. It was on the kitchen table. At the very end, she didn't carry it with her."

"We found it on the table when we arrived from San Diego," Clarise recalled. "Beside her breakfast plate."

Joe was surprised. "She'd eaten breakfast?"

"I know what you're thinking," Clarise said. "If she was going to kill herself, why bother with breakfast? It's even weirder than that, Joe. She'd made an omelet with Cheddar and chopped scallions and ham. Toast on the side. A glass of fresh-squeezed orange juice. She was halfway through eating it when she got up and went outside with the camcorder."

"The woman you described on the video was deeply depressed or in an altered state of some kind. How could she have had the mental clarity or the patience to make such a complicated breakfast?"

Clarise said, "And consider this—the *Los Angeles Times* was open beside her plate—"

"—and she was reading the comics," Bob finished.

For a moment they were silent, pondering the imponderable.

Then Bob said, "You see what I meant earlier when I said we have a thousand questions of our own."

As though they were friends of long acquaintance, Clarise put her arms around Joe and hugged him. "I hope this Rose is a good person, like you think. I hope you find her. And whatever she has to tell you, I hope it brings you some peace, Joe."

Moved, he returned her embrace. "Thanks, Clarise."

Bob had written their Miramar address and telephone number on a page from a note pad. He gave the folded slip of paper to Joe. "In case you have any more questions . . . or if you learn anything that might help us understand."

They shook hands. The handshake became a brotherly hug.

Clarise said, "What'll you do now, Joe?"

He checked the luminous dial of his watch. "It's only a few minutes past nine. I'm going to try to see another of the families tonight."

"Be careful," she said.

"I will."

"Something's wrong, Joe. Something's wrong big time."

"I know."

Bob and Clarise were still standing on the porch, side by side, watching Joe as he drove away.

Although he'd finished more than half of his second drink, Joe felt no effect from the 7-and-7. He had never seen a picture of Nora Vadance; nevertheless, the mental image he held of a faceless woman in a patio chair with a butcher knife was sufficiently sobering to counter twice the amount of whiskey that he had drunk.

The metropolis glowed, a luminous fungus festering along the coast. Like spore clouds, the sour-yellow radiance rose and smeared the sky. Only a few stars were visible: icy, distant light.

A minute ago, the night had seemed gracious, and he had seen nothing to fear in it. Now it *loomed*, and he repeatedly checked his rearview mirror.

8

Charles and Georgine Delmann lived in an enormous Georgian house on a half-acre lot in Hancock Park. A pair of magnolia trees framed the entrance to the front walk, which was flanked by knee-high box hedges so neatly groomed that they appeared to have been trimmed by legions of gardeners with cuticle scissors. The extremely rigid geometry of the house and grounds revealed a need for order, a faith in the superiority of human arrangement over the riot of nature.

The Delmanns were physicians. He was an internist specializing in cardiology, and she was both internist and ophthalmologist. They were prominent in the community, because in addition to their regular medical practices, they had founded and continued to oversee a free clinic for children in East Los Angeles and another in South Central.

When the 747-400 fell, the Delmanns lost their eighteen-year-old daughter, Angela, who had been returning from an invitation-only, six-week watercolor workshop at a university in New York, to prepare for her first year at art school in San Francisco. Apparently, she had been a talented painter with considerable promise.

Georgine Delmann herself answered the door. Joe recognized her from her photo in one of the *Post* articles about the crash. She was in her late forties, tall and slim,

118

with richly glowing dusky skin, masses of curly dark hair, and lively eyes as purple-black as plums. Hers was a wild beauty, and she assiduously tamed it with steel-frame eyeglasses instead of contacts, no makeup, and gray slacks and white blouse that were manly in style.

When Joe told her his name, before he could say that his family had been on Flight 353, she exclaimed, to his surprise, "My God, we were just talking about you!"

"Me?"

Grabbing his hand, pulling him across the threshold into the marble-floored foyer, pushing the door shut with her hip, she didn't take her astonished gaze from him. "Lisa was telling us about your wife and daughters, about how you just dropped out, went away. But now here you are, here you are."

"Lisa?" he said, perplexed.

This night, at least, the sober-physician disguise of her severe clothes and steel-rimmed spectacles could not conceal the sparkling depths of Georgine Delmann's natural ebullience. She threw her arms around Joe and kissed him on the cheek so hard that he was rocked back on his heels. Then face-to-face with him, searching his eyes, she said excitedly, "She's been to see you too, hasn't she?"

"Lisa?"

"No, no, not Lisa. *Rose.*"

An inexplicable hope skipped like a thrown stone across the lake-dark surface of his heart. "Yes. But—"

"Come, come with me." Clutching his hand again, pulling him out of the foyer and along a hall toward the back of the house, she said, "We're back here, at the kitchen table—me and Charlie and Lisa."

At meetings of The Compassionate Friends, Joe had never seen any bereaved parent capable of this *effervescence.* He'd never heard of such a creature, either. Parents who lost young children spent five or six years—sometimes a decade or even more—striving, often fruitlessly, merely to overcome the conviction that they themselves should be dead instead of their offspring, that outliving their children was sinful or selfish—or even monstrously wicked. It wasn't much different for those who, like the Delmanns, had lost an eighteen-year-old. In fact, it was no different for a sixty-year-old parent who lost a thirty-year-old child. Age had nothing to do with it. The loss of a child at any stage of life is unnatural, so *wrong* that purpose is difficult to rediscover. Even when acceptance is achieved and a degree of happiness attained, joy often remains elusive forever, like a promise of water in a dry well once brimming but now holding only the deep, damp smell of past sustenance.

Yet here was Georgine Delmann, flushed and sparkling, girlishly excited, as she pulled Joe to the end of the hallway and through a swinging door. She seemed not merely to have recovered from the loss of her daughter in one short year but to have transcended it.

Joe's brief hope faded, for it seemed to him that Georgine Delmann must be either out of her mind or incomprehensibly shallow. Her apparent joy shocked him.

The lights were dimmed in the kitchen, but he could see that the space was cozy in spite of being large, with a maple floor, maple cabinetry, and sugar-brown granite counters. From overhead racks, in the low amber light, gleaming copper pots and pans and utensils dangled like festoons of temple bells waiting for the vespers hour.

Leading Joe across the kitchen to a breakfast table in a bay-window alcove, Georgine Delmann said, "Charlie, Lisa, look who's here! It's almost a miracle, isn't it?"

Beyond the beveled-glass windows was a backyard and pool, which outdoor lighting had transformed into a storybook scene full of sparkle and glister. On the oval table this side of the window were three decorative glass oil lamps with flames adance on floating wicks.

Beside the table stood a tall, good-looking man with thick silver hair: Dr. Charles Delmann.

As Georgine approached with Joe in tow, she said, "Charlie, it's Joe Carpenter. *The* Joe Carpenter."

Staring at Joe with something like wonder, Charlie Delmann came forward and vigorously shook his hand. "What's happening here, son?"

"I wish I knew," Joe said.

"Something strange and wonderful is happening," Delmann said, as transported by emotion as was his wife.

Rising from a chair at the table, blond hair further gilded by the lambent light of the oil lamps, was the Lisa to whom Georgine had referred. She was in her forties, with the smooth face of a college girl and faded-denim eyes that had seen more than one level of Hell.

Joe knew her well. Lisa Peccatone. She worked for the *Post*. A former colleague. An investigative reporter specializing in stories about particularly heinous criminals— serial killers, child abusers, rapists who mutilated their victims—she was driven by an obsession that Joe had never fully understood, prowling the bleakest chambers of the human heart, compelled to immerse herself in stories of blood and madness, seeking meaning in the most meaningless acts of human savagery. He sensed that a long time ago she had endured unspeakable offenses, had come out of childhood with a beast on her back, and could not shrive herself of the demon memory other than by struggling to *understand* what could never be understood. She was one of the kindest people he had ever known and one of the angriest, brilliant and deeply troubled, fearless but haunted, able to write prose so fine that it could lift the hearts of angels or strike terror into the hollow chests of devils. Joe admired the hell out of her. She was one of his best friends, yet he had abandoned her with all of his other friends when he had followed his lost family into a graveyard of the heart.

"Joey," she said, "you worthless sonofabitch, are you back on the job or are you here just because you're part of the story?"

"I'm on the job *because* I'm part of the story. But I'm not writing again. Don't have much faith in the power of words anymore."

"I don't have much faith in anything else."

"What're you doing here?" he asked.

"We called her just a few hours ago," said Georgine. "We asked her to come."

"No offense," Charlie said, clapping a hand on Joe's shoulder, "but Lisa's the only reporter we ever knew that we have a lot of respect for."

"Almost a decade now," Georgine said, "she's been doing eight hours a week of volunteer work at one of the free clinics we operate for disadvantaged kids."

Joe hadn't known this about Lisa and wouldn't have suspected it.

She could not repress a crooked, embarrassed smile. "Yeah, Joey, I'm a regular Mother Teresa. But listen, you shithead, don't you ruin my reputation by telling people at the *Post.*"

"I want some wine. Who wants wine? A good Chardonnay, maybe a Cakebread or a Grgich Hills," Charlie enthused. He was infected with his wife's inappropriate good cheer, as if they were gathered on this solemn night of nights to *celebrate* the crash of Flight 353.

"Not for me," Joe said, increasingly disoriented.

"I'll have some," Lisa said.

"Me too," Georgine said. "I'll get the glasses."

"No, honey, sit, you sit here with Joe and Lisa," Charlie said. "I'll take care of everything."

As Joe and the women settled into chairs around the table, Charlie went to the far end of the kitchen.

Georgine's face was aglow with light from the oil lamps. "This is incredible, just incredible. Rose has been to see him too, Lisa."

Lisa Peccatone's face was half in lamplight but half in shadow. "When, Joe?"

"Today in the cemetery. Taking photographs of Michelle's and the girls' graves. She said she wasn't ready to talk to me yet . . . and went away."

Joe decided to reserve the rest of his story until he heard theirs, both in the interest of hastening their revelations and to ensure that their recitations were not colored too much by what he revealed.

"It can't have been her," Lisa said. "She died in the crash."

"That's the official story."

"Describe her," Lisa requested.

Joe went through the standard catalogue of physical details, but he spent as much time trying to convey the black woman's singular presence, the magnetism that almost seemed to bend her surroundings to her personal lines of force.

The eye in the shadowed side of Lisa's smooth face was dark and enigmatic, but the eye in the lamplit half revealed emotional turmoil as she responded to the description that Joe gave her. "Rosie always was charismatic, even in college."

Surprised, Joe said, "You know her?"

"We went to UCLA together too long ago to think about. We were roomies. We stayed reasonably close over the years."

"That's why Charlie and I decided to call Lisa a little while ago," said Georgine. "We knew she'd had a friend on Flight 353. But it was in the middle of the night, hours after Rose left here, that Charlie remembered Lisa's friend was also named Rose. We knew they must be one and the same, and we've been trying all day to decide what to do about Lisa."

"When was Rose here?" Joe asked.

"Yesterday evening," Georgine said. "She showed up just as we were on our way out to dinner. Made us promise to tell no one what she told us . . . not until she'd had a chance to see a few more of the victims' families here in L.A. But Lisa had been so depressed last year, with the news, and since she and Rose were such friends, we didn't see what harm it could do."

"I'm not here as a reporter," Lisa told Joe.

"You're always a reporter."

Georgine said, "Rose gave us this."

From her shirt pocket she withdrew a photograph and put it on the table. It was a shot of Angela Delmann's gravestone.

Eyes shining expectantly, Georgine said, "What do you see there, Joe?"

"I think the real question is what *you* see."

Elsewhere in the kitchen, Charlie Delmann opened drawers and sorted through the clattering contents, evidently searching for a corkscrew.

"We've already told Lisa." Georgine glanced across the room. "I'll wait until Charlie's here to tell you, Joe."

Lisa said, "It's damned weird, Joey, and I'm not sure what to make of what they've said. All I know is it scares the crap out of me."

"Scares you?" Georgine was astonished. "Lisa, dear, how on earth could it scare you?"

"You'll see," Lisa told Joe. This woman, usually blessed with the strength of stones, shivered like a reed. "But I guarantee you, Charlie and Georgine are two of the most level-headed people I know. Which you're sure going to need to keep in mind when they get started."

Picking up the Polaroid snapshot, Georgine gazed needfully at it, as though she wished not merely to burn it into her memory but to absorb the image and make it a physical part of her, leaving the film blank.

With a sigh, Lisa launched into a revelation: "I have my own weird piece to add to the puzzle, Joey. A year ago tonight, I was at LAX, waiting for Rosie's plane to land."

Georgine looked up from the photo. "You didn't tell us that."

"I was about to," Lisa said, "when Joey rang the doorbell."

At the far end of the kitchen, with a soft *pop*, a stubborn cork came free from a wine bottle, and Charlie Delmann grunted with satisfaction.

"I didn't see you at the airport that night, Lisa," Joe said.

"I was keeping a low profile. Torn up about Rosie but also . . . flat out scared."

"You were there to pick her up?"

"Rosie called me from New York and asked me to be at LAX with Bill Hannett."

Hannett was the photographer whose images of natural and man-made disasters hung on the walls of the reception lounge at the *Post*.

The pale-blue fabric of Lisa's eyes was worn now with worry. "Rosie desperately needed to talk to a reporter, and I was the only one she knew she could trust."

"Charlie," Georgine said, "you've got to come hear this."

"I can hear, I can hear," Charlie assured her. "Just pouring now. A minute."

"Rosie also gave me a list—six other people she wanted there," Lisa said. "Friends from years back. I managed to locate five of them on short notice and bring them with me that night. They were to be witnesses."

Rapt, Joe said, "Witnesses to what?"

"I don't know. She was so guarded. Excited, really *excited* about something, but also frightened. She said she was going to be getting off that plane with something that would change all of us forever, change the world."

"Change the world?" Joe said. "Every politician with a scheme and every actor with a rare thought thinks he can change the world these days."

"Oh, but in this case, Rose was right," Georgine said. Barely contained tears of excitement or joy shone in her eyes as she showed him the gravestone photo once more. "It's wonderful."

If he had fallen down the White Rabbit's hole, Joe didn't notice the plunge, but the territory in which he now found himself was increasingly surrealistic.

The flames in the oil lamps, which had been steady, flared and writhed in the tall glass chimneys, drawn upward by a draft that Joe could not feel.

Salamanders of yellow light wriggled across the previously dark side of Lisa's face. When she looked at the lamps, her eyes were as yellow as moons low on the horizon.

Quickly the flames subsided, and Lisa said, "Yeah, sure, it sounded melodramatic. But Rosie is no bullshit artist. And she *has* been working on something of enormous importance for six or seven years. I believed her."

Between the kitchen and the downstairs hall, the swinging door made its distinctive sound. Charlie Delmann had left the room without explanation.

"Charlie?" Georgine rose from her chair. "Now where's he gone? I can't believe he's missing this."

To Joe, Lisa said, "When I spoke to her on the phone a few hours before she boarded Flight 353, Rosie told me they were looking for her. She didn't think they would expect her to show up in L.A. But just in case they figured out what flight she was on, in case they were waiting for her, Rosie wanted *us* there too, so we could surround her the minute she got off the plane and prevent them from silencing her. She was going to give me the whole story right there at the debarkation gate."

"They?" Joe asked.

Georgine had started after Charlie to see where he'd gone, but interest in Lisa's story got the better of her, and she returned to her chair.

Lisa said, "Rosie was talking about the people she works for."

"Teknologik."

"You've been busy today, Joey."

"Busy trying to understand," he said, his mind now swimming through a swamp of hideous possibilities.

"You and me and Rosie all connected. Small world, huh?"

Sickened to think there were people murderous enough to kill three hundred and twenty-nine innocent bystanders merely to get at their true target, Joe said, "Lisa, dear God, tell me you don't think that plane was brought down just because Rose Tucker was on it."

Staring out at the shimmering blue light of the pool, Lisa thought about her answer before giving it. "That night I was sure of it. But then . . . the investigation showed no sign of a bomb. No probable cause really fixed. If anything, it was a combination of a minor mechanical error and human error on the part of the pilots."

"At least that's what we've been told."

"I spent time quietly looking into the National Transportation Safety Board, not on this crash so much as in general. They have an impeccable record, Joey. They're good people. No corruption. They're even pretty much above politics."

Georgine said, "But I believe Rose thinks she was responsible for what happened. She's convinced that her being there was the cause of it."

"But if she's even indirectly responsible for the death of your daughter," Joe said, "why do you find her so wonderful?"

Georgine's smile was surely no different from the one with which she had greeted—and charmed—him at the front door. To Joe, however, in his growing disorientation, her expression seemed to be as strange and unsettling as might be the smile on a clown encountered in a fog-threaded alley after midnight, alarming because it was so profoundly out of place. Through her disturbing smile, she said, "You want to know why, Joe? Because this is the end of the world as we know it."

To Lisa, Joe said exasperatedly, "Who *is* Rose Tucker, what does she do for Teknologik?"

"She's a geneticist, and a brilliant one."

"Specializing in recombinant DNA research." Georgine held up the Polaroid again, as if Joe should be able to grasp at once how the photo of a gravestone and genetic engineering were related.

"Exactly what she was doing for Teknologik," Lisa said, "I never knew. That's what she was going to tell me when she landed at LAX a year ago tonight. Now, because of what she told Georgine and Charlie yesterday . . . I can pretty much figure it out. I just don't know how to believe it."

Joe wondered about her odd locution: not *whether* to believe it, but *how* to believe it.

"What is Teknologik—besides what it appears to be?" he asked.

Lisa smiled thinly. "You have a good nose, Joe. A year

off hasn't dulled your sense of smell. From things Rosie said over the years, vague references, I think you're looking at a singularity in a capitalist world—a company that can't fail."

"Can't fail?" Georgine asked.

"Because behind it there's a generous partner that covers all the losses."

"The military?" Joe wondered.

"Or some branch of government. Some organization with deeper pockets than any individual in the world. I got the sense, from Rosie, that this project wasn't funded with just a hundred million of research and development funds. We're talking major capital on the line here. There were billions behind this."

From upstairs came the boom of a gunshot.

Even muffled by intervening rooms, the nature of the sound was unmistakable.

The three of them came to their feet as one, and Georgine said, "Charlie?"

Perhaps because he had so recently sat with Bob and Clarise in that cheery yellow living room in Culver City, Joe immediately thought of Nora Vadance naked in the patio chair, the butcher knife grasped in both hands with the point toward her abdomen.

In the wake of the gunshot's echo, the silence settling down through the house seemed as deadly as the invisible and weightless rain of atomic radiation in the sepulchral stillness following nuclear thunder.

Alarm growing, Georgine shouted, "Charlie!"

As Georgine started away from the table, Joe restrained her. "No, wait, wait. I'll go. Call 911, and I'll go."

Lisa said, "Joey—"

"I know what this is," he said, sharply enough to forestall further discussion.

He hoped that he was wrong, that he didn't know what

was happening here, that it had nothing to do with what
Nora Vadance had done to herself. But if he was right,
then he couldn't allow Georgine to be the first on the
scene. In fact, she shouldn't have to see the aftermath at
all, not now or later.

"I know what this is. Call 911," Joe repeated as he
crossed the kitchen and pushed through the swinging
door into the downstairs hall.

In the foyer, the chandelier dimmed and brightened,
dimmed and brightened, like the flickering lights in one
of those old prison movies when the governor's call
came too late and the condemned man was fried in the
electric chair.

Joe ran to the foot of the stairs but then was slowed by
dread as he ascended toward the second floor, terrified
that he would find what he expected.

A plague of suicide was as irrational a concept as any
brewed in the stew-pot minds of those people who thought
that the mayor was a robot and that evil aliens were
watching them every moment of the day. Joe couldn't
comprehend how Charlie Delmann could have gone from
near euphoria to despair in the space of two minutes—as
Nora Vadance had gone from a pleasant breakfast and the
newspaper comics pages to self-evisceration without even
pausing to leave a note of explanation.

If Joe was right about the meaning of the shot, however, there was a slim chance that the doctor was still
alive. Maybe he hadn't done himself in with only one
round. Maybe he could still be saved.

The prospect of saving a life, after so many had
slipped like water through his hands, pushed Joe forward
in spite of his dread. He climbed the rest of the stairs two
at a time.

On the second floor, with barely a glance, he passed

unlighted rooms and closed doors. At the end of the hallway, from behind a half-open door, came ruddy light.

The master suite was entered through a small foyer of its own. Beyond lay the bedroom, furnished with bone-colored contemporary upholstery. The graceful pale-green curves of Sung Dynasty pottery, displayed on glass shelves, imposed serenity on the chamber.

Dr. Charles Delmann was sprawled on a Chinese sleigh bed. Across him lay a Mossberg 12-gauge, pump-action, pistol-grip shotgun. Because of the short barrel, he had been able to put the muzzle between his teeth and easily reach the trigger. Even in the poor light, Joe could see there was no reason to check for a pulse.

The celadon lamp on the farther of the two nightstands provided the only illumination. The glow was ruddy because the shade was splashed with blood.

On a Saturday night ten months ago, in the course of covering a story, Joe had visited the city morgue, where the bagged bodies on the gurneys and the naked bodies on the autopsy tables waited for the attention of over-worked pathologists. Abruptly he was gripped by the irrational conviction that the cadavers surrounding him were those of his wife and children; *all* of them were Michelle and the girls, as though Joe had wandered into a scene in a science fiction movie about clones. And from within the body-size drawers of the stainless-steel coolers, where more of the dead rested between destina-tions, arose the muffled voices of Michelle, Chrissie, little Nina, pleading with him to release them to the world of the living. Beside him, a coroner's assistant zipped open a body bag, and Joe looked down into the winter-white face of a dead woman, her painted mouth like a poinsettia leaf crumpled on snow, and he saw Michelle, Chrissie, Nina. The dead woman's blind blue eyes were mirrors of his own soaring madness. He had walked out of the morgue and submitted his resignation to Caesar Santos, his editor.

Now, he quickly turned away from the bed before any beloved faces materialized over that of the dead physician.

An eerie wheezing came to his attention, and for an instant he thought that Delmann was straining to draw breath through his shattered face. Then he realized that he was listening to his own ragged breathing.

On the nearer nightstand, the lighted green numbers on a digital clock were flashing. Time changes were occurring at a frantic pace: ten minutes with every flash, the hours reversing through the early evening and backward into the afternoon.

Joe had the crazy thought that the malfunctioning clock—which must have been hit by a stray shotgun pellet—might magically undo all that had happened, that Delmann might rise from death as the pellets rattled backward into the barrel and torn flesh reknit, that in a moment Joe himself might be on the Santa Monica beach once more, in the sun, and then back in his one-room apartment in the moon-deep night, on the telephone with Beth in Virginia, and backward, still backward, until Flight 353 had not yet gone down in Colorado.

From downstairs came a scream, imploding his desperate fantasy. Then another scream.

He thought it was Lisa. As tough as she was, she had probably never before screamed in her life, yet this was a cry of sheerest child-like terror.

He had been gone from the kitchen for at most a minute. What could have happened in a minute, so fast?

He reached toward the shotgun, intending to pluck it off the corpse. The magazine might contain other rounds.

No. Now it's a suicide scene. Move the weapon, and it looks like a murder scene. With me as the suspect.

He left the gun untouched.

Out of the thin blood-filtered light, into the hallway where a funerary stillness of shadows stood sentinel, toward the enormous chandelier that hung in a perpetual crystal rain above the foyer staircase, he ran.

The shotgun was useless. He wasn't capable of firing it at anyone. Besides, who was in the house but Georgine and Lisa? No one. No one.

Down the stairs two at a time, three at a time, under the crystal cascade of beveled teardrops, he grabbed at the banister to keep his balance. His palm, slick with cold sweat, slid across the mahogany.

Along the lower hall in a thunder of footsteps, he heard jangly music, and as he slammed through the swinging door, he saw pendulous copper pots and pans swinging on the racks overhead, gently clinking together.

The kitchen was as softly lit as it had been when he left. The overhead halogen downlights were dimmed so low as to be all but extinguished.

At the far end of the room, backlit by the quivering glow of the three decorative oil lamps on the table, Lisa stood with her fists pressed to her temples, as if struggling to contain a skull-cracking pressure. No longer screaming, she sobbed, groaned, shuddered out whispery words that might have been *Oh God, oh God.*

Georgine was not in sight.

As the copper chimes subsided like the soft dissonant music in a dream of trolls, Joe hurried toward Lisa, and from the corner of his eye, he glimpsed the open wine bottle where Charlie Delmann had left it on the island counter. Beside the bottle were three glasses of Chardonnay. The tremulous surface of each serving glimmered jewel-like, and Joe wondered fleetingly if something had been in the wine—poison, chemical, drug.

When Lisa saw Joe approaching, she lowered her

hands from her temples and opened her fists, wet and red, rose-petal fingers adrip with dew. A stinging salt of sounds shook from her, pure animal emotion, more raw with grief and burning hotter with terror than any words could have.

At the end of the center island, on the floor in front of Lisa, Georgine Delmann was on her side in the fetal position, curled not in an unborn's anticipation of life but in an embrace of death, both hands still impossibly clenched on the handle of the knife that was her cold umbilical. Her mouth was twisted in a scream never voiced. Her eyes were wide, welling with terminal tears, but without depth.

The stink of evisceration hit Joe hard enough to knock him to the edge of an anxiety attack: the familiar sense of falling, falling as from a great height. If he succumbed to it, he would be of no use to anyone, no help to Lisa or to himself.

With little effort, he looked away from the horror on the floor. With a much greater effort, he willed himself back from the brink of emotional dissolution.

He turned toward Lisa to hold her, to comfort her, to move her away from the sight of her dead friend, but her back was now toward him.

Glass shattered, and Joe flinched. He thought wildly that some murderous adversary was breaking into the kitchen through the windows.

The breaking was not windows but glass oil lamps, which Lisa had grasped like bottles, by their tall chimneys. She had smashed the bulbous bases together, and a viscous spray of oil had burst from them.

Bright points of flame irised wider on the tabletop, became glaring pools of fire.

Joe grabbed her and tried to pull her away from the

spreading blaze, but without a word, she wrenched loose of him and seized the third lamp.

"Lisa!"

Granite and bronze ignited in the Polaroid of Angela Delmann's grave, image and medium curling like a black burnt leaf.

Lisa tipped the third lamp, pouring the oil and the floating wick across the front of her dress.

For an instant Joe was immobilized by shock.

The oil washed Lisa, but somehow the slithering spot of flame slipped along the bodice and waist of her dress and was extinguished in the skirt.

On the table, the blazing pools overlapped, and molten streams flowed to all edges. Incandescent drizzle sizzled to the floor.

Joe reached for her again, but as if dipping into a wash basin, she scooped handfuls of flames off the table, splashing them against her breast. As Lisa's oil-soaked clothes exploded with fire, Joe snatched his hand back from her and cried, *"No!"*

Without a scream, which at least she had managed in reaction to Georgine's suicide, without a groan or even as much as a whimper, she raised her hands, in which balls of flame roiled. She stood briefly like the ancient goddess Diana with fiery moons balanced on her palms, and she brought her hands to her face, to her hair.

Joe reeled backward from the burning woman, from the sight that scorched his heart, from the hideous stench that withered him, from an insoluble mystery that left him empty of hope. He collided with cabinetry.

Remaining miraculously on her feet, as calm as though standing only in a cool rain, reflected in every angle of the big bay window, Lisa turned as if to look at Joe through her fuming veil. Mercifully, he could see nothing of her face.

Paralyzed by horror, he realized he was going to die next, not from the flames that licked the maple flooring around his shoes but by his own hand, in some fashion as monstrous as a self-inflicted shotgun wound, self-evisceration, self-immolation. The plague of suicide had not yet infected him, but it would claim him the moment that Lisa, entirely dead, crumpled in a heap on the floor—and yet he could not move.

Wrapped in a whirlwind of tempestuous flames, she flung off phantoms of light and ghosts of shadow, which crawled up the walls and swarmed across the ceiling, and some shadows were shadows, but some were unspooling ribbons of soot.

The bone-piercing shriek of the kitchen smoke alarm cracked the ice in Joe's marrow. He was jarred out of his trance.

He ran with the phantoms and the ghosts, out of that hell, past suspended copper pots like bright blank faces in a forge light, past three glasses of Chardonnay sparkling with images of flames and now the color of claret.

Through the swinging door, along the hallway, across the foyer, Joe felt closely pursued by something more than the blatting of the smoke alarm, as though a killer had been in the kitchen, after all, standing so still in a darkish corner that he had watched unnoticed. At the front door, as Joe grasped the knob, he expected a hand to drop upon his shoulder, expected to be spun around and confronted by a smiling assassin.

From behind him came not a hand and not, as he might have expected, a blast of heat, but a hissing cold that first prickled the nape of his neck and then seemed to drill into the summit of his spine, through the base of his skull. He was so panicked that he did not remember opening the door or leaving the house, but found himself crossing the porch, casting off the chill.

He hurried along the brick walk between the perfect box hedges. When he reached the pair of matched magnolias, where large flowers like the white faces of monkeys peered from among the glossy leaves, he glanced back. He was not, after all, being pursued by anyone.

The residential street was quiet but for the muffled blaring of the smoke alarms in the Delmann house: no traffic at the moment, no one out for a walk in the warm August night. On nearby porches and lawns, no one had yet been drawn outside by the commotion. Here the properties were so large and the stately houses so solidly built, with thick walls, that the screams might not have penetrated to the attention of the neighbors, and even the single gunshot might have been apprehended only as a car door slamming or a truck backfiring.

He considered waiting for the firemen and police, but he could not imagine how he would convincingly describe what had transpired in that house in a mere three or four hellish minutes. As he had lived those feverish events, they had seemed hallucinatory, from the sound of the shotgun to the moment when Lisa swathed herself in flames; and now they were like fragments of a deeper dream in the ongoing nightmare of his life.

The fire would destroy much of the evidence of suicide, and the police would detain him for questioning—then possibly on suspicion of murder. They would see a deeply troubled man who had lost his way after losing his family, who held no job, who lived in one room above a garage, who was gaunt from weight loss, whose eyes were haunted, who kept twenty thousand dollars in cash in the spare-tire well in the trunk of his car. His circumstances and his psychological profile would not dispose them to believe him even if his story had not been so far beyond the bounds of reason.

Before Joe could win his freedom, Teknologik and its

associates would find him. They had tried to shoot him down merely because Rose *might* have told him something they didn't want known—and now he knew more than he'd known then, even if he didn't have any idea what the hell to make of it. Considering Teknologik's suspected connections to political and military power grids, Joe more likely than not would be killed in jail during a meticulously planned altercation with other prisoners well paid to waste him. If he survived jail, he would be followed on his release and eliminated at the first opportunity.

Trying not to break into a run and thereby draw attention to himself, he walked to the Honda across the street.

At the Delmann house, kitchen windows exploded. Following the brief ringing of falling glass, the shriek of the smoke alarm was considerably more audible than previously.

Joe glanced back and saw fire writhing out of the back of the house. The lamp oil served as an accelerant: Just inside the front door, which he had left standing open, tongues of fire already licked the walls of the downstairs hallway.

He got in the car. Pulled the door shut.

He had blood on his right hand. Not his own blood.

Shuddering, he popped open the console between the seats and tore a handful of tissues from a box of Kleenex. He scrubbed at his hand.

He stuffed the wadded tissues into the bag that had contained the burgers from McDonald's.

Evidence, he thought, although he was guilty of no crime.

The world had turned upside down. Lies were truth, truth was a lie, facts were fiction, the impossible was possible, and innocence was guilt.

He dug in his pockets for keys. Started the engine.

Through the broken-out window in the backseat, he heard not only the smoke alarms, several of them now, but neighbors shouting at one another, cries of fright in the summer night.

Trusting that their attention would be on the Delmann place and that they would not even notice him departing, Joe switched on the headlights. He swung the Honda into the street.

The lovely old Georgian house was now the domicile of dragons, where bright presences with incendiary breath prowled from room to room. While the dead lay in shrouds of fire, multiple sirens rose like lamentations in the distance.

Joe drove away into a night grown too strange to comprehend, into a world that no longer seemed to be the one into which he had been born.

THREE
ZERO POINT

9

This Halloween light in August, as orange as pumpkin lanterns but leaping high from pits in the sand, made even the innocent seem like debauched pagans in its glow.

On a stretch of beach where bonfires were permitted, ten blazed. Large families gathered at some, parties of teenagers and college students at others.

Joe walked among them. The beach was one he favored on nights when he came to the ocean for therapy, although usually he kept his distance from the bonfires.

Here the decibels of chatter were off the top of the scale, and barefoot couples danced in place to old tunes by the Beach Boys. But here a dozen listeners sat enthralled as a stocky man with a mane of white hair and a reverberant voice spun a ghost story.

The day's events had altered Joe's perception of everything, so it seemed he was looking at the world through a pair of peculiar glasses won in a game of chance on the midway of a mysterious carnival that traveled from venue to venue in whisper-quiet black trains, spectacles with the power not to distort the world but to reveal a secret dimension that was enigmatic, cold, and fearsome.

The dancers in bathing suits, bare limbs molten-bronze from the firelight, shook their shoulders and rolled their hips, dipped and swayed, beat their supple arms like

wings or clawed at the radiant air, and to Joe each cele-
brant seemed to be two entities at the same time. Each
was a real person, yes, but each was also a marionette,
controlled by an unseen puppet master, string-tugged into
postures of jubilation, winking glass eyes and cracking
wooden smiles and laughing with the thrown voices of
hidden ventriloquists, for the sole purpose of deceiving
Joe into believing that this was a benign world that mer-
ited delight.

He passed a group of ten or twelve young men in swimming trunks. Their discarded wetsuits glistened like piles
of sealskins or flayed eels or some other harvest of the
sea. Their upended surfboards cast Stonehenge shadows
across the sand. Testosterone levels were so high among
them that the air virtually smelled of it, so high that it
made them not rowdy but slow and murmurous, almost
somnambulant with primal male fantasies.

The dancers, the storyteller and his audience, the surfers,
and everyone else whom Joe passed watched him warily.
This was not his imagination. Though their glances were
mostly surreptitious, he was aware of their attention.

He wouldn't have been surprised if all of them worked
for Teknologik or for whoever funded Teknologik.

On the other hand, although wading deep in paranoia,
he was still sane enough to realize that he carried with
him the unspeakable things he had seen at the Delmann
house—and that these horrors were visible in him. The
experience carved his face, painted a dull sheen of desolation in his eyes, and sculpted his body into angles of
rage and dread. When he passed, the people on the beach
saw a tormented man, and they were all city dwellers
who understood the danger of tormented men.

He found a bonfire surrounded by twenty or more
utterly silent young men and women with shaved heads.
Each of them wore a sapphire-blue robe and white tennis

shoes, and each had a gold ring in his or her left ear. The men were beardless. The women were without makeup. Many of both sexes were so strikingly attractive and so stylish in their raiment that he instantly thought of them as the Cult of the Beverly Hills Children.

He stood among them for a few minutes, watching them as they watched their fire in meditative silence. When they returned his attention, they had no fear of what they perceived in him. Their eyes were, without exception, calm pools in which he saw humbling depths of acceptance and a kindness like moonlight on water— but perhaps only because that was what he needed to see.

He was carrying the McDonald's bag that contained the wrappers of two cheeseburgers, an empty soft drink container, and the Kleenex with which he had scrubbed the blood off his hand. Evidence. He tossed the bag into the bonfire, and he watched the cultists as they watched the bag burst into flame, blacken, and vanish.

When he walked away, he wondered briefly what they believed the purpose of life to be. His fantasy was that in the mad spiral and plummet of modern life, these blue-robed faithful had learned a truth and achieved an enlightened state that gave meaning to existence. He didn't ask them, for fear their answer would be nothing other than one more version of the same sad longing and wishful thinking on which so many others based their hope.

A hundred yards up the beach from the bonfires, where the night ruled, he hunkered down at the purling edge of the surf and washed his hands in the inch-deep salty water. He picked up wet sand and scrubbed with it, scouring any lingering traces of blood from the creases in his knuckles and from under his fingernails.

After a final rinse of his hands, without bothering to take off his socks and Nikes or to roll up his jeans, he walked into the sea. He moved into the black tide and stopped after he passed the break line of the quiet surf, where the water was above his knees.

The gentle waves wore only thin frayed collars of phosphorescent foam. Curiously, though the night was clear and pierced by a moon, within a hundred yards the sea rolled naked, black, invisible.

Denied the pacifying vista that had drawn him to the shore, Joe found some solace in the surging tide that pressed against his legs and in the low, dumb grumble of the great watery machine. Eternal rhythms, meaningless motions, the peace of indifference.

He tried not to think about what had happened at the Delmann house. Those events were incomprehensible. Thinking about them would not lead to understanding.

He was dismayed to feel no grief and so little anguish about the Delmanns' and Lisa's deaths. At meetings of The Compassionate Friends, he had learned that following the loss of a child, parents often reported a disturbing inability to care about the suffering of others. Watching television news of freeway wrecks, apartment-building fires, and heinous murders, one sat numb and unaffected. Music that had once stirred the heart, art that had once touched the soul, now had no effect. Some people overcame this loss of sensitivity in a year or two, others in five years or ten, but others—never.

The Delmanns had seemed like fine people, but he had never really known them.

Lisa was a friend. Now she was dead. So what? Everyone died sooner or later. Your children. The woman who was the love of your life. Everyone.

The hardness of his heart frightened him. He felt loathsome. But he could not force himself to feel the pain of others. Only his own.

From the sea he sought the indifference to his losses that he already felt to the losses of others.

Yet he wondered what manner of beast he would become if even the deaths of Michelle and Chrissie and Nina no longer mattered to him. For the first time, he considered that utter indifference might inspire not inner peace but a limitless capacity for evil.

∎

The busy service station and the adjacent twenty-four-hour convenience store were three blocks from his motel. Two public telephones were outside, near the rest rooms.

A few fat moths, white as snowflakes, circled under the cone-shaped downlights that were mounted along the building eaves. Vastly enlarged and distorted shadows of their wings swooped across the white stucco wall.

Joe had never bothered to cancel his phone-company credit card. With it, he placed several long-distance calls that he dared not make from his motel room if he hoped to remain safe there.

He wanted to speak to Barbara Christman, the IIC— Investigator in Charge—of the probe of Flight 353. It was eleven o'clock here on the West Coast and two o'clock Sunday morning in Washington, D.C. She would not be in her office, of course, and although Joe might be able to reach a duty officer at the National Transportation Safety Board even at this hour, he would never be given Christman's home number.

Nevertheless, he got the NTSB's main number from information and placed the call. The Board's new auto-mated phone system gave him extensive options, including the opportunity to leave voice mail for any Board member, senior crash investigator, or executive-level civil servant. Supposedly, if he entered the first initial and first four let-ters of the surname of the party for whom he wished to leave a message, he would be connected. Though he carefully entered B-C-H-R-I, he was routed not to voice mail but to a recording that informed him no such extension existed. He tried again, with the same result.

Either Barbara Christman was no longer an employee or the voice-mail system wasn't functioning properly.

Although the IIC at any crash scene was a senior investigator operating out of the NTSB headquarters in Washington, other members of a Go-Team could be culled from specialists in field offices all over the country: Anchorage, Atlanta, Chicago, Denver, Fort Worth, Los Angeles, Miami, Kansas City, New York City, and Seattle. From the computer at the *Post*, Joe had obtained a list of most if not all of the team members, but he didn't know where even one of them was based.

Because the crash site was a little more than a hundred miles south of Denver, he assumed at least a few of the team had been drawn from that office. Using his list of eleven names, he sought phone numbers from directory assistance in Denver.

He obtained three listings. The other eight people were either unlisted or not Denver-area residents.

The ceaseless swelling and shrinking and swelling again of moth shadows across the stucco wall of the service station teased at Joe's memory. They reminded him of something, and increasingly he sensed that the recollection was as important as it was elusive. For a moment he stared intently at the swooping shadows, which were as amorphous as the molten forms in a Lava lamp, but he could not make the connection.

Though it was past midnight in Denver, Joe called all three men whose numbers he'd obtained. The first was the Go-Team meteorologist in charge of considering weather factors pertinent to the crash. His phone was picked up by an answering machine, and Joe didn't leave a message. The second was the man who had overseen the team division responsible for sifting the wreckage for metallurgical evidence. He was surly, possibly awakened by the phone, and uncooperative. The third man provided the link to Barbara Christman that Joe needed.

His name was Mario Oliveri. He had headed the human-performance division of the team, searching for errors possibly committed by the flight crew or air-traffic controllers.

In spite of the hour and the intrusion on his privacy, Oliveri was cordial, claiming to be a night owl who never went to bed before one o'clock. "But, Mr. Carpenter, I'm sure you'll understand that I do not speak to reporters about Board business, the details of any investigation. It's public record anyway."

"That's not why I've called, Mr. Oliveri. I'm having trouble reaching one of your senior investigators, whom I need to talk with urgently, and I'm hoping you can put me in touch. Something's wrong with her voice mail at your Washington offices."

"*Her* voice mail? We have no current senior investigators who are women. All six are men."

"Barbara Christman."

Oliveri said, "That had to be who it was. But she took early retirement months ago."

"Do you have a phone number for her?"

Oliveri hesitated. Then: "I'm afraid I don't."

"Maybe you know if she resides in D.C. itself or which suburb. If I knew where she lived, I might be able to get a phone—"

"I heard she came home to Colorado," Oliveri said. "She started out in the Denver field office a lot of years ago, was transferred out to Washington, and worked her way up to senior investigator."

"So she's in Denver now?"

Again Oliveri was silent, as if the very subject of Barbara Christman troubled him. At last he said, "I believe her actual home was Colorado Springs. That's about seventy miles south of Denver."

And it was less than forty miles from the meadow where the doomed 747 had come to a thunderous end.

"She's in Colorado Springs now?" Joe asked.

"I don't know."

"If she's married, the phone might be in a husband's name."

"She's been divorced for many years. Mr. Carpenter . . . I am wondering if . . ."

After long seconds during which Oliveri failed to complete his thought, Joe gently prodded: "Sir?"

"Is this related to Nationwide Flight 353?"

"Yes, sir. A year ago tonight."

Oliveri fell into silence once more.

Finally Joe said, "Is there something about what happened to Flight 353 . . . something unusual?"

"The investigation is public record, as I said."

"That's not what I asked."

The open line was filled with a silence so deep that Joe could half believe that he was connected not to Denver but to the far side of the moon.

"Mr. Oliveri?"

"I don't really have anything to tell you, Mr. Carpenter. But if I thought of something later . . . is there a number where I could reach you?"

Rather than explain his current circumstances, Joe said, "Sir, if you're an honest man, then you might be endangering yourself by calling me. There are some damned nasty people who would suddenly be interested in you if they knew we were in touch."

"What people?"

Ignoring the question, Joe said, "If something's on your mind—or on your conscience—take time to think about it. I'll get back to you in a day or two."

Joe hung up.

Moths swooped. Swooped. Batted against the flood-lamps above. Clichés on the wing: moths to the flame.

The memory continued to elude Joe.

He called directory assistance in Colorado Springs. The operator provided him with a number for Barbara Christman.

She answered on the second ring. She did not sound as though she had been awakened.

Perhaps some of these investigators, who had walked through the unspeakable carnage of major air disasters, did not always find their way easily into sleep.

Joe told her his name and where his family had been one year ago this night, and he implied that he was still an active reporter with the *Post*.

Her initial silence had the cold, moon-far quality of Oliveri's. Then she said, "Are you here?"

"Excuse me?"

"Where are you calling from? Here in Colorado Springs?"

"No. Los Angeles."

"Oh," she said, and Joe thought he heard the faintest breath of regret when she exhaled that word.

He said, "Ms. Christman, I have some questions about Flight 353 that I would—"

"I'm sorry," she interrupted. "I know you've suffered terribly, Mr. Carpenter. I can't even conceive the depth of your anguish, and I know it's often difficult for family members to accept their losses in these horrible incidents, but there's nothing I could say to you that would help you find that acceptance or—"

"I'm not trying to learn acceptance, Ms. Christman. I'm trying to find out what *really* happened to that airliner."

"It's not unusual for people in your position to take refuge in conspiracy theories, Mr. Carpenter, because otherwise the loss seems so pointless, so random and inexplicable. Some people think we're covering up for airline incompetence or that we've been bought off by the Airline Pilots Association and that we've buried proof the flight crew was drunk or on drugs. This was just an accident, Mr. Carpenter. But if I were to spend a lot of time with you on the phone, trying to persuade you of that, I'd never convince you, and I'd be encouraging you in this denial fantasy. You have my deepest sympathy, you really do, but you need to be talking to a therapist, not to me."

Before Joe could reply, Barbara Christman hung up.

He called her again. Although he waited while the phone rang forty times, she did not answer it.

For the moment, he had accomplished all that was possible by telephone.

Halfway back to his Honda, he stopped. He turned and studied the side of the service station again, where the exaggerated and weirdly distorted shadows of moths washed across the white stucco, like nightmare phantoms gliding through the pale mists of a dream.

Moths to the flame. Three points of fire in three oil lamps. Tall glass chimneys.

In memory, he saw the three flames leap higher in the chimneys. Yellow lamplight glimmered across Lisa's somber face, and shadows swooped up the walls of the Delmanns' kitchen.

At the time, Joe had thought only that a vagrant draft had abruptly drawn the flames higher in the lamps, though the air in the kitchen had been still. Now, in retrospect, the serpentine fire, shimmering several inches upward from the three wicks, impressed him as possessing greater importance than he previously realized.

The incident had significance.

He watched the moths but pondered the oil wicks, standing beside the service station but seeing around him the kitchen with its maple cabinetry and sugar-brown granite counters.

Enlightenment did not rise in him as the flames had briefly risen in those lamps. Strive as he might, he could not identify the significance that he intuited.

He was weary, exhausted, battered from the trauma of the day. Until he was rested, he could not trust either his senses or his hunches.

■

On his back in the motel bed, head on a foam pillow, heart on a rock of hard memory, Joe ate a chocolate bar that he'd bought at the service station.

Until the final mouthful, he could discern no flavor whatsoever. With the last bite, the taste of blood flooded his mouth, as though he had bitten his tongue.

His tongue was not cut, however, and what plagued him was the familiar taste of guilt. Another day had ended, and he was still alive and unable to justify his survival.

Except for the light of the moon at the open balcony door and the green numerals of the digital alarm clock, the room was dark. He stared at the ceiling light fixture, which was vaguely visible—and only visible at all because the convex disk of glass was lightly frosted with moonglow. It floated like a ghostly visitant above him.

He thought of the luminous Chardonnay in the three glasses on the counter in the Delmanns' kitchen. No explanation there. Though Charlie might have tasted the wine before pouring it, Georgine and Lisa had never touched their glasses.

Thoughts like agitated moths swooped and fluttered through his mind, seeking light in his darkness.

He wished that he could talk with Beth in Virginia. But they might have her phone tapped and trace his call to find him. Besides, he was concerned that he would be putting Beth and Henry in jeopardy if he told them anything about what had happened to him since he'd found himself under surveillance at the beach.

Lulled by the maternal heart sound of the rhythmic surf, weighed down by weariness, wondering why he had escaped the plague of suicide at the Delmanns' house, he slipped into sleep with nightmares.

Later, he half woke in darkness, lying on his side, facing the alarm clock on the nightstand. The glowing green numbers reminded him of those on the clock in Charles Delmann's bloodied bedroom: time flashing backward in ten-minute increments.

Joe had supposed that a stray shotgun pellet must have struck the clock, damaging it. Now, in a swoon of sleep, he perceived that the explanation was different from what he had thought—something more mysterious and more significant than a mere bead of lead.

The clock and the oil lamps.

Numbers flashing, flames leaping.

Connections.

Significance.

Dreams reclaimed him briefly, but the alarm woke him long before dawn. He had been out less than three and a half hours, but after a year of restless nights, he was refreshed even by this much sleep.

Following a quick shower, as Joe dressed, he studied the digital clock. Revelation eluded him now as it had eluded him when he had been sotted with sleep.

Joe drove to LAX while the coast was still waiting for dawn.

He purchased a same-day, round-trip ticket to Denver. The return flight would bring him back to Los Angeles in time to keep the six-o'clock meeting with Demi—she of the sexy-smoky voice—at the coffeehouse in Westwood.

As he was on his way to the gate where his plane was already boarding, he saw two young men in blue robes at the check-in desk for a flight to Houston. Their shaved heads, the gold rings in their left ears, and their white tennis shoes identified them as members of the same cult as the group that he had encountered around the bonfire on the beach only hours earlier.

One of these men was black, the other was white, and both were carrying NEC laptops. The black man checked his wristwatch, which appeared to be a gold Rolex. Whatever their religious beliefs might be, they evidently didn't take vows of poverty or have much in common with the Hare Krishnas.

Although this was the first time Joe had been aboard an aircraft since receiving the news about Michelle and the girls a year earlier, he was not nervous during the trip to Denver. Initially he worried that he would have an anxiety attack and begin to relive the plunge of Flight 353 as he had so often imagined it, but after just a few minutes, he knew that he would be all right.

He wasn't apprehensive about dying in another crash. Perversely, if he perished in the same way that his wife and daughters had been taken, he would be calm and without fear on the long ride down into the earth, because such a fate would seem like a welcome return to balance in the universe, an open circle closed, a wrongness made right at last.

Of greater concern to him was what he might learn from Barbara Christman at the far end of his journey.

He was convinced that she didn't trust the privacy of telephone conversations but would talk with him face-to-face. He didn't think he had imagined the note of disappointment in her voice when she learned that he was not calling her from Colorado Springs. Likewise, her speech about the dangers of believing in conspiracy theories and the need for grief therapy, although compassionate and well stated, sounded to Joe as though it had been intended less for him than for the ears of eavesdroppers.

If Barbara Christman was carrying a burden that she longed to put down, the solution to the mystery of Flight 353 might be close at hand.

Joe wanted to know the whole truth, *needed* to know, but dreaded knowing. The peace of indifference would forever be beyond his reach if he learned that men, not fate, had been responsible for taking his family from him. The journey toward this particular truth was not an ascension toward a glorious light but a descent into darkness, chaos, the maelstrom.

He'd brought the printouts of four articles about Teknologik, which he had gotten from Randy Colway's computer at the *Post*. The business-section prose was so dry, however—and his attention span so short after only three and a half hours of sleep—that he wasn't able to concentrate.

He dozed fitfully across the Mojave Desert and the Rockies: two hours and fifteen minutes of half-formed dreams lit by oil lamps and the glow of digital clocks, in which understanding seemed about to wash over him but from which he woke still thirsty for answers.

In Denver, the humidity was unusually high and the sky overcast. To the west, the mountains lay buried under slow avalanches of early-morning fog.

In addition to his driver's license, he had to use a credit card as ID to obtain a rental car. He put down a cash deposit, however, trying to avoid the actual use of the card, which might leave a trail of plastic for anyone who was tracking him.

Though no one on the plane or in the terminal had seemed to be especially interested in him, Joe parked the car at a shopping center not far from the airport and searched it inside and out, under the hood and in the trunk, for a transponder like the one that he had found on his Honda the previous day. The rental Ford was clean.

From the shopping center, he wove a tangled course along surface streets, checking his rearview mirror for a tail. Convinced that he was not being followed, he finally picked up Interstate 25 and drove south.

Mile by mile, Joe pushed the Ford harder, eventually ignoring the speed limit, because he became increasingly convinced that if he didn't get to Barbara Christman's house in time, he would find her dead by her own hand. Eviscerated. Immolated. Or with the back of her head blown out.

10

In Colorado Springs, Joe found Barbara Christman's address in the telephone book. She lived in a diminutive jewel-box Victorian, Queen Anne style, exuberantly decorated with elaborate millwork.

When she came to the door in answer to the bell, she spoke before Joe had a chance to identify himself. "Even sooner than I expected you."

"Are you Barbara Christman?"

"Let's not do this here."

"I'm not sure you know who I—"

"Yes, I know. But not here."

"Where?"

"Is that your car at the curb?" she asked.

"The rental Ford."

"Park it in the next block. Two blocks. Wait there, and I'll pick you up."

She closed the door.

Joe stood on the porch a moment longer, considering whether he should ring the bell again. Then he decided that she wasn't likely to be planning to run out on him.

Two blocks south of Christman's house, he parked beside a grade-school playground. The swings, seesaws, and jungle gyms were unused on this Sunday morning. Otherwise, he would have parked elsewhere, to be safe from the silvery laughter of children.

He got out of the car and looked north. There was no sign of the woman yet.

Joe consulted his wristwatch. Ten minutes till ten o'clock, Pacific time, an hour later here.

In eight hours, he would have to be back in Westwood to meet Demi—and Rose.

Along the sleepy street came a cat's paw of warm wind searching the boughs of the pine trees for hidden birds. It rustled the leaves on the branches of a nearby group of paper birches with trunks as luminous white as choirboys' surplices.

Under a sky gray-white with lowering mist to the west and drear with gunmetal thunderheads to the east, the day seemed to carry a heavy freight of dire portents. The flesh prickled on the nape of Joe's neck, and he began to feel as exposed as a red bull's-eye target on a shooting range.

When a Chevy sedan approached from the south and Joe saw three men in it, he moved casually around to the passenger's side of the rental car, using it for cover in the event that they opened fire on him. They passed without glancing in his direction.

A minute later, Barbara Christman arrived in an emerald-green Ford Explorer. She smelled faintly of bleach and soap, and he suspected she had been doing the laundry when he'd rung her bell.

As they headed south from the grade school, Joe said, "Ms. Christman, I'm wondering—where have you seen a photograph of me?"

"Never have," she said. "And call me Barbara."

"So, Barbara . . . when you opened your door a bit ago, how did you know who I was?"

"Hasn't been a stranger at my door in ages. Anyway, last night when you called back and I didn't answer, you let it ring more than thirty times."

"Forty."

"Even a persistent man would have given up after twenty. When it kept ringing and ringing, I knew you were more than persistent. Driven. I knew you'd come soon."

She was about fifty, dressed in Rockports, faded jeans, and a periwinkle-blue chambray shirt. Her thick white hair looked as if it had been cut by a good barber rather than styled by a beautician. Well tanned, with a broad face as open and inviting as a golden field of Kansas wheat, she appeared honest and trustworthy. Her stare was direct, and Joe liked her for the aura of efficiency that she projected and for the crisp self-assurance in her voice.

"Who are you afraid of, Barbara?"

"Don't know who they are."

"I'm going to get the answer somewhere," he warned.

"What I'm telling you is the truth, Joe. Never have known who they are. But they pulled strings I never thought could *be* pulled."

"To control the results of a Safety Board investigation?"

"The Board still has integrity, I think. But these people . . . they were able to make some evidence disappear."

"What evidence?"

Braking to a halt at a red traffic signal, she said, "What finally made you suspicious, Joe, after all this time? What about the story didn't ring true?"

"It all rang true—until I met the sole survivor."

She stared blankly at him, as though he had spoken in a foreign language of which she had no slightest knowledge.

"Rose Tucker," he said.

There seemed to be no deception in her hazel eyes but

genuine puzzlement in her voice when she said, "Who's she?"

"She was aboard Flight 353. Yesterday she visited the graves of my wife and daughters while I was there."

"Impossible. No one survived. No one *could* have survived."

"She was on the passenger manifest."

Speechless, Barbara stared at him.

He said, "And some dangerous people are hunting for her—and now for me. Maybe the same people who made that evidence disappear."

A car horn blared behind them. The traffic signal had changed to green.

While she drove, Barbara reached to the dashboard controls and lowered the fan speed of the air conditioning, as though chilled. "No one could have survived," she insisted. "This was not your usual hit-and-skip crash, where there's a greater or lesser chance of any survivors depending on the angle of impact and lots of other factors. This was straight down, head-in, catastrophic."

"Head-in? I always thought it tumbled, broke apart."

"Didn't you read any newspaper accounts?"

He shook his head. "Couldn't. I just imagined . . ."

"Not a hit-and-skip, like most," she repeated. "Almost straight into the ground. Sort of similar to Hopewell, September '94. A USAir 737 went down in Hopewell Township, on its way to Pittsburgh, and was just . . . obliterated. Being aboard Flight 353 would have been . . . I'm sorry, Joe, but it would have been like standing in the middle of a bomb blast. A big bomb blast."

"There were some remains they were never able to identify."

"So little left *to* identify. The aftermath of something like this . . . it's more gruesome than you can imagine, Joe. Worse than you want to know, believe me."

He recalled the small caskets in which his family's remains had been conveyed to him, and the strength of the memory compressed his heart into a small stone.

Eventually, when he could speak again, he said, "My point is that there were a number of passengers for whom the pathologists were unable to find any remains. People who just . . . ceased to exist in an instant. Disappeared."

"A large majority of them," she said, turning onto State Highway 115 and heading south under a sky as hard as an iron kettle.

"Maybe this Rose Tucker didn't just . . . didn't just disintegrate on impact like the others. Maybe she disappeared because she walked away from the scene."

"Walked?"

"The woman I met wasn't disfigured or crippled. She appeared to have come through it without a scar."

Adamantly shaking her head, Barbara said, "She's lying to you, Joe. Flat out lying. She wasn't on that plane. She's playing some sort of sick game."

"I believe her."

"Why?"

"Because of things I've seen."

"What things?"

"I don't think I should tell you. Knowing . . . that might put you as deep in the hole as I am. I don't want to endanger you any more than I have to. Just by coming here, I might be causing you trouble."

After a silence, she said, "You must have seen something pretty extraordinary to make you believe in a survivor."

"Stranger than you can imagine."

"Still . . . I don't believe it," she said.

"Good. That's safer."

They had driven out of Colorado Springs, through

suburbs, into an area of ranches, traveling into increasingly rural territory. To the east, high plains dwindled into an arid flatness. To the west, the land rose gradually through fields and woods toward foothills half screened by gray mist.

He said, "You're not just driving aimlessly, are you?"

"If you want to fully understand what I'm going to tell you, it'll help to see." She glanced away from the road, and her concern for him was evident in her kind eyes. "Do you think you can handle it, Joe?"

"We're going . . . there."

"Yes. If you can handle it."

Joe closed his eyes and strove to suppress a welling anxiety. In his imagination, he could hear the screaming of the airliner's engines.

The crash scene was thirty to forty miles south and slightly west of Colorado Springs.

Barbara Christman was taking him to the meadow where the 747 had shattered like a vessel of glass.

"Only if you can handle it," she said gently.

The substance of his heart seemed to condense even further, until it was like a black hole in his chest.

The Explorer slowed. She was going to pull to the shoulder of the highway.

Joe opened his eyes. Even the thunderhead-filtered light seemed too bright. He willed himself to be deaf to the airplane-engine roar in his mind.

"No," he said. "Don't stop. Let's go. I'll be all right. I've got nothing to lose now."

■

They turned off the state highway onto an oiled-gravel road and soon off the gravel onto a dirt lane that led west through tall poplars with vertical branches streaming skyward like green fire. The poplars gave way to tamarack and birches, which surrendered the ground to white pines as the lane narrowed and the woods thickened.

Increasingly pitted and rutted, wandering among the trees as though weary and losing its way, the lane finally pulled a blanket of weeds across itself and curled up to rest under a canopy of evergreen boughs.

Parking and switching off the engine, Barbara said, "We'll walk from here. It's no more than half a mile, and the brush isn't especially thick."

Although the forest was not as dense and primeval as the vast stands of pine and spruce and fir on the fog-robed mountains looming to the west, civilization was so far removed that the soulful hush was reminiscent of a cathedral between services. Broken only by the snapping of twigs and the soft crunch of dry pine needles underfoot, this prayerful silence was, for Joe, as oppressive as the imagined roar of jet engines that sometimes shook him into an anxiety attack. It was a stillness full of eerie, disturbing expectation.

He trailed Barbara between columns of tall trees, under green vaults. Even in the late morning, the shadows were as deep as those in a monastery cloister.

The air was crisp with the aroma of pine. Musty with the scent of toadstools and natural mulch.

Step by step, a chill as damp as ice melt seeped from his bones and through his flesh, then out of his brow, his scalp, the nape of his neck, the curve of his spine. The day was warm, but he was not.

Eventually he could see an end to the ranks of trees, an open space past the last of the white pines. Though the forest had begun to seem claustrophobic, he was now reluctant to forsake the crowding greenery for the revelation that lay beyond.

Shivering, he followed Barbara through the last trees into the bottom of a gently rising meadow. The clearing was three hundred yards wide from north to south—and twice that long from the east, where they had entered it, to the wooded crest at the west end.

The wreckage was gone, but the meadow felt haunted.

The previous winter's melting snow and the heavy spring rains had spread a healing poultice of grass across the torn, burnt land. The grass and a scattering of yellow wildflowers, however, could not conceal the most terrible wound in the earth: a ragged-edged, ovate depression approximately ninety yards by sixty yards. This enormous crater lay uphill from them, in the northwest quadrant of the meadow.

"Impact point," Barbara Christman said.

They set out side by side, walking toward the precise place where three-quarters of a million pounds had come screaming out of the night sky into the earth, but Joe quickly fell behind Barbara and then came to a stop altogether. His soul was as gouged as this field, plowed by pain.

Barbara returned to Joe and, without a word, slipped her hand into his. He held tightly to her, and they set out again.

As they approached the impact point, he saw the fire-blackened trees along the north perimeter of the forest, which had served as backdrop to the crash-scene photograph in the *Post*. Some pines had been stripped bare of needles by the flames; their branches were charred stubs. A score of seared aspens, as brittle as charcoal, imprinted a stark geometry on the dismal sky.

They stopped at the eroded rim of the crater; the uneven floor below them was as deep as a two-story house in some places. Although patches of grass bristled from the sloping walls, it did not thrive on the bottom of the depression, where shattered slabs of gray stone showed through a thin skim of dirt and brown leaves deposited by the wind.

Barbara said, "It hit with enough force to blast away thousands of years of accumulated soil and still fracture the bedrock beneath."

Even more shaken by the power of the crash than he had expected to be, Joe turned his attention to the somber sky and struggled to breathe.

An eagle appeared out of the mountain mists to the west, flying eastward on a course as unwaveringly straight as a latitude line on a map. Silhouetted against the gray-white overcast, it was almost as dark as Poe's raven, but as it passed under that portion of sky that was blue-black with a still-brewing storm, it appeared to grow as pale as a spirit.

Joe turned to watch the bird as it passed overhead and away.

"Flight 353," Barbara said, "was tight on course and free of problems when it passed the Goodland navigational beacon, which is approximately a hundred and seventy air miles east of Colorado Springs. By the time it ended here, it was twenty-eight miles off course."

Encouraging Joe to stay with her on a slow walk around the crater rim, Barbara Christman summarized the known details of the doomed 747 from its takeoff until its premature descent.

Out of John F. Kennedy International Airport in New York City, Flight 353, bound for Los Angeles, ordinarily would have followed a more southerly corridor than the one it traveled that August evening. Due to thunderstorms throughout the South and tornado warnings in the southern

Midwest, another route was considered. More important, the headwinds on the northerly corridor were considerably less severe than those on the southern; by taking the path of least resistance, flight time and fuel consumption could be substantially reduced. Consequently, the Nationwide flight-route planning manager assigned the aircraft to Jet Route 146.

Departing JFK only four minutes behind schedule, the nonstop to LAX sailed high over northern Pennsylvania, Cleveland, the southern curve of Lake Erie, and southern Michigan. Routed south of Chicago, it crossed the Mississippi River from Illinois to Iowa at the city of Davenport. In Nebraska, passing the Lincoln navigational beacon, Flight 353 adjusted course southwest toward the next major forward beacon, at Goodland in the northwest corner of Kansas.

The battered flight-data recorder, salvaged from the wreckage, eventually revealed that the pilot made the proper course correction from Goodland toward the next major forward beacon, at Blue Mesa, Colorado. But about a hundred and ten miles past Goodland, something went wrong. Although it experienced no loss of altitude or airspeed, the 747 began to veer off its assigned flight path, now traveling west-southwest at a seven-degree deviation from Jet Route 146.

For two minutes, nothing more happened—and then the aircraft made a sudden three-degree heading change, nose right, as if the pilot had begun to recognize that he was off course. But just three seconds later, this was followed by an equally sudden four-degree heading change, nose left.

Analysis of all thirty parameters covered by this particular flight-data recorder seemed to confirm that the heading changes were either yawing of the craft or resulted in yawing. First the tail section had swung to the left—or port—while the nose had gone right—starboard—and then the tail had swung to the right and the nose to the left, skidding in midair almost as a car might fishtail on an icy highway.

Post-crash data analysis also gave rise to the suspicion that the pilot might have used the rudder to execute these abrupt changes of heading—which made no sense. Virtually all yaws result from movements of the rudder, the vertical panel in the tail, but pilots of commercial jets eschew use of the rudder out of consideration for their passengers. A severe yaw creates lateral acceleration, which can throw standing passengers to the floor, spill food and drinks, and induce a general state of alarm.

Captain Delroy Blane and his copilot, Victor Santorelli, were veterans with forty-two years of commercial piloting between them. For all heading changes, they would have used the ailerons—hinged panels on the trailing edge of each wing—which facilitate gentle banking turns. They would have resorted to the rudder only in the event of engine failure on takeoff or when landing in a strong crosswind.

The flight-data recorder had shown that eight seconds after the first yawing incident, Flight 353's heading again abruptly changed three degrees, nose left, followed two seconds later by a second and even more severe shift of seven degrees to the left. Both engines were at full performance and bore no responsibility for the heading change or the subsequent disaster.

As the front of the plane swung sharply to port, the starboard wing would have been moving faster through the air, rapidly gaining lift. When the starboard wing lifted, it forced the port wing down. During the next fateful twenty-two seconds, the banking angle grew to one hundred forty-six degrees, while the nose-down pitch reached eighty-four degrees.

In that incredibly short span of time, the 747 went from earth-parallel flight to a deadly roll while virtually standing on end.

Pilots with the experience of Blane and Santorelli should have been able to correct the yaw quickly, before it became a roll. Even then, they should have been able to pull the aircraft out of the roll before it became an inevitable plunge. Under any scenario that the human-performance experts could conceive, the captain would have turned the control wheel hard to the right and would have used the ailerons to bring the 747 back to level flight.

Instead, perhaps because of a singular hydraulic-systems failure that defeated the pilots' efforts, Nationwide Flight 353 rolled into a steep dive. With all jet engines still firing, it *rocketed* into this meadow, splashing millennia of accumulated soil as if it were water, boring to the bedrock with an impact powerful enough to crack the steel blades of the Pratt and Whitney power plants as though they were made of balsa wood, sufficiently loud to shake all the winged residents out of the trees halfway up the slopes of distant Pikes Peak.

█

Halfway around the impact crater, Barbara and Joe stopped, now facing east toward beetling thunderheads, less concerned about the pending storm than about the brief thunder of that year-ago night.

Three hours after the crash, the headquarters contingent of the investigating team departed Washington from National Airport. They made the journey in a Gulfstream jet owned by the Federal Aviation Administration.

During the night, Pueblo County fire and police officials

had quickly ascertained that there were no survivors. They pulled back so as not to disturb evidence that might help the NTSB arrive at an understanding of the cause of the disaster, and they secured the perimeter of the crash site.

By dawn, the Go-Team arrived in Pueblo, Colorado, which was closer to the incident than Colorado Springs. They were met by regional FAA officials, who were already in possession of the flight-data recorder and cockpit-voice recorder from Nationwide 353. Both devices emitted signals by which they could be located; therefore, swift retrieval from the wreckage had been possible even in darkness and even from the relative remoteness of the site.

"The recorders were put on the Gulfstream and flown back to the Safety Board's labs in Washington," Barbara said. "The steel jackets were badly battered, even breached, but we were hopeful the data could be extracted."

In a caravan of four-wheel-drive vehicles driven by county emergency-response personnel, the Safety Board team was conveyed to the crash site for its initial survey. The secured perimeter extended to the gravel road that turned off State Highway 115, and gathered along both sides of the paved highway in that vicinity were fire trucks, black-and-whites, ambulances, drab sedans from federal and state agencies, coroners' vans, as well as scores of cars and pickups belonging to the genuinely concerned, the curious, and the ghoulish.

"It's always chaos," Barbara said. "Lots of television vans with satellite dishes. Nearly a hundred and fifty members of the press. They clamored for statements when they saw us arrive, but we didn't have anything to say yet, and we came directly up here to the site."

Her voice trailed away. She shoved her hands into the pockets of her jeans.

No wind was at play. No bees moved among the wild-flowers. The surrounding woods were full of motionless monk trees, which had taken vows of silence.

Joe lowered his gaze from the silent storm clouds, black with throttled thunder, to the crater where the thunder of Flight 353 was now only a memory held deep in fractured stone.

"I'm okay," he assured Barbara, though his voice was thick. "Go on. I need to know what it was like."

After another half minute of silence, during which she gathered her thoughts and decided how much to tell him, Barbara said, "When you arrive with the Go-Team, the first impression is always the same. Always. The smell. You never ever forget the stench. Jet fuel. Smoldering vinyl and plastic—even the new blended thermoplastics and the phenolic plastics burn under extreme conditions. There's the stink of seared insulation, melted rubber, and . . . roasted flesh, biological wastes from the ruptured lavatory holding tanks and from the bodies."

Joe forced himself to continue looking into the pit, because he would need to go away from this place with a new strength that would make it possible for him to seek justice against all odds, regardless of the power of his adversaries.

"Ordinarily," Barbara said, "in even terribly violent crashes, you see some pieces of wreckage large enough to allow you to envision the aircraft as it once was. A wing. The empennage. A long section of fuselage. Depending on the angle of impact, you sometimes even have the nose and cockpit mostly intact."

"In the case of Flight 353?"

"The debris was so finely chopped, so gnarled, so compacted, that on first look it was impossible to see that it had been a plane. It seemed to us that a huge portion of the mass must be missing. But it was all here in the meadow and scattered some distance into the trees uphill, west and north. All here . . . but for the most part there was nothing bigger than a car door. All I saw that I could identify at first glance was a portion of an engine and a three-unit passenger-seat module."

"Was this the worst crash in your experience?" Joe asked.

"Never seen one worse. Only two others to equal it— including the Pennsylvania crash in '94, Hopewell, USAir Flight 427, en route to Pittsburgh. The one I mentioned earlier. I wasn't the IIC on that one, but I saw it."

"The bodies here. How were they when you arrived?"

"Joe . . ."

"You said no one could have survived. Why are you so sure?"

"You don't want to know the *why*." When he met her eyes, she looked away from him. "These are images that haunt your sleep, Joe. They wear away a part of your soul."

"The bodies?" he insisted.

With both hands, she pressed her white hair back from her face. She shook her head. She put her hands in her pockets again.

Joe drew a deep breath, exhaled with a shudder, and repeated his question. "The bodies? I need to know everything I can learn. Any detail about this might be helpful. And even if this isn't much help . . . it'll keep my anger high. Right now, Barbara, I need the anger to be able to go on."

"No bodies intact."

"None at all?"

"None even close to intact."

"How many of the three hundred and thirty were the pathologists finally able to identify . . . to find at least a few teeth from, body parts, something, anything, to tell who they were?"

Her voice was flat, studiedly emotionless, but almost a whisper. "I think slightly more than a hundred."

"Broken, severed, mangled," he said, hammering himself with the hard words.

"Far worse. All that immense hurtling energy released in an instant . . . you don't even recognize most of the biological debris as being human. The risk of infectious disease was high from blood and tissue contamination, so we had to pull out and revisit the site only in biologically secure gear. Every piece of wreckage had to be carted away and documented by the structural specialists, of course—so to protect them we had to set up four decontamination stations out along the gravel road. Most of the wreckage had to be processed there before it moved on to a hangar at Pueblo Airport."

Being brutal to prove to himself that his anguish would never again get the better of his anger until this quest was completed, Joe said, "It was pretty much like putting them through one of those tree-grinding machines."

"Enough, Joe. Knowing more details can't *ever* help you."

The meadow was so utterly soundless that it might have been the ignition point of all Creation, from which God's energies had long ago flowed toward the farthest ends of the universe, leaving only a mute vacuum.

■

A few fat bees, enervated by the August heat that was unable to penetrate Joe's chill, forsook their usual darting urgency and traveled languidly across the meadow from wildflower to wildflower, as though flying in their sleep and acting out a shared dream about collecting nectar. He could hear no buzzing as the torpid gatherers went about their work.

"And the cause," he asked, "was hydraulic-control failure—that stuff with the rudder, the yawing and then the roll?"

"You really haven't read about it, have you?"

"Couldn't."

She said, "The possibility of a bomb, anomalous weather, the wake vortex from another aircraft, and various other factors were eliminated pretty early. And the structures group, twenty-nine specialists in that division of the investigation alone, studied the wreckage in the hangar in Pueblo for eight months without being able to pin down a probable cause. They suspected lots of different things at one time or another. Malfunctioning yaw dampers, for one. Or an electronics-bay door failure. Engine-mount failure looked good to them for a while. And malfunctioning thrust reversers. But they eliminated each suspicion, and no official probable cause was found."

"How unusual is that?"

"Unusual. But sometimes we can't pin it down. Like Hopewell in '94. And, in fact, another 737 that went down on its approach to Colorado Springs in '91, killing everyone aboard. So it happens, we get stumped."

Joe realized there had been a disturbing qualifier in what she had said: no *official* probable cause.

Then a second realization struck him: "You took early retirement from the Safety Board about seven months ago. That's what Mario Oliveri told me."

"Mario. Good man. He headed the human-performance group in this investigation. But it's been almost nine months since I quit."

"If the structures group was still sifting the wreckage eight months after the crash . . . then you didn't stay to oversee the entire inquiry, even though you were the original IIC on it."

"Bailed out," she acknowledged. "When it all turned sour, when evidence disappeared, when I started to make some noise about it . . . they put the squeeze on me. At first I tried to stay on, but I just couldn't handle being part of a fraud. Couldn't do the *right* thing and spill the beans, either, so I bailed. Not proud of it. But I've got a hostage to fortune, Joe."

"Hostage to fortune. A child?"

"Denny. He's twenty-three now, not a baby anymore, but if I ever lost him . . ."

Joe knew too well how she would have finished that sentence. "They threatened your son?"

Although Barbara stared into the crater before her, she was seeing a potential disaster rather than the aftermath of a real one, a personal catastrophe rather than one involving three hundred and thirty deaths.

"It happened two weeks after the crash," she said. "I was in San Francisco, where Delroy Blane—the captain on Flight 353—had lived, overseeing a pretty intense investigation into his personal history, trying to discover any signs of psychological problems."

"Finding anything?"

"No. He seemed like a rock-solid guy. This was also at the time when I was pressing the hardest to go public with what had happened to certain evidence. I was staying in a hotel. I'm a reasonably sound sleeper. At two-thirty in the morning, someone switched on my nightstand lamp and put a gun in my face."

■

After years of waiting for Go-Team calls, Barbara had long ago overcome a tendency to shed sleep slowly. She woke to the click of the lamp switch and the flood of light as she would have awakened to the ringing telephone: instantly alert and clearheaded.

She might have cried out at the sight of the intruder, except that her shock pinched off her voice and her breath.

The gunman, about forty, had large sad eyes, hound-dog eyes, a nose bashed red by the slow blows of two decades of drink, and a sensuous mouth. His thick lips never quite closed, as though waiting for the next treat that couldn't be resisted—cigarette, whiskey, pastry, or breast.

His voice was as soft and sympathetic as a mortician's but with no unctuousness. He indicated that the pistol was fitted with a sound suppressor, and he assured her that if she tried to call for help, he would blow her brains out with no concern that anyone beyond the room would hear the shot.

She tried to ask who he was, what he wanted.

Hushing her, he sat on the edge of her bed.

He had nothing against her personally, he said, and it would depress him to have to kill her. Besides, if the IIC of the probe of Flight 353 were to be found murdered, inconvenient questions might be asked.

The sensualist's bosses, whoever they might be, could not afford inconvenient questions at this time, on this issue.

Barbara realized that a second man was in the room. He had been standing in the corner near the bathroom door, on the other side of the bed from the gunman.

This one was ten years younger than the first. His smooth pink face and choirboy eyes gave him an innocent demeanor that was belied by a disquietingly eager smile that came and went like the flickering of a serpent's tongue.

The older man pulled the covers off Barbara and politely asked her to get out of bed. They had a few things to explain to her, he said. And they wanted to be certain that she was alert and attentive throughout, because lives depended on her understanding and believing what they had come to tell her.

In her pajamas, she stood obediently while the younger man, with a flurry of brief smiles, went to the desk, withdrew the chair from the kneehole, and stood it opposite the foot of the bed. She sat as instructed.

She had been wondering how they had gotten in, as she'd engaged both the deadbolt and the security chain on the door to the corridor. Now she saw that both of the doors between this hotel room and the next—which could be connected to form a suite for those guests who required more space—stood open. The mystery remained, however, for she was certain that the door on this side had been securely locked with a deadbolt when she had gone to bed.

At the direction of the older man, the younger produced a roll of strapping tape and a pair of scissors. He secured Barbara's wrists tightly to the arms of the straight-back chair, wrapping the tape several times.

Frightened of being restrained and helpless, Barbara nonetheless submitted because she believed that the sad-eyed man would deliver on his threat to shoot her point-blank in the head if she resisted. With his sensuous mouth, as though sampling the contents of a bonbon box, he had savored the words *blow your brains out*.

When the younger man cut a six-inch length of tape and pressed it firmly across Barbara's mouth, then secured that piece by winding a continuous length of tape twice around her head, she panicked for a moment but then regained control of herself. They were not going to pinch her nose shut and smother her. If they had come here to kill her, she would be dead already.

As the younger man retreated with his tremulous smiles to a shadowy corner, the sensualist sat on the foot of the bed, opposite Barbara. Their knees were no more than a few inches apart.

Putting his pistol aside on the rumpled sheets, he took a knife from a jacket pocket. A switchblade. He flicked it open.

Her fear soaring again, Barbara could manage to draw only quick, shallow breaths. The resultant whistling in her nose amused the man sitting with her.

From another jacket pocket, he withdrew a snack-size round of Gouda cheese. Using the knife, he removed the cellophane wrapper and then peeled off the red wax skin that prevented the Gouda from developing mold.

Carefully eating thin slivers of cheese off the wickedly sharp blade, he told Barbara that he knew where her son, Denny, lived and worked. He recited the addresses.

He also knew that Denny had been married to Rebekah for thirteen months, nine days, and—he consulted his watch, calculated—fifteen hours. He knew that Rebekah was six months pregnant with their first child, a girl, whom they were going to name Felicia.

To prevent harm from befalling Denny and his bride, Barbara was expected to accept the official story about what had happened to the tape from the cockpit-voice recorder on Flight 353—a story that she had rejected in discussions with her colleagues and that she had set out to disprove. She was also expected to forget what she had heard on the enhanced version of that tape.

If she continued to seek the truth of the situation or attempted to express her concerns to either the press or the public, Denny and Rebekah would disappear. In the deep basement of a private redoubt soundproofed and equipped for prolonged and difficult interrogations, the sensualist and his associates would shackle Denny, tape open his eyes, and force him to watch while they killed Rebekah and the unborn child.

Then they would surgically remove one of his fingers every day for ten days—taking elaborate measures to control bleeding, shock, and infection. They would keep him alive and alert, though steadily less whole. On the eleventh and twelfth days, they would remove his ears.

They had a full month of imaginative surgery planned.

Every day, as they took another piece of him, they would tell Denny that they would release him to his mother without further harm if she would only agree to cooperate with them in a conspiracy of silence that was, after all, in the national interest. Vitally important defense matters were involved here.

This would not be entirely true. The part about the national interest was true, from their point of view, at least, even though they could not, of course, explain to Barbara how the knowledge she possessed was a threat to her country. The part about her being able to earn Denny's release by cooperation would not be true, however, because once she failed to honor a pledge of silence, she would not be given a second chance, and her son would be forever lost to her. They would deceive Denny solely to ensure that he would spend the last month of his life desperately wondering why his mother had so stubbornly condemned him to such excruciating pain and horrible disfigurement. By the end, half mad or worse, in deep spiritual misery, he would curse her vehemently and beg God to let her rot in Hell.

As he continued to carve the tiny wheel of Gouda and serve himself off the dangerous point of the blade, the sensualist assured Barbara that no one—not the police, not the admittedly clever FBI, not the mighty United

States Army—could keep Denny and Rebekah safe forever. He claimed to be employed by an organization with such bottomless resources and extensive connections that it was capable of compromising and subverting any institution or agency of the federal or state governments.

He asked her to nod if she believed him.

She did believe him. Implicitly. Without reservation. His seductive voice, which seemed to lick each of his hideous threats to savor the texture and astringency of it, was filled with the quiet confidence and smug superiority of a megalomaniac who carries the badge of a secret authority, receives a comfortable salary with numerous fringe benefits, and knows that in his old age he will be able to rely upon the cushion of a generous civil-service pension.

He then asked her if she intended to cooperate.

With guilt and humiliation but also with utter sincerity, she nodded again. Yes. She would cooperate. Yes.

Studying a pale oval of cheese like a tiny filleted fish on the point of the blade, he said that he wanted her to be deeply impressed with his determination to ensure her cooperation, so impressed that she would be in no danger of forsaking the pledge she had just made to him. Therefore, on their way out of the hotel, he and his partner would select, at random, an employee or perhaps a guest—someone who just happened to cross their path—and would kill that person on the spot. Three shots: two in the chest, one in the head.

Stunned, Barbara protested from behind the gag, contorting her face in an effort to twist the tape and free her mouth. But it was pulled cruelly tight, and her lips were stuck firmly to the adhesive, and the only argument that she could get out was a pained, muffled, wordless pleading. She didn't want to be responsible for anyone's death. She was going to cooperate. There was no reason to impress her with their seriousness. No reason. She already *believed* in their seriousness.

Never taking his great sad eyes from her, without saying another word, he slowly finished his cheese.

His unwavering stare seemed to cause a power back-flow, draining her of energy. Yet she could not look away.

When he had consumed the final morsel, he wiped the blade of his knife on the sheets. Then he folded it into the handle and returned the weapon to his pocket.

Sucking on his teeth and rolling his tongue slowly around his mouth, he gathered up the shredded cellophane and the peels of red wax. He rose from the bed and deposited the trash in the waste basket beside the desk.

The younger man stepped out of the shadowy corner. His thin but eager smile no longer fluttered uncertainly; it was fixed.

From behind the strapping tape, Barbara was still attempting to protest the murder of an innocent person when the older man returned to her and, with the edge of his right hand, chopped hard at the side of her neck.

As a scintillant darkness sprayed across her field of vision, she started to slump forward. She felt the chair tipping sideways. She was unconscious before her head hit the carpet.

For perhaps twenty minutes she dreamed of severed fingers in preserving sheaths of red wax. In shrimp-pink faces, fragile smiles broke like strings of pearls, the bright teeth bouncing and rolling across the floor, but in the black crescent between the curved pink lips, new pearls formed, and a choirboy eye blinked blue. There were hound-dog eyes too, as black and shiny as leeches, in which she saw not her reflection but images of Denny's screaming, earless face.

When she regained consciousness, she was slumped in the chair, which had been set upright again. Either the sensualist or his pearl-toothed companion had taken pity on her.

Her wrists were taped to the arms of the chair in such a fashion as to allow her to wrench loose if she applied herself diligently. She needed less than ten minutes to free her right hand, much less to slip the bonds on the left.

She used her own cuticle scissors to snip through the tape wound around her head. When she gingerly pulled it off her lips, it took far less skin than she expected.

Liberated and able to talk, she found herself at the telephone with the receiver in her hand. But she could think of no one whom she dared to call, and she put the phone down.

There was no point in warning the hotel's night manager that one of his employees or guests was in danger. If the gunman had kept his threat to impress her with a senseless, random killing, he had pulled the trigger already. He and his companion would have left the hotel at least half an hour ago.

Wincing at the throbbing pain in her neck, she went to the door that connected her room with theirs. She opened it and checked the inner face. Her privacy deadbolt latch was backed by a removable brass plate fixed in place with screws, which allowed access to the mechanism of her lock from the other side. The other room's door featured no such access plate.

The shiny brass looked new. She was certain that it had been installed shortly before she checked into the hotel—by the gunman and his companion acting either clandestinely or with the assistance of a hotel engineer. A clerk at the front desk was paid or coerced to put her in this room rather than any other.

Barbara was not much of a drinker, but she raided the honor bar for a two-shot miniature of vodka and a cold bottle of orange juice. Her hands were shaking so badly she could barely pour the ingredients into a glass. She drank the screwdriver straight down, opened another miniature, mixed a second drink, took a swallow of it—then went into the bathroom and threw up.

She felt unclean. With dawn less than an hour away, she took a long shower, scrubbing herself so hard and standing in water so hot that her skin grew red and stung unbearably.

Although she knew that it was pointless to change hotels, that they could find her again if they wanted her, she couldn't stay any longer in this place. She packed and, an hour after first light, went down to the front desk to pay her bill.

The ornate lobby was full of San Francisco policemen—uniformed officers and plainclothes detectives.

From the wide-eyed cashier, Barbara learned that sometime after three o'clock in the morning, a young room-service waiter had been shot to death in a service corridor near the kitchen. Twice in the chest and once in the head.

The body had not been discovered immediately because, curiously, no one had heard gunfire.

Harried by fear that seemed to push her forward like a rude hand in the back, she checked out. She took a taxi to another hotel.

The day was high and blue. The city's famous fog was already pulling back across the bay into a towering palisade beyond the Golden Gate, of which she had a limited view from her new room.

She was an aeronautical engineer. A pilot. She held a master's degree in business administration from Columbia University. She had worked hard to become the only current female IIC working air crashes for the National Transportation Safety Board. When her husband had walked out on her seventeen years ago, she had raised Denny alone and raised him well. Now all that she had achieved seemed to have been gathered into the hand of the sad-eyed sensualist, wadded with the cellophane and the peels of red wax, and thrown into the trash can.

After canceling her appointments for the day, Barbara hung the *Do Not Disturb* sign on the door. She closed the draperies and curled on the bed in her new room.

Quaking fear became quaking grief. She wept uncontrollably for the dead room-service waiter whose name she didn't know, for Denny and Rebekah and unborn Felicia whose lives now seemed perpetually suspended on a slender thread, for her own loss of innocence and self-respect, for the three hundred and thirty people aboard Flight 353, for justice thwarted and hope lost.

■

A sudden wind groaned across the meadow, playing with old dry aspen leaves, like the devil counting souls and casting them away.

"I can't let you do this," Joe said. "I can't let you tell me what was on the cockpit-voice recorder if there's any chance it's going to put your son and his family in the hands of people like that."

"It's not for you to decide, Joe."

"The hell it's not."

"When you called from Los Angeles, I played dumb because I've got to assume my phone is permanently tapped, every word recorded. Actually, I don't think it is. I don't think they feel any *need* to tap it, because they know by now that they've got me muzzled."

"If there's even a chance—"

"And I know for certain I'm not being watched. My house isn't under observation. I'd have picked up on that long ago. When I walked out on the investigation, took early retirement, sold the house in Bethesda, and came back to Colorado Springs, they wrote me off, Joe. I was broken, and they knew it."

"You don't seem broken to me."

She patted his shoulder, grateful for the compliment. "I've rebuilt myself some. Anyway, if you weren't followed—"

"I wasn't. I lost them yesterday. No one could have followed me to LAX this morning."

"Then I figure there's no one to know we're here or to know what I tell you. All I ask is you never say you got it from me."

"I wouldn't do that to you. But there's still such a risk you'll be taking," he worried.

"I've had months to think about it, to live with it, and the way it seems to me is . . . They probably think I told Denny some of it, so he would know what danger he's in, so he'd be careful, watchful."

"Did you?"

"Not a word. What kind of a life could they have, knowing?"

"Not a normal one."

"But now Denny, Rebekah, Felicia, and I are going to be hanging by a thread as long as this cover-up continues. Our only hope is for someone else to blow it wide open, so then what little I know about it won't matter any more."

The storm clouds were not only in the east now. Like an armada of incoming starships in a film about futuristic warfare, ominous black thunderheads slowly resolved out of the white mists overhead.

"Otherwise," Barbara continued, "a year from now or two years from now, even though I've kept my mouth shut, they'll decide to tie up all the loose ends. Flight 353 will be such old news that no one will connect my death or Denny's or a handful of others to it. No suspicions will be raised if something happens to those of us with incriminating bits of information. These people, whoever the hell they are . . . they'll buy insurance with a car accident here, a fire there. A faked robbery to cover a murder. A suicide."

Through Joe's mind passed the waking-nightmare images of Lisa burning, Georgine dead on the kitchen floor, Charlie in the blood-tinted light.

He couldn't argue with Barbara's assessment. She probably had it figured right.

■

In a sky waiting to snarl and crackle, menacing faces formed in the clouds, blind and open-mouthed, choked with anger.

Taking her first fateful step toward revelation, Barbara said, "The flight-data recorder and the cockpit-voice recorder arrived in Washington on the Gulfstream and were in the labs by three o'clock Eastern Time the day after the crash."

"You were still just getting into the investigation here."

"That's right. Minh Tran—he's an electronics engineer with the Safety Board—and a few colleagues opened the Fairchild recorder. It's almost as large as a shoe box, jacketed in three-eighths of an inch of stainless steel. They cut it carefully, with a special saw. This particular unit had endured such violent impact that it was compressed four inches end to end—the steel just crunched up like cardboard—and one corner had been crushed, resulting in a small breach."

"And it still functioned?"

"No. The recorder was completely destroyed. But inside

the larger box is the steel memory module. It contains the tape. It was also breached. A small amount of moisture had penetrated all the way into the memory module, but the tape wasn't entirely ruined. It had to be dried, processed, but that didn't take long, and then Minh and a few others gathered in a soundproof listening room to run it from the beginning. There were almost three hours of cockpit conversation leading up to the crash—"

Joe said, "They don't just run it fast forward to the last few minutes?"

"No. Something earlier in the flight, something that seemed to be of no importance to the pilots at the time, might provide clues that help us understand what we're hearing in the moments immediately before the plane went down."

Steadily rising, the warm wind was brisk enough now to foil the lethargic bees on their lazy quest from bloom to bloom. Surrendering the field to the oncoming storm, they departed for secret nests in the woods.

"Sometimes we get a cockpit tape that's all but useless to us," Barbara continued. "The recording quality's lousy for one reason or another. Maybe the tape's old and abraded. Maybe the microphone is the hand-held type or isn't functioning as well as it should, too much vibration. Maybe the recording head is worn and causing distortion."

"I would think there'd be daily maintenance, weekly replacement, when it's something as important as this."

"Remember, as a percentage of flights, planes rarely go down. There are costs and flight-time delays to be considered. Anyway, commercial aviation is a human enterprise, Joe. And what human enterprise ever operates to ideal standards?"

"Point taken."

"This time there was good and bad," she said. "Both Delroy Blane and Santorelli were wearing headsets with boom microphones, which is real damn good, much better than a hand-held. Those along with the overhead cockpit mike gave us three channels to study. On the bad side, the tape wasn't new. It had been recorded over a lot of times and was more deteriorated than we would have liked. Worse, whatever the nature of the moisture that reached the tape, it had caused some patchy corrosion to the recording surface."

From a back pocket of her jeans, she took a folded paper but didn't immediately hand it to Joe.

She said, "When Minh Tran and the others listened, they found that some portions of the tape were clearly audible and others were so full of scratchy static, so garbled, they could only discern one out of four or five words."

"What about the last minute?"

"That was one of the worst segments. It was decided that the tape would have to be cleaned and rehabilitated. Then the recording would be electronically enhanced to whatever extent possible. Bruce Laceroth, head of the Major Investigations Division, had been there to listen to the whole tape, and he called me in Pueblo, at a quarter past seven, Eastern Time, to tell me the status of the recording. They were stowing it for the night, going to start work with it again in the morning. It was depressing."

High above them, the eagle returned from the east, pale against the pregnant bellies of the clouds, still flying straight and true with the weight of the pending storm on its wings.

"Of course, that whole day had been depressing," Barbara said. "We'd brought in refrigerated trucks from Denver to collect all the human remains from the site, which had to be completed before we could begin to deal with the pieces of the plane itself. There was the usual organizational meeting, which is always exhausting, because so many interest groups—the airline, the manufacturer of the plane, the supplier of the power plants, the Airline Pilots Association, lots of others—all want to bend the proceedings to serve their interests as much as possible. Human nature—and not the prettier part of it. So you have to be reasonably diplomatic but also damn tough to keep the process truly impartial."

"And there was the media," he said, condemning his own kind so she wouldn't have to do it.

"Everywhere. Anyway, I'd only slept less than three hours the previous night, before I'd been awakened by the Go-Team call, and there was no chance even to doze on the Gulfstream from National to Pueblo. I was like the walking dead when I hit the sheets a little before midnight—but back there in Washington, Minh Tran was still at it."

"The electronics engineer who cut open the recorder?"

Staring at the folded white paper that she had taken from her hip pocket, turning it over and over in her hands, Barbara said, "You have to understand about Minh. His family were Vietnamese boat people. Survived the communists after the fall of Saigon and then pirates at sea, even a typhoon. He was ten at the time, so he knew early that life was a struggle. To survive and prosper, he *expected* to give a hundred and ten percent."

"I have friends . . . had friends who were Vietnamese immigrants," Joe said. "Quite a culture. A lot of them have a work ethic that would break a plow horse."

"Exactly. When everyone else went home from the labs that night at a quarter past seven, they'd put in a long day. People at the Safety Board are pretty dedicated . . . but Minh more so. He didn't leave. He made a dinner of whatever he could get out of the vending machines, and he stayed to clean the tape and then to work on the last minute of it. Digitize the sound, load it in a computer, and then try to separate the static and other extraneous noises from the voices of the pilots and from the actual sounds that occurred aboard the aircraft. The layers of static proved to be so specifically patterned that the computer was able to help strip them away fairly quickly. Because the boom mikes had delivered strong signals to the recorder, Minh was able to clarify the pilots' voices under the junk noise. What he heard was extraordinary. Bizarre."

She handed the folded white paper to Joe.

He accepted but didn't open it. He was half afraid to see what it contained.

"At ten minutes till four in the morning Washington time, ten till two in Pueblo, Minh called me," Barbara said. "I'd told the hotel operator to hold all calls, I needed my sleep, but Minh talked his way through. He played the tape for me . . . and we discussed it. I always have a cassette recorder with me, because I like to tape all meetings myself and have my own transcripts prepared. So I got my machine and held it to the phone to make my own copy. I didn't want to wait until Minh got a clean tape to me by courier. After Minh hung up, I sat at the desk in my room and listened to the last exchanges between the pilots maybe ten or twelve times. Then I got out my notebook and made a handwritten transcript of it, because sometimes things appear different to you when you read them than when you listen. Occasionally the eye sees nuances that the ear misses."

Joe now knew what he held in his hand. He could tell by the thickness that there were three sheets of paper.

Barbara said, "Minh had called me first. He intended to call Bruce Laceroth, then the chairman and the vice chairman of the Board—if not all five Board members— so each of them could hear the tape himself. It wasn't standard protocol, but this was a strange and unprecedented situation. I'm sure Minh got to at least one of those people—though they all deny hearing from him. We'll never know for sure, because Minh Tran died in a fire at the labs shortly before six o'clock that same morning, approximately two hours after he called me in Pueblo."

"Jesus."

"A very intense fire. An impossibly intense fire."

■

Surveying the trees that surrounded the meadow, Joe expected to see the pale faces of watchers in the deep shadows of the woods. When he and Barbara had first arrived, the site had struck him as remote, but now he felt as exposed and vulnerable as if he had been standing in the middle of any intersection in L.A.

He said, "Let me guess—the original tape from the cockpit recorder was destroyed in the lab fire."

"Supposedly burned to powder, vanished, no trace, gone, good-bye," Barbara said.

"What about the computer that was processing the digitized version?"

"Scorched garbage. Nothing in it salvageable."

"But you still have your copy."

She shook her head. "I left the cassette in my hotel room while I went to a breakfast meeting. The contents of the cockpit tape were so explosive, I didn't intend to share it right away with everyone on the team. Until we'd had time to think it through, we needed to be careful about when and how we released it."

"Why?"

"The pilot was dead, but his reputation was at stake. His family would be devastated if he was blamed. We had to be absolutely sure. If the cause was laid in Captain

Blane's lap, then tens of millions—even hundreds of millions—of dollars' worth of wrongful-death litigation would ensue. We had to act with due diligence. My plan was to bring Mario back to my room after breakfast to hear the tape, just the two of us."

"Mario Oliveri," Joe said, referring to the man in Denver who had told him last night that Barbara had retired and moved back to Colorado Springs.

"Yeah. As head of the human-performance group, Mario's thoughts were more important to me at that moment than anyone's. But just as we were finishing breakfast, we got word about the fire at the labs—about poor Minh. By the time I got back to my room with Mario, the copy of the tape I'd made over the phone was blank."

"Stolen and replaced."

"Or just erased on my own machine. I guess Minh told someone that I'd duped it long-distance."

"Right then you must have known."

She nodded. "Something was very wrong. Something stank."

Her mop of hair was as white as the feathers on the head of the eagle that had overflown them, but until this moment she had seemed younger than fifty. Now she suddenly seemed older.

"Something wrong," he said, "but you couldn't quite believe it."

"My life was the Safety Board. I was proud to be part of it. Still am, Joe. They're damn good people."

"Did you tell Mario what was on the tape?"

"Yeah."

"What was his reaction?"

"Amazement. Disbelief, I think."

"Did you show him the transcript you'd made?"

She was silent a moment. Then: "No."

"Why not?"

"My hackles were up."

"You didn't trust anyone."

"A fire that intense . . . there must have been an accelerant."

"Arson," Joe said.

"But no one ever raised the possibility. Except me. I don't have faith in the integrity of their investigation of that lab fire at all. Not at all."

"What did the autopsy on Minh reveal? If he was murdered and the fire set to cover it—"

"If he was, they couldn't prove it by what was left of the body. He was virtually cremated. The thing is . . . he was a really nice guy, Joe. He was sweet. He loved his job because he believed what he did would save lives, help to prevent other crashes. I hate these people, whoever they are."

Among the white pines at the foot of the meadow, near where Joe and Barbara had first entered the clearing, something moved: a shadow gliding through deeper shadows, dun against purple.

Joe held his breath. He squinted but could not identify what he had briefly glimpsed.

Barbara said, "I think it was just a deer."

"If it wasn't?"

"Then we're dead whether we finish this talk or not," she said in a matter-of-fact tone that revealed the bleak and paranoid new world order in which she lived following Flight 353.

He said, "The fact that your tape was erased—didn't that raise anyone's suspicions?"

"The consensus was that I'd been tired. Three hours' sleep the night of the crash—then only a few hours the next night before Minh called and woke me. Poor bleary-eyed

Barbara. I'd sat listening to the tape over and over, over and over, and at the end I must have pressed the wrong button—you know?—and erased it without realizing what I'd done." Her face twisted with sarcasm. "You can see how it must have happened."

"Any chance of that?"

"None whatsoever."

Though Joe unfolded the three sheets of paper, he didn't yet begin to read them.

He said, "Why didn't they believe you when you told them what you'd heard on the tape? They were your colleagues. They knew you to be a responsible person."

"Maybe some of them did believe it—and didn't want to. Maybe some of them just chalked it up to my fatigue. I'd been fighting an ear infection for weeks, and it had worn me down even before Pueblo. Maybe they took that into account. I don't know. And there's one or two who just plain don't like me. Who among us is universally loved? Not me. Too pushy. Too opinionated. Anyway, it was all moot—because without a tape, there was no proof of the exchanges between Blane and Santorelli."

"When did you finally tell someone you'd made a transcript word for word?"

"I was saving that. I was trying to figure the right moment, the right context in which to mention it—preferably once the investigation turned up some detail that would support what I said had been on the tape."

"Because by itself your transcript isn't real proof."

"Exactly. Sure, it's better than nothing, better than memory alone, but I needed to augment it with something. Then those two creeps woke me in the hotel in San Francisco, and after that . . . Well, I just wasn't much of a crusader any more."

Out of the eastern forest, two deer leaped in tandem into

the bottom of the meadow, a buck and a doe. They raced across the corner of the clearing, quickly disappearing into the trees on the northern perimeter.

Under the skin on the back of Joe's neck, ticks of apprehension still burrowed and twitched.

The movement he had glimpsed earlier must have been the two deer. From their volatile entrance into the meadow, however, he inferred that they had been flushed from the trees by something—or someone—that had frightened them.

He wondered if any corner of the world would ever feel safe to him again. But he knew the answer even as the question passed through his mind: no.

No corner. Not anywhere.

Not ever.

■

He said, "Who do you suspect—inside the Safety Board? Who did Minh call next after you? Because that person is probably the one who told him not to pass the word any further—and then arranged to have him killed and the evidence burned."

"It could have been any of them he was intending to call. They were all his superiors, and he would have obeyed their instructions. I'd like to think it can't be Bruce Laceroth, because he's a bedrock guy. He started out a grunt like the rest of us did, worked his way up. The five Board members, on the other hand, are presidential appointees, approved by the Senate for five-year terms."

"Political hacks."

"No, actually, the great majority of the board members over the years have been straight shooters, trying to do their best. Most of them are a credit to the agency, and others we just endure. Once in a while, yeah, one of them is slime in a suit."

"What about the current chairman and vice chairman? You said Minh Tran was going to call them—supposing he wasn't able to reach Laceroth first."

"They're not your ideal public servants. Maxine Wulce is the chairman. An attorney, young and politically ambitious, looking out for number one, a real piece of work. Wouldn't give you two cents for her."

"Vice chairman?"

"Hunter Parkman. Pure political patronage. He's old money, so he doesn't need the job, but he likes being a presidential appointee and talking crash lore at parties. Give you fifteen cents for him."

Although he had continued to study the woods at the foot of the meadow, Joe had seen no further movement among those trees.

Far to the east, a vein of lightning pulsed briefly through the dark muscle of the storm.

He counted the seconds between the silver flash and the rumble of thunder, translating time to distance, and judged that the rain was five or six miles from them.

Barbara said, "I've given you only a Xerox of the transcript I wrote down that night. I've hidden the original away. God knows why, since I'll never use it."

Joe was torn between a rage to know and a fear of knowing. He sensed that in the exchanges between Captain Blane and First Officer Santorelli, he would discover new dimensions to the terror that his wife and daughters had endured.

Finally Joe focused his attention on the first page, and Barbara watched over his shoulder as he followed the text with one finger to allow her to see where he was reading.

*Sounds of First Officer Santorelli returning to his
seat from the lavatory. His initial comments are
captured by the overhead cockpit microphone before
he puts on his headset with the boom mike.*

SANTORELLI: Get to L.A. (unintelligible), I'm going to
chow down on so much (unintelligible), hummus, tab-
bouleh, lebne with string cheese, big plateful of kibby
till I bust. There's this Armenian place, it's the best.
You like Middle East food?

Three seconds of silence.

SANTORELLI: Roy? Somethin' up?

Two seconds of silence.

SANTORELLI: What's this? What're we . . . Roy, you
off the autopilot?

BLANE: One of their names is Dr. Louis Blom.

SANTORELLI: What?

BLANE: One of their names is Dr. Keith Ramlock.

SANTORELLI: (with audible concern) What's this on
the McDoo? You been in the FMC, Roy?

When Joe inquired, Barbara said, "The 747-400s use
digitized avionics. The instrument panel is dominated
by six of the largest cathode-ray tubes made, for the display of data. And the McDoo means MCDU, the multi-
function control and display unit. There's one beside each
pilot's seat, and they're interconnected, so anything one
pilot enters is updated on the other's unit. They control
the Honeywell/Sperry FMC, the flight management computer. The pilots input the flight plan and the load sheet

through the MCDU keyboards, and all en route flight-plan changes are also actuated with the McDoos."

"So Santorelli comes back from the john and sees that Blane has made changes to the flight plan. Is that unusual?"

"Depends on weather, turbulence, unexpected traffic, holding patterns because of airport problems at the destination . . ."

"But at this point in a coast-to-coast flight—little past the midpoint—in pretty good weather, with everything apparently ticking along routinely?"

Barbara nodded. "Yeah, Santorelli would wonder why they were making flight-plan changes under the circumstances. But I think the concern in his voice results more from Blane's unresponsiveness and from something unusual he saw on the McDoo, some plan change that didn't make sense."

"Which would be?"

"As I said earlier, they were seven degrees off course."

"Santorelli wouldn't have felt that happening when he was in the lavatory?"

"It started soon after he was off the flight deck, and it was a gradual, really gentle bank. He might have sensed something, but there's no reason he would have realized the change was so big."

"Who are these doctors—Blom and Ramlock?"

"I don't have a clue. But read on. It gets weirder."

BLANE: They're doing bad things to me.

SANTORELLI: Captain, what's wrong here?

BLANE: They're mean to me.

SANTORELLI: Hey, are you with me here?

BLANE: Make them stop.

Barbara said, "Blane's voice changes there. It's sort of odd all the way through this, but when he says, 'Make them stop,' there's a tremor in it, a fragility, as if he's actually in . . . not pain so much but emotional distress."

SANTORELLI: Captain . . . Roy, I'm taking over here now.

BLANE: Are we recording?

SANTORELLI: What?

BLANE: Make them stop hurting me.

SANTORELLI: (worriedly) Gonna be—

BLANE: Are we recording?

SANTORELLI: Gonna be all right now—

A hard sound like a punch. A grunt, apparently from Santorelli. Another punch. Santorelli falls silent.

BLANE: Are we recording?

As a timpani of thunder drummed an overture in the east, Joe said, "He sucker-punched his copilot?"

"Or hit him with some blunt object, maybe something he'd taken out of his flight bag and hidden beside his seat while Santorelli was in the lav, something he was ready with."

"Premeditation. What the hell?"

"Probably hit him in the face, because Santorelli went right out. He's silent for ten or twelve seconds, and then"— she pointed to the transcript—"we hear him groaning."

"Dear God."

"On the tape, Blane's voice now loses the tremor, the fragility. There's a bitterness that makes your skin crawl."

BLANE: Make them stop or when I get the chance . . . when I get the chance, I'll kill everybody. Everybody. I will. I'll do it. I'll kill everybody, and I'll like it.

The transcript rattled in Joe's hands.

He thought of the passengers on 353: some dozing in their seats, others reading books, working on laptops, leafing through magazines, knitting, watching a movie, having a drink, making plans for the future, all of them complacent, none aware of the terrifying events occurring in the cockpit.

Maybe Nina was at the window, gazing out at the stars or down at the top of the cloud cover below them; she liked the window seat. Michelle and Chrissie might have been playing a game of Go Fish or Old Maid; they traveled with decks for various games.

He was torturing himself. He was good at it because a part of him believed that he deserved to be tortured.

Forcing those thoughts out of his mind, Joe said, "What was going on with Blane, for God's sake? Drugs? Was his brain fried on something?"

"No. That was ruled out."

"How?"

"It's always a priority to find something of the pilots' remains to test for drugs and alcohol. It took some time in this case," she said, as with a sweep of one hand she indicated the scorched pines and aspens uphill, "because a lot of the organic debris was scattered as much as a hundred yards into the trees west and north of the impact."

An internal darkness encroached on Joe's field of vision, until he seemed to be looking at the world through a tunnel. He bit his tongue almost hard enough to draw blood, breathed slowly and deeply, and tried not to let Barbara see how shaken he was by these details.

She put her hands in her pockets. She kicked a stone into the crater. "Really need this stuff, Joe?"

"Yes."

She sighed. "We found a portion of a hand we suspected was Blane's because of a half-melted wedding band that was fused to the ring finger, a relatively unique gold band. There was some other tissue as well. With that we identified—"

"Fingerprints?"

"No, those were burned off. But his father's still alive, so the Armed Forces DNA Identification Laboratory was able to confirm it was Blane's tissue through a DNA match with a blood sample that his dad supplied."

"Reliable?"

"A hundred percent. Then the remains went to the toxicologists. There were minute amounts of ethanol in both Blane and Santorelli, but that was just the consequence of putrefaction. Blane's partial hand was in those woods more than seventy-two hours before we found it. Santorelli's remains—four days. Some ethanol related to tissue decay was to be expected. But otherwise, they both passed all the toxicologicals. They were clean and sober."

Joe tried to reconcile the words on the transcript with the toxicological findings. He couldn't.

He said, "What're the other possibilities? A stroke?"

"No, it just didn't sound that way on the tape I listened to," Barbara said. "Blane speaks clearly, with no slurring of the voice whatsoever. And although what he's saying is damn bizarre, it's nevertheless coherent—no transposition of words, no substitution of inappropriate words."

Frustrated, Joe said, "Then what the hell? A nervous breakdown, psychotic episode?"

Barbara's frustration was no less than Joe's: "But where the hell did it come from? Captain Delroy Michael Blane was the most rock-solid psychological specimen you'd ever want to meet. Totally stable guy."

"Not totally."

"Totally stable guy," she insisted. "Passed all the company psychological exams. Loyal family man. Faithful husband. A Mormon, active in his church. No drinking, no drugs, no gambling. Joe, you can't find *one person* out there who ever saw him in a single moment of aberrant behavior. By all accounts he wasn't just a good man, not just a solid man—but a *happy* man."

Lightning glimmered. Wheels of rolling thunder clattered along steel rails in the high east.

Pointing to the transcript, Barbara showed Joe where the 747 made the first sudden three-degree heading change, nose right, which precipitated a yaw. "At that point, Santorelli was groaning but not fully conscious yet. And just before the maneuver, Captain Blane said, 'This is fun.' There are these other sounds on the tape—here, the rattle and clink of small loose objects being flung around by the sudden lateral acceleration."

This is fun.

Joe couldn't take his eyes off those words.

Barbara turned the page for him. "Three seconds later, the aircraft made another violent heading change, of four degrees, nose left. In addition to the previous clatter, there were now sounds from the aircraft—a thump and a low shuddery noise. And Captain Blane is laughing."

"Laughing," Joe said with incomprehension. "He was going to go down with them, and he was laughing?"

"It wasn't anything you'd think of as a *mad* laugh, either. It was . . . a pleasant laugh, as if he were genuinely enjoying himself."

This is fun.

Eight seconds after the first yawing incident, there was another abrupt heading change of three degrees, nose left, followed just two seconds later by a severe shift of seven degrees, nose right. Blane laughed as he executed the first maneuver and, with the second, said, *Oh, wow!*

"This is where the starboard wing lifted, forcing the port wing down," Barbara said. "In twenty-two seconds the craft was banking at a hundred and forty-six degrees, with a downward nose pitch of eighty-four degrees."

"They were finished."

"It was deep trouble but not hopeless. There was still a chance they might have pulled out of it. Remember, they were above twenty thousand feet. Room for recovery."

Because he had never read about the crash or watched television reports of it, Joe had always pictured fire in the aircraft and smoke filling the cabin. A short while ago, when he had realized that the passengers were spared that particular terror, he'd hoped that the long journey down had been less terrifying than the imaginary plunge that he experienced in some of his anxiety attacks. Now, however, he wondered which would have been worse: the gush of smoke and the instant recognition of impending doom that would have come with it—or clean air and the hideously attenuated false hope of a last-minute correction, salvation.

The transcript indicated the sounding of alarms in the cockpit. An altitude alert tone. A recorded voice repeatedly warning *Traffic!* because they were descending through air corridors assigned to other craft.

Joe asked, "What's this reference to the 'stick-shaker alarm'?"

"It makes a loud rattling, a scary sound nobody's

going to overlook, warning the pilots that the plane has lost lift. They're going into a stall."

Gripped in the fist of fate punching toward the earth, First Officer Victor Santorelli abruptly stopped mumbling. He regained consciousness. Perhaps he saw clouds whipping past the windshield. Or perhaps the 747 was already below the high overcast, affording him a ghostly panorama of onrushing Colorado landscape, faintly luminous in shades of gray from dusty pearl to charcoal, with the golden glow of Pueblo scintillant to the south. Or maybe the cacophony of alarms and the radical data flashing on the six big display screens told him in an instant all that he needed to know. He had said, *Oh, Jesus.*

"His voice was wet and nasal," Barbara said, "which might have meant that Blane broke his nose."

Even reading the transcript, Joe could hear Santorelli's terror and his frantic determination to survive.

SANTORELLI: Oh, Jesus. No, Jesus, no.

BLANE: (laughter) Whoooaaa. Here we go, Dr. Ramlock. Dr. Blom, here we go.

SANTORELLI: Pull!

BLANE: (laughter) Whoooaaa. (laughter) Are we recording?

SANTORELLI: Pull up!

Santorelli is breathing rapidly, wheezing. He's grunting, struggling with something, maybe with Blane, but it sounds more like he's fighting the control wheel. If Blane's respiration rate is elevated at all, it's not registering on the tape.

SANTORELLI: Shit, shit!

BLANE: Are we recording?

Baffled, Joe said, "Why does he keep asking about it being recorded?"

Barbara shook her head. "I don't know."

"He's a pilot for how long?"

"Over twenty years."

"He'd know the cockpit-voice recorder is always working. Right?"

"He should know. Yeah. But he's not exactly in his right mind, is he?"

Joe read the final words of the two men.

SANTORELLI: Pull!

BLANE: Oh, wow.

SANTORELLI: Mother of God . . .

BLANE: Oh, yeah.

SANTORELLI: No.

BLANE: (child-like excitement) Oh, yeah.

SANTORELLI: Susan.

BLANE: Now. Look.

Santorelli begins to scream.

BLANE: Cool.

Santorelli's scream is three and a half seconds long, lasting to the end of the recording, which is terminated by impact.

Wind swept the meadow grass. The sky was swollen with a waiting deluge. Nature was in a cleansing mood.

Joe folded the three sheets of paper. He tucked them into a jacket pocket.

For a while he couldn't speak.

Distant lightning. Thunder. Clouds in motion.

Finally, gazing into the crater, Joe said, "Santorelli's last word was a name."

"Susan."

"Who is she?"

"His wife."

"I thought so."

At the end, no more entreaties to God, no more pleas for divine mercy. At the end, a bleak acceptance. A name said lovingly, with regret and terrible longing but perhaps also with a measure of hope. And in the mind's eye not the cruel earth hurtling nearer or the darkness after, but a cherished face.

Again, for a while, Joe could not speak.

11

From the impact crater, Barbara Christman led Joe farther up the sloping meadow and to the north, to a spot no more than twenty yards from the cluster of dead, charred aspens.

"Here somewhere, in this general area, if I remember right," she said. "But what does it matter?"

When Barbara first arrived in the meadow on the morning after the crash, the shredded and scattered debris of the 747-400 had not resembled the wreckage of an airliner. Only two pieces had been immediately recognizable: a portion of one engine and a three-unit passenger-seat module.

He said, "Three seats, side by side?"

"Yes."

"Upright?"

"Yes. What's your point?"

"Could you identify what part of the plane the seats were from?"

"Joe—"

"From what part of the plane?" he repeated patiently.

"Couldn't have been from first class, and not from business class on either the main deck or the upper, because those are all two-seat modules. The center rows in economy class have four seats, so it had to come from the port or starboard rows in economy."

"Damaged?"

"Of course."

"Badly?"

"Not as badly as you'd expect."

"Burned?"

"Not entirely."

"Burned at all?"

"As I remember . . . there were just a few small scorch marks, a little soot."

"In fact, wasn't the upholstery virtually intact?"

Her broad, clear face now clouded with concern. "Joe, no one survived this crash."

"Was the upholstery intact?" he pressed.

"As I remember . . . it was slightly torn. Nothing serious."

"Blood on the upholstery?"

"I don't recall."

"Any bodies in the seats?"

"No."

"Body parts?"

"No."

"Lap belts still attached?"

"I don't remember. I suppose so."

"If the lap belts were attached—"

"No, it's ridiculous to think—"

"Michelle and the girls were in economy," he said.

Barbara chewed on her lip, looked away from him, and stared toward the oncoming storm. "Joe, your family wasn't in those seats."

"I know that," he assured her. "I know."

But how he *wished*.

She met his eyes again.

He said, "They're dead. They're gone. I'm not in denial here, Barbara."

"So you're back to this Rose Tucker."

"If I can find out where she was sitting on the plane, and if it was either the port or starboard side in economy—that's at least some small corroboration."

"Of what?"

"Her story."

"Corroboration," Barbara said disbelievingly.

"That she survived."

Barbara shook her head.

"You didn't meet Rose," he said. "She's not a flake. I don't think she's a liar. She has such . . . power, presence."

On the wind came the ozone smell of the eastern lightning, that theater-curtain scent which always rises immediately before the rain makes its entrance.

In a tone of tender exasperation, Barbara said, "They came down four miles, straight in, nose in, no hit-and-skip, the whole damn plane *shattering* around Rose Tucker, unbelievable explosive force—"

"I understand that."

"God knows, I really don't mean to be cruel, Joe—but *do* you understand? After all you've heard, do you? Tremendous explosive force all around this Rose. Impact force great enough to pulverize stone. Other passengers and crew . . . in most cases the flesh is literally *stripped* off their bones in an instant, stripped away as clean as if boiled off. Shredded. Dissolved. Disintegrated. And the bones themselves splintered and crushed like breadsticks. Then in the second instant, even as the plane is still hammering into the meadow, a spray of jet fuel—a spray as fine as an aerosol mist—explodes. Everywhere fire. Geysers of fire, rivers of fire, rolling tides of inescapable fire. Rose Tucker didn't float down in her seat like a bit of dandelion fluff and just stroll away through the inferno."

Joe looked at the sky, and he looked at the land at his feet, and the land was the brighter of the two.

He said, "You've seen pictures, news film, of a town hit by a tornado, everything smashed flat and reduced to rubble so small that you could almost sift it through a colander—and right in the middle of the destruction is one house, untouched or nearly so."

"That's a weather phenomenon, a caprice of the wind. But this is simple physics, Joe. Laws of matter and motion. Caprice doesn't play a role in physics. If that whole damn town had been dropped four miles, then the one surviving house would have been rubble too."

"Some of the families of survivors . . . Rose has shown them something that lifts them up."

"What?"

"I don't know, Barbara. I want to see. I want her to show me too. But the point is . . . they believe her when she says she was aboard that airplane. It's more than mere belief." He remembered Georgine Delmann's shining eyes. "It's a profound conviction."

"Then she's a con artist without equal."

Joe only shrugged.

A few miles away, a tuning fork of lightning vibrated and broke the storm clouds. Shatters of gray rain fell to the east.

"For some reason," Barbara said, "you don't strike me as a devoutly religious man."

"I'm not. Michelle took the kids to Sunday school and church every week, but I didn't go. It was the one thing I didn't share with them."

"Hostile to religion?"

"No. Just no passion for it, no interest. I was always as indifferent to God as He seemed to be to me. After the crash . . . I took the one step left in my 'spiritual journey' from disinterest to disbelief. There's no way to reconcile the idea of a benign God with what happened to everyone on that plane . . . and to those of us who're going to spend the rest of our lives missing them."

"Then if you're such an atheist, why do you insist on believing in this miracle?"

"I'm not saying Rose Tucker's survival was a miracle."

"Damned if I can see what *else* it would be. Nothing but God Himself and a rescue team of angels could have pulled her out of that in one piece," Barbara insisted with a note of sarcasm.

"No divine intervention. There's another explanation, something amazing but logical."

"Impossible," she said stubbornly.

"Impossible? Yeah, well . . . so was everything that happened in the cockpit with Captain Blane."

She held his gaze while she searched for an answer in the deep and orderly files of her mind. She was not able to find one.

Instead, she said, "If you don't believe in anything—then what is it that you expect Rose to tell you? You say that what she tells them 'lifts them up.' Don't you imagine it's got to be something of a spiritual nature?"

"Not necessarily."

"What else would it be?"

"I don't know."

Repeating Joe's own words heavily colored with exasperation, she said, "'Something amazing but logical.'"

He looked away from her, toward the trees along the northern edge of the field, and he realized that in the fire-blasted aspen cluster was a sole survivor, reclothed in foliage. Instead of the characteristic smooth pale trunk, it had scaly black bark, which would provide a dazzling contrast when its leaves turned brilliant yellow in the autumn.

"Something amazing but logical," he agreed.

Closer than ever, lightning laddered down the sky, and the boom of thunder descended rung to rung.

"We better go," Barbara said. "There's nothing more here anyway."

Joe followed her down through the meadow, but he paused again at the rim of the impact crater.

The few times that he had gone to meetings of The Compassionate Friends, he had heard other grieving parents speak of the Zero Point. The Zero Point was the instant of the child's death, from which every future event would be dated, the eye blink during which crushing loss reset your internal gauges to zero. It was the moment at which your shabby box of hopes and wants—which had once seemed to be such a fabulous chest of bright dreams—was turned on end and emptied into an abyss, leaving you with zero expectations. In a clock tick, the future was no longer a kingdom of possibility and wonder, but a yoke of obligation—and only the unattainable past offered a hospitable place to live.

He had existed at the Zero Point for more than a year, with time receding from him in both directions, belonging to neither the days ahead nor those behind. It was as though he had been suspended in a tank of liquid nitrogen and lay deep in cryogenic slumber.

Now he stood at another Zero Point, the physical one, where his wife and daughters had perished. He wanted so badly to have them back that the wanting tore like eagle's claws at his viscera. But at last he wanted something else as well: justice for them, justice which could not give meaning to their deaths but which might give meaning to his.

He had to get all the way up from his cryogenic bed, shake the ice out of his bones and veins, and not lie down again until he had dug the truth out of the grave in which it had been buried. For his lost women, he would burn palaces, pull down empires, and waste the world if necessary for the truth to be found.

And now he understood the difference between justice and mere vengeance: genuine justice would bring him no relief of his pain, no sense of triumph; it would only allow him to step out of the Zero Point and, with his task completed, die in peace.

Down through the vaulted conifers came fluttering white wings of storm light, and again, and still more, as if the cracking sky were casting out a radiant multitude. Thunder and the rush of wind beat like pinions at Joe's ears, and by the many thousands, feathered shadows swooped and shuddered between the tree trunks and across the forest floor.

Just as he and Barbara reached her Ford Explorer, at the weedy end of the narrow dirt lane, a great fall of rain hissed and roared through the pines. They piled inside, their hair and faces jeweled, and her periwinkle-blue blouse was spattered with spots as dark as plum skin.

They didn't encounter whatever had frightened the deer from cover, but Joe was pretty sure now that the culprit had been another animal. In the run to beat the rain, he had sensed only wild things crouching—not the far deadlier threat of men.

Nevertheless, the crowding conifers seemed to provide ideal architecture for assassins. Secret bowers, blinds, ambushments, green-dark lairs.

As Barbara started the Explorer and drove back the way they had come, Joe was tense. Surveying the woods. Waiting for the bullet.

When they reached the gravel road, he said, "The two men that Blane named on the cockpit tape . . ."

"Dr. Blom and Dr. Ramlock."

"Have you tried to find out who they are, launched a search for them?"

"When I was in San Francisco, I was prying into Delroy Blane's background. Looking for any personal problems that might have put him in a precarious psychological condition. I asked his family and friends if they'd heard those names. No one had."

"You checked Blane's personal records, appointment calendars, his checkbook?"

"Yeah. Nothing. And Blane's family physician says he never referred his patient to any specialists with those names. There's no physician, psychiatrist, or psychologist in the San Francisco area by those names. That's as far as I carried it. Because then I was awakened by those bastards in my hotel room, a pistol in my face, and told to butt out."

■

To the end of the gravel road and onto the paved state route, where sizzling silver rain danced in a froth on the blacktop, Barbara fell into a troubled silence. Her brow was creased, but not—Joe sensed—because the inclement weather required that she concentrate on her driving.

The lightning and thunder had passed. Now the storm threw all its energy into wind and rain.

Joe listened to the monotonous thump of the windshield wipers.

He listened as well to the hard-driven drops snapping against the glass, which seemed at first to be a meaningless random rattle; but gradually he began to think that he perceived hidden patterns even in the rhythms of the rain.

Barbara found perhaps not a pattern but an intriguing puzzle piece that she had overlooked. "I'm remembering something peculiar, but . . ."

Joe waited.

" . . . but I don't want to encourage you in this weird delusion of yours."

"Delusion?"

She glanced at him. "This idea that there might have been a survivor."

He said, "Encourage me. Encouragement isn't something I've had much of in the past year."

She hesitated but then sighed. "There was a rancher not far from here who was already asleep when Flight 353 went down. People who work the land go to bed early in these parts. The explosion woke him. And then someone came to his door."

"Who?"

"The next day, he called the county sheriff, and the sheriff's office put him in touch with the investigation command center. But it didn't seem to amount to much."

"Who came to his door in the middle of the night?"

"A witness," Barbara said.

"To the crash?"

"Supposedly."

She looked at him but then quickly returned her attention to the rain-swept highway.

In the context of what Joe had told her, this recollection seemed by the moment to grow more disturbing to Barbara. Her eyes pinched at the corners, as if she were straining to see not through the downpour but more clearly into the past, and her lips pressed together as she debated whether to say more.

"A witness to the crash," Joe prompted.

"I can't remember why, of all places, she went to this ranch house or what she wanted there."

"She?"

"The woman who claimed to have seen the plane go down."

"There's something more," Joe said.

"Yeah. As I recall . . . she was a black woman."

His breath went stale in his lungs, but at last he exhaled and said, "Did she give this rancher her name?"

"I don't know."

"If she did, I wonder if he'd remember it."

■

At the turnoff from the state route, the entrance road to the ranch was flanked by tall white posts that supported an overhead sign bearing graceful green letters on a white background: LOOSE CHANGE RANCH. Under those three words, in smaller letters and in script: *Jeff and Mercy Ealing.* The gate stood open.

The oiled-gravel lane was flanked by white ranch fencing that divided the fields into smaller pastures. They passed a big riding ring, exercise yards, and numerous white stables trimmed in green.

Barbara said, "I wasn't here last year, but one of my people gave me a report on it. Coming back to me now . . . It's a horse ranch. They breed and race quarter horses. Also breed and sell some show horses like Arabians, I think."

The pasture grass, alternately churned by wind and flattened by the pounding rain, was not currently home to any horses. The riding ring and the exercise yards were deserted.

In some of the stables, the top of the Dutch door at each stall was open. Here and there, from the safety of their quarters, horses peered out at the storm. Some were nearly as dark as the spaces in which they stood, but others were pale or dappled.

The large and handsome ranch house, white clapboard with green shutters, framed by groupings of aspens, had the deepest front porch that Joe had ever seen. Under the heavy cape of gloom thrown down by the thunderheads, a yellow glow as welcoming as hearth light filled some of the windows.

Barbara parked in the driveway turnaround. She and Joe ran through the rain—previously as warm as bath water but now cooler—to the screened porch. The door swung inward with a creak of hinges and the singing of a worn tension spring, sounds so rounded in tone that they were curiously pleasing; they spoke of time passed at a gentle pace, of gracious neglect rather than dilapidation.

The porch furniture was white wicker with green cushions, and ferns cascaded from wrought-iron stands.

The house door stood open, and a man of about sixty, in a black rain slicker, waited to one side on the porch. The weather-thickened skin of his sun-darkened face was well creased and patinaed like the leather of a long-used saddlebag. His blue eyes were as quick and friendly as his smile. He raised his voice to be heard above the drumming of the rain on the roof. "Mornin'. Good day for ducks."

"Are you Mr. Ealing?" Barbara asked.

"That would be me," said another man in a black slicker as he appeared in the open doorway.

He was six inches taller and twenty years younger than the man who had commented on the weather. But a life on horseback, in hot sun and dry wind and the nip of winter, had already begun to abrade the smooth, hard planes of youth and bless him with a pleasantly worn and appealing face that spoke of deep experience and rural wisdom.

Barbara introduced herself and Joe, implying that she still worked for the Safety Board and that Joe was her associate.

"You poking into that after a whole year?" Ealing asked.

"We weren't able to settle on a cause," Barbara said. "Never like to close a file until we know what happened. Why we're here is to ask about the woman who knocked on your door that night."

"Sure, I remember."

"Could you describe her?" Joe asked.

"Petite lady. About forty or so. Pretty."

"Black?"

"She was, yes. But also a touch of something else. Mexican maybe. Or more likely Chinese. Maybe Vietnamese."

Joe remembered the Asian quality of Rose Tucker's eyes. "Did she tell you her name?"

"Probably did," Ealing said. "But I don't recall it."

"How long after the crash did she show up here?" Barbara asked.

"Not too long." Ealing was carrying a leather satchel similar to a physician's bag. He shifted it from his right hand to his left. "The sound of the plane coming down woke me and Mercy before it hit. Louder than you ever hear a plane in these parts, but we knew what it had to be. I got out of bed, and Mercy turned on the light. I said, 'Oh, Lordy,' and then we heard it, like a big far-off quarry blast. The house even shook a little."

The older man was shifting impatiently from foot to foot.

Ealing said, "How is she, Ned?"

"Not good," Ned said. "Not good at all."

Looking out at the long driveway that dwindled through the lashing rain, Jeff Ealing said, "Where the hell's Doc

Sheely?" He wiped one hand down his long face, which seemed to make it longer.

Barbara said, "If we've come at a bad time—"

"We've got a sick mare, but I can give you a minute," Ealing said. He returned to the night of the crash. "Mercy called Pueblo County Emergency Rescue, and I quick got dressed and drove the pickup out to the main road, headed south, trying to figure where it went down and could I help. You could see the fire in the sky—not direct but the glow. By the time I got oriented and into the vicinity, there was already a sheriff's car blocking the turnoff from the state route. Another pulled up behind me. They were setting up a barrier, waiting for the search-and-rescue teams, and they made it clear this wasn't a job for untrained do-gooders. So I came home."

"How long were you gone?" Joe asked.

"Couldn't have been more than forty-five minutes. Then I was in the kitchen here with Mercy for maybe half an hour, having some decaf with a shot of Bailey's, wide awake and listening to the news on the radio and wondering was it worth trying to get back to sleep, when we heard the knocking at the front door."

Joe said, "So she showed up an hour and fifteen minutes after the crash."

"Thereabouts."

Its engine noise masked by the heavy downpour and by the shivery chorus of wind-shaken aspens, the approaching vehicle didn't attract their attention until it was almost upon them. A Jeep Cherokee. As it swung into the turnaround in front of the house, its headlights, like silver swords, slashed at the chain-mail rain.

"Thank God!" Ned exclaimed, pulling up the hood on his slicker. The screen door sang as he pushed through it and into the storm.

"Doc Sheely's here," Jeff Ealing said. "Got to help

him with the mare. But Mercy knows more about that woman than I do anyway. You go ahead and talk to her."

■

Mercy Ealing's graying blond hair was for the most part held away from her face and off her neck by three butterfly barrettes. She had been busy baking cookies, however, and a few curling locks had slipped loose, hanging in spirals along her flushed cheeks.

Wiping her hands on her apron and then, more thoroughly, on a dish towel, she insisted that Barbara and Joe sit at the breakfast table in the roomy kitchen while she poured coffee for them. She provided a plate heaped with freshly baked cookies.

The back door was ajar. An unscreened rear porch lay beyond. The cadenced rain was muffled here, like the drumming for a funeral cortege passing out on the highway.

The air was warm and redolent of oatmeal batter, chocolate, and roasting walnuts.

The coffee was good, and the cookies were better.

On the wall was a pictorial calendar with a Christian theme. The painting for August showed Jesus on the seashore, speaking to a pair of fishermen brothers, Peter and Andrew, who would cast aside their nets and follow Him to become fishers of men.

Joe felt as if he had fallen through a trapdoor into a different reality from the one in which he'd been living for a year, out of a cold strange place into the normal world with its little day-to-day crises, pleasantly routine tasks, and simple faith in the rightness of all things.

As she checked the cookies in the two ovens, Mercy recalled the night of the crash. "No, not Rose. Her name was Rachel Thomas."

Same initials, Joe realized. Maybe Rose walked out of the crash suspecting that somehow the plane had been brought down because she was aboard. She might be anxious to let her enemies think that she was dead. Keeping the same initials probably helped her remember the false name that she had given.

"She'd been driving from Colorado Springs to Pueblo when she saw the plane coming down, right over her," Mercy said. "The poor thing was so frightened, she jammed on the brakes, and the car spun out of control. Thank God for the seat belts. Went off the road, down an embankment, and turned over."

Barbara said, "She was injured?"

Spooning lumps of thick dough on greased baking sheets, Mercy said, "No, both fine and dandy, just shaken up some. It was only a little embankment. Rachel, she had dirt on her clothes, bits of grass and weeds stuck to her, but she was okay. Oh, shaky as a leaf in a gale but okay. She was such a sweet thing, I felt so sorry for her."

To Joe, Barbara said meaningfully, "So back then she was claiming to be a witness."

"Oh, I don't think she was making it up," Mercy said. "She was a witness, for sure. Very rattled by what she saw."

A timer buzzed. Diverted, Mercy slipped one hand into a baker's quilted mitten. From the oven, she withdrew a sheet filled with fragrant brown cookies.

"The woman came here that night for help?" Barbara asked.

Putting the hot aluminum tray on a wire cooling rack, Mercy said, "She wanted to call a taxi service in Pueblo, but I told her they never in a million years come way out here."

"She didn't want to get a tow truck for her car?" Joe asked.

"She didn't figure to be able to get it done at that hour of the night, all the way from Pueblo. She expected to come back the next day with the tow-truck driver."

Barbara said, "What did she do when you told her there was no way to get taxi service from out here?"

Sliding a sheet of raw dough drops into the oven, Mercy said, "Oh, then I drove them into Pueblo myself."

"All the way to Pueblo?" Barbara asked.

"Well, Jeff had to be up earlier than me. Rachel didn't want to stay over here, and it wasn't but an hour to get there, with my heavy foot on the pedal," Mercy said, closing the oven door.

"That was extraordinarily kind of you," Joe said.

"Was it? No, not really. The Lord wants us to be Samaritans. It's what we're here for. You see folks in trouble like this, you have to help them. And this was a real nice lady. All the way to Pueblo, she couldn't stop talking about the poor people on that plane. She was all torn up about it. Almost like it was her fault, what happened to them, just because she saw it a few seconds before it hit. Anyway, it was no big deal going to Pueblo . . . though coming back home that night was the devil's own trip, because there was so much traffic going to the crash site. Police cars, ambulances, fire trucks. Lots of lookie-loos too. Standing along the side of the road by their cars and pickups, hoping to see blood, I guess. Give me the creeps. Tragedy can bring out the best in people, but it also brings out the worst."

"On the way to Pueblo, did she show you where her car had gone off the highway?" Joe asked.

"She was too rattled to recognize the exact spot in the darkness and all. And we couldn't be stopping every half mile or whatever to see if maybe this was the right embankment, or then we'd never get the poor girl home to bed."

Another timer buzzed.

Putting on the quilted mitten again and opening the door on the second oven, Mercy said, "She was so pooped, all sleepy-eyed. She didn't care about tow trucks, just about getting home to bed."

Joe felt certain that there had been no car. Rose walked out of the burning meadow, into the woods, all but blind as she left the blaze for the dark, but desperately determined to get away before anyone discovered that she was alive, somehow sure that the 747 had been brought down because of her. Terrified, in a state of shock, horrified by the carnage, lost in the wilds, she had preferred to risk death from starvation and exposure rather than be found by a rescue team and perhaps fall into the hands of her eerily powerful enemies. Soon, by great good luck, she reached a ridge from which she was able to see, through the trees, the distant lights of the Loose Change Ranch.

Pushing aside her empty coffee cup, Barbara said, "Mercy, where did you take this woman in Pueblo? Do you remember the address?"

Holding the baking sheet half out of the oven to examine the cookies, Mercy said, "She never told me an address, just directed me street to street until we got to the house."

No doubt it was one that Rose had chosen at random, as it was unlikely that she knew anyone in Pueblo.

"Did you see her go inside?" Joe asked.

"I was going to wait until she unlocked the door and was inside. But she thanked me, said God bless, and I should scoot back home."

"Could you find the place again?" Barbara asked.

Deciding that the cookies needed an additional minute, Mercy slid the tray back into the oven, pulled off the mitten, and said, "Sure. Nice big house in a real nice neighborhood. But it wasn't Rachel's. It belonged to her partner in the medical practice. Did I say she was a doctor down in Pueblo?"

"But you didn't actually see her go into this place?" Joe asked. He assumed that Rose waited until Mercy was out of sight, then walked away from the house and found transportation out of Pueblo.

Mercy's face was red and dewy from the oven heat. Plucking two paper towels off a roll and blotting the sweat from her brow, she said, "No. Like I said, I dropped them off in front, and they went up the walk."

"Them?"

"The poor sleepy little thing. Such a dear. She was the daughter of Rachel's partner."

Startled, Barbara glanced at Joe, then leaned forward in her chair toward Mercy. "There was a child?"

"Such a little angel, sleepy but not cranky at all."

Joe flashed back to Mercy's mention of "seat belts," plural, and to other things she had said that suddenly required a more literal interpretation than he had given them. "You mean Rose . . . Rachel had a child with her?"

"Well, didn't I say?" Mercy looked puzzled, tossing the damp paper towel into a waste can.

"We didn't realize there was a child," Barbara said.

"I told you," Mercy said, perplexed by their confusion. "Back a year ago, when the fella came around from your Board, I told him all about Rachel and the little girl, about Rachel being a witness."

Looking at Joe, Barbara said, "I didn't remember that. I guess I did well even to remember this place at all."

Joe's heart turned over, turned like a wheel long stilled on a rusted axle.

Unaware of the tremendous impact that her revelation had on Joe, Mercy opened the oven door to check the cookies once more.

"How old was the girl?" he asked.

"Oh, about four or five," Mercy said.

Premonition weighed on Joe's eyes, and when he closed them, the darkness behind his lids swarmed with possibilities that he was terrified to consider.

"Can you . . . can you describe her?"

Mercy said, "She was just a little slip of a doll of a thing. Cute as a button—but then they're all pretty darn cute at that age, aren't they?"

When Joe opened his eyes, Barbara was staring at him, and her eyes brimmed with pity for him. She said, "Careful, Joe. It can't lead where you hope."

Mercy placed the hot baking sheet full of finished cookies on a second wire rack.

Joe said, "What color was her hair?"

"She was a little blonde."

He was moving around the table before he realized that he had risen from his chair.

Having picked up a spatula, Mercy was scooping the cookies off the cooler of the two baking sheets, transferring them to a large platter.

Joe went to her side. "Mercy, what color were this little girl's eyes?"

"Can't say I remember."

"Try."

"Blue, I guess," she said, sliding the spatula under another cookie.

"You guess?"

"Well, she was blond."

He surprised her by taking the spatula from her and putting it aside on the counter. "Look at me, Mercy. This is important."

From the table, Barbara warned him again. "Easy, Joe. Easy."

He knew that he should heed her warning. Indifference was his only defense. Indifference was his friend and his consolation. Hope is a bird that always flies, the light that always dies, a stone that crushes when it can't be carried any farther. Yet with a recklessness that frightened him, he felt himself shouldering that stone, stepping into the light, reaching toward those white wings.

"Mercy," he said, "not all blondes have blue eyes, do they?"

Face-to-face with him, captured by his intensity, Mercy Ealing said, "Well . . . I guess they don't."

"Some have green eyes, don't they?"

"Yes."

"If you think about it, I'm sure you've even seen blondes with brown eyes."

"Not many."

"But some," he said.

Premonition swelled in him again. His heart was a bucking horse now, iron-shod hooves kicking the stall boards of his ribs.

"This little girl," he said, "are you sure she had blue eyes?"

"No. Not sure at all."

"Could her eyes have been gray?"

"I don't know."

"Think. Try to remember."

Mercy's eyes swam out of focus as memory pulled her vision to the past, but after a moment, she shook her head. "I can't say they were gray, either."

"Look at my eyes, Mercy."

She was looking.

He said, "They're gray."

"Yes."

"An unusual shade of gray."

"Yes."

"With just the faintest touch of violet to them."

"I see it," she said.

"Could this girl . . . Mercy, could this child have had eyes like mine?"

She appeared to know what answer he needed to hear, even if she could not guess why. Being a goodhearted woman, she wanted to please him. At last, however, she said, "I don't really know. I can't say for sure."

A sinking sensation overcame Joe, but his heart continued to knock hard enough to shake him.

Keeping his voice calm, he said, "Picture the girl's face." He put his hands on Mercy's shoulders. "Close your eyes and try to see her again."

She closed her eyes.

"On her left cheek," Joe said. "Beside her earlobe. Only an inch in from her earlobe. A small mole."

Mercy's eyes twitched behind her smooth lids as she struggled to burnish her memory.

"It's more of a beauty mark than a mole," Joe said. "Not raised but flat. Roughly the shape of a crescent moon."

After a long hesitation, she said, "She might have had a mark like that, but I can't remember."

"Her smile. A little lopsided, a little crooked, turned up at the left corner of her mouth."

"She didn't smile that I remember. She was so sleepy . . . and a little dazed. Sweet but withdrawn."

Joe could not think of another distinguishing feature that might jar Mercy Ealing's memory. He could have regaled her for hours with stories about his daughter's grace, about her charm, about her humor and the musical quality of her laughter. He could have spoken at length of her beauty: the smooth sweep of her forehead, the coppery gold of her eyebrows and lashes, the pertness of her nose, her shell-like ears, the combination of fragility and stubborn strength in her face that sometimes made his heart ache when he watched her sleeping, the inquisitiveness and unmistakable intelligence that informed her every expression. Those were subjective impressions, however, and no matter how detailed such descriptions were, they could not lead Mercy to the answers that he had hoped to get from her.

He took his hands from her shoulders.

She opened her eyes.

Joe picked up the spatula he had taken from her. He put it down again. He didn't know what he was doing.

She said, "I'm sorry."

"It's okay. I was hoping . . . I thought . . . I don't know. I'm not sure what I was thinking."

Self-deceit was a suit that didn't fit him well, and even as he lied to Mercy Ealing, he stood naked to himself, excruciatingly aware of what he had been hoping, thinking. He'd been in a fit of searching behavior again, not chasing anyone into a convenience store this time, not stalking an imagined Michelle through a mall or department store, not rushing to a schoolyard fence for a closer glimpse of a Chrissie who was not Chrissie after all, but heart-deep in searching behavior nonetheless. The coincidence of this mystery child sharing his lost daughter's age and hair color had been all that he needed to send him racing pell-mell once more in pursuit of false hope.

"I'm sorry," Mercy said, clearly sensing the precipitous downward spiral of his mood. "Her eyes, the mole, the smile . . . just don't ring a bell. But I remember her name. Rachel called her Nina."

Behind Joe, at the table, Barbara got up so fast that she knocked over her chair.

12

At the corner of the back porch, the water falling through the downspout produced a gargle of phantom voices, eager and quarrelsome, guttural and whispery, spitting out questions in unknown tongues.

Joe's legs felt rubbery. He leaned with both hands on the wet railing. Rain blew under the porch eaves, spattering his face.

In answer to his question, Barbara pointed toward the low hills and the woods to the southwest. "The crash site was that way."

"How far?"

Mercy stood in the open kitchen door. "Maybe half a mile as the crow flies. Maybe a little farther."

Out of the torn meadow, into the forest where the fire died quickly because it had been a wet summer that year, farther into the darkness of the trees, thrashing through the thin underbrush, eyes adjusting grudgingly to the gloom, perhaps onto a deer trail that allowed easy passage, perhaps across another meadow, to the hilltop from which the ranch lights could be seen, Rose might have led—or mostly carried—the child. Half a mile as the crow flies, but twice or three times as far when one followed the contours of the land and the way of the deer.

"One and a half miles on foot," Joe said.

"Impossible," Barbara said.

"Very possible. She could have done it."

"I'm not talking about the hike." She turned to Mercy and said, "Mrs. Ealing, you have been an enormous help to us already, a really enormous help, but we've got a confidential matter to discuss here for a minute or two."

"Oh, of course, I understand. You just take all the time you want," said Mercy, hugely curious but still too polite to intrude. She backed off the threshold and closed the kitchen door.

"Only a mile and a half," Joe repeated.

"On the horizontal," Barbara said, moving close to him, putting a hand on his shoulder. "Only a mile and a half on the horizontal, but more than four miles on the vertical, straight down, sky to ground. *That's* the part I can't accept, Joe."

He was struggling with it himself. To believe in survivors required faith or something very like it, and he was without faith by choice and by necessity. To put faith in a God would require him to see meaning in the suffering that was the weft of human experience, and he could see no meaning to it. On the other hand, to believe that this miracle of survival resulted somehow from the scientific research in which Rose was engaged, to contemplate that humankind could reach successfully for god-like power— Shadrach saving Shadrach from the furnace, Lazarus raising Lazarus from the grave—required him to have faith in the transcendent spirit of humankind. Its goodness. Its beneficent genius. After fourteen years as a crime reporter, he knew men too well to bend his knee before the altar in the First Church of Humanity the Divine. Men had a genius for arranging their damnation, but few if any were capable of their own salvation.

With her hand still on Joe's shoulder, being tough with him but in the spirit of sisterly counseling, she said,

"First you want me to believe there was one survivor of that holocaust. Now it's two. I stood in the smoking ruins, in the slaughterhouse, and I *know* that the odds against anyone walking out of there on her own two feet are billions to one."

"Granted."

"No—greater than billions to one. Astronomical, immeasurable."

"All right."

"So there simply are no odds whatsoever that *two* could have come through it, none, not even an infinitesimal chance."

He said, "There's a lot I haven't told you, and most of it I'm not going to tell you now, because you're probably safer not knowing. But one thing . . . this Rose Tucker is a scientist who's been working on something big for years, government or military financing behind it, something secret and very damn big."

"What?"

"I don't know. But before she boarded the flight in New York, she called a reporter out in Los Angeles, an old friend of hers, and set up an interview, with trusted witnesses, at the arrival gate at LAX. She said she was bringing something with her that would change the world forever."

Barbara searched his eyes, obviously seeking some sign that he was not serious about this change-the-world-overnight fantasy. She was a woman of logic and reason, impressed by facts and details, and experience had shown her that solutions were found at an inchworm's pace, in a journey of countless small steps. As an investigator, for years she'd dealt with puzzles that presented her with literally millions of pieces and that were hugely more complex than virtually any homicide case to which any police detective was ever assigned, mysteries of human action and machine failure that were solved not with miracles but with drudgery.

Joe understood the look in her eyes, because investigative journalism was not unlike her own work.

"Just what are you saying?" she pressed. "That when the plane rolls and plummets, Rose Tucker takes a squeeze bottle out of her purse, some fabulous new topical lotion that confers temporary invulnerability on the user, sort of like a sunscreen, and quickly coats herself?"

Joe almost laughed. This was the first time he'd felt like laughing in ages. "No, of course not."

"Then what?"

"I don't know. Something."

"Sounds like a big nothing."

"Something," he insisted.

With the forge fire of lightning now gone and with the crack of thunder silenced, the churning clouds had an iron-dark beauty.

In the distance the low, wooded hills were veiled in mists of enigma—the hills across which she had come that night, untouched out of fire and destruction.

Skirling wind made cottonwoods and aspens dance, and across the fields, billows of rain whirled like skirts in a tarantella.

He had hope again. It felt good. Exhilarating. Of course, that was why hope was dangerous. The glorious lifting up, the sweet sense of soaring, always too brief, and then the terrible fall that was more devastating because of the sublime heights from which it began.

But maybe it was worse never to hope at all.

He was filled with wonder and quickening expectation.

He was scared too.

"Something," he insisted.

He took his hands off the railing. His legs were sturdy again. He blotted his wet hands on his jeans. He wiped his rain-spattered face on the sleeve of his sportcoat.

Turning to Barbara, he said, "Somehow safe to the meadow, then a mile and a half to the ranch. A mile and a half in an hour and fifteen minutes, which might be just about right in the darkness, with a small child to carry or help along."

"I hate to be always the pin in the balloon—"

"Then don't be."

"—but there's one thing you have to consider."

"I'm listening."

Barbara hesitated. Then: "Just for the sake of argument, let's accept that there were survivors. That this woman was on the plane. Her name is Rose Tucker . . . but she told Mercy and Jeff that she was Rachel Thomas."

"So?"

"If she doesn't give them her real name, why does she give them Nina's real name?"

"These people who're after Rose . . . they're not after Nina, they don't care about Nina."

"If they find out Rose somehow saved the girl, and if she saved the girl because of this strange, radical news-truth-thing-whatever that she was bringing with her to the press interview in Los Angeles, then maybe somehow that makes the girl as big a danger to them as Rose herself seems to be."

"Maybe. I don't know. I don't care right now."

"My point is—she'd use another name for Nina."

"Not necessarily."

"She would," Barbara insisted.

"So what's the difference?"

"So maybe *Nina* is a false name."

He felt slapped. He didn't reply.

"Maybe the child who came to this house that night is really named Sarah or Mary or Jennifer . . ."

"No," Joe said firmly.

"Just like Rachel Thomas is a false name."

"If the child wasn't Nina, what an amazing coincidence it would be for Rose to pluck my daughter's name out of thin air. Talk about billion-to-one odds!"

"That plane could have been carrying more than one little blond girl going on five."

"Both of them named Nina? *Jesus*, Barbara."

"*If* there were survivors, and if one of them was a little blond girl," Barbara said, "you've at least got to prepare yourself for the possibility that she wasn't Nina."

"I know," he said, but he was angry with her for forcing him to say it. "I know."

"Do you?"

"Yes, of course."

"I'm worried for you, Joe."

"Thank you," he said sarcastically.

"Your soul's broken."

"I'm okay."

"You could fall apart so easy."

He shrugged.

"No," she said. "Look at yourself."

"I'm better than I was."

"She might not be Nina."

"She might not be Nina," he admitted, hating Barbara for this relentless insistence, even though he knew that she was genuinely concerned for him, that she was prescribing this pill of reality as a vaccine against the total collapse that he might experience if his hopes, in the end, were not realized. "I'm ready to face that she might turn out not to be Nina. Okay? Feel better? I can handle it if that's the case."

"You say it, but it's not true."

He glared at her. "It is true."

"Maybe a tiny piece of your heart knows she might not be Nina, a thin fiber, but the rest of your heart is right now pounding, *racing* with the conviction that she is."

He could feel his own eyes shining with—stinging with—the delirious expectation of a miraculous reunion.

Her eyes, however, were full of a sadness that infuriated him so much he was nearly capable of striking her.

■

Mercy making peanut-butter dough balls. A new curiosity—and wariness—in her eyes. Having seen, through the window, the emotional quality of the discussion on the porch. Perhaps catching a few words through the glass, even without attempting to eavesdrop.

Nevertheless, she was a Samaritan, with Jesus and Andrew and Simon Peter marking the month of August as a reminder for her, and she still wanted to do her best to help.

"No, actually, the girl never said her name. Rachel introduced her. The poor child never spoke two words. She was so tired, you see, so sleepy. And maybe in shock a little from the car rolling over. Not hurt, mind you. Not a mark on her. But her little face was as white and shiny as candle wax. Heavy-eyed and not really with us. Half in a sort of trance. I worried about her, but Rachel said she was okay, and Rachel was a doctor, after all, so then I didn't worry about it that much. The little doll slept in the car all the way to Pueblo."

Mercy rolled a ball of dough between her palms. She put the pale sphere on a baking sheet and flattened it slightly with the gentle pressure of her thumb.

"Rachel had been to Colorado Springs to visit family

for the weekend, and she'd taken Nina with her because Nina's dad and mom were on an anniversary cruise. At least that's how I understood it." Mercy began to fill a brown paper lunch bag with the cooled cookies that were stacked on the platter.

"Not the usual thing—I mean, a black doctor and a white doctor in practice together in these parts, and not usual, either, to see a black woman with a white child around here. But I take all that to mean the world's getting to be a better place at last, more tolerant, more loving."

She folded the top of the bag twice and handed it to Barbara.

"Thank you, Mercy."

To Joe, Mercy Ealing said, "I'm sure sorry I couldn't be more help to you."

"You've been a lot of help," he assured her. He smiled. "And there's cookies."

She looked toward the kitchen window that was on the side of the house rather than on the back of it. One of the stables was visible through the pall of rain.

She said, "A good cookie does lift the spirit, doesn't it? But I sure wish I could do more than make cookies for Jeff today. He dearly loves that mare."

Glancing at the calendar with the religious theme, Joe said, "How do you hold on to your faith, Mercy? How in a world with so much death, planes falling out of the sky and favorite mares being taken for no reason?"

She didn't seem surprised or offended by the question. "I don't know. Sometimes it's hard, isn't it? I used to be so angry that we couldn't have kids. I was working at some record for miscarriages, and then I just gave up. You want to scream at the sky sometimes. And there's nights you lie awake. But then I think . . . well, this life has its joys too. And, anyway, it's nothing but a place we have to pass through on our way to somewhere better. If we live forever, it doesn't matter so much what happens to us here."

Joe had been hoping for a more interesting answer. Insightful. Penetrating. Homespun wisdom. Something he could believe.

He said, "The mare will matter to Jeff. And it matters to you because it matters so much to him."

Picking up another lump of dough, rolling it into a pale moon, a tiny planet, she smiled and said, "Oh, if I understood it, Joe, then I wouldn't be me. I'd be God. And that's a job I sure wouldn't want."

"How so?"

"It's got to be even sadder than our end of things, don't you think? He knows our potential but has to watch us forever falling short, all the cruel things we do to one another, the hatred and the lies, the envy and greed and the endless coveting. We see only the ugliness people do to those around us, but He sees it all. The seat He's in has a sadder view than ours."

She put the ball of dough on the cookie sheet and impressed upon it the mark of her thumb: a moment of pleasure waiting to be baked, to be eaten, to lift the spirit.

The veterinarian's Jeep station wagon was still in the driveway, parked in front of the Explorer. A Weimaraner was lying in the back of the vehicle. As Joe and Barbara climbed into the Ford and slammed the doors, the dog raised its noble silver-gray head and stared at them through the rear window of the Jeep.

By the time that Barbara slipped the key into the ignition and started the Explorer, the humid air was filled with the aromas of oatmeal-chocolate-chip cookies and damp denim. The windshield quickly clouded with the condensation of their breath.

"If it's Nina, your Nina," Barbara said, waiting for the air conditioner to clear the glass, "then where has she been for this whole year?"

"With Rose Tucker somewhere."

"And why would Rose keep your daughter from you? Why such awful cruelty?"

"It's not cruelty. You hit on the answer yourself, out there on the back porch."

"Why do I suspect the only time you listen to me is when I'm full of shit?"

Joe said, "Somehow, since Nina survived with Rose, survived *because* of Rose, now Rose's enemies will want Nina too. If Nina had been sent home to me, she'd have been a target. Rose is just keeping her safe."

The pearly condensation retreated toward the edges of the windshield.

Barbara switched on the wipers.

From the rear window of the Jeep Cherokee, the Weimaraner still watched them without getting to its feet. Its eyes were luminous amber.

"Rose is keeping her safe," he repeated. "That's why I've got to learn everything I can about Flight 353 and stay alive long enough to find a way to break the story wide open. When it's exposed, when the bastards behind all of this are ruined and on their way to prison or the gas chamber, then Rose will be safe and Nina can . . . she can come back to me."

"If this Nina is your Nina," she reminded him.

"If she is, yes."

Under the somber yellow gaze of the dog, they swung past the Cherokee and circled the oval bed of blue and purple delphiniums around which the terminus of the driveway turned.

"You think we should have asked Mercy to help us find the house in Pueblo where she dropped Rose and the girl that night?" Barbara wondered.

"No point. Nothing there for us. They never went inside that house. As soon as Mercy drove out of sight, they moved on. Rose was just using Mercy to reach the nearest sizable town, where she could get transportation, maybe call a trusted friend in Los Angeles or somewhere. How large is Pueblo?"

"About a hundred thousand people."

"That's large enough. Plenty of ways in and out of a city that size. Bus, maybe train, rental car, even by air."

As they headed down the gravel driveway toward the paved road, Joe saw three men in hooded rain slickers exiting a stable stall beyond an exercise yard. Jeff Ealing, Ned, and the veterinarian.

They left both the lower and the upper halves of the Dutch door standing open. No horse followed them.

Huddled against the downpour, heads bowed as if they were a procession of monks, they moved toward the house. No clairvoyance was required to know that their shoulders were slumped not only under the weight of the storm but under the weight of defeat.

Now a call to the knackery. A beloved mare to be transported and rendered. Another summer afternoon on the Loose Change Ranch—never to be forgotten.

Joe hoped that the years, the toil, and the miscarriages had not caused any distance to open between Jeff and Mercy Ealing. He hoped that in the night they still held each other.

The gray storm light was so dim that Barbara switched on the headlights. In those twin beams, as they reached the paved highway, the silvery rain glittered like flensing knives.

In Colorado Springs, a network of shallow lakes had formed on the grammar-school playground next to which Joe had parked his rental car. In the gray-rinsed light, rising from the rain-dimpled water, the jungle gyms and the seesaws and the elaborate swing sets appeared strange to Joe, not at all like what they were, but like a steel-pipe Stonehenge more mysterious even than the ancient rock megaliths and trilithons on England's Salisbury Plain.

Everywhere he turned his eyes now, this world was different from the one that he had inhabited all his life. The change had begun the previous day, when he'd gone to the cemetery. Ever since, a *shift* seemed to be progressing with gathering power and speed, as though the world of Einsteinian laws had intersected with a universe where the rules of energy and matter were so different as to baffle the wisest mathematicians and the proudest physicists.

This new reality was both more piercingly beautiful and more fearsome than the one that it replaced. He knew the change was subjective and would never reverse itself. Nothing this side of death would ever again seem simple to him; the smoothest surface hid unknowable depths and complexities.

Barbara stopped in the street beside his rental car, two blocks from her house. "Well. I guess this is as far as we go."

"Thank you, Barbara. You've taken such risks—"

"I don't want you to worry about that. You hear me? It was my decision."

"If not for your kindness and your courage, I'd never have had a hope of getting to the bottom of this. Today you've opened a door for me."

"But a door to what?" she worried.

"Maybe to Nina."

Barbara looked weary and frightened and sad. She wiped one hand across her face, and then she looked only frightened and sad.

"Joe, you keep my voice in your head. Wherever you go from here, you remember to listen for me at the back of your mind. I'll be an old nag, telling you that even if two people somehow came out of that crash alive, it's damn unlikely that one of them is your Nina. Don't swing the sword on yourself, don't you be the one to cut yourself off at the knees."

He nodded.

"Promise me," she said.

"Promise."

"She's gone, Joe."

"Maybe."

"Armor your heart."

"We'll see."

"Better go," she said.

He opened the door and got out into the rain.

"Good luck," Barbara said.

"Thanks."

He slammed the door, and she drove away.

As he unlocked his rental car, Joe heard the Explorer's brakes bark less than half a block away. When he looked up, the Ford was reversing toward him, its red taillights shimmering on the slick blacktop.

She got out of the Explorer, came to him, put her arms around him, and held him tight. "You're a dear man, Joe Carpenter."

He embraced her too, but no words came to him. He remembered how badly he had wanted to strike her when she had pressed him to forsake the idea that Nina might be alive. He was ashamed by the hatred that he had felt for her then, ashamed and confused—but he was also touched by her friendship, which meant more to him now than he could have imagined when he first rang her doorbell.

"How can I have known you only a few short hours," she wondered, "and feel as if you're my son?"

She left him for the second time.

He got into his car as she drove away.

He watched the dwindling Explorer in the rearview mirror until it turned left into Barbara's driveway, two blocks behind him, and disappeared into her garage.

Across the street, the white trunks of the paper birches glowed like painted doorjambs, the deep moody shadows between like open doors to futures best left unvisited.

Soaked, he drove back to Denver with no regard for the speed limit, alternately using the heater and the air conditioner, trying to dry out his clothes.

He was electrified by the prospect of finding Nina.

In spite of what he had said to Barbara, in spite of what he had promised her, he knew that Nina was alive. One thing in this eerily altered world seemed absolutely right again at last: Nina alive, Nina out there somewhere. She was a warm light upon his skin, a spectrum of light beyond the ability of his eyes to detect, as were infrared and ultraviolet, but though he could not see her, he could feel her shining in the world.

This wasn't at all similar to the portentous feeling that had so often sent him spiraling into searching behavior, chasing after ghosts. This hope was rock under his hand, not mist.

He was as close to happiness as he had been in more than a year, but each time that his heart swelled too full with excitement, his mood was dampened by a pang of guilt. Even if he found Nina—*when* he found Nina—he would not also regain Michelle and Chrissie. They were gone forever, and it seemed callous of him to be too happy about reclaiming only one of three.

Nevertheless, the desire to learn the truth, which had motivated him to come to Colorado, was the tiniest fraction as powerful as the wrenching need to find his younger daughter, which now raged in him to a degree beyond the measurements used to define mere compulsion or obsession.

At Denver International Airport, he returned the car to the agency, paid the bill in cash, and retrieved his signed credit-card form. He was in the terminal again fifty minutes before his flight was scheduled to depart.

He was starving. But for two cookies in Mercy's kitchen, he had eaten nothing since the two cheeseburgers the previous evening on his way to the Vadance house and later a chocolate bar.

He found the nearest restaurant in the terminal. He ordered a club sandwich with french fries and a bottle of Heineken.

Bacon had never tasted half as good as it did now. He licked mayonnaise from his fingertips. The fries had a satisfying crunch, and the crisp dill pickle snapped with a spray of sour juice. For the first time since another August, he not only consumed his food but *relished* it.

On his way to the boarding gate, with twenty minutes to spare, he suddenly took a detour to the men's room. He thought he was going to be sick.

By the time he got into a stall and latched the door, his nausea passed. Instead of throwing up, he leaned his back against the door and wept.

He hadn't cried in many months, and he didn't know why he was crying now. Maybe because he was on the trembling edge of happiness with the thought of seeing Nina again. Or maybe because he was scared of never finding her or of losing her a second time. Maybe he was grieving anew for Michelle and Chrissie. Maybe he had learned too many dreadful details about what had happened to Flight 353 and to the people on it.

Maybe it was all those things.

He was on a runaway rocket of emotion, and he needed to regain control of himself. He wasn't going to be effective in his search for Rose and Nina if he swung wildly between euphoria and despair.

Red-eyed but recovered, he boarded the plane for Los Angeles as they issued the final call.

As the 737 took off, to Joe's surprise his heart made a hollow racket in his ears, like running footsteps descending stairs. He clutched the arms of his seat as though he might tumble forward and fall headlong.

He hadn't been afraid on the flight to Denver, but now he was in the lap of terror. Coming eastward, he would have welcomed death, for the wrongness of outliving his family had been heavy on his mind—but now, westward bound, he had a reason to live.

Even when they had reached cruising altitude and leveled off, he remained edgy. He could too easily imagine one of the pilots turning to the other and saying, *Are we recording?*

Since Joe could not get Captain Delroy Blane out of his mind anyway, he withdrew the three folded pages of the transcript from an inner jacket pocket. Reviewing it, he might see something that he had missed before—and he needed to keep his mind occupied, even if with this.

The flight wasn't heavily booked, a third of the seats

empty. He had a window seat with no immediate neighbor, so he was afforded the privacy he needed.

In response to his request, a flight attendant brought a pen and note pad.

As he read through the transcript, he extracted Blane's dialogue and printed it on the note pad. Standing apart from First Officer Victor Santorelli's increasingly frantic statements and shorn of Barbara's descriptions of sounds and pauses, the captain's words might allow for the discovery of nuances otherwise not easy to spot.

When he was done, Joe folded the transcript and returned it to his coat pocket. Then he read from the note pad:

> *One of their names is Dr. Louis Blom.*
>
> *One of their names is Dr. Keith Ramlock.*
>
> *They're doing bad things to me.*
>
> *They're mean to me.*
>
> *Make them stop.*
>
> *Are we recording?*
>
> *Make them stop hurting me.*
>
> *Are we recording?*
>
> *Are we recording?*
>
> *Make them stop or when I get the chance . . . when I get the chance, I'll kill everybody. Everybody. I will. I'll do it. I'll kill everybody, and I'll like it.*
>
> *This is fun.*
>
> *Whoooaaa. Here we go, Dr. Ramlock. Dr. Blom, here we go.*

Whoooaaa. Are we recording?

Are we recording?

Oh, wow.

Oh, yeah.

Oh, yeah.

Now. Look.

Cool.

Joe didn't see anything new in the material, but something he had noticed before was more obvious when Blane's dialogue was read in this extracted format. Although the captain was speaking in the voice of an adult, some of the things he was saying had a distinct childlike quality.

They're doing bad things to me. They're mean to me. Make them stop. Make them stop hurting me.

This was neither the phrasing nor the word choice most adults would use to accuse tormentors or to ask for help.

His longest speech, a threat to kill everybody *and like it*, was petulant and childish as well—especially when immediately followed by the observation *This is fun.*

Whoooaaa. Here we go . . . Whoooaaa. Oh, wow. Oh, yeah.

Blane's reaction to the roll and plunge of the 747 was like that of a boy thrilling to the arrival of a roller coaster at the crown of the first hill on the track and, then, to the first stomach-rolling drop. According to Barbara, the captain had sounded unafraid; and there was no more terror in his words than in his tone of voice.

Now. Look.

Those words were spoken three and a half seconds before impact, as Blane watched the nightscape bloom like a black rose beyond the windscreen. He seemed gripped not by fear but by a sense of wonder.

Cool.

Joe stared at that final word for a long time, until the shiver it caused had passed, until he could consider all the implications of it with a measure of detachment.

Cool.

To the end, Blane reacted like a boy on an amusement-park ride. He had exhibited no more concern for his passengers and crew than a thoughtless and arrogant child might exhibit for the insects that he tortured with matches.

Cool.

Even a thoughtless child, as selfish as only the very young and the incurably immature can be, would nonetheless have shown some fear for *himself.* Even a determinedly suicidal man, having leaped off a high ledge, would cry out in mortal fear if not regret as he hurtled toward the pavement. Yet this captain, in whatever altered state he occupied, watched oblivion approach with no apparent concern, even with delight, as though he recognized no physical threat to himself.

Cool.

Delroy Blane. Family man. Faithful husband. Devout Mormon. Stable, loving, kind, compassionate. Successful, happy, healthy. Everything to live for. Cleared by the toxicological tests.

What's wrong with this picture?

Cool.

A useless anger rose in Joe. It was not aimed at Blane, who surely was a victim too—though he didn't initially appear to be one. This was the simmering anger of his childhood and adolescence, undirected and therefore likely to swell like the ever-hotter steam in a boiler with no pressure-release valve.

He tucked the note pad into his jacket pocket.

His hands curled into fists. Unclenching them was difficult. He wanted to strike something. Anything. Until he broke it. Until his knuckles split and bled.

This blind anger always reminded Joe of his father.

■

Frank Carpenter had not been an angry person. The opposite. He never raised his voice in other than amusement and surprise and happy exclamation. He was a good man—inexplicably good and oddly optimistic, considering the suffering with which fate saddled him.

Joe, however, had been perpetually angry *for* him.

He could not remember his dad with two legs. Frank had lost the left one when his car was broadsided by a pickup truck driven by a nineteen-year-old drunk with lapsed insurance. Joe was not yet three years old at the time.

Frank and Donna, Joe's mother, had been married with little more than two paychecks and their work clothes. To save money, they carried only liability coverage with their car. The drunk driver had no assets, and they received no compensation from any insurance company for the loss of the limb.

The leg was amputated halfway between knee and hip. In those days there were no highly effective prostheses. Besides, a false leg with any sort of functioning knee was expensive. Frank became so agile and quick with one leg and a crutch that he joked about entering a marathon.

Joe had never been ashamed of his father's difference. He knew his dad not as a one-legged man with a peculiar lurching gait, but as a bedtime storyteller, an indefatigable player of Uncle Wiggly and other games, a patient softball coach.

The first serious fight he'd gotten into was when he was six, in first grade. A kid named Les Olner had referred to Frank as a "stupid cripple." Although Olner was a bully and bigger than Joe, his superior size was an insufficient advantage against the savage animal fury with which he was confronted. Joe beat the shit out of him. His intention was to put out Olner's right eye, so he would know what it was like to live with one of two, but a teacher pulled him off the battered kid before he could half blind him.

Afterward, he felt no remorse. He still felt none. He was not proud of this. It was just the way he felt.

Donna knew that her husband's heart would break a little if he learned his boy had gotten into trouble over him. She devised and enforced Joe's punishment herself, and together they concealed the incident from Frank.

That was the beginning of Joe's secret life of quiet rage and periodic violence. He grew up looking for a fight and usually finding one, but he chose the moment and the venue to ensure that his dad was unlikely to learn of it.

Frank was a roofer, but there was no scrambling up ladders and hustling from eaves to ridgeline with one leg. He was loath to take disability from the government, but he accepted it for a while, until he found a way to turn a talent for woodworking into an occupation.

He made jewelry boxes, lamp bases, and other items inlaid with exotic woods in intricate patterns, and he found shops that would carry his creations. For a while he cleared a few dollars more than the disability payments, which he relinquished.

A seamstress in a combination tailor's shop and dry cleaner, Donna came home from work every day with hair curled from the steam-press humidity and smelling of benzine and other liquid solvents. To this day, when

Joe entered a dry-cleaning establishment, his first breath brought vividly to mind his mother's hair and her honey-brown eyes, which as a child he'd thought were faded from a darker brown by steam and chemicals.

Three years after losing the leg, Frank began suffering pain in his knuckles and then his wrists. The diagnosis was rheumatoid arthritis.

A vicious thing, this disease. And in Frank, it progressed with uncommon speed, a fire spreading through him: the spinal joints in his neck, his shoulders, hips, his one remaining knee.

He shut down his woodworking business. There were government programs providing assistance, though never enough and always with the measure of humiliation that bureaucrats dished out with a hateful—and often unconscious—generosity.

The Church helped too, and charity from the local parish was more compassionately provided and less humbling to receive. Frank and Donna were Catholics. Joe went to Mass with them faithfully but without faith.

In two years, already hampered by the loss of one leg, Frank was in a wheelchair.

Medical knowledge has advanced dramatically in thirty years, but in those days, treatments were less effective than they are now—especially in cases as severe as Frank's. Nonsteroidal anti-inflammatory drugs, injections of gold salts, and then much later penicillamine. Still the osteoporosis progressed. More cartilage and tendon tissue were lost from the chronic inflammation. Muscles continued to atrophy. Joints ached and swelled. The immunosuppressant corticosteroids available at the time somewhat slowed but did not halt the deformation of joints, the frightening loss of function.

By the time Joe was thirteen, his daily routine included

helping his dad dress and bathe when his mother was at work. From the first, he never resented any tasks that fell to him; to his surprise, he found within himself a tenderness that was a counterweight to the omnipresent anger that he directed at God but that he inadequately relieved on those unlucky boys with whom he periodically picked fights. For a long time Frank was mortified to have to rely on his son for such private matters, but eventually the shared challenge of bathing, grooming, and toilet brought them closer, deepened their feelings for each other.

By the time Joe was sixteen, Frank was suffering with fibrousankylosis. Huge rheumatoid nodules had formed at several joints, including one the size of a golf ball on his right wrist. His left elbow was deformed by a nodule almost as large as the softball that he had thrown so many hundreds of times in backyard practices when Joe had been six years old and getting into Little League.

His dad lived now for Joe's achievements, so Joe was an honor student in spite of a part-time job at McDonald's. He was a star quarterback on the high-school football team. Frank never put any pressure on him to excel. Love motivated Joe.

In the summer of that year, he joined the YMCA Youth Athletics Program: the boxing league. He was quick to learn, and the coach liked him, said he had talent. But in his first two practice matches, he continued hammering punches into opponents after they were sagging on the ropes, beaten and defenseless. He'd had to be pulled off. To them, boxing was recreation and self-defense, but to Joe it was savage therapy. He didn't want to hurt anyone, not any specific individual, but he *did* hurt people; consequently, he was not permitted to compete in the league.

Frank's chronic pericarditis, arising from the rheumatoid arthritis, led to a virulent infection of the pericardium, which ultimately led to heart failure. Frank died two days before Joe's eighteenth birthday.

The week following the funeral Mass, Joe visited the church after midnight, when it was deserted. He'd had too many beers. He sprayed black paint on all the stations of the cross. He overturned a cast-stone statue of Our Lady and smashed a score of the ruby-red glasses from the votive-candle rack.

He might have done considerably more damage if he had not quickly been overcome by a sense of futility. He could not teach remorse to God. He could not express his pain with sufficient power to penetrate the steel veil between this world and the next—if there was a next.

Slumping in the front pew, he wept.

He sat there less than a minute, however, because suddenly he felt that weeping in the church might seem to be an admission of his powerlessness. Ludicrously, he thought it important that his tears not be misconstrued as an acceptance of the cruelty with which the universe was ruled.

He left the church and was never apprehended for the vandalism. He felt no guilt about what he'd done—and, again, no pride.

For a while he was crazy, and then he went to college, where he fit in because half of the student body was crazy too, with youth, and the faculty with tenure.

His mother died just three years later, at the age of forty-seven. Lung cancer, spreading to the lymphatic system. She had never been a smoker. Neither had his father. Maybe it was the fumes of the benzine and other solvents in the dry cleaner's shop. Maybe it was weariness, loneliness, and a way out.

The night she died, Joe sat at her bedside in the hospital, holding her hand, putting cold compresses on her brow, and slipping slivers of ice into her parched mouth when she asked for them, while she spoke sporadically, half coherently, about a Knights of Columbus dinner dance to which Frank had taken her when Joe was only two, the year before the accident and amputation. There was a big band with eighteen fine musicians, playing genuine dance music, not just shake-in-place rock-'n'-roll. She and Frank were self-taught in the fox-trot, swing, and the cha-cha, but they weren't bad. They knew each other's moves. How they laughed. There were balloons, oh, hundreds of balloons, suspended in a net from the ceiling. The centerpiece on each table was a white plastic swan holding a fat candle surrounded by red chrysanthemums. Dessert was ice cream in a sugar swan. It was a night of swans. The balloons were red and white, hundreds of them. Holding her close in a slow dance, he whispered in her ear that she was the most beautiful woman in the room, and oh, how he loved her. A revolving ballroom chandelier cast off splinters of colored light, the balloons came down, red and white, and the sugar swan tasted of almonds when it crunched between the teeth. She was twenty-nine years old the night of the dance, and she relished this memory and no other through the final hour of her life, as though it had been the last good time she could recall.

Joe buried her from the same church that he had vandalized three years earlier. The stations of the cross had been restored. A new statue of the Holy Mother watched over a full complement of votive glasses on the tiered rack.

Later, he expressed his grief in a bar fight. His nose was broken, but he did worse damage to the other guy.

He stayed crazy until he met Michelle.

On their first date, as he had returned her to her apartment, she had told him that he had a wild streak a foot wide. When he'd taken that as a compliment, she had told him that only a moron, a hormone-crazed pubescent boy, or an ape in the zoo would be witless enough to take pride in it.

Thereafter, by her example, she taught him everything that was to shape his future. That love was worth the risk of loss. That anger harms no one more than he who harbors it. That both bitterness and true happiness are choices that we make, not conditions that fall upon us from the hands of fate. That peace is to be found in the acceptance of things that we are unable to change. That friends and family are the blood of life, and that the purpose of existence is caring, commitment.

Six days before their wedding, in the evening, Joe went alone to the church from which he'd buried his parents. Having calculated the cost of the damage he'd done years before, he stuffed a wad of hundred-dollar bills into the poor box.

He made the contribution neither because of guilt nor because his faith was regained. He did it for Michelle, though she would never know of the vandalism or of this act of restitution.

Thereafter, his life had begun.

And then ended one year ago.

Now Nina was in the world again, waiting to be found, waiting to be brought home.

With the hope of finding Nina as balm, Joe was able to take the heat out of his anger. To recover Nina, he must be totally in control of himself.

Anger harms no one more than he who harbors it.

He was ashamed by how quickly and absolutely he had turned away from all the lessons that Michelle had taught him. With the fall of Flight 353, he too had fallen, had plummeted out of the sky into which Michelle had lifted him with her love, and had returned to the mud of bitterness. His collapse was a dishonor to her, and now he felt a sting of guilt as sharp as he might have felt if he'd betrayed her with another woman.

Nina, mirror of her mother, offered him the reason and the chance to rebuild himself into a reflection of the person he had been before the crash. He could become again a man worthy of being her father.

Nine-ah, Neen-ah, have you seen her?

He leafed slowly through his treasure trove of mental images of Nina, and the effect was soothing. Gradually, his clenched hands relaxed.

He began the last hour of the flight by reading two of the four printouts of articles about Teknologik that he had retrieved from the *Post* computer the previous afternoon.

In the second, he came upon a piece of information that stunned him. Thirty-nine percent of Teknologik's stock, the largest single block, was owned by Nellor et Fils, a Swiss holding company with extensive and diverse interests in drug research, medical research, medical publishing, general publishing, and the film and broadcasting industries.

Nellor et Fils was the principal vehicle by which Horton Nellor and his son, Andrew, invested the family fortune, which was thought to be in excess of four billion dollars. Nellor was not Swiss, of course, but American. He had taken his base of operations offshore a long time ago. And more than twenty years ago, Horton Nellor had founded the *Los Angeles Post*. He still owned it.

For a while, Joe fingered his astonishment as though he were a whittler with an intriguingly shaped piece of driftwood, trying to decide how best to carve it. As in raw wood, something waited here to be discovered by the craftsman's hand; his knives were his mind and his journalistic instinct.

Horton Nellor's investments were widespread, so it might mean nothing whatsoever that he owned pieces of both Teknologik and the *Post*. Probably pure coincidence.

He owned the *Post* outright and was not an absentee publisher concerned only about profit; through his son, he exerted control over the editorial philosophy and the reportorial policies of the newspaper. He might not be so intimately involved, however, with Teknologik, Inc. His stake in that corporation was large but not in itself a controlling interest, so perhaps he was not engaged in the day-to-day operations, treating it only as a stock investment.

In that case, he was not necessarily personally aware of the top-secret research Rose Tucker and her associates had undertaken. And he was not necessarily carrying any degree of responsibility for the destruction of Flight 353.

Joe recalled his encounter the previous afternoon with Dan Shavers, the business-page columnist at the *Post*. Shavers pungently characterized the Teknologik executives: *infamous self-aggrandizers, think of themselves as some kind of business royalty, but they are no better than us. They, too, answer to He Who Must Be Obeyed.*

He Who Must Be Obeyed. Horton Nellor. Reviewing the rest of the brief conversation, Joe realized that Shavers had assumed that Joe knew of Nellor's interest in Teknologik. And the columnist seemed to have been implying that Nellor asserted his will at Teknologik no less than he did at the *Post*.

Joe also flashed back to something Lisa Peccatone had

said in the kitchen at the Delmann house when the relationship between Rose Tucker and Teknologik was mentioned: *You and me and Rosie all connected. Small world, huh?*

At the time, he had thought she was referring to the fact that Flight 353 had become a spring point in the arcs of all their lives. Maybe what she really meant was that all of them worked for the same man.

Joe had never met Horton Nellor, who had become something of a recluse over the years. He'd seen photographs, of course. The billionaire, now in his late sixties, was silver-haired and round-faced, with pleasing if somewhat blurred features. He looked like a muffin on which, with icing, a baker had painted a grandfather face.

He did not appear to be a killer. He was known as a generous philanthropist. His reputation was not that of a man who would hire assassins or condone murder in the maintenance or expansion of his empire.

Human beings, however, were different from apples and oranges: The flavor of the peel did not reliably predict the taste of the pulp.

The fact remained that Joe and Michelle had worked for the same man as those who now wanted to kill Rose Tucker and who—in some as yet incomprehensible manner—had evidently destroyed Nationwide 353. The money that had long supported his family was the same money that had financed their murders.

His response to this revelation was so complexly tangled that he could not quickly unknot it, so dark that he could not easily see the entire shape of it.

Greasy fingers of nausea seined his guts.

Although he stared out the window for perhaps half an hour, he was not aware of the desert surrendering to the suburbs or the suburbs to the city. He was surprised when he realized that they were descending toward LAX.

On the ground, as they taxied to the assigned gate and as the telescoping mobile corridor was linked like an umbilical between the 737 and the terminal, Joe checked his wristwatch, considered the distance to Westwood, and calculated that he would be at least half an hour early for his meeting with Demi. Perfect. He wanted enough time to scope the meeting place from across the street and a block away before committing himself to it.

Demi should be reliable. She was Rose's friend. He had gotten her number from the message that Rose had left for him at the *Post*. But he wasn't in the mood to trust anyone.

After all, even if Rose Tucker's motives had been pure, even if she had kept Nina with her to prevent Teknologik from killing or kidnapping the girl, she had nevertheless withheld Joe's daughter from him for a year. Worse, she had allowed him to go on thinking that Nina—like Michelle and Chrissie—was dead. For reasons that he could not yet know, perhaps Rose would *never* want to return his little girl to him.

Trust no one.

As he got up from his seat and started forward toward the exit, he noticed a man in white slacks, white shirt, and white Panama hat rise from a seat farther forward in the cabin and glance back at him. The guy was about fifty, stockily built, with a thick mane of white hair that made him look like an aging rock star, especially under that hat.

This was no stranger.

For an instant, Joe thought that perhaps the man was, in fact, a lowercase celebrity—a musician in a famous band or a character actor from television. Then he was certain that he had seen him not on screen or stage but elsewhere, recently, and in significant circumstances.

Mr. Panama looked away from him after a fraction of a

second of eye contact, stepped into the aisle, and moved forward. Like Joe, he was not burdened by any carry-on luggage, as though he had been on a day trip.

Eight or ten passengers were between the day-tripper and Joe. He was afraid he would lose track of his quarry before he figured out where he had previously seen him. He couldn't push along the narrow aisle past the intervening passengers without causing a commotion, however, and he preferred not to let Mr. Panama know that he had been spotted.

When Joe tried to use the distinctive hat as a prod to memory, he came up blank, but when he pictured the man without the hat and focused on the flowing white hair, he thought of the blue-robed cult members with the shaven heads. The connection eluded him, seemed absurd.

Then he thought of the bonfire around which the cultists had been standing last night on the beach, where he had disposed of the McDonald's bag that contained the Kleenex damp with Charlie Delmann's blood. And the lithe dancers in bathing suits around another bonfire. A third fire and the gathering of surfers inside the totemic ring of their upended boards. And still another fire, around which sat a dozen enthralled listeners as a stocky man with a broad charismatic face and a mane of white hair narrated a ghost story in a reverberant voice.

This man. The storyteller.

Joe had no doubt that they were one and the same.

He also knew there was no chance whatsoever that he had crossed this man's path on the beach last night and again here sheerly by chance. All is intimately interwoven in this most conspiratorial of all worlds.

They must have been conducting surveillance on him for weeks or months, waiting for Rose to contact him, when he had finally become aware of them on Santa

Monica Beach, Saturday morning. During that time they had learned all his haunts, which were not numerous: the apartment, a couple of coffee shops, the cemetery, and a few favorite beaches where he went to learn indifference from the sea.

After he had disabled Wallace Blick, invaded their van, and then fled the cemetery, they had lost him. He had found the transponder on his car and thrown it into the passing gardener's truck, and they had lost him. They'd almost caught up with him again at the *Post*, but he'd slipped away minutes ahead of them.

So they had staked out his apartment, the coffee shops, the beaches—waiting for him to show up somewhere. The group being entertained by the ghost story had been ordinary civilians, but the storyteller who had insinuated himself into their gathering was not in the least ordinary.

They had picked Joe up once more the past night on the beach. He knew the correct surveillance jargon: They had *reacquired* him on the beach. Followed him to the convenience store from which he had telephoned Mario Oliveri in Denver and Barbara in Colorado Springs. Followed him to his motel.

They could have killed him there. Quietly. While he slept or after waking him with a gun to his head. They could have made it look like a drug overdose—or like suicide.

In the heat of the moment, they had been eager to shoot him down at the cemetery, but they were no longer in a hurry to see him dead. Because maybe, just maybe, he would lead them again to Rose Marie Tucker.

Evidently they weren't aware that he had been at the Delmann house, among other places, during the hours when they had lost contact with him. If they knew he'd seen what had happened to the Delmanns and to Lisa—

even though he could not understand it—they probably would terminate him. Take no chances. Terminate him "with extreme prejudice," as their kind phrased it.

During the night, they had placed another tracking device on his car. In the hour before dawn, they followed him to LAX, always at a distance where they were in no danger of being spotted. Then to Denver and perhaps beyond.

Jesus.

What had frightened the deer in the woods?

Joe felt stupid and careless, although he knew that he was not either. He couldn't expect to be as good at this game as they were; he'd never played it before, but they played it every day.

He was getting better, though. He was getting better.

Farther up the aisle, the storyteller reached the exit door and disappeared into the debarkation umbilical.

Joe was afraid of losing his stalker, but it was imperative that they continue to believe that he was unaware of them.

Barbara Christman was in terrible danger. First thing, he had to find a phone and warn her.

Faking patience and boredom, he shuffled forward with the other passengers. In the umbilical, which was much wider than the aisle in the airplane, he finally slipped past them without appearing to be alarmed or in a hurry. He didn't realize that he was holding his breath until he exhaled hard with relief when he spotted his quarry ahead of him.

The huge terminal was busy. At the gates, the ranks of chairs were filled with passengers waiting to catch a late-afternoon flight in the fast-fading hours of the weekend. Chattering, laughing, arguing, brooding in silence, shuffling-striding-strolling-limping-ambling, arriving passengers poured out of other gates and along the concourse.

There were singles, couples, entire families, blacks and whites and Asians and Latinos and four towering Samoan men, all with black porkpie hats, beautiful sloe-eyed women, willow graceful in their turquoise or ruby or sapphire saris, others in chadors and others in jeans, men in business suits, men in shorts and bright polo shirts, four young Hasidic Jews arguing (but joyfully) over the most mystical of all documents (a Los Angeles freeway map), uniformed soldiers, giggling children and shrieking children and two placid octogenarians in wheelchairs, a pair of tall Arab princes in akals and kaffiyehs and flowing djellabas, preceded by fierce bodyguards and trailed by retinues, beacon-red tourists drifting homeward on the astringent fumes of medicated sunburn lotion, pale tourists arriving with the dampish smell of cloudy country clinging to them—and, like a white boat strangely serene in a typhoon, the man in the Panama hat, sailing imperiously through the polygenic sea.

As far as Joe was concerned, they might all be stage dressing, every one of them an agent of Teknologik or of institutions unknown, all watching him surreptitiously, snapping photographs of him with trick cameras concealed in their purses and attaché cases and tote bags, all conferring by hidden microphones as to whether he should be permitted to proceed or be gunned down on the spot.

He had never before felt so alone in a crowd.

Dreading what might happen—might even now *be* happening—to Barbara, he tried to keep the storyteller in sight while also searching for a telephone.

FOUR

PALE FIRE

13

The public telephone, one in a cluster of four, was not in
a booth, but the wings of a sound shield provided a small
measure of privacy.

As he entered Barbara's Colorado Springs number on
the keypad, Joe ground his teeth together as though he
could bite off the noise of the crowded terminal and chew
it into a silence that would allow him to concentrate. He
needed to think through what he would say to her, but he
had neither the time nor the solitude to craft the ideal
speech, and he was afraid of committing a blunder that
would pitch her deeper into trouble.

Even if her phone had not been tapped the previous
evening, it was surely being monitored now, following
his visit to her. His task was to warn her of the danger
while simultaneously convincing the eavesdroppers that
she had never broken the pledge of silence that would
keep her and Denny safe.

As the telephone began to ring in Colorado, Joe
glanced toward the storyteller, who had taken up a position farther along—and on the opposite side of—the concourse. He was standing outside the entrance to an airport
newsstand and gift shop, nervously adjusting his Panama
hat, and conversing with a Hispanic man in tan chinos, a
green madras shirt, and a Dodgers cap.

Through the screen of passing travelers, Joe pretended

not to watch the two men while they pretended, less convincingly, not to watch him. They were less circumspect than they should have been, because they were over-confident. Although they might give him credit for being industrious and clever, they thought that he was basically a jerk civilian in fast-running water way over his head.

He was exactly what they thought him to be, of course, but he hoped he was also more than they believed. A man driven by paternal love—and therefore dangerous. A man with a passion for justice that was alien to their world of situational ethics, in which the only morals were the morals of convenience.

Barbara answered the phone on the fifth ring, just as Joe was beginning to despair.

"It's me, Joe Carpenter," he said.

"I was just—"

Before Barbara could say anything that might reveal the extent of the revelations she'd made to him, Joe said, "Listen, I wanted to thank you again for taking me to the crash site. It wasn't easy, but it was something I had to do, had to see, if I was ever going to have any peace. I'm sorry if I badgered you about what *really* happened to that airplane. I was a little crazy, I guess. A couple of odd things have happened lately, and I just let my imagination run wild. You were right when you said most of the time things are exactly what they appear to be. It's just hard to accept that you can lose your family to anything as stupid as an accident, mechanical failure, human error, whatever. You feel like it just *has* to be a lot more significant than an accident because . . . well, because *they* were so significant to you. You know? You think there have to be villains somewhere, that it can't be just fate, because *God* wouldn't allow this to happen. But you started me thinking when you said the only place there's always villains is in the movies. If I'm going to get over this, I'm going to have to accept that these things just happen, that no one's to blame. Life is risk, right? God *does* let innocent people die, lets children die. It's that simple."

Joe was tense, waiting to hear what she would say, whether she had understood the urgent message that he was striving to convey so indirectly.

After a brief hesitation, Barbara said, "I hope you find peace, Joe, I really do. It took a lot of guts for you to go out there, right to the impact site. And it takes guts to face the fact that there's no one to blame in the end. As long as you're stuck in the idea that there's someone who's guilty of something, someone who's got to be brought to justice . . . well, then you're full of vengeance, and you're not healing."

She understood.

Joe closed his eyes and tried to gather his unraveled nerves into a tight bundle again.

He said, "It's just . . . we live in such weird times. It's easy to believe in vast conspiracies."

"Easier than facing hard truths. Your real argument isn't with the pilots or the maintenance crew. It isn't with the air-traffic controllers or with the people who built the airplane. Your real argument's with God."

"Which I can't win," he said, opening his eyes.

In front of the newsstand, the storyteller and the Dodgers fan finished their conversation. The storyteller departed.

"We're not supposed to understand why," Barbara said. "We just have to have faith that there's a reason. If you can learn to accept that, then you really might find peace. You're a very nice man, Joe. You don't deserve to be in such torment. I'll be praying for you."

"Thanks, Barbara. Thanks for everything."

"Good luck, Joe."

He almost wished her good luck as well, but those two words might be a tip-off to whoever was listening.

Instead, he said, "Good-bye."

Still hummingbird tense, he hung up.

Simply by going to Colorado and knocking on Barbara's door, he had put her, her son, and her son's entire family in terrible jeopardy—although he'd had no way of knowing this would be the consequence of his visit. Anything might happen to her now—or nothing—and Joe felt a chill of blame coil around his heart.

On the other hand, by going to Colorado, he had learned that Nina was miraculously alive. He was willing to take the moral responsibility for a hundred deaths in return for the mere hope of seeing her again.

He was aware of how monstrous it was to regard the life of his daughter as more precious than the lives of any hundred strangers—two hundred, a thousand. He didn't care. He would kill to save her, if that was the extreme to which he was driven. Kill anyone who got in his way. Any number.

Wasn't it the human dilemma to dream of being part of the larger community but, in the face of everlasting death, always to operate on personal and family imperatives? And he was, after all, too human.

Joe left the public telephones and followed the concourse toward the exit. As he reached the head of the escalators, he contrived to glance back.

The Dodgers fan followed at a discreet distance, well disguised by the ordinariness of his dress and demeanor. He wove himself into the crowd so skillfully that he was no more evident than any single thread in a coat of many colors.

Down the escalator and through the lower floor of the terminal, Joe did not look back again. Either the Dodgers fan would be there or he would have handed Joe over to another agent, as the storyteller had done.

Given their formidable resources, they would have a substantial contingent of operatives at the airport. He could never escape them here.

He had exactly an hour until he had to meet Demi, who he hoped would take him to Rose Tucker. If he didn't make the rendezvous in time, he had no way to reestablish contact with the woman.

His wristwatch seemed to be ticking as loudly as a grandfather clock.

■

Tortured faces melted into the mutant forms of strange animals and nightmare landscapes in the Rorschach stains on the walls of the vast, drab concrete parking structure. Engine noise from cars in other aisles, on other levels, echoed like a Grendel grumble through these man-made caverns.

His Honda was where he'd left it.

Although most of the vehicles in the garage were cars, three vans—none white—an old Volkswagen minibus with curtained windows, and a pickup truck with a camper shell were parked near enough to him to serve as surveillance posts. He didn't give any of them a second look.

He opened the car trunk, and using his body to block the view of any onlooker, he quickly checked the spare-tire well for the money. He had taken two thousand to Colorado, but he had left the bulk of his funds in the Honda. He was afraid the bank's manila envelope with the brass clasp would be gone, but it was where he'd left it.

He slipped the envelope under the waistband of his jeans. He considered taking the small suitcase as well, but if he transferred it to the front seat, the people watching him would not be suckered by the little drama he had planned for them.

In the driver's seat, he took the envelope out of his waistband, opened it, and tucked the packets of hundred-dollar bills in the various pockets of his corduroy jacket. He folded the empty envelope and put it in the console box.

When he backed out of the parking space and drove away, none of the suspect vehicles followed him immediately. They didn't need to be quick. Hidden somewhere on the Honda, another transponder was sending the surveillance team a signal that made constant visual contact unnecessary.

He drove down three levels to the exit. Departing vehicles were lined up at the cashiers' booths.

As he inched forward, he repeatedly checked his rearview mirror. Just as he reached the cashier, he saw the pickup with the camper shell pull into line six cars behind him.

■

Driving away from the airport, he held his speed slightly below the legal limit and made no effort to beat traffic lights as they turned yellow ahead of him. He didn't want to put too much distance between himself and his pursuers.

Preferring surface streets rather than the freeways, he headed toward the west side of the city. Block by block through a seedy commercial district, he searched for a setup that would serve his purposes.

The summer day was warm and clear, and the sunshine was diffused in matching parabolic rainbow arcs across the dirty windshield. The soapy washer spray and the wipers cleared the glass somewhat but not sufficiently.

Squinting through the glare, Joe almost failed to give the used-car dealership due consideration. Gem Fittich Auto Sales. Sunday was a car-shopping day, and the lot was open, though perhaps not for long. Realizing that this was precisely what he needed, he pulled to the right-hand curb and stopped half a block past the place.

He was in front of a transmission-repair shop. The business was housed in a badly maintained stucco and corrugated-steel building that appeared to have been blown *together* by a capricious tornado, using parts of several other structures that it had previously torn asunder. Fortunately, the shop was closed; he didn't want any good-Samaritan mechanics coming to his rescue.

He shut off the engine and got out of the Honda.

The pickup with the camper shell was not yet within sight on the street behind him.

He hurried to the front of the car and opened the hood.

The Honda was of no use to him anymore. This time they would have concealed the transponder so well that he would need hours to find it. He couldn't drive it to Westwood and lead them to Rose, but he couldn't simply abandon it, either, because then they would know that he was onto them.

He needed to disable the Honda in such a fashion that it would appear to be not sabotage but genuine mechanical failure. Eventually the people following him would open the hood, and if they spotted missing spark plugs or a disconnected distributor cap, they would know that they had been tricked.

Then Barbara Christman would be in deeper trouble than ever. They would realize that Joe had recognized the storyteller on the airplane, that he knew they'd been following him in Colorado—and that everything he'd said to Barbara on the phone had been designed to warn her and to convince them that she had not told him anything important when, in fact, she had told him everything.

He carefully unplugged the ignition control module but left it sitting loosely in its case. A casual inspection would not reveal that it was disengaged. Even if later they searched until they found the problem, they were more likely to assume that the ICM had worked loose on its own rather than that Joe had fiddled with it. At least they would be left with the element of doubt, affording Barbara some protection.

The pickup with the camper shell drove past him.

He didn't look directly at the truck but recognized it from the corner of his eye.

For a minute or two he pretended to study various things in the engine compartment. Poking this. Wiggling that. Scratching his head.

Leaving the hood up, he got behind the wheel again and tried to start the Honda, but of course he had no luck.

He got out of the car and went to look at the engine again.

Peripherally, he saw that the camper truck had turned off the street at the end of the block. It had stopped in the shallow parking area in front of an empty industrial building that featured a real-estate agency's large *For Sale* sign on the front.

He studied the engine another minute, cursing it with energy and color, just in case they had directional microphones trained on him.

Finally he slammed the hood and looked worriedly at his watch. He stood indecisively for a moment. Consulted his watch again. He said, "Shit."

He walked back the street in the direction he had come. When he arrived at the used-car lot, he hesitated for effect, then walked directly to the sales office.

Gem Fittich Auto Sales operated under numerous criss-crossing stringers of yellow and white and red plastic pennants faded by a summer of sun. In the breeze, they snapped like the flapping wings of a perpetually hovering flock of buzzards over more than thirty cars that ranged from good stock to steel carrion.

The office was in a small prefab building painted yellow with red trim. Through the large picture window, Joe could see a man lounging in a spring-back chair, watching a small television, loafer-clad feet propped on a desk.

As he climbed the two steps and went through the open doorway, he heard a sportscaster doing color commentary on a baseball game.

The building consisted of a single large room with a rest room in one corner, visible beyond the half-open door. The two desks, the four chairs, and the bank of metal file cabinets were cheap, but everything was clean and neatly kept.

Joe had been hoping for dust, clutter, and a sense of quiet desperation.

The fortyish salesman was cheery-looking, sandy-haired, wearing tan cotton slacks and a yellow polo shirt. He swung his feet off the desk, got up from his chair, and offered his hand. "Howdy! Didn't hear you drive up. I'm Gem Fittich."

Shaking his hand, Joe said, "Joe Carpenter. I need a car."

"You came to the right place." Fittich reached toward the portable television that stood on his desk.

"No, that's okay, leave it on," Joe said.

"You're a fan, you might not want to see this one. They're getting their butts kicked."

Right now the transmission-repair shop next door blocked them from the surveillance team. If the camper truck appeared across the street, however, as Joe more than half expected, and if directional microphones were trained on the big picture window, the audio from the baseball game might have to be turned up to foil the listeners.

Positioning himself so he could talk to Fittich and look past him to the sales lot and the street, Joe said, "What's the cheapest set of wheels you've got ready to roll?"

"Once you consider my prices, you're going to realize you can get plenty of value without having to settle for—"

"Here's the deal," Joe said, withdrawing packets of hundred-dollar bills from a jacket pocket. "Depending on how it performs on a test drive, I'll buy the cheapest car you have on the lot right now, one hundred percent cash money, no guarantee required."

Fittich liked the look of the cash. "Well, Joe, I've got this Subaru, she's a long road from the factory, but she's still got life in her. No air conditioning but radio and—"

"How much?"

"Well, now, I've done some work on her, have her tagged at twenty-one hundred fifty, but I'll let you have her for nineteen seventy-five. She—"

Joe considered offering less, but every minute counted, and considering what he was going to ask of Fittich, he decided that he wasn't in a position to bargain. He interrupted the salesman to say, "I'll take it."

After a disappointingly slow day in the iron-horse trade, Gem Fittich was clearly torn between pleasure at the prospect of a sale and uneasiness at the way in which they had arrived at terms. He smelled trouble. "You don't want to take a test drive?"

Putting two thousand in cash on Fittich's desk, Joe said, "That is exactly what I want to do. Alone."

Across the street, a tall man appeared on foot, coming from the direction in which the camper truck was parked.

He stood in the shade of a bus-stop shelter. If he'd sat on the shelter bench, his view of the sales office would have been hampered by the merchandise parked in front of it.

"Alone?" Fittich asked, puzzled.

"You've got the whole purchase price there on the desk," Joe said. From his wallet, he withdrew his driver's license and handed it to Fittich. "I see you have a Xerox. Make a copy of my license."

The guy at the bus stop was wearing a short-sleeve shirt and slacks, and he wasn't carrying anything. Therefore, he wasn't equipped with a high-power, long-range listening device; he was just keeping watch.

Fittich followed the direction of Joe's gaze and said, "What trouble am I getting into here?"

Joe met the salesman's eyes. "None. You're clear. You're just doing business."

"Why's that fella at the bus stop interest you?"

"He doesn't. He's just a guy."

Fittich wasn't deceived. "If what's actually happening here is a *purchase*, not just a test drive, then there're state forms we have to fill out, sales tax to be collected, legal procedures."

"But it's just a test drive," Joe said.

He checked his wristwatch. He wasn't pretending to be worried about the hour now; he was genuinely concerned.

"All right, look, Mr. Fittich, no more bullshit. I don't have time. This is going to be even better for you than a sale, because here's what's going to happen. You take that money and stick it in the back of a desk drawer. Nobody ever has to know I gave it to you. I'll drive the Subaru to where I have to go, which is only someplace on the West Side. I'd take my own car, but they've got a tracking device on it, and I don't want to be followed. I'll abandon the Subaru in a safe area and call you by tomorrow to let you know where it is. You bring it back, and all that's happened is you've rented your cheapest car for one day for two thousand bucks tax free. The worst that happens is I don't call. You've still got the money—and a theft write-off."

Fittich turned the driver's license over and over in his hand. "Is somebody going to ask me why I'd let you make a test drive alone even with a copy of your license?"

"The guy looked honest to me," Joe said, feeding Fittich the lines he could use. "It was his picture on the license. And I just couldn't leave, 'cause I expected a call from a hot prospect who came in earlier and might buy the best piece of iron I have on the lot. Didn't want to risk missing that call."

"You got it all figured out," Fittich said.

His manner changed. The easygoing, smiley-faced salesman was a chrysalis from which another Gem Fittich was emerging, a version with more angles and harder edges.

He stepped to the Xerox and switched it on.

Nevertheless, Joe sensed that Fittich had not yet made up his mind. "The fact is, Mr. Fittich, even if they come in here and ask you some questions, there's nothing they could do to you—and nothing they'd want to bother doing."

"You in the drug trade?" Fittich asked bluntly.

"No."

"'Cause I hate people who sell drugs."

"I do too."

"Ruining our kids, ruining what's left of our country."

"I couldn't agree more."

"Not that there *is* much left." Fittich glanced through the window at the man at the bus stop. "They cops?"

"Not really."

"'Cause I support the cops. They got a hard job these

days, trying to uphold the law when the biggest criminals are some of our own elected officials."

Joe shook his head. "These aren't any kind of cops you've ever heard of."

Fittich thought for a while, and then he said, "That was an honest answer."

"I'm being as truthful with you as I can be. But I'm in a hurry. They probably think I'm in here to call a mechanic or a tow truck or something. If I'm going to get that Subaru, I want it to be *now*, before they maybe tumble to what I'm really doing."

After glancing at the window and the bus stop across the street, Fittich said, "They government?"

"For all intents and purposes—yeah."

"You know why the drug problem just grows?" Fittich said. "It's because half this current group of politicians, they've been paid off to let it happen, and hell, a bunch of the bastards are even users themselves, so they don't care."

Joe said nothing, for fear that he would say the *wrong* thing. He didn't know the cause of Fittich's anger with authority. He could easily misspeak and be viewed suddenly as not a like thinker but as one of the enemy.

Frowning, Gem Fittich made a Xerox copy of the driver's license. He returned the laminated card to Joe, who put it away in his wallet.

At the desk again, Fittich stared at the money. He seemed to be disturbed about cooperating—not because he was worried about getting in trouble but because the moral dimension, in fact, was of concern to him. Finally he sighed, opened a drawer, and slid the two thousand into it.

From another drawer, he withdrew a set of keys and handed them to Joe.

Taking them gratefully, Joe said, "Where is it?"

Fittich pointed at the car through the window. "Half an hour, I probably got to call the cops and report it stolen, just to cover myself."

"I understand. With luck, I'll be where I'm going by then."

"Hell, don't worry, they won't even look for it anyway. You could use it a week and never get nailed."

"I *will* call you, Mr. Fittich, and tell you exactly where I left it."

"I expect you will." As Joe reached the open door, Fittich said, "Mr. Carpenter, do you believe in the end of all things?"

Joe paused on the threshold. "Excuse me?"

The Gem Fittich who had emerged from the chrysalis of the cheerful salesman was not merely harder edged and edgier; he also had peculiar eyes—eyes different from what they had been, full of not anger but an unnerving pensiveness. "The end of time in our time, the end of this mess of a world we've made, all of it just suddenly rolled up and put away like an old moth-eaten rug."

"I suppose it's got to end someday," Joe said.

"Not someday. Soon. Doesn't it seem to you that wrong and right have all got turned upside down, that we don't even half know the difference anymore?"

"Yes."

"Don't you wake up sometimes in the middle of the night and feel it coming? Like a tidal wave a thousand miles high, hanging over us, darker than the night and cold, going to crash over us and sweep us all away?"

"Yes," Joe said softly and truthfully. "Yes, I've often felt just that in the middle of the night."

The tsunami looming over Joe in dark hours was of an entirely personal nature, however: the loss of his family, towering so high that it blocked the stars and prevented him from seeing the future. He had often *longed* to be swept away by it.

He sensed that Fittich, sunk in some deep moral weariness, also longed for a delivering apocalypse. Joe was disquieted and surprised to discover he shared this melancholy with the car salesman.

The discovery disturbed him, because this expectation that the end of all things loomed was profoundly dysfunctional and antisocial, an illness from which he himself was only beginning to recover with great difficulty, and he feared for a society in which such gloom was widespread.

"Strange times," Fittich said, as Joe had said *weird times* to Barbara a short while ago. "They scare me." He went to his chair, put his feet on the desk, and stared at the ball game on television. "Better go now."

With the flesh on the nape of his neck as crinkled as crepe paper, Joe walked outside to the yellow Subaru.

Across the street, the man at the bus stop looked impatiently left and right, as though disgruntled about the unreliability of public transportation.

The engine of the Subaru turned over at once, but it sounded tinny. The steering wheel vibrated slightly. The upholstery was worn, and pine-fragrant solvents didn't quite mask the sour scent of cigarette smoke that over the years had saturated the vinyl and the carpet.

Without looking at the man in the bus-stop shelter, Joe drove out of the lot. He turned right and headed up the street past his abandoned Honda.

The pickup with the camper shell was still parked in front of the untenanted industrial building.

When Joe reached the intersection just past the camper truck, there was no cross-traffic. He slowed, did not come to a full stop, and instead put his foot down heavily on the accelerator.

In the rearview mirror, he saw the man from the bus stop hurrying toward the camper, which was already backing into the street. Without the transponder to guide them, they would have to maintain visual contact and risk following him close enough to blow their cover—which they thought they still enjoyed.

Within four miles Joe lost them at a major intersection when he sped through a yellow traffic signal that was changing to red. When the camper tried to follow him, it was thwarted by the surging cross-traffic. Even over the whine and rattle of the Subaru engine, he heard the sharp bark of their brakes as they slid to a halt inches short of a collision.

Twenty minutes later, he abandoned the Subaru on Hilgarde Street near the UCLA campus, as far as he dared from the address where he was to meet Demi. He walked fast to Westwood Boulevard, trying not to break into a run and draw attention to himself.

Not long ago Westwood Village had been an island of quaint charm in the more turbulent sea of the city around it, a mecca for shoppers and theatergoers. Amidst some of the most interesting small-scale architecture of any Los Angeles commercial district and along the tree-lined streets had thrived trendy clothing stores, galleries, restaurants, prosperous theaters featuring the latest cutting-edge dramas and comedies, and popular movie houses. It was a place to have fun, people-watch, and be seen.

Then, during a period when the city's ruling elite was in one of its periodic moods to view certain forms of sociopathic behavior as a legitimate protest, vagrancy increased, gang members began to loiter in groups, and open drug dealing commenced. A few shootings occurred in turf disputes, and many of the fun lovers and shoppers decided that the scene was *too* colorful and that to be seen here was to be marked as a victim.

Now Westwood was struggling back from the precipice. The streets were safer than they had been for a while. Many shops and galleries had closed, however, and new businesses had not moved into all of the empty storefronts. The lingering atmosphere of despair might take years to dissipate entirely. Built at the solemn pace of coral reefs, civilization could be destroyed with frightening swiftness, even by a blast of good intentions, and all that was lost could be regained, if ever, only with determination.

The gourmet coffeehouse was busy. From the open door came the delicious aromas of several exotic brews and the music of a lone guitarist playing a New Age tune that was mellow and relaxing though filled with tediously repetitive chords.

Joe intended to scout the meeting place from across the street and farther along the block, but he arrived too late to do so. At two minutes past six o'clock, he stood outside the coffeehouse as instructed, to the right of the entrance, and waited to be contacted.

Over the noise of the street traffic and the guitar, he heard a soft tuneless jangling-tinkling. The sound instantly alarmed him, for reasons he could not explain, and he looked around nervously for the source.

Above the door were wind chimes crafted from at least twenty spoons of various sizes and materials. They clinked together in the light breeze.

Like a mischievous childhood playmate, memory taunted him from hiding place after hiding place in a deep garden of the past dappled by light and shadow.

Then suddenly he recalled the ceiling-mounted rack of copper pots and pans in the Delmanns' kitchen.

Returning from Charlie Delmann's bedroom, in answer to Lisa's scream, Joe had heard the cookware clinking and softly clanging as he had hurried along the downstairs hall. Coming through the door into the kitchen, he saw the pots and pans swinging like pendulums from their hooks.

By the time he reached Lisa and saw Georgine's corpse on the floor, the cookware had settled into silence. But what set those items in motion in the first place? Lisa and Georgine were at the far end of the long room, nowhere near the dangling pots.

Like the flashing green numbers on the digital clock at Charlie Delmann's bedside, like the swelling of flames in the three oil lamps on the kitchen table, this coppery music was important.

He felt as though a hard rap of insight was about to crack the egg of his ignorance.

Holding his breath, mentally reaching for the elusive connection that would make sense of these things, Joe realized that the shell-cracking insight was receding. He strained to bring it back. Then, maddeningly, it was gone.

Perhaps *none* of these things was important: not the oil lamps, not the digital clock, not the jangling cookware. In a world viewed through lenses of paranoia—a pair of distorting spectacles that he had been wearing with good reason for the past day and a half—every falling leaf, every whisper of wind, and every fretwork of shadows was invested with a portentous meaning that, in reality, it did not possess. He was not merely a neutral observer, not merely a reporter this time, but a victim, central to his own story, so maybe he could not trust his journalistic instincts when he saw significance in these small, if admittedly strange, details.

Along the sidewalk came a tall black kid, college age,

wearing shorts and a UCLA T-shirt, gliding on Roller-blades. Joe, puzzling over clues that might not be clues at all, paid little attention to the skater, until the kid spun to a stop in front of him and handed him a cellular phone.

"You'll need this," said the skater, in a bass voice that would have been pure gold to any fifties doo-wop group.

Before Joe could respond, the skater rolled away with powerful pushes of his muscular legs.

The phone rang in Joe's hand.

He surveyed the street, searching for the surveillance post from which he was being watched, but it was not obvious.

The phone rang again, and he answered it. "Yeah?"

"What's your name?" a man asked.

"Joe Carpenter."

"Who're you waiting for?"

"I don't know her name."

"What do you call her?"

"Demi."

"Walk a block and a half south. Turn right at the corner and keep going until you come to a bookstore. It's still open. Go in, find the biography section."

The caller hung up.

After all, there wasn't going to be a pleasant get-acquainted chat over coffee.

■

According to the business hours posted on the glass door, the bookstore closed on Sundays at six o'clock. It was a quarter past six. Through the big display windows, Joe saw that the fluorescent panels toward the front of the store were dark; only a few at the back were lighted, but when he tried the door, it was unlocked.

Inside, a single clerk waited at the cashiers' counter. He

was black, in his late thirties, as small and wiry as a jockey, with a mustache and goatee. Behind the thick lenses of his horn-rimmed glasses, his eyes were as large as those of a persistent interrogator in a dream of inquisition.

"Biographies?" Joe asked.

Coming out from behind the counter, the clerk pointed to the right rear corner of the store, where light glowed beyond ranks of shadowed shelves.

As he headed deeper into the maze of books, Joe heard the front door being locked behind him.

In the biography aisle, another black man was waiting. He was a huge slab of ebony—and appeared capable of being an irresistible force or an immovable object, whichever was required. His face was as placid as that of Buddha.

He said, "Assume the position."

At once Joe knew he was dealing with a cop or former cop.

Obediently, he faced a wall of books, spread his legs wide, leaned forward with both hands against the shelves, and stared at the spines of the volumes in front of him. One in particular caught his attention: a massive biography of Henry James, the writer.

Henry James.

For some reason even that name seemed significant. Everything *seemed* significant, but nothing was. Least of all, the name of a long-dead writer.

The cop frisked him quickly and professionally, searching for a weapon or a transmitter. When he found neither, he said, "Show me some ID."

Joe turned away from the shelves and fished his driver's license from his wallet.

The cop compared the photo on the license with Joe's face, read his vital statistics and compared them to the reality, then returned the card. "See the cashier."

"What?"

"The guy when you came in."

The wiry man with the goatee was waiting by the front door. He unlocked it as Joe approached. "You still have the phone?"

Joe offered it to him.

"No, hold on to it," the cashier said. "There's a black Mustang parked at the curb. Drive it down to Wilshire and turn west. You'll be contacted."

As the cashier opened the door and held it, Joe stared at the car and said, "Whose is it?"

From behind the bottle-thick lenses, the magnified eyes studied him as though he were a bacterium at the lower end of a microscope. "What's it matter whose?"

"Doesn't, I guess."

Joe went outside and got into the Mustang. The keys were in the ignition.

At Wilshire Boulevard, he turned west. The car was almost as old as the Subaru that he had gotten from Gem Fittich. The engine sounded better, however, the interior was cleaner, and instead of pine-scented disinfectant masking the stink of stale cigarette smoke, the air held a faint tang of menthol aftershave.

Shortly after he drove through the underpass at the San Diego Freeway, the cellular phone rang. "Yeah?"

The man who had sent him to the bookstore now said, "You're going all the way to the ocean in Santa Monica. When you get there, I'll ring you with more directions."

"All right."

"Don't stop anywhere along the way. You understand?"

"Yes."

"We'll know if you do."

They were somewhere in the traffic around him, in front or behind—or both. He didn't bother to look for them.

The caller said, "Don't try to use your phone to call anyone. We'll know that too."

"I understand."

"Just one question. The car you're driving—why did you want to know whose it was?"

Joe said, "Some seriously unpleasant bastards are looking for me. If they find me, I don't want to get any innocent people in trouble just because I was using their car."

"Whole world's already in trouble, man. Haven't you noticed?" the caller asked, and then he disconnected.

With the exception of the cop—or former cop—in the bookstore, these people who were hiding Rose Tucker and providing security for her were amateurs with limited resources compared to the thugs who worked for Teknologik. But they were thoughtful and clever amateurs with undeniable talent for the game.

■

Joe was not halfway through Santa Monica, with the ocean still far ahead, when an image of the book spine rose in his mind—the name *Henry James*.

Henry James. So what?

Then the title of one of James's best-known works came to him. *The Turn of the Screw*. It would be on any short list of the most famous ghost stories ever written.

Ghost.

The inexplicable welling of the oil-lamp flames, the flashing of the numbers on the clock, the jangling pots and pans now seemed as if they might have been linked, after all. And as he recalled those images, it was easy in retrospect to discern a supernatural quality to them— although he was aware that his imagination might be enhancing the memories in that regard.

He remembered, as well, how the foyer chandelier had dimmed and brightened and dimmed repeatedly as he had hurried upstairs in response to the shotgun blast that killed Charlie Delmann. In the fearsome turmoil that followed, he'd forgotten that odd detail.

Now he was reminded of countless séance scenes in old movies and television programs, in which the opening of the door between this world and the realm of spirits was marked by the pulsing of electric lights or the guttering of candles without the presence of a draft.

Ghost.

This was absurd speculation. Worse than absurd. Insane. There were no such things as ghosts.

Yet now he recalled another disquieting incident that occurred as he'd fled the Delmann house.

Racing from the kitchen with the smoke alarm blaring behind him, along the hallway and across the foyer to the door. His hand on the knob. From behind comes a hissing cold, prickling his neck, drilling through the base of his skull. Then he is crossing the porch without any memory of having opened the door.

This seemed to be a meaningful incident as long as he considered it to be meaningful—but as soon as skepticism reasserted itself, the moment appeared to be utterly without import. Yes, if he had felt anything at the back of his neck, it should have been the heat of the fire, not a piercing chill. And, yes, this cold had been different from anything that he had ever felt before: not a spreading chill but like the tip of an icicle—indeed, more finely pointed yet, like a stiletto of steel taken from a freezer, a wire, a *needle*. A needle inserted into the summit of his spine. But this was a subjective perception of something that he had *felt*, not a journalist's measured observation of a concrete phenomenon. He'd been in a state of sheer panic, and he'd felt a lot of peculiar things; they were nothing but normal physiological responses to extreme stress. As for the few seconds of blank memory between the time when he'd put his hand on the doorknob and when he'd found himself most of the way across the porch . . . Well, that was also easily explained by panic, by stress, and by the blinding power of the overwhelming animal instinct to survive.

Not a ghost.

Rest in peace, Henry James.

As he progressed through Santa Monica toward the ocean, Joe's brief embrace of superstition loosened, lost all passion. Reason returned.

Nevertheless, something about the *concept* of a ghost continued to seem significant to him. He had a hunch that eventually he would arrive at a rational explanation derived from this consideration of the supernatural, a provable theory that would be as logical as the meticulously structured prose of Henry James.

A needle of ice. Piercing to the gray matter in the center of the spine. An injection, a quick cold squirt of . . . something.

Did Nora Vadance feel that ghost needle an instant before she got up from the breakfast table to fetch the camcorder?

Did the Delmanns feel it?

And Lisa?

Did Captain Delroy Blane feel it too, before he disengaged the autopilot, clubbed his first officer in the face, and calmly piloted Flight 353 straight into the earth?

Not a ghost, perhaps, but something fully as terrifying and as malevolent as any evil spirit returned from the abyss of the damned . . . something *akin* to a ghost.

◼

When Joe was two blocks from the Pacific, the cell phone rang for the third time.

The caller said, "Okay, turn right on the Coast Highway and keep driving until you hear from us again."

To Joe's left, less than two hours of sunlight lay over the ocean, like lemon sauce cooking in a pan, gradually thickening to a deeper yellow.

In Malibu, the phone rang again. He was directed to a turnoff that would take him to Santa-Fe-by-the-Sea, a Southwest restaurant on a bluff overlooking the ocean.

"Leave the phone on the passenger's seat and give the car to the valet. He knows who you are. The reservation is in your name," said the caller, and he hung up for the last time.

The big restaurant looked like an adobe lodge transported from New Mexico, with turquoise window trim, turquoise doors, and walkways of red-clay tiles. The landscaping consisted of cactus gardens in beds of white pebbles—and two large sorrel trees with dark-green foliage and sprays of white flowers.

The Hispanic valet was more handsome by far than any current or past Latin movie star, affecting a moody and smoldering stare that he had surely practiced in front of a mirror for eventual use in front of a camera. As the man on the phone had promised, the valet was expecting Joe and didn't give him a claim check for the Mustang.

Inside, Santa-Fe-by-the-Sea featured massive lodgepole-pine ceiling beams, vanilla-colored plaster, and more red-clay pavers. The chairs and tables and other furnishings, which fortunately didn't push the Southwest theme to extremes, were J. Robert Scott knockoffs though not inexpensive, and the decorator's palette was restricted to pastels used to interpret classic Navajo motifs.

A fortune had been spent here; and Joe was acutely aware that by comparison to the decor, he was a scruffy specimen. He hadn't shaved since leaving for Colorado more than twelve hours ago. Because most contemporary male movie stars and directors indulged in a perpetually adolescent lifestyle, blue jeans were acceptable attire even at many tony establishments in Los Angeles. But his new corduroy jacket was wrinkled and baggy from having been rain-soaked earlier, and he had the rumpled look of a traveler—or a lush coming off a bender.

The young hostess, as beautiful as any famous actress and no doubt passing time in food service while waiting for the role that would win her an Oscar, seemed to find nothing about his appearance to disdain. She led him to a window table set for two.

Glass formed the entire west wall of the building. Tinted plastic blinds softened the power of the declining sun. The view of the coastline was spectacular as it curved outward to both the north and the south—and the sea was the sea.

"Your associate has been delayed," the hostess said, evidently referring to Demi. "She's asked that you have dinner without her, and she'll join you afterwards."

Joe didn't like this development. Didn't like it at all. He was eager to make the connection with Rose, eager to learn what she had to tell him—eager to find Nina.

He was playing by their rules, however. "All right. Thanks."

If Tom Cruise had undergone cosmetic surgery to improve his appearance, he might have been as handsome as Joe's waiter. His name was Gene, and he seemed to have had a twinkle surgically inserted in each of his gas-flame-blue eyes.

After ordering a Corona, Joe went to the men's room and winced at the mirror. With his beard stubble, he resembled one of the criminal Beagle Boys in old Scrooge McDuck comics. He washed his hands and face, combed his hair, and smoothed his jacket. He still looked like he should be seated at not a window table but a Dumpster.

Back at his table, sipping ice-cold beer, he surveyed the other patrons. Several were famous.

An action-movie hero three tables away was even more stubbled than Joe, and his hair was matted and tousled like that of a small boy just awakened from a nap. He was dressed in tattered black jeans and a pleated tuxedo shirt.

Nearer was an Oscar-nominated actor and well-known heroin addict in an eccentric outfit fumbled from the closet in a state of chemical bliss: black loafers without socks, green-plaid golf pants, a brown-checkered sports jacket, and a pale-blue denim shirt. In spite of his ensemble, the most colorful things about him were his bloodshot eyes and his swollen, flame-red eyelids.

Joe relaxed and enjoyed dinner. Puréed corn and black-bean soup were poured into the same dish in such a way as to form a yellow and black yin-and-yang pattern. The mesquite-grilled salmon was on a bed of mango-and-red-pepper salsa. Everything was delicious.

While he ate, he spent as much time watching the customers as he did staring at the sea. Even those who were not famous were colorful, frequently ravishing, and generally engaged in one sort of performance or another.

Los Angeles was the most glamorous, tackiest, most elegant, seediest, most clever, dumbest, most beautiful, ugliest, forward-looking, retro-thinking, altruistic, self-absorbed, deal-savvy, politically ignorant, artistic-minded, criminal-loving, meaning-obsessed, money-grubbing, laid-back, frantic city on the planet. And any two slices of it, as different as Bel Air and Watts, were nevertheless uncannily alike in essence: rich with the same crazy hungers, hopes, and despairs.

By the time he was finishing dinner with mango bread

pudding and jalapeño ice cream, Joe was surprised to realize how much he enjoyed this people-watching. He and Michelle had spent afternoons strolling places as disparate as Rodeo Drive and City Walk, checking out the "two-footed entertainment," but he had not been interested in other people for the past year, interested only in himself and his pain.

The realization that Nina was alive and the prospect of finding her were slowly bringing Joe out of himself and back to life.

A heavyset black woman in a red and gold muumuu and two pounds of jewelry had been spelling the hostess. Now she escorted two men to a nearby table.

Both of these new patrons were dressed in black slacks, white silk shirts, and black leather jackets as supple as silk. The older of the two, approximately forty, had enormous sad eyes and a mouth sufficiently sensuous to assure him a contract to star in Revlon lipstick advertisements. He would have been handsome enough to be a waiter— except that his nose was red and misshapen from years of heavy drinking, and he never quite closed his mouth, which gave him a vacuous look. His blue-eyed companion, ten years younger, was as pink-faced as if he had been boiled—and plagued by a nervous smile that he couldn't control, as if chronically unsure of himself.

The willowy brunette having dinner with the movie star–slash–heroin addict developed an instant attraction for the guy with the Mick Jagger mouth, in spite of his rose-bloom nose. She stared at him so hard and so insistently that he responded to her as quickly as a trout would respond to a fat bug bobbing on the surface of a stream— though it was difficult to say which of these two was the trout and which the tender morsel.

The actor-addict became aware of his companion's infatuation, and he, too, began to stare at the man with the

melancholy eyes—though he was glaring rather than
flirting. Suddenly he rose from the table, almost knocking
over his chair, and weaved across the restaurant, as if
intending either to strike or regurgitate upon his rival.
Instead, he curved away from the two men's table and
disappeared into the hall that led to the rest rooms.

By this time, the sad-eyed man was eating baby
shrimps on a bed of polenta. He speared each tiny crus-
tacean on the point of his fork and studied it apprecia-
tively before sucking it off the tines with obscene relish.
As he leisurely savored each bite, he looked toward the
brunette as if to say that if he ever got a chance to bed
her, she could rest assured that she would wind up as
thoroughly shelled and de-veined as the shrimps.

The brunette was aroused or repulsed. Hard to tell
which. With some Angelenos, those two emotions were
as inextricably entwined as the viscera of inoperable
Siamese twins. Anyway, she departed the actor-addict's
table and drew up a chair to sit with the two men in
leather jackets.

Joe wondered how interesting things would get when
the wasted actor returned—no doubt with a white dust
glowing around the rims of his nostrils, since current
heroin was sufficiently pure to snort. Before events could
develop, the waiter, Gene of the twinkling eyes, stopped
by to tell him there would be no charge for dinner and
that Demi was waiting for him in the kitchen

Surprised, he left a tip and followed Gene's directions
toward the hallway that served the rest rooms and the
cookery.

The late-summer twilight had finally arrived. On the
griddle-flat horizon, a sun like a bloody yolk cooked
toward a darker hue.

As Joe crossed the restaurant, where all of the tables
were now occupied, something about that three-person

tableau—the brunette, the two men in leather jackets—
teased his memory. By the time that he reached the
hallway to the kitchen, he was puzzled by a full-blown
case of déjà vu.

Before stepping into the hall, Joe turned for one look
back. He saw the seducer with fork raised, savoring
a speared shrimp with his sad eyes, while the brunette
murmured something and the nervous pink-faced man
watched.

Joe's puzzlement turned to alarm.

For an instant, he could not understand why his mouth
went dry or why his heart began to race. Then in his
mind's eye he saw the fork metamorphose into a stiletto,
and the shrimp became a sliver of Gouda cheese.

Two men and a woman. Not in a restaurant but in
a hotel room. Not this brunette but Barbara Christman.
If not these two men, then two astonishingly similar
to them.

Of course Joe had never seen them, only listened to
Barbara's brief but vivid descriptions. The hound-dog
eyes, the nose that was "bashed red by . . . decades of
drink," the thick-lipped mouth. The younger of the two:
pink-faced, with the ceaselessly flickering smile.

Joe was more than twenty-four hours past the ability
ever to believe in coincidence again.

Impossibly, Teknologik was *here*.

■

He hurried along the hallway, through one of two swinging doors, and into a roomy antechamber used as a salad-
prep area. Two white-uniformed men, artfully and rapidly
arranging plates of greenery, never even glanced at him.

Beyond, in the main kitchen, the heavyset black

woman in the voluminous muumuu was waiting for him. Even her bright dress and the cascades of glittering jewelry could not disguise her anxiety. Her big-mama, jazz-singer face was pretty and lively and made for mirth, but there was no song or laughter in her now.

"My name's Mahalia. Real sorry I couldn't have dinner with you, Presentable Joe. That would've been a treat." Her sexy-smoky voice pegged her as the woman whom he had named Demi. "But there's been a change of plans. Follow me, honey."

With the formidable majesty of a great ship leaving its dock, Mahalia set out across the busy and immaculate kitchen crowded with chefs, cooks, and assistants, past cooktops and ovens and griddles and grills, through steam and meat smoke and the eye-watering fragrance of sautéing onions.

Hurrying after her, Joe said, "Then you know about them?"

"Sure do. Been on the TV news today. The news people show you stuff to curl your hair, then try to sell you Fritos. This awful business changes everythin'."

He put an arm on her shoulder, halted her. "TV news?"

"Some people been murdered after she talks to them."

Even with the large culinary staff in white flurries of activity around them, they were afforded privacy for their conversation by the masking clang of pots, rattle of skillets, whir of mixers, swish of whisks, clatter of dishes, buzz, clink, tink, ping, pop, scrape, chop, sizzle.

"They call it somethin' else on the news," Mahalia said, "but it's murder sure enough."

"That's not what I mean," he said. "I'm talking about the men in the restaurant."

She frowned. "What men?"

"Two of them. Black slacks, white silk shirts, black leather jackets—"

"I walked 'em to their table."

"You did, yeah. I just recognized them a minute ago."

"Bad folks?"

"The worst."

Baffled, she shook her head. "But, sugar, we know you weren't followed."

"I wasn't, but maybe *you* were. Or maybe someone else who's protecting Rose was followed."

"Devil himself would have a hard time finding Rosie if he had to depend on getting to her through us."

"But somehow they've figured out who's been hiding her for a year, and now they're closing in."

Glowering, wrapped by bulletproof confidence, Mahalia said, "Nobody's gonna lay one little finger on Rosie."

"Is she here?"

"Waitin' for you."

A cold tide washed through his heart. "You don't understand—the two in the restaurant won't have come alone. There's sure to be more outside. Maybe a small army of them."

"Yeah, maybe, but they don't know what they're dealin' with, honey." Thunderheads of resolve massed in her dark face. "We're Baptists."

Certain that he could not have heard the woman correctly, Joe hurried after her as she continued through the kitchen.

At the far end of the big room, they went through an open door into a sparkling scullery where fruits and vegetables were cleaned and trimmed before being sent in to the main cookery. This late in the restaurant's day, no one was at work here.

Beyond the scullery was a concrete-floored receiving room that smelled of raw celery and peppers, damp wood and damp cardboard. On pallets along the right-hand wall, empty fruit and vegetable crates, boxes, and cases of empty beer bottles were stacked almost to the low ceiling.

Directly ahead, under a red *Exit* sign, was a wide steel exterior door, closed now, beyond which suppliers' trucks evidently parked to make deliveries. To the left was an elevator.

"Rose is down below." Mahalia pressed the call button, and the elevator doors slid open at once.

"What's under us?"

"Well, one time, this was the service elevator to a banquet room and deck, where you could have big parties right on the beach, but we can't use it like the joint did before us. Coastal Commission put a hard rule on us. Now it's just a storeroom. Once you go down, I'll have some boys come move the pallets and empty crates to this wall. We'll cover the elevator real nice. Nobody'll know it's even here."

Uneasy about being cornered, Joe said, "Yeah, but what if they come looking and they *do* find the elevator?"

"Gonna have to stop callin' you Presentable Joe. Better would be Worryin' Joe."

"After a while, they *will* come looking. They won't just wait till closing time and go home. So once I'm down there, do I have another way out?" he persisted.

"Never tore apart the front stairs, where the customers used to go down. Just covered the openin' with hinged panels so you don't really see it. You come up that way, though, you'll be right across from the hostess station, in the middle of plain view."

"No good."

"So if somethin' goes wrong, best to skedaddle out the lower door onto the deck. From there you have the beach, the whole coast."

"They could be covering that exit too."

"It's down at the base of the bluff. From the upper

level, they can't know it's there. You should just try to relax, sugar. We're on the righteous side, which counts for somethin'."

"Not much."

"Worryin' Joe."

He stepped into the elevator but blocked the sliding door with his arm in case it tried to close. "How're you connected with this place, Mahalia?"

"Half owner."

"The food's great."

"You can look at me the way I am and think I don't *know*?" she asked good-naturedly.

"What're you to Rose?"

"Gonna call you Curious Joe pretty soon. Rosie married my brother Louis about twenty-two years ago. They met in college. Wasn't truly surprised when Louis turned out smart enough to go to college, but I was sure surprised he had the brains to fall for someone like Rosie. Then, of course, the man proved he was a pure fool, after all, when he up and divorced her four years later. Rosie couldn't have kids, and havin' kids was important to Louis—though with less air in his skull and any common sense at all, the man would've realized Rosie was more treasure than a houseful of babies."

"She hasn't been your sister-in-law for eighteen years, but you're willing to put yourself on the line for her?"

"Why not? You think Rosie turned into a vampire when Louis, the fool, divorced her? She's been the same sweet lady ever I met her. I love her like a sister. Now she's waitin', Curious Joe."

"One more thing. Earlier, when you told me these people don't know who they're dealing with . . . You didn't say 'We're Baptists'?"

"That's exactly what I did say. 'Tough' and 'Baptists' don't go together in your head—is that it?"

"Well—"

"Mama and Daddy stood up to the Klan down in Mississippi when the Klan had a whole lot more teeth than they do now, and so did my grandma and grandpap before them, and they never let fear weigh 'em down. When I was a little girl, we went through hurricanes off the Gulf of Mexico and Delta floods and encephalitis epidemics and poor times when we didn't know where tomorrow's food was comin' from, but we rode it out and still sung loud in the choir every Sunday. Maybe the United States Marines are some tougher than your average Southern black Baptist, Joe, but not by much."

"Rose is a lucky woman with a friend like you."

"I'm the lucky one," said Mahalia. "She lifts me up—now more than ever. Go on, Joe. And stay down there with her till we close this place and figure a way we can slip you two out. I'll come for you when it's time."

"Be ready for trouble long before that," he warned her. "Go."

Joe let the doors slide shut.

The elevator descended.

14

Here now, at last and alone, at the far end of the long room, was Dr. Rose Marie Tucker, in one of four folding chairs at a scarred worktable, leaning forward, forearms on the table, hands clasped, waiting and silent, her eyes solemn and full of tenderness, this diminutive survivor, keeper of secrets that Joe had been desperate to learn but from which he suddenly shied.

Some of the recessed-can fixtures in the ceiling contained dead bulbs, and the live ones were haphazardly angled, so the floor that he slowly crossed was mottled with light and shadow as if it were an underwater realm. His own shadow preceded him, then fell behind, but again preceded him, flowed here into a pool of gloom and vanished like a soul into oblivion, only to swim into view three steps later. He felt as though he were a condemned man submerged in the concrete depths of an inescapable prison, on a long death-row walk toward lethal punishment—yet simultaneously he believed in the possibility of clemency and rebirth. As he approached the revelation that had lifted Georgine and Charlie Delmann from despair to euphoria, as he drew nearer the truth about Nina, his mind churned with conflicting currents, and hope like schools of bright koi darted through his internal darkness.

Against the left-hand wall were boxes of restaurant provisions, primarily paper towels for the rest rooms, candles for the tables, and janitorial supplies purchased in bulk. The right-hand wall, which faced the beach and the ocean beyond, featured two doors and a series of large windows, but the coast was not visible because the glass was protected by metal Rolladen security shutters. The banquet room felt like a bunker.

He pulled out a chair and sat across the table from Rose.

As in the cemetery the previous day, this woman radiated such extraordinary charismatic power that her petite stature was a source of continual surprise. She seemed more physically imposing than Joe—yet her wrists were as dainty as those of a twelve-year-old girl. Her magnetic eyes held him, touched him, and some knowledge in them humbled him in a way that no man twice his size could have humbled him—yet her features appeared so fragile, her throat so slender, her shoulders so delicate that she should have seemed as vulnerable as a child.

Joe reached across the table toward her.

She gripped his hand.

Dread fought with hope for his voice, and while the battle raged, he could not speak to ask about Nina.

More solemn now than she had been in the cemetery, Rose said, "It's all going so badly. They're killing everyone I talk to. They'll stop at nothing."

Relieved of the obligation to ask, first, the fateful question about his younger daughter, Joe found his voice. "I was there at the house in Hancock Park with the Delmanns . . . and Lisa."

Her eyes widened in alarm. "You don't mean . . . when it happened?"

"Yes."

Her small hand tightened on his. "You saw?"

He nodded. "They killed themselves. Such terrible . . . such violence, madness."

"Not madness. Not suicide. Murder. But how in the name of God did you survive?"

"I ran."

"While they were still being killed?"

"Charlie and Georgine were already dead. Lisa was still burning."

"So she wasn't dead yet when you ran?"

"No. Still on her feet and burning but not screaming, just quietly . . . quietly burning."

"Then you got out just in time. A miracle of your own."

"How, Rose? How was it done to them?"

Lowering her gaze from his eyes to their entwined hands, she didn't answer Joe's question. More to herself than to him, she said, "I thought this was the way to begin the work—by bringing the news to the families who'd lost loved ones on that airliner. But because of me . . . all this blood."

"You really were aboard Flight 353?" he asked.

She met his eyes again. "Economy class. Row sixteen, seat B, one away from the window."

The truth was in her voice as sure as rain and sunshine are in a green blade of grass.

Joe said, "You really walked away from the crash unharmed."

"Untouched," she said softly, emphasizing the miraculousness of her escape.

"And you weren't alone."

"Who told you?"

"Not the Delmanns. Not anyone else you've spoken with. They have all kept faith with you, held tight to whatever secrets you've told them. How I found out goes all the way back to that night. Do you remember Jeff and Mercy Ealing?"

A faint smile floated across her mouth and away as she said, "The Loose Change Ranch."

"I was there early this afternoon," he said.

"They're nice people."

"A lovely quiet life."

"And you're a good reporter."

"When the assignment matters to me."

Her eyes were midnight-dark but luminous lakes, and Joe could not tell whether the secrets sunk in them would drown or buoy him.

She said, "I'm so sorry about all the people on that plane. Sorry they went before their time. So sorry for their families . . . for you."

"You didn't realize that you were putting them in jeopardy—did you?"

"God, no."

"Then you've no guilt."

"I feel it, though."

"Tell me, Rose. Please. I've come a long, long way around to hear it. Tell me what you've told the others."

"But they're killing everyone I tell. Not just the Delmanns but others, half a dozen others."

"I don't care about the danger."

"But I care. Because now I *do* know the jeopardy I'm putting you in, and I've got to consider it."

"No jeopardy. None whatsoever. I'm dead anyway," he said. "Unless what you have to tell me is something that gives me a life again."

"You're a good man. In all the years you have left, you can contribute so much to this screwed-up world."

"Not in my condition."

Her eyes, those lakes, were sorrow given substance. Suddenly they scared him so profoundly that he wanted to look away from them—but could not.

Their conversation had given him time to approach the

question from which at first he'd cringed, and now he knew that he must ask it before he lost his courage again. "Rose . . . Where is my daughter Nina?"

Rose Tucker hesitated. Finally, with her free hand, she reached into an inner pocket of her navy-blue blazer and withdrew a Polaroid photograph.

Joe could see that it was a picture of the flush-set headstone with the bronze plaque bearing the names of his wife and daughters—one of those she had taken the previous day.

With a squeeze of encouragement, she let go of his hand and pressed the photograph into it.

Staring at the Polaroid, he said, "She's not here. Not in the ground. Michelle and Chrissie, yes. But not Nina."

Almost in a whisper, she said, "Open your heart, Joe. Open your heart and your mind—and what do you see?"

At last she was bringing to him the transforming gift that she had brought to Nora Vadance, to the Delmanns, and to others.

He stared at the Polaroid.

"What do you see, Joe?"

"A gravestone."

"Open your mind."

With expectations that he could not put into words but that nevertheless caused his heart to race, Joe searched the image in his hand. "Granite, bronze . . . the grass around."

"Open your heart," she whispered.

"Their three names . . . the dates . . ."

"Keep looking."

" . . . sunshine . . . shadows . . ."

"Open your heart."

Although Rose's sincerity was evident and could not be doubted, her little mantra—*Open your mind, open your heart*—began to seem silly, as though she were not a scientist but a New Age guru.

"Open your mind," she persisted gently.

The granite. The bronze. The grass around.

She said, "Don't just look. *See.*"

The sweet milk of expectation began to curdle, and Joe felt his expression turning sour.

Rose said, "Does the photo feel strange to you? Not to your eyes . . . to your fingertips? Does it feel peculiar against your skin?"

He was about to tell her no, that it felt like nothing more than what it was, like a damned Polaroid, glossy and cool—but then it *did* feel peculiar.

First he became conscious of the elaborate texture of his own skin to an extent that he had never before experienced or imagined possible. He felt every arch, loop, and whorl as it pressed against the photo, and each tiny ridge and equally tiny trough of skin on each finger pad seemed to have its own exquisitely sensitive array of nerve endings.

More tactile data flowed to him from the Polaroid than he was able to process or understand. He was overwhelmed by the smoothness of the photograph, but also by the thousands of microscopic pits in the film surface that were invisible to the unassisted eye, and by the *feel* of the dyes and fixatives and other chemicals of which the graveyard image was composed.

Then to his touch, although not to his eye, the image on the Polaroid acquired depth, as if it were not merely a two-dimensional photograph but a window with a view of the grave, a window through which he was able to reach. He felt warm summer sun on his fingers, felt granite and bronze and a prickle of grass.

Weirder still: Now he *felt* a color, as if wires had crossed in his brain, jumbling his senses, and he said,

"Blue," and immediately he *felt* a dazzling burst of light, and as if from a distance, he heard himself say, "Bright."

The feelings of blueness and light quickly became actual visual experiences: The banquet room began to fade into a bright blue haze.

Gasping, Joe dropped the photograph as if it had come alive in his hand.

The blue brightness *snapped* to a small point in the center of his field of vision, like the picture on a television screen when the Off switch is clicked. This point shrank until the final pixel of light hung starlike for an instant but then silently imploded and was gone.

Rose Tucker leaned across the table toward him.

Joe peered into her commanding eyes—and perceived something different from what he had seen before. The sorrow and the pity, yes. They remained. The compassion and the intelligence were still there, in as full measure as ever. But now he saw—or thought he saw—some part of her that rode a mad horse of obsession at a gallop toward a cliff over which she wanted him to follow.

As though reading his thoughts, she said, "Joe, what you're afraid of has nothing to do with me. What you're truly afraid of is *opening your mind* to something you've spent your life refusing to believe."

"Your voice," he said, "the whisper, the repetitive phrases—*Open your heart, open your mind*—like a hypnotist."

"You don't really believe that," she said as calmly as ever.

"Something on the Polaroid," he said, and heard the quiver of desperation in his voice.

"What do you mean?" she asked.

"A chemical substance."

"No."

"A hallucinogenic drug. Absorbed through the skin."

"No."

"Something I absorbed through the skin," he insisted, "put me in an altered state of consciousness." He rubbed his hands on his corduroy jacket.

"Nothing on the photograph could have entered your bloodstream through your skin *so quickly*. Nothing could have affected your mind in mere seconds."

"I don't know that to be true."

"I do."

"I'm no pharmacologist."

"Then consult one," she said without enmity.

"Shit." He was as irrationally angry with her as he had briefly been angry with Barbara Christman.

The more rattled he became, the deeper her equanimity. "What you experienced was synesthesia."

"What?"

All scientist now, Rose Tucker said, "Synesthesia. A sensation produced in one modality when a stimulus is applied in a different modality."

"Mumbo-jumbo."

"Not at all. For instance, a few bars of a familiar song are played—but instead of hearing them, you might see a certain color or smell an associated aroma. It's a rare condition in the general population, but it's what most people first feel with these photos—and it's common among mystics."

"Mystics!" He almost spat on the floor. "I'm no mystic, Dr. Tucker. I'm a crime reporter—or was. Only the facts matter to me."

"Synesthesia isn't simply the result of religious mania, if that's what you're thinking, Joe. It's a scientifically documented experience even among nonbelievers, and some well-grounded people think it's a glimpse of a higher state of consciousness."

Her eyes, such cool lakes before, seemed hot now, and

when he peered into them, he looked at once away, afraid that her fire would spread to him. He was not sure if he saw evil in her or only wanted to see it, and he was thoroughly confused.

"If it was some skin-permeating drug on the photograph," she said, as maddeningly soft-spoken as any devil ever had been, "then the effect would have lingered after you dropped it."

He said nothing, spinning in his internal turmoil.

"But when you released the photo, the effect ceased. Because what you're confronted with here is nothing as comforting as mere illusion, Joe."

"Where's Nina?" he demanded.

Rose indicated the Polaroid, which now lay on the table where he had dropped it. "Look. See."

"No."

"Don't be afraid."

Anger surged in him, boiled. This was the savage anger that had frightened him before. It frightened him now, too, but he could not control it.

"Where's Nina, damn it?"

"Open your heart," she said quietly.

"This is bullshit."

"Open your mind."

"Open it how far? Until I've emptied out my head? Is that what you want me to be?"

She gave him time to get a grip on himself. Then: "I don't want you to be anything, Joe. You asked me where Nina is. You want to know about your family. I gave you the photograph so you could see. So you could see."

Her will was stronger than his, and after a while he found himself picking up the photograph.

"Remember the feeling," she encouraged him. "Let it come to you again."

It did not come to him again, however, although he

turned the photograph over and over in his hands. He slid his fingertips in circles across the glossy image but could not feel the granite, the bronze, the grass. He summoned the blueness and the brightness, but they did not appear.

Tossing the photograph aside in disgust, he said, "I don't know what I'm doing with this."

Infuriatingly patient, she smiled compassionately and held out a hand to him.

He refused to take it.

Although he was frustrated by what he now perceived as her New Age proclivities, he also felt that somehow, by not being able to lose himself a second time in the phantasmal blue brightness, he had failed Michelle and Chrissie and Nina.

But if his experience had been only a hallucination, induced with chemicals or hypnosis, then it had no significance, and giving himself to the waking dream once again could not bring back those who were irretrievably lost.

A fusillade of confusions ricocheted through his mind.

Rose said, "It's okay. The imbued photograph is usually enough. But not always."

"Imbued?"

"It's okay, Joe. It's okay. Once in a while there's someone . . . someone like you . . . and then the only thing that convinces is galvanic contact."

"I don't know what you're talking about."

"The touch."

"What touch?"

Instead of answering him, Rose picked up the Polaroid snapshot and stared at it as though she could clearly see something that Joe could see not at all. If turmoil touched her heart and mind, she hid it well, for she seemed as tranquil as a country pond in a windless twilight.

Her serenity only inflamed Joe. "Where's Nina, damn it? Where is my little girl?"

Calmly she returned the photograph to her jacket pocket.

She said, "Joe, suppose that I was one of a group of scientists engaged in a revolutionary series of medical experiments, and then suppose we unexpectedly discovered something that could prove there was some kind of life after death."

"I might be a hell of a lot harder to convince than you."

Her softness was an irritating counterpoint to his sharpness: "It's not as outrageous an idea as you think. For the past couple of decades, discoveries in molecular biology and certain branches of physics have seemed ever more clearly to point toward a *created* universe."

"You're dodging my question. Where are you keeping Nina? Why have you let me go on thinking she's dead?"

Her face remained in an almost eerie repose. Her voice was still soft with a Zen-like sense of peace. "If science gave us a way to perceive the truth of an afterlife, would you really want to see this proof? Most people would say *yes* at once, without thinking how such knowledge would change them forever, change what they have always considered important, what they intend to do with their lives. And then . . . what if this were a revelation with an unnerving edge? Would you want to see this truth—even if it was as frightening as it was uplifting, as fearsome as it was joyous, as deeply and thoroughly strange as it was enlightening?"

"This is just a whole lot of babble to me, Dr. Tucker, a whole lot of nothing—like healing with crystals and channeling spirits and little gray men kidnapping people in flying saucers."

"Don't just look. See."

Through the red lenses of his defensive anger, Joe perceived her calmness as a tool of manipulation. He got up from his chair, hands fisted at his sides. "What were you bringing to L.A. on that plane, and why did Teknologik and its friends kill three hundred and thirty people to stop you?"

"I'm trying to tell you."

"Then *tell* me!"

She closed her eyes and folded her small brown hands, as though waiting for this storm in him to pass—but her serenity only fed the winds of his tempest.

"Horton Nellor. Once your boss, once mine. How does he figure in this?" Joe demanded.

She said nothing.

"Why did the Delmanns and Lisa and Nora Vadance and Captain Blane commit suicide? And how can their suicides be murder, like you say? Who're those men upstairs? What the *hell* is this all about?" He was shaking. *"Where is Nina?"*

Rose opened her eyes and regarded him with sudden concern, her tranquillity at last disturbed. "What men upstairs?"

"Two thugs who work for Teknologik or some secret damn police agency, or someone."

She turned her gaze toward the restaurant. "You're sure?"

"I recognized them, having dinner."

Getting quickly to her feet, Rose stared at the low ceiling as though she were in a submarine sinking out of control into an abyss, furiously calculating the enormity of the crushing pressure, waiting for the first signs of failure in the hull.

"If two of them are inside, you can bet others are outside," Joe said.

"Dear God," she whispered.

"Mahalia's trying to figure a way to slip us past them after closing time."

"She doesn't understand. We've got to get out of here now."

"She's having boxes stacked in the receiving room to cover the entrance of the elevator—"

"I don't care about those men or their damn guns," Rose said, rounding the end of the table. "If they come down here after us, I can face that, handle that. I don't care about dying that way, Joe. But they don't really need to come after us. If they know we're somewhere in this building right now, they can remote us."

"What?"

"Remote us," she said fearfully, heading toward one of the doors that served the deck and the beach.

Following her, exasperated, Joe said, "What does that mean—remote us?"

The door was secured by a pair of thumb-turn dead-bolts. She disengaged the upper one.

He clamped his hand over the lower lock, preventing her from opening it. "Where's Nina?"

"Get out of the way," she demanded.

"Where's Nina?"

"Joe, for God's sake—"

This was the first time that Rose Tucker had seemed vulnerable, and Joe was going to take advantage of the moment to get what he most wanted. "Where's Nina?"

"Later. I promise."

"Now."

From upstairs came a loud clatter.

Rose gasped, turned from the door, and pressed her gaze upon the ceiling again as if it might crash down on them.

Joe heard voices raised in argument, filtered through the elevator shaft—Mahalia's and those of at least two or three men. He was sure that the clatter was the sound of empty packing crates and pallets being dragged and tossed away from the cab door.

When the men in the leather jackets discovered the elevator and knew there was a lower floor to the building, they might realize that they had left an escape gate open by not covering the beach. Indeed, others might even now be looking for a way down the sheer forty-foot bluff, with the hope of cutting off that route.

Nevertheless, face-to-face with Rose, recklessly determined to have an answer at any cost, fiercely insistent, Joe pressed his question: "Where's Nina?"

"Dead," she said, seeming to wrench the word from herself.

"Like hell she is."

"Please, Joe—"

He was furious with her for lying to him, as so many others had lied to him during the past year. "Like *hell* she is. No way. No damn way. I've talked to Mercy Ealing. Nina was alive that night and she's alive now, somewhere."

"If they know we're in this building," Rose repeated in a voice that now shook with urgency, "they can *remote* us. Like the Delmanns. Like Lisa. Like Captain Blane!"

"Where is Nina?"

The elevator motor rumbled to life, and the cab began to hum upward through the shaft.

"Where is Nina?"

Overhead, the banquet room lights dimmed, probably because the elevator drew power from their circuit.

At the dimming of the lights, Rose cried out in terror, threw her body against Joe, trying to knock him off his feet, and clawed frenziedly at the hand that he had clamped over the lower deadbolt.

Her nails gouged his flesh, and he hissed in pain and let go of the lock, and she pulled open the door. In came a breeze that smelled of the ocean, and out went Rose into the night.

Joe rushed after her, onto a twenty-foot-wide, eighty-foot-long, elevated wood deck overhung by the restaurant. It reverberated like a kettledrum with each footfall.

The scarlet sun had bled into a grave on the far side of Japan. The sky and the sea to the west were raven meeting crow, as feathery smooth and sensuous and inviting as death.

Rose was already at the head of the stairs.

Following her, Joe found two flights that led down fourteen or sixteen feet to the beach.

As dark as Rose was, and darkly dressed, she all but vanished in the black geometry of the steps below him. When she reached the pale sand, however, she regained some definition.

The strand was more than a hundred feet across at this point, and the phosphorescent tumble of surf churned out a low white noise that washed like a ghost sea around him. This was not a swimming or surfing beach, and there were no bonfires or even Coleman lanterns in sight in either direction.

To the east, the sky was a pustulant yellow overlaid on black, full of the glow of the city, as insistent as it was meaningless. Cast from high above, the pale-yellow rectangles of light from the restaurant windows quilted part of the beach.

Joe did not try to stop Rose or to slow her. Instead, when he caught up with her, he ran at her side, shortening his stride to avoid pulling ahead of her.

She was his only link to Nina. He was confused by her apparent mysticism, by her sudden transit from beatific calm to superstitious terror, and he was furious that she would lie to him about Nina now, after she had led him to believe, at the cemetery, that she would ultimately tell him the full truth. Yet his fate and hers were inextricably linked, because only she could ever lead him to his younger daughter.

As they ran north through the soft sand and passed the corner of the restaurant, someone rushed at them from ahead and to the right, from the bluff, a shadow in the night, quick and big, like the featureless beast that seeks us in nightmares, pursuer through corridors of dreams.

"Look out," Joe warned Rose, but she also saw the oncoming assailant and was already taking evasive action.

Joe attempted to intervene when the hurtling dark shape moved to cut Rose off—but he was blindsided by a second man, who came at him from the direction of the sea. This guy was as big as a professional football line-backer, and they both went down so hard that the breath should have been knocked out of Joe, but it wasn't, not entirely—he was wheezing but breathing—because the sand in which they landed was deep and soft, far above the highest lapping line of the compacting tide.

He kicked, flailed, ruthlessly used knees and elbows and feet, and rolled out from under his attacker, scrambling to his feet as he heard someone shout at Rose farther along the strand—*"Freeze, bitch!"*—after which he heard a shot, hard and flat. He didn't want to think about that shot, a whip of sound snapping across the beach to the growling sea, didn't want to think about Rose with a bullet in her head and his Nina lost again forever, but he couldn't avoid thinking about it, the possibility like a lash burn branded forever across the surface of his brain. His own assailant was cursing him and pushing up now from the sand, and as Joe spun around to deal with the threat, he was full of the meanness and fury that had gotten him thrown out of the youth boxing league twenty years ago, seething with church-vandalizing rage—he was an animal now, a heartless predator, cat-quick and savage—and he reacted as though this stranger were personally responsible for poor Frank's being crippled with rheumatoid arthritis, as if this son of a bitch had worked some hoodoo to make Frank's joints swell and deform, as if this wretched thug were the *sole perpetrator* who had somehow put a funnel in Captain Blane's ear and poured an elixir of madness into his head, so Joe kicked him in the crotch, and when the guy grunted and began to double over, Joe grabbed the bastard's head and at the same time drove a knee upward, shoving the face down into the knee and jamming the knee up hard into the face, a ballet of violence, and he actually heard the crunch of the man's nose disintegrating and felt the bite of teeth breaking against his kneecap. The guy collapsed backward on the beach, all at once choking and spitting blood and gasping for breath and crying like a small child, but this wasn't enough for Joe, because he was wild now, wilder than any animal, as wild as weather, a cyclone of anger and grief and frustration, and he kicked where he thought ribs would be, which hurt him almost as much as it hurt the broken man who received the blow, because Joe was only wearing Nikes, not hard-toed shoes, so he tried to stomp the guy's throat and crush his windpipe, but stomped his chest instead—and would have tried again, would have killed him, not quite realizing that he was doing so, but then he was rammed from behind by a third attacker.

Joe slammed facedown onto the beach, with the weight of this new assailant atop him, at least two hundred pounds pinning him down. Head to one side, spitting sand, he tried to heave the man off, but this time his breath *was* knocked out of him; he exhaled all of his strength with it, and he lay helpless.

Besides, as he gasped desperately for air, he felt his attacker thrust something cold and blunt against the side of his face, and he knew what it must be even before he heard the threat.

"You want me to blow your head off, I'll do it," the stranger said, and his reverberant voice had a ragged homicidal edge. "I'll do it, you asshole."

Joe believed him and stopped resisting. He struggled only for his breath.

Silent surrender wasn't good enough for the angry man atop him. "Answer me, you bastard. You want me to blow your damn head off? Do you?"

"No."

"Do you?"

"No."

"Going to behave?"

"Yes."

"I'm out of patience here."

"All right."

"Son of a bitch," the stranger said bitterly.

Joe said nothing more, just spit out sand and breathed deeply, getting his strength back with his wind, though trying to stave off the return of the brief madness that had seized him.

Where is Rose?

The man atop Joe was breathing hard too, expelling foul clouds of garlic breath, not only giving Joe time to calm down but getting his own strength back. He smelled of a lime-scented cologne and cigarette smoke.

What's happened to Rose?

"We're going to get up now," the guy said. "Me first. Getting up, I got this piece aimed at your head. You stay flat, dug right into the sand the way you are, just the way you are, until I step back and tell you it's okay to get up." For emphasis, he pressed the muzzle of the gun more deeply into Joe's face, twisting it back and forth; the inside of Joe's cheek pressed painfully against his teeth. "You understand, Carpenter?"

"Yes."

"I can waste you and walk away."

"I'm cool."

"Nobody can touch me."

"Not me anyway."

"I mean, I got a badge."

"Sure."

"You want to see it? I'll pin it to your damn lip."

Joe said nothing more.

They hadn't shouted *Police*, which didn't prove that they were phony cops, only that they didn't want to advertise. They hoped to do their business quickly, cleanly— and get out before they were required to explain their presence to the local authorities, which would at least tangle them in inter-jurisdictional paperwork and might result in troubling questions about what legitimate laws they were enforcing. If they weren't strictly employees of Teknologik, they had some measure of federal power behind them, but they hadn't shouted *FBI* or *DEA* or *ATF* when they had burst out of the night, so they were probably operatives with a clandestine agency paid for out of those many billions of dollars that the government dispensed off the accounting books, from the infamous Black Budget.

Finally the stranger eased off Joe, onto one knee, then stood and backed away a couple of steps. "Get up."

Rising from the sand, Joe was relieved to discover that his eyes were rapidly adapting to the darkness. When he had first come out of the banquet room and run north along the beach, hardly two minutes ago, the gloom had seemed deeper than it was now. The longer he remained night blind to any degree, the less likely he would be to see an advantage and to be able to seize it.

Although his rakish Panama hat was gone, and in spite of the darkness, the gunman was clearly recognizable: the storyteller. In his white slacks and white shirt, with his long white hair, he seemed to draw the meager ambient light to himself, glowing softly like an entity at a séance.

Joe glanced back and up at Santa-Fe-by-the-Sea. He saw the silhouettes of diners at their tables, but they probably couldn't see the action on the dark beach.

Crotch-kicked, face-slammed, the disabled agent still sprawled nearby on the sand, no longer choking but gagging, in pain, and still spitting blood. He was striving to squeeze off his flow of tears by wheezing out obscenities instead of sobs.

Joe shouted, "Rose!"

The white-clad gunman said, "Shut up."

"Rose!"

"Shut up and turn around."

Silent in the sand, a new man loomed behind the storyteller and, instead of proving to be another Teknologik drone, said, "I have a Desert Eagle .44 magnum just one inch from the back of your skull."

The storyteller seemed as surprised as Joe was, and Joe was *dizzied* by this turn of events.

The man with the Desert Eagle said, "You know how powerful this weapon is? You know what it'll do to your head?"

Still softly radiant but now also as powerless as a ghost, the astonished storyteller said, "Shit."

"Pulverize your skull, take your fat head right off your neck, is what it'll do," said the new arrival. "It's a doorbuster. Now toss your gun in the sand in front of Joe."

The storyteller hesitated.

"Now."

Managing to surrender with arrogance, the storyteller

threw the gun as if disdaining it, and the weapon thudded into the sand at Joe's feet.

The savior with the .44 said, "Pick it up, Joe."

As Joe retrieved the pistol, he saw the new arrival use the Desert Eagle as a club. The storyteller dropped to his knees, then to his hands and knees, but did not go all the way out until struck with the pistol a second time, whereupon he plowed the sand with his face, planting his nose like a tuber. The stranger with the .44—a black man dressed entirely in black—stooped to turn the white-maned head gently to one side to ensure that the unconscious thug would not suffocate.

The agent with the knee-smashed face stopped cursing. Now that no witnesses of his own kind were able to hear, he sobbed miserably again.

The black man said, "Come on, Joe."

More impressed than ever with Mahalia and her odd collection of amateurs, Joe said, "Where's Rose?"

"This way. We've got her."

With the disabled agent's sobs purling eerily across the strand behind them, Joe hurried with the black man north, in the direction that he and Rose had been heading when they were assaulted.

He almost stumbled over another unconscious man lying in the sand. This was evidently the first one who had rushed them, the one who had fired a gun.

Rose was on the beach but in the inky shadow of the bluff. Joe could barely see her in the murk, but she seemed to be hugging herself as though she were shivering and cold on this mild summer night.

He was half surprised by the wave of relief that washed through him at the sight of her, not because she was his only link to Nina but because he was genuinely glad that she was alive and safe. For all that she had frustrated and angered and sorely confused him, she was still special, for he recalled, as well, the kindness in her eyes when she had encountered him in the cemetery, the tenderness and pity. Even in the darkness, small as she was, she had an imposing presence, an aura of mystery but also of consequence and prodigious wisdom, probably the same power with which great generals and holy women alike elicited sacrifice from their followers. And here, now, on the shore of the night sea, it was almost possible to believe that she had walked out of the deeps to the west, having breathed water as easily as she now breathed air, come to land with the wonderful secrets of another realm.

With her was a tall man in dark clothes. He was little more than a spectral form—except for masses of curly blond hair that shone faintly like sinuous strands of phosphorate seaweed.

Joe said, "Rose, are you all right?"

"Just got . . . battered around a little," she said in a voice taut with pain.

"I heard a shot," he worried. He wanted to touch her, but he wasn't sure that he should. Then he found himself with his arms around her, holding her.

She groaned in pain, and Joe started to let go of her, but she put one arm around him for a moment, embracing him to let him know that in spite of her injuries she was grateful for his expression of concern. "I'm fine, Joe. I'll be okay."

Shouting rose in the distance, from the bluff top beside the restaurant. And from the beach to the south, the disabled agent replied, calling feebly for help.

"Gotta get out of here," said the blond guy. "They're coming."

"Who are you people?" Rose asked.

Surprised, Joe said, "Aren't they Mahalia's crew?"

"No," Rose said. "Never saw them before."

"I'm Mark," said the man with the curly blond hair, "and he's Joshua."

The black man—Joshua—said something that sounded like: "We're both in finna face."

Rose said, "I'll be damned."

"Who, what? You're in what?" Joe asked.

"It's all right, Joe," Rose said. "I'm surprised, but I probably shouldn't be."

Joshua said, "We believe we're fighting on the same side, Dr. Tucker. Anyway, we have the same enemies."

Out of the distance, at first as soft as the murmur of a heart, but then like the approaching hooves of a headless horseman's steed, came the *whump-whump-whump* of helicopter rotors.

15

Having stolen nothing but their own freedom, they raced like fleeing thieves alongside the bluffs, which soared and then declined and then soared high again, almost as if mirroring Joe's adrenaline levels.

While they were on the move, with Mark in the lead and Rose at his heels, Joe heard Joshua talking urgently to someone. He glanced back and saw the black man with a cell phone. Hearing the word *car*, he realized that their escape was being planned and coordinated even as it was unfolding.

Just when they seemed to have gotten away, the thumping promise of the helicopter became a bright reality to the south. Like a beam from the jewel eye of a stone-temple god angered by desecration, a searchlight pierced the night and swept the beach. Its burning gaze arced from the sandy cliffs to the foaming surf and back again, moving relentlessly toward them.

Because the sand was soft near the base of the palisades, they left shapeless impressions in it. Their aerial pursuers, however, wouldn't be able to follow them by their footprints. Because this sand was never raked, as it might have been on a well-used public beach, it was disturbed by the tracks of many others who had come before them. If they had walked nearer the surf, in the area where higher tides had compacted the sand and left it smooth, their route would have been as clearly marked as if they'd left flares.

They passed several sets of switchback stairs leading to great houses on the bluffs above, some of masonry pinned to the cliff face with steel, some of wood bolted to deep pylons and vertical concrete beams. Joe glanced back once and saw the helicopter hovering by one staircase, the searchlight shimmering up the treads and across the railings.

He figured that a team of hunters might already have driven north from the restaurant and gone by foot to the beach to work methodically southward. Ultimately, if Mark kept them on the strand like this, they would be trapped between the northbound chopper and the southbound searchers.

Evidently the same thought occurred to Mark, because he suddenly led them to an unusual set of redwood stairs rising through a tall box frame. The structure was reminiscent of an early rocket gantry as built back when Cape Kennedy had been called Cape Canaveral, the spacecraft gone now and the architecture surrounding a curious void.

While they ascended, they were putting no additional distance between themselves and the chopper, but it continued to approach. Two, four, six, eight flights of steep stairs brought them to a landing where they seemed horribly exposed. The helicopter, after all, was hovering no more than a hundred feet above the beach—which put it perhaps forty feet above them as they stood atop the bluff—and hardly a hundred and fifty yards to the south. The house next door had no stairs to the shore, which made this platform even more prominent. If either the pilot or the copilot looked to the right and at the bluff top instead of at the searchlight-splashed sand below, discovery could not be avoided.

The upper landing was surrounded by a six-foot-tall,

wrought-iron, gated security fence with a sharply inward-angled, spiked top to prevent unwanted visitors from gaining access by way of the beach below. It had been erected long ago, in the days when the Coastal Commission didn't control such things.

The helicopter was now little more than a hundred yards to the south, moving forward slowly, all but hovering. Its screaming engine and clattering rotors were so loud that Joe could not have made himself heard to his companions unless he shouted.

There was no easy way to climb the fence, not in the minute or two of grace they might have left. Joshua stepped forward with the doorbuster Desert Eagle, fired one round into the lock, and kicked the gate open.

The men in the helicopter could not have heard the gunshot, and it was unlikely that the sound was perceived in the house as anything more than additional racket caused by the aircraft. Indeed, every window was dark, and all was as still as though no one was home.

They passed through the gate into an expansive, estate-size property with low box hedges, formal rose gardens, bowl fountains currently dry, antique French terra-cotta walkways lit by bronze-tulip path lights, and multilevel terraces with limestone balustrades rising to a Mediterranean mansion. There were phoenix palms, ficus trees. Massive California live oaks were underlit by landscape spots: magisterial, frost-and-black, free-form scaffoldings of branches.

Because of the artfulness of the landscape lighting, no glare spoiled any corner. The romantic grounds cast off tangled shawls of shadow, intricate laces of soft light and hard darkness, in which the four of them surely could not be seen by the pilots even as the helicopter now drew almost even with the bluff on which the estate made its bed.

As he followed Rose and Mark up stone steps onto the lowest terrace, Joe hoped that security-system motion detectors were not installed on the exterior of the enormous house, only within its rooms. If their passage activated kleigs mounted high in the trees or atop the perimeter walls, the sudden dazzle would draw the pilots' attention.

He knew how difficult it could be even for a lone fugitive on foot to escape the bright eye of a police search chopper with a good and determined pilot—especially in comparatively open environs such as this neighborhood, which didn't offer the many hiding places of a city's mazes. The four of them would be altogether too easy to keep pinpointed once they had been spotted.

Earlier, an onshore breeze had come with the grace of gull wings from the sea; currently, the flow was offshore and stronger. This was one of those hot winds, called Santa Anas, born in the mountains to the east, out of the threshold of the Mojave, dry and blustery and curiously wearing on the nerves. Now a loud whispering rose from the oaks, and the great fronds of the phoenix palms hissed and rattled and creaked as though the trees were warning one another of gales that might soon descend.

Joe's fear of an outer security line seemed unwarranted as they hurriedly climbed another short flight of stone steps to the upper terrace. The grounds remained subtly lighted, heavily layered with sheltering shadows.

Out beyond the bluff's edge, the search chopper was parallel with them, moving slowly northward. The pilots' attention remained focused on the beach below.

Mark led them past an enormous swimming pool. The oil-black water glimmered with fluid arabesques of silver, as though schools of strange fish with luminous scales were swimming just beneath the surface.

They were still passing the pool when Rose stumbled.

She almost fell but regained her balance. She halted, swaying.

"Are you all right?" Joe asked worriedly.

"Yes, fine, I'll be okay," she said, but her voice was thin, and she still appeared to be unsteady.

"How badly were you hurt back there?" Joe pressed as Mark and Joshua gathered around.

"Just knocked on my ass," she said. "Bruised a little."

"Rose—"

"I'm okay, Joe. It's just all this running, all those damn stairs up from the beach. I guess I'm not in as good a shape as I should be."

Joshua was talking sotto voce on the cell phone again.

"Let's go," Rose said. "Come on, come on, let's go."

Beyond the bluff, above the beach, the helicopter was almost past the estate.

Mark led the way again, and Rose followed with renewed energy. They dashed under the roof of the arched loggia against the rear wall, where they were no longer in any danger of being spotted by the chopper pilots, and then to the corner of the house.

As they moved single file along the side of the mansion on a walkway that serpentined through a small grove of shaggy-barked melaleucas, they were abruptly pinned in the bright beam of a big flashlight. Blocking the path ahead of them, a watchman said, "Hey, who the hell are—"

Acting without hesitation, Mark began to move even as the beam flicked on. The stranger was still speaking when Mark collided with him. The two men grunted from the impact.

The flashlight flew against the trunk of a melaleuca, rebounded onto the walkway, and spun on the stone, making shadows whirl like a pack of tail-chasing dogs.

Mark swiveled the startled watchman around, put a

hammerlock on him, bum-rushed him off the sidewalk and through bordering flower beds, and slammed him against the side of the house so hard that the nearby windows rattled.

Scooping up the flashlight, Joshua directed it on the action, and Joe saw that they had been challenged by an overweight uniformed security guard of about fifty-five. Mark pressed him to his knees and kept a hand on the back of his head to force his face down and away from them, so he couldn't describe them later.

"He's not armed," Mark informed Joshua.

"Bastards," the watchman said bitterly.

"Ankle holster?" Joshua wondered.

"Not that, either."

The watchman said, "Stupid owners are pacifists or some damn thing. Won't have a gun on the place, even for me. So now here I am."

"We're not going to hurt you," Mark said, pulling him backward from the house and forcing him to sit on the ground with his back against the trunk of a melaleuca.

"You don't scare me," the watchman said, but he sounded scared.

"Dogs?" Mark demanded.

"Everywhere," the guard said. "Dobermans."

"He's lying," Mark said confidently.

Even Joe could hear the bluff in the watchman's voice.

Joshua gave the flashlight to Joe and said, "Keep it pointed at the ground." Then he produced handcuffs from a fanny pack.

Mark directed the guard to reach in back of himself and clasp his hands behind the tree. The trunk was only about ten inches in diameter, so the guard didn't have to contort himself, and Joshua snapped the cuffs on his wrists.

"The cops are on the way," the watchman gloated.

"No doubt riding Dobermans," Mark said.

"Bastard," said the watchman.

From his fanny pack, Mark withdrew a tightly rolled Ace bandage. "Bite on this," he told the guard.

"Bite on *this*," the guard said, indulging in one last bleat of hopeless bravado, and then he did as he was told.

Three times, Joshua wound electrician's tape around the guard's head and across his mouth, fixing the Ace bandage firmly in place.

From the watchman's belt, Mark unclipped what appeared to be a remote control. "This open the driveway gate?"

Through his gag, the watchman snarled something obscene, which issued as a meaningless mumble.

"Probably the gate."

To the guard, Joshua said, "Just relax. Don't chafe your wrists. We're not robbing the place. We're really not. We're only passing through."

Mark said, "When we've been gone half an hour, we'll call the cops so they can come and release you."

"Better get a dog," Joshua advised.

Taking the watchman's flashlight, Mark led them toward the front of the house.

Whoever these guys were, Joe was glad that they were on his side.

The estate occupied at least three acres. The huge house was set two hundred feet back from the front property wall at the street. In the eye of the wide, looping driveway was a four-tier marble fountain: four broad scalloped bowls, each supported by three leaping dolphins, bowls and dolphins diminishing in scale as they ascended. The bowls were full of water, but the pump was silent, and there were no spouts or cascades.

"We'll wait here," Mark said, leading them to the dolphins.

The dolphins and bowls rose out of a pool with a two-foot-high wall finished with a broad cap of limestone. Rose sat on the edge—and then so did Joe and Mark.

Taking the remote control they had gotten from the watchman, Joshua walked along the driveway toward the entrance gate, talking on the cellular phone as he went.

Dogs of warm Santa Ana wind chased cat-quick leaves and curls of papery melaleuca bark along the blacktop.

"How do you even know about me?" Rose asked Mark.

"When any enterprise is launched with a one-billion-dollar trust fund, like ours," Mark said, "it sure doesn't take long to get up to speed. Besides, computers and data technology are what we're about."

"What enterprise?" Joe asked.

The answer was the same mystifying response that Joshua had given on the beach, "In finna face."

"And what's that mean?"

"Later, Joe," Rose promised. "Go on, Mark."

"Well, so, from day one, we've had the funds to try to keep track of all promising research in every discipline, worldwide, that could conceivably lead to the epiphany we expect."

"Maybe so," Rose said, "but you people have been around two years, while the largest part of my research for the past *seven* years has been conducted under the tightest imaginable security."

"Doctor, you showed enormous promise in your field until you were about thirty-seven—and then suddenly your work appeared to come almost to a complete halt, except for a minor paper published here or there from time to time. You were a Niagara of creativity—and then went dry overnight."

"And that indicates what to you?"

"It's the signature pattern of a scientist who's been co-opted by the defense establishment or some other branch of government with sufficient power to enforce a total information blackout. So when we see something like that, we start trying to find out exactly where you're at work. Finally we located you at Teknologik, but not at any of their well-known and accessible facilities. A deep subterranean, biologically secure complex near Manassas, Virginia. Something called 'Project 99.'"

While he listened intently to the conversation, Joe watched as, out at the end of the long driveway, the ornate electric gate rolled aside.

"How much do you know about what we do on Project 99?" Rose asked.

"Not enough," Mark said.

"How can you know anything at all?"

"When I say we track ongoing research worldwide, I don't mean that we limit ourselves to the same publications and shared data banks that any science library has available to it."

With no animosity, Rose said, "That's a nice way of saying you try to penetrate computer security systems, hack your way in, break encryptions."

"Whatever. We don't do it for profit. We don't economically exploit the information we acquire. It's simply our mission, the search we were created to undertake."

Joe was surprised by his own patience. Although he was learning things by listening to them talk, the basic mystery only grew deeper. Yet he was prepared to wait for answers. The bizarre experience with the Polaroid snapshot in the banquet room had left him shaken. Now that he'd had time to think about what had happened, the synesthesia seemed to be but prelude to some revelation that was going to be more shattering and humbling than he had previously imagined. He remained committed to learning the truth, but now instinct warned him that he should allow the revelations to wash over him in small waves instead of in one devastating tsunami.

Joshua had gone through the open gate and was standing along the Pacific Coast Highway.

Over the eastern hills, the swollen moon ascended yellow-orange, and the warm wind seemed to blow down out of it.

Mark said, "You were one of thousands of researchers whose work we followed—though you were of somewhat special interest because of the extreme secrecy at Project 99. Then, a year ago, you left Manassas with something from the project, and overnight you were the most wanted person in the country. Even after you supposedly died aboard that airliner in Colorado. Even then . . . people were looking for you, lots of people, expending considerable resources, searching frantically for a dead woman—which seemed pretty weird to us."

Rose said nothing to encourage him. She seemed tired.

Joe took her hand. She was trembling, but she squeezed his hand as if to assure him that she was all right.

"Then we began to intercept reports from a certain clandestine police agency . . . reports that said you were alive and active in the L.A. area, that it involved families who'd lost loved ones on Flight 353. We set up some surveillance of our own. We're pretty good at it. Some of us are ex-military. Anyway, you could say we watched the watchers who were keeping tab on people like Joe here. And now . . . I guess it's a good thing we did."

"Yes. Thank you," she said. "But you don't know what you're getting into here. There's not just glory . . . there's terrible danger."

"Dr. Tucker," Mark persisted, "there are over nine thousand of us now, and we've committed our lives to what we do. We're not afraid. And now we believe that you may have found the interface—and that it's very different from anything we quite anticipated. If you've actually made that breakthrough . . . if humanity is at that pivot point in history when everything is going to change radically and forever . . . then *we* are your natural allies."

"I think you are," she agreed.

Gently but persistently selling her on this alliance, Mark said, "Doctor, we both have set ourselves against those forces of ignorance and fear and self-interest that want to keep the world in darkness."

"Remember, I once worked for them."

"But turned."

A car swung off Pacific Coast Highway and paused to pick up Joshua. It was followed through the gate and along the driveway by a second car.

Rose, Mark, and Joe got to their feet as the two vehicles—a Ford trailed by a Mercedes—circled the fountain and stopped in front of them.

Joshua stepped from the passenger door of the Ford, and a young brunette woman got out from behind the steering wheel. The Mercedes was driven by an Asian man of about thirty.

They all gathered before Rose Tucker, and for a moment everyone stood in silence.

The steadily escalating wind no longer spoke merely through the rustling foliage of the trees, through the cricket-rasping branches of the shrubbery, and through the hollow flute-like music issuing from the eaves of the mansion, for now it also enjoyed a voice of its own: a haunted keening that curled chillingly in listening ears, akin to the muted but frightful ululant crying of coyote packs chasing down prey in some far canyon of the night.

In the landscape lights, the shuddering greenery cast nervous shadows, and the gradually paling moon gazed at itself in the shiny surfaces of the automobiles.

Watching these four people as they watched Rose, Joe realized that they regarded the scientist not solely with curiosity but with wonder, perhaps even with awe, as though they stood in the presence of someone transcendent. Someone holy.

"I'm surprised to see every one of you in mufti," Rose said.

They smiled, and Joshua said, "Two years ago, when we first set out on this mission, we were reasonably quiet about it. Didn't want to excite a lot of media interest . . . because we thought we'd largely be misunderstood. What we didn't expect was that we'd have enemies. And enemies so violent."

"So powerful," Mark said.

"We thought everyone would want to know the answers we were seeking—if we ever found them. Now we know better."

"Ignorance is a bliss that some people will kill for," said the young woman.

"So a year ago," Joshua continued, "we adopted the robes as a distraction. People understand us as a cult—or think they do. We're more acceptable when we're viewed as fanatics, neatly labeled and confined to a box. We don't make people quite so nervous."

Robes.

Astonished, Joe said, "You wear blue robes, shave your heads."

Joshua said, "Some of us do, yes, as of a year ago—and those in the uniform pretend to be the entire membership. That's what I meant when I said the robes are a distraction—the robes, the shaved heads, the earrings, the visible communal enclaves. The rest of us have gone underground, where we can do the work without being spied on, subjected to harassment, and easily infiltrated."

"Come with us," the young woman said to Rose. "We

know you may have found the way, and we want to help you bring it to the world—without interference."

Rose moved to her and put a hand against her cheek, much as she had touched Joe in the cemetery. "I might be with you soon, but not tonight. I need more time to think, to plan. And I'm in a hurry to see a young girl, a child, who is at the center of what is happening."

Nina, Joe thought, and his heart shuddered like the shadows of the wind-shaken trees.

Rose moved to the Asian man and touched him too. "I can tell you this much . . . we stand on the threshold you foresaw. We will go through that door, maybe not tomorrow or the day after tomorrow or next week, but in the years ahead."

She went to Joshua. "Together we will see the world change forever, bring the light of knowledge into the great dark loneliness of human existence. *In our time*."

And finally she approached Mark. "I assume you brought two cars because you were prepared to give one to Joe and me."

"Yes. But we hoped—"

She put a hand on his arm. "Soon but not tonight. I've got urgent business, Mark. Everything we hope to achieve hangs in the balance right now, hangs so precariously—until I can reach the little girl I mentioned."

"Wherever she is, we can take you to her."

"No. Joe and I must do this alone—and quickly."

"You can take the Ford."

"Thank you."

Mark withdrew a folded one-dollar bill from his pocket and gave it to Rose. "There are just eight digits in the serial number on this bill. Ignore the fourth digit, and the other seven are a phone number in the 310 area code."

Rose tucked the bill into her jeans.

"When you're ready to join us," Mark said, "or if you're ever in trouble you can't get out of, ask for me at that number. We'll come for you no matter where you are."

She kissed him on the cheek. "We've got to go." She turned to Joe. "Will you drive?"

"Yes."

To Joshua, she said, "May I take your cell phone?"

He gave it to her.

Wings of furious wind beat around them as they got into the Ford. The keys were in the ignition.

As Rose pulled the car door shut, she said, "Oh, Jesus," and leaned forward, gasping for breath.

"You *are* hurt."

"Told you. I got knocked around."

"Where's it hurt?"

"We've got to get across the city," Rose said, "but I don't want to go back past Mahalia's."

"You could have a broken rib or two."

Ignoring him, she sat up straight, and her breathing improved as she said, "The creeps won't want to risk setting up a roadblock and a traffic check without cooperation from the local authorities, and they don't have time to get that. But you can bet your ass they'll be watching passing cars."

"If you've got a broken rib, it could puncture a lung."

"Joe, damn it, we don't have *time*. We've got to move if we're going to keep our girl alive."

He stared at her. "Nina?"

She met his eyes. She said, "Nina," but then a fearful look came into her face, and she turned from him.

"We can head north from here on PCH," he said, "then inland on Kanan-Dume Road. That's a county route up to Augora Hills. There we can get the 101 east to the 210."

"Go for it."

Faces powdered by moonlight, hair wind-tossed, the four who would leave in the Mercedes stood watching, backdropped by leaping stone dolphins and thrashing trees.

This tableau struck Joe as both exhilarating and ominous—and he could not identify the basis of either perception, other than to admit that the night was charged with an uncanny power that was beyond his understanding. Everything his gaze fell upon seemed to have monumental significance, as if he were in a state of heightened consciousness, and even the moon appeared different from any moon that he had ever seen before.

As Joe put the Ford in gear and began to pull away from the fountain, the young woman came forward to place her hand against the window beside Rose Tucker's face. On this side of the glass, Rose matched her palm to the other. The young woman was crying, her lovely face glimmering with moon-bright tears, and she moved with the car along the driveway, hurrying as it picked up speed, matching her hand to Rose's all the way to the gate before at last pulling back.

Joe felt almost as if somewhere earlier in the night he had stood before a mirror of madness and, closing his eyes, had passed through his own reflection into lunacy. Yet he did not want to return through the silvered surface to that old gray world. This was a lunacy that he found increasingly agreeable, perhaps because it offered him the one thing he desired most and could find only on this side of the looking glass—hope.

Slumped in the passenger seat beside him, Rose Tucker said, "Maybe all this is more than I can handle, Joe. I'm so tired—and so scared. I'm nobody special enough to do what needs doing, not nearly special enough to carry a weight like this."

"You seem pretty special to me," he said.

"I'm going to screw it up," she said as she entered a phone number on the keypad of the cellular phone. "I'm scared shitless that I'm not going to be strong enough to open that door and take us all through it." She pushed the Send button.

"Show me the door, tell me where it goes, and I'll help you," he said, wishing she would stop speaking in metaphors and give him the hard facts. "Why is Nina so important to whatever's happening? Where is she, Rose?"

Someone answered the cellular call, and Rose said, "It's me. Move Nina. Move her now."

Nina.

Rose listened for a moment but then said firmly, "No, now, move her right now, in the next five minutes, even sooner if you can. They linked Mahalia to me . . . yeah, and in spite of all the precautions we'd taken. It's only a matter of time now—and not very much time—until they make the connection to you."

Nina.

Joe turned off the Pacific Coast Highway onto the county road to Augora Hills, driving up through a rumpled bed of dark land from which the Santa Ana wind flung sheets of pale dust.

"Take her to Big Bear," Rose told the person on the phone.

Big Bear. Since Joe had talked to Mercy Ealing in Colorado—could it be less than nine hours ago?—Nina had been back in the world, miraculously returned, but in some corner where he could not find her. Soon, however, she would be in the town of Big Bear on the shores of Big Bear Lake, a resort in the nearby San Bernardino Mountains, a place he knew well. Her return was more real to him now that she was in a place that he could *name*, the byways of which he had walked, and he was flooded with such sweet anticipation that he wanted to shout to relieve the pressure of it. He kept his silence, however, and he rolled the name between the fingers of his mind, rolled it over and over as if it were a shiny coin: *Big Bear.*

Rose spoke into the phone: "If I can . . . I'm going to be there in a couple of hours. I love you. Go. Go *now.*"

She terminated the call, put the phone on the seat between her legs, closed her eyes, and leaned against the door.

Joe realized that she was not making much use of her left hand. It was curled in her lap. Even in the dim light from the instrument panel, he could see that her hand was shaking uncontrollably.

"What's wrong with your arm?"

"Give it a rest, Joe. It's sweet of you to be concerned, but you're getting to be a nag. I'll be fine once we get to Nina."

He was silent for half a mile. Then: "Tell me everything. I deserve to know."

"You do, yes. It's not a long story . . . but where do I begin?"

16

Great bristling balls of tumbleweed, robbed of their green by the merciless Western sun, cracked from their roots by the withering dryness of the California summer, torn from their homes in the earth by the shrieking Santa Ana wind, now bounded out of the steep canyons and across the narrow highway, silver-gray in the headlights, a curiously melancholy sight, families of thistled skeletons like starved and harried refugees fleeing worse torment.

Joe said, "Start with those people back there. What kind of cult are they?"

She spelled it for him: *Infiniface.*

"It's a made word," she said, "shorthand for 'Interface with the Infinite.' And they're not a cult, not in any sense you mean it."

"Then what are they?"

Instead of answering immediately, she shifted in her seat, trying to get more comfortable.

Checking her wristwatch, she said, "Can you drive faster?"

"Not on this road. In fact, better put on your safety belt."

"Not with my left side feeling like it does." Having adjusted her position, she said, "Do you know the name Loren Pollack?"

"The software genius. The poor man's Bill Gates."

"That's what the press sometimes calls him, yes. But I don't think the word *poor* should be associated with someone who started from scratch and made seven billion dollars by the age of forty-two."

"Maybe not."

She closed her eyes and slumped against the door, supporting her weight on her right side. Sweat beaded her brow, but her voice was strong. "Two years ago, Loren Pollack used a billion dollars of his money to form a charitable trust. Named it Infiniface. He believes many of the sciences, through research facilitated by new generations of superfast computers, are approaching discoveries that will bring us face-to-face with the reality of a Creator."

"Sounds like a cult to me."

"Oh, plenty of people think Pollack is a flake. But he's got a singular ability to grasp complex research from a wide variety of sciences—and he has vision. You know, there's a whole movement of modern physics that sees evidence of a created universe."

Frowning, Joe said, "What about chaos theory? I thought that was the big thing."

"Chaos theory doesn't say the universe is random and chaotic. It's an extremely broad theory that among many other things notes strangely complex relationships in *apparently* chaotic systems—like the weather. Look deeply enough in any chaos, and you find hidden regularities."

"Actually," he admitted, "I don't know a damn thing about it—just the way they use the term in the movies."

"Most movies are stupidity machines—like politicians. So . . . if Pollack was here, he'd tell you that just eighty years ago, science mocked religion's assertion that the universe was created *ex nihilo*, out of nothing. Everyone *knew* something couldn't be created from nothing—a violation of all the laws of physics. Now we understand more about molecular structure—and particle physicists create matter *ex nihilo* all the time." Inhaling with a hiss through clenched teeth, she leaned forward, popped open the glove box, and rummaged through its contents. "I was hoping for aspirin or Excedrin. I'd chew them dry."

"We could stop somewhere—"

"No. Drive. Just drive. Big Bear's so far . . ." She closed the glove box but remained sitting forward, as though that position gave her relief. "Anyway, physics and biology are the disciplines that most fascinate Pollack—especially molecular biology."

"Why molecular biology?"

"Because the more we understand living things on a molecular level, the clearer it becomes that everything is intelligently designed. You, me, mammals, fish, insects, plants, everything."

"Wait a second. Are you tossing away evolution here?"

"Not entirely. Wherever molecular biology takes us, there might still be a place for Darwin's theory of evolution—in some form."

"You're not one of those strict fundamentalists who believe we were created exactly five thousand years ago in the Garden of Eden."

"Hardly. But Darwin's theory was put forth in 1859, before we had any knowledge of atomic structure. He thought the smallest unit of a living creature was the cell—which he saw as just a lump of adaptable albumen."

"Albumen? You're losing me."

"The origin of this basic living matter, he thought, was most likely an accident of chemistry—and the origin of all species was explained through evolution. But we now know cells are enormously complex structures of such clockwork design that it's impossible to believe they are accidental in nature."

"We do? I guess I've been out of school a long time."

"Even in the matter of the species . . . Well, the two axioms of Darwinian theory—the continuity of nature and adaptable design—have never been validated by a single empirical discovery in nearly a hundred and fifty years."

"Now you *have* lost me."

"Let me put it another way." She still leaned forward, staring out at the dark hills and the steadily rising glow of the sprawling suburbs beyond. "Do you know who Francis Crick is?"

"No."

"He's a molecular biologist. In 1962, he shared the Nobel Prize in Medicine with Maurice Wilkins and James Watson for discovering the three-dimensional molecular structure of DNA—the double helix. Every advancement in genetics since then—and the countless revolutionary cures for diseases we're going to see over the next twenty years—spring directly from the work of Francis Crick and his colleagues. Crick is a scientist's scientist, Joe, to no degree a spiritualist or mystic. But do you know what he suggested a few years ago? That life on earth may well have been designed by an extra-terrestrial intelligence."

"Even highbrows read the *National Enquirer*, huh?"

"The point is—Crick was unable to square what we now know of molecular biology's complexity with the theory of natural selection, but he was unwilling to suggest a Creator in any spiritual sense."

"So . . . enter the ever-popular god-like aliens."

"But it totally begs the issue, you see? Even if every form of life on this planet was designed by extraterrestrials . . . who designed *them?*"

"It's the chicken or the egg all over again."

She laughed softly, but the laughter mutated into a cough that she couldn't easily suppress. She eased back, leaning against the door once more—and glared at him when he tried to suggest that she needed medical attention.

When she regained her breath, she said, "Loren Pollack believes the purpose of human intellectual striving—the purpose of science—is to increase our understanding of the universe, not just to give us better physical control of our environment or to satisfy curiosity, but to solve the puzzle of existence God has put before us."

"And by solving it to become like gods ourselves."

She smiled through her pain. "Now you're tuned to the Pollack frequency. Pollack thinks we're living in the time when some key scientific breakthrough will prove there is a Creator. Something that is . . . an interface with the infinite. This will bring the soul back to science—lifting humanity out of its fear and doubt, healing our divisions and hatreds, finally uniting our species on one quest that's both of the spirit and of the mind."

"Like *Star Trek*."

"Don't make me laugh again, Joe. It hurts too much."

Joe thought of Gem Fittich, the used-car dealer. Both Pollack and Fittich sensed an approaching end to the world as they knew it, but the oncoming tidal wave that Fittich perceived was dark and cold and obliterating, while Pollack foresaw a wave of purest light.

"So Pollack," she said, "founded Infiniface to facilitate this quest, to track research worldwide with an eye toward projects with . . . well, with metaphysical aspects that the scientists themselves might not recognize. To ensure that key discoveries were shared among researchers. To encourage specific projects that seemed to be leading to a breakthrough of the sort Pollack predicts."

"Infiniface isn't a religion at all."

"No. Pollack thinks all religions are valid to the extent that they recognize the existence of a created universe and a Creator—but that then they bog down in elaborate interpretations of what God expects of us. What's wanted of us, in Pollack's view, is to work together to learn, to understand, to peel the layers of the universe, to find God . . . and in the process to become His equals."

By now they were out of the dark hills and into suburbs again. Ahead was the entrance to the freeway that would take them east across the city.

As he drove up the ramp, heading toward Glendale and Pasadena, Joe said, "I don't believe in anything."

"I know."

"No loving god would allow such suffering."

"Pollack would say that the fallacy of your thinking lies in its narrow human perspective."

"Maybe Pollack is full of shit."

Whether Rose began to laugh again or fell directly victim to the cough, Joe couldn't tell, but she needed even longer than before to regain control of herself.

"You need to see a doctor," he insisted.

She was adamantly opposed. "Any delay . . . and Nina's dead."

"Don't make me choose between—"

"There *is* no choice. That's my point. If it's me or Nina . . . then she comes first. Because she's the future. She's the hope."

■

Orange-faced on first appearance, the moon had lost its blush and, stage fright behind it, had put on the stark white face of a smugly amused mime.

Sunday night traffic on the moon-mocked freeway was heavy as Angelenos returned from Vegas and other points in the desert, while desert dwellers streamed in the opposite direction, returning from the city and its beaches: ceaselessly restless, these multitudes, always seeking a greater happiness—and often finding it, but only for a weekend or an afternoon.

Joe drove as fast and as recklessly as he dared, weaving from lane to lane, but keeping in mind that they could not risk being stopped by the highway patrol. The car wasn't registered in either his name or Rose's. Even if they could prove it had been loaned to them, they would lose valuable time in the process.

"What is Project 99?" he asked her. "What the hell are they doing in that subterranean facility outside Manassas?"

"You've heard about the Human Genome Project."

"Yeah. Cover of *Newsweek*. As I understand it, they're figuring out what each human gene controls."

"The greatest scientific undertaking of our age," Rose said. "Mapping all one hundred thousand human genes and detailing the DNA alphabet of each. And they're making incredibly fast progress."

"Find out how to cure muscular dystrophy, multiple sclerosis—"

"Cancer, everything—given time."

"You're part of that?"

"No. Not directly. At Project 99 . . . we have a more exotic assignment. We're looking for those genes that seem to be associated with unusual talents."

"What—like Mozart or Rembrandt or Michael Jordan?"

"No. Not creative or athletic talents. Paranormal talents. Telepathy. Telekinesis. Pyrokinesis. It's a long strange list."

His immediate reaction was that of a crime reporter, not of a man who had recently seen the fantastic in action: "But there aren't such talents. That's science fiction."

"There are people who score far higher than chance on a variety of tests designed to disclose psychic abilities. Card prediction. Calling coin tosses. Thought-image transmission."

"That stuff they used to do at Duke University."

"That and more. When we find people who perform exceptionally well in these tests, we take blood samples from them. We study their genetic structure. Or children in poltergeist situations."

"Poltergeists?"

"Poltergeist phenomena—weeding out the hoaxes—aren't really ghosts. There's always one or more children in houses where this happens. We think the objects flying around the room and the ectoplasmic apparitions are caused by these children, by their unconscious exercise of powers they don't even know they have. We take samples from these kids when we can find them. We're building a library of unusual genetic profiles, looking for common patterns among people who have had all manner of paranormal experiences."

"And have you found something?"

She was silent, perhaps waiting for another spasm of pain to pass, though her face revealed more mental anguish than physical suffering. At last she said, "Quite a lot, yes."

If there had been enough light for Joe to see his reflection in the rearview mirror, he knew that he could have watched as his tan faded and his face turned as white as the moon, for he suddenly knew the essence of what Project 99 was all about. "You haven't just *studied* this."

"Not just. No."

"You've applied the research."

"Yes."

"How many work on Project 99?"

"Over two hundred of us."

"Making monsters," he said numbly.

"People," she said. "Making people in a lab."

"They may look like people, but some of them are monsters."

She was silent for perhaps a mile. Then she said, "Yes." And after another silence: "Though the true monsters are those of us who made them."

■

Fenced and patrolled, identified at the highway as a think tank called the Quartermass Institute, the property encompasses eighteen hundred acres in the Virginia countryside: meadowed hills where deer graze, hushed woods of birch and beeches where a plenitude of small game thrives beyond the rifle reach of hunters, ponds with ducks, and grassy fields with nesting plovers.

Although security appears to be minimal, no animal larger than a rabbit moves across these acres without being monitored by motion detectors, heat sensors, microphones, and cameras, which feed a continuous river of data to a Cray computer for continuous analysis. Unauthorized visitors are subject to immediate arrest, and on those rare occasions when hunters or adventurous teenagers scale the fence, they are halted and taken into custody within five hundred feet of the point of intrusion.

Near the geographical center of these peaceful acres is the orphanage, a cheerless three-story brick structure that resembles a hospital. Forty-eight children currently reside herein, every one below the age of six—though some appear older. They are all residents by virtue of having been born without mothers or fathers in any but the chemical sense. None of them was conceived in love, and none entered the world through a woman's womb. As fetuses, they were nurtured in mechanical wombs, adrift in amniotic fluid brewed in a laboratory.

As with laboratory rats and monkeys, as with dogs

whose skulls are cut open and brains exposed for days
during experiments related to the central nervous system,
as with all animals that further the cause of knowledge,
these orphans have no names. To name them would be to
encourage their handlers to develop emotional attach-
ments to them. The handlers—who include everyone
from those security men who double as cooks to the scientists who bring these children into the world—must
remain morally neutral and emotionally detached in
order to do their work properly. Consequently, the children are known by letter and number codes that refer to
the specific indices in Project 99's genetic-profile library
from which their special abilities were selected.

Here on the third floor, southwest corner, in a room of
her own, sits ATX-12-23. She is four years old, catatonic,
and incontinent. She waits in her crib, in her own wastes
until her nurse changes her, and she never complains.
ATX-12-23 has never spoken a single word or uttered any
sound whatsoever. As an infant, she never cried. She
cannot walk. She sits motionlessly, staring into the middle
distance, sometimes drooling. Her muscles are partially
atrophied even though she is given manipulated exercise
three times a week. If her face were ever enlivened by
expression, she might be beautiful, but the unrelieved
slackness of her features gives her a chilling aspect. Cameras cover every inch of her room and record around the
clock, which might seem to be a waste of videotape—
except that from time to time, inanimate objects around
ATX-12-23 become animated. Rubber balls of various
colors levitate and spin in the air, float from wall to wall
or circle the child's head for ten or twenty minutes at a
time. Window blinds raise and lower without a hand
touching them. Lights dim and flare, the digital clock
speeds through the hours, and a teddy bear that she has
never touched sometimes walks around the room on its

stubby legs as if it contains the mechanical system that would allow it to do so.

Now come here, down to the second floor, to the third room east of the elevators, where lives a five-year-old male, KSB-22-09, who is neither physically nor mentally impaired. Indeed, he is an active redheaded boy with a genius-level IQ. He loves to learn, receives extensive tutoring daily, and is currently educated to a ninth-grade equivalent. He has numerous toys, books, and movies on video, and he participates in supervised play sessions with the other orphans, because it is deemed essential by the project architects that all subjects with normal mental faculties and full physical abilities be raised in as social an atmosphere as possible, given the limitations of the Institute. Sometimes when he tries hard (and sometimes when he is not trying at all), KSB-22-09 is able to make small objects—pencils, ball bearings, paper clips, thus far nothing larger than a glass of water—vanish. Simply vanish. He sends them elsewhere, into what he calls "The All Dark." He is not able to bring them back and cannot explain what The All Dark may be—though he does not like the place. He must be sedated to sleep, because he frequently suffers vivid nightmares in which he uncontrollably sends himself, piece by piece, into The All Dark—first a thumb, and then a toe, and then his left foot, a tooth and another tooth, one eye gone from a suddenly empty socket, and then an ear. Lately, KSB-22-09 is experiencing memory lapses and spells of paranoia, which are thought to be related to the long-term use of the sedative that he receives before bed each night.

Of the forty-eight orphans residing at the Institute, only seven exhibit any paranormal powers. The other forty-one, however, are not regarded as failures. Each of the seven successes first revealed his or her talent at a different age—one as young as eleven months, one as old as five. Consequently, the possibility remains that many of the forty-one will blossom in years to come—perhaps not until they experience the dramatic changes in body chemistry related to puberty. Eventually, of course, those subjects who age without revealing any valuable talent will have to be removed from the program, as even Project 99's resources are not infinite. The project's architects have not yet determined the optimum point of termination.

■

Although the steering wheel was hard under his hands and slick with his cold sweat, although the sound of the engine was familiar, although the freeway was solid under the spinning tires, Joe felt as if he had crossed into another dimension as treacherously amorphous and inimical to reason as the surreal landscapes in Salvador Dalí's paintings.

As his horror grew, he interrupted Rose: "This place you're describing is Hell. You . . . you couldn't have been part of anything like this. You're not that kind of person."

"Aren't I?"

"No."

Her voice grew thinner as she talked, as though the strength supporting her had been the secrets she kept, and as she revealed them one by one, her vitality ebbed as it had for Samson lock by lock. In her increasing weariness was a sweet relief like that dispensed in a confessional, a weakness that she seemed to embrace—but that was nonetheless colored by a gray wash of despair. "If I'm not that kind of person now . . . I must have been then."

"But how? Why? Why would you want to be involved with these . . . these atrocities?"

"Pride. To prove that I was as good as they thought I was, good enough to take on this unprecedented challenge. Excitement. The thrill of being involved with a program even better funded than the Manhattan Project. Why did the people who invented the atomic bomb work on it . . . knowing what they were making? Because others, elsewhere in the world, will do it if we don't . . . so maybe we have to do it to save ourselves from them?"

"Save ourselves by selling our souls?" he asked.

"There's no defense I can offer that should ever exonerate me," Rose said. "But it is true that when I signed on, there was no consensus that we would carry the experiments this far, that we would *apply* what we learned with such . . . zeal. We entered into the creation of the children in stages . . . down a slippery slope. We intended to monitor the first one just through the second trimester of the fetal stage—and, after all, we don't consider a fetus to be an actual human being. So it wasn't like we were experimenting on a *person*. And when we brought one of them to full term . . . there were intriguing anomalies in its EEG graphs, strangeness in its brainwave patterns that might have indicated heretofore unknown cerebral function. So we had to keep it alive to see . . . to see what we had achieved, to see if maybe we had moved evolution forward a giant step."

"Jesus."

Though he had first met this woman only thirty-six hours ago, his feelings for her had been rich and intense, ranging from virtual adoration to fear and now to repulsion. Yet from his repulsion came pity, because for the first time he saw in her one of the many cloves of human weakness that, in other forms, were so ripe in himself.

"Fairly early on," she said, "I *did* want out. So I was invited for a private chat with the project director, who made it clear to me that there was no quitting now. This had become a job with lifetime tenure. Even to attempt to leave Project 99 is to commit suicide—and to put the lives of your loved ones at risk as well."

"But couldn't you have gone to the press, broken the story wide open, shut them down?"

"Probably not without physical evidence, and all I had was what was in my head. Anyway, a couple of my colleagues had the idea that they could bring it all down, I think. One of them suffered a timely stroke. The other was shot three times in the head by a mugger—who was never caught. For a while . . . I was so depressed I considered killing myself and saving them the trouble. But then . . . along came CCY-21-21. . . ."

First, born a year ahead of CCY-21-21 was male subject SSW-89-58. He exhibits prodigious talents in every regard and his story is of importance to you because of your own recent experiences with people who eviscerate themselves and set themselves afire—and because of your losses in Colorado.

By the time he is forty-two months old, SSW-89-58 possesses the language skills of the average first-year college student and is able to read a three-hundred-page volume in one to three hours, depending on the complexity of the text. Higher math comes to him as easily as eating ice cream, as do foreign languages from French to Japanese. His physical development proceeds at an accelerated rate as well, and by the time he is four, he stands as tall and is as proportionately developed as the average seven-year-old. Paranormal talents are anticipated, but researchers are surprised by 89-58's great breadth of more ordinary genius—which includes the ability to play any piece of piano music after hearing it once—and by his physical precocity, for which no genetic selection has been made.

When 89-58 begins to exhibit paranormal abilities, he proves to be phenomenally endowed. His first startling achievement is remote viewing. As a game, he describes to researchers the rooms in their own homes, where he has never visited. He walks them through tours of museums to which he has never been admitted. When he is shown a photograph of a Wyoming mountain in which is buried a top-secret Strategic Air Command defense center, he describes in accurate detail the missile-status display boards in the war room. He is considered an espionage asset of incalculable value—until, fortunately by degrees, he discovers that he is able to step into a human mind as easily as he steps into distant rooms. He takes mental control of his primary handler, makes the man undress, and sends him through the halls of the orphanage, crowing like a rooster. When SSW-89-58 relinquishes control of the handler and what he's done is discovered, he is punished severely. He resents the punishment, resents it deeply. That night he conducts a remote viewing of the handler's home and enters the handler's mind at a distance of forty-six miles. Using the handler's body, he brutally murders the man's wife and daughter, and then he walks the handler through suicide.

Following this episode, SSW-89-58 is subdued by the use of a massive dose of tranquilizers administered by a dart gun. Two employees of Project 99 perish in the process.

Thereafter, for a period of eighteen days, he is maintained in a drug-induced coma while a team of scientists designs and oversees the urgent construction of a suitable habitat for their prize—one which will sustain his life but assure that he remains controlled. A faction of the staff suggests immediate termination of SSW-89-58, but this advice is considered and rejected. Every endeavor is at some point troubled by pessimists.

Here, now, come into the security room in the southeast corner of the first floor of the orphanage. In this place—if you were an employee—you must present yourself for the scrutiny of three guards, because this post is never manned by fewer, regardless of the hour. You must place your right hand on a scanner that will identify you by your fingerprints. You must peer into a retina scanner as well, which will compare your retinal patterns to those recorded in the scan taken when you first accepted employment.

From here you descend in an elevator past five subterranean levels, where much of the work of Project 99 is conducted. You are interested, however, in the sixth and lowest level, where you walk to the end of a long corridor and through a gray metal door. You stand in a plain room with simple institutional furnishings, with three security men, none of whom is interested in you. These men work six-hour shifts to ensure that they remain alert not only to what is happening in this room and the next but to nuances in one another's behavior.

One wall of this room features a large window that looks into the adjoining chamber. Frequently you will see Dr. Louis Blom or Dr. Keith Ramlock—or both—at work beyond this glass, for they are the designers of SSW-89-58 and oversee the exploration and the utilization of his gifts. When neither Dr. Blom nor Dr. Ramlock is present, at least three other members of their immediate staff are in attendance.

SSW-89-58 is never left unsupervised.

They were transitioning from Interstate 210 to Interstate 10 when Rose interrupted herself to say, "Joe, could
you find an exit with a service station? I need to use a rest
room."

"What's wrong?"

"Nothing. I just need . . . a rest room. I hate to waste
the time. I want to get to Big Bear as quick as we can.
But I don't want to wet my pants, either. No hurry. Just
somewhere in the next few miles, okay?"

"All right."

She conducted him, once more, on her version of a
remote viewing of Project 99 outside Manassas.

■

Onward, please, through the connecting door and into
the final space, where stands the elaborate containment
vessel in which 89-58 now lives and, barring any unfore-
seen and calamitous developments, in which he will spend
the rest of his unnatural life. This is a tank that somewhat
resembles the iron lungs which, in more primitive decades,
were used to sustain victims of polio. Nestled like a pecan
in its shell, 89-58 is entirely enclosed, pressed between
the mattress-soft halves of a lubricated body mold that
restricts all movement, including even the movement
of each finger, limiting him to facial expressions and
twitches—which no one can see anyway. He is supplied
with bottled air directly through a nose clip from tanks
outside the containment vessel. Likewise, he is pierced by
redundant intravenous-drip lines, one in each arm and one
in his left thigh, through which he receives life-sustaining
nourishment, a balance of fluids, and a variety of drugs as
his handlers see fit to administer them. He is permanently
catheterized for the efficient elimination of waste. If any of
these IV drips or other lifelines works loose or otherwise

fails, an insistent alarm immediately alerts the handlers, and in spite of the existence of redundant systems, repairs are undertaken without delay.

The researchers and their assistants conduct conversations as necessary with 89-58 through a speakerphone. The clamshell body mold in which he lies inside the steel tank is equipped with audio feed to both of his ears and a microphone over his mouth. The staff is able to reduce 89-58's words to a background whisper whenever they wish, but he does not enjoy an equivalent privilege to tune them out. A clever video feed allows images to be transmitted by glass fiber to a pair of lenses fitted to 89-58's sockets; consequently, he can be shown photographs—and if necessary the geographical coordinates—of buildings and places in which he is required to conduct remote viewings. Sometimes he is shown photographs of individuals against whom it is desired that he take one form of action or another.

During a remote viewing, 89-58 describes in vivid detail what he sees in whatever far place they have sent him, and he dutifully answers questions that his handlers put to him. By monitoring his heart rate, blood pressure, respiratory rate, brainwaves, eyelid movements, and changes in the electrical conductivity of his skin, they are able to detect a lie with better than ninety-nine-percent accuracy. Furthermore, they test him from time to time by remoting him to places on which extensive, reliable intelligence has already been gathered; his answers are subsequently compared to the material currently in file.

He has been known to be a bad boy. He is not trusted.

When 89-58 is instructed to enter the mind of a specific person and either eliminate that individual or use him to eliminate another—which is most often a foreign national—the assignment is referred to as a "wet mission." This term is used partly because blood is spilled but largely because 89-58 is plunged not into the comparative dryness of faraway rooms but into the murky depths of a human mind. As he conducts a wet mission, 89-58 describes it to Dr. Blom or Dr. Ramlock, at least one of whom is always present during the event. After numerous such missions, Blom and Ramlock and their associates are adept at identifying deception even before the polygraph signals trouble.

For his handlers, video displays of electrical activity in 89-58's brain clearly define the activity in which he is engaged at every moment. When he is only remote viewing, the patterns are radically different from those that arise when he is engaged in wet work. If he is assigned only to observe some distant place and, while viewing, disobediently occupies the mind of someone in that remote location, either as an act of rebellion or sheerly for sport, this is known at once to his handlers.

If SSW-89-58 refuses an instruction, exceeds the parameters of an assignment, or exhibits any other signs of rebellion, he can be punished in numerous ways. Electrical contacts in the body mold—and in his catheter—can be activated to deliver painful shocks to selected tender points head to foot or over his entire skin surface. Piercing electronic squeals at excruciating volume may be blasted into his ears. Disgusting odors are easily introduced with his air supply. A variety of drugs are available to precipitate painful and terrifying physiological symptoms—such as violent muscle spasms and inflamed nerve sheaths—which pose no danger to the life of this valuable asset. Inducing claustrophobic panic by cutting off his air supply is also a simple but effective disciplinary technique.

If he is obedient, 89-58 can be rewarded in one of five ways. Although he receives his primary nutrients—carbohydrates, proteins, vitamins, minerals—through IV drips, a feeding tube can be extruded from the body mold and between his lips, to allow him to enjoy tasty liquids, from Coca-Cola to apple juice to chocolate milk. Second, because he is a piano prodigy and takes great pleasure from music, he can be rewarded with anything from the Beatles to Beethoven. Third, entire movies can be transmitted to the lenses over his eyes—and from such an intimate perspective, he seems to be virtually in the middle of the cinematic experience. Fourth, he can receive mood-elevating drugs that make him as happy, in some ways, as any boy in the world. Fifth, and best of all, he is sometimes allowed to go remote viewing in places that he would like to experience, and during these glorious expeditions, guided by his own interests, he knows freedom—or as much of it as he can imagine.

Routinely, no fewer than three staff monitor the containment vessel and its occupant, because 89-58 can control only one mind at a time. If any of the three were to turn suddenly violent or exhibit any unusual behavior, either of the other two could, with the flip of a switch, administer sufficient sedatives through the intravenous feeds to drop 89-58 into a virtually instant, deep, and powerless sleep. In the unlikely event that this should fail, a doomsday button follows the sedative with a lethal dose of nerve toxin that kills in three to five seconds.

The three guards on the other side of the observation window have similar buttons available for use at their discretion.

SSW-89-58 is not able to read minds. He is not a telepath. He can only repress the personality of the person he inhabits and take control of the physical plant. There is disagreement among the staff of Project 99 as to whether 89-58's lack of telepathic ability is a disappointment or a blessing.

Furthermore, when sent on a wet mission, he must

know where his target is located before being able to invade its mind. He cannot search at will across the populations of the world but must be guided by his handlers, who first locate his prey. Once shown an image of the building or vehicle in which the target can be found—and when that place is geographically sited in his mind—he can act.

Thus far, he is also limited to the walls of that structure and cannot effectively pursue a wanted mind beyond the boundaries that are initially established. No one knows why this limitation should exist, though theories abound. Perhaps it is because the invisible psychic self, being only a wave energy of some type, responds to open spaces in much the manner of heat contained in a hot stone placed in a cold room: It radiates outward, dissipating, dispersing itself, and cannot be conserved in a coherent form. He is able to practice remote viewing of outdoor locations—but only for short periods of time. This shortcoming frustrates 89-58's handlers, but they believe and hope that his abilities in this regard may improve with time.

If you can bear to watch, the containment vessel is opened twice each week to allow the handlers to clean their asset. He is without fail deeply sedated for this procedure—and remains connected to the doomsday button. He is given a thorough sponge bath, irritations of the skin are treated, the minimal solid waste that he produces is evacuated from the bowel, teeth are cleaned, eyes are examined for infection and then are flushed with antibiotic, and other maintenance is performed. Although 89-58 receives daily low-voltage electrical stimulation of his muscles to ensure a minimal life-sustaining mass, he resembles one of the starving children of any third-world country racked by drought and evil politics. He is as pale as any job on a mortician's table, withered, with elfin bones grown thin from lack of use; and when unconsciously he curls his feeble fingers around the hands of ministering attendants, his grip is no stronger than that of a cradled newborn baby struggling to hold fast to its mother's thumb.

Sometimes, in this profound sedation, he murmurs wordlessly but forlornly, mewls, and even weeps, as if adrift in a soft sad dream.

■

At the Shell station, only three vehicles were at the self-service pumps. Tending to their cars, the motorists squinted and ducked their heads to keep wind-blown grit out of their eyes.

The lighting was as bright as that on a movie set, and though Joe and Rose were not being sought by the type of police agency that would distribute their photographs to local television news programs, Joe preferred to stay out of the glare. He parked along the side of the building, near the rest rooms, where huddled shadows survived.

Joe was in emotional turmoil, felt slashed across the heart, because now he knew the exact cause of the catastrophic crash, knew the murderer's identity and the twisted details. The knowledge was like a scalpel that pared off what thin scabs had formed over his pain. His grief felt fresh, the loss more recent than it really was.

He switched off the engine and sat speechless.

"I don't understand how the hell they found out I was on that flight," Rose said. "I'd taken such precautions. . . . But I knew when he remote-viewed the passenger cabin, looking for us, because there was an odd dimming of lights, a problem with my wristwatch, a vague sense of a *presence*—signs I'd learned to read."

"I've met a National Transportation Safety Board

investigator who's heard the tape from the cockpit voice recorder, before it was destroyed in a convenient sound-lab fire. This boy was inside the captain's head, Rose. I don't understand . . . Why didn't he take out just *you?*"

"He had to get us both, that was his assignment, me and the girl—and while he could've nailed me without any problem, it wouldn't have been easy with her."

Utterly baffled, Joe said, "Nina? Why would they have been interested in her then? She was just another passenger, wasn't she? I thought they were after her later because . . . well, because she survived with you."

Rose would not meet his eyes. "Get me the key to the women's rest room, Joe. Will you, please? Let me have a minute here. I'll tell you the rest of it on the way to Big Bear."

He went into the sales room and got the key from the cashier. By the time he returned to the Ford, Rose had gotten out. She was leaning against a front fender, back turned and shoulders hunched to the whistling Santa Ana wind. Her left arm was curled against her breast, and her hand was still shaking. With her right hand, she pulled the lapels of her blazer together, as though the warm August wind felt cold to her.

"Would you unlock the door for me?" she asked.

He went to the women's room. By the time he unlocked the door and switched on the light, Rose had arrived at his side.

"I'll be quick," she promised, and slipped past him.

He had a glimpse of her face in that brightness, just before the door fell shut. She didn't look good.

Instead of returning to the car, Joe leaned against the wall of the building, beside the lavatory door, to wait for her.

According to nurses in asylums and psychiatric wards, a greater number of their most disturbed patients responded to the Santa Ana winds than ever reacted to the sight of a full moon beyond a barred window. It wasn't simply the baleful sound, like the cries of an unearthly hunter and the unearthly beasts that it pursued; it was also the subliminal alkaline scent of the desert and a queer electrical charge, different from those that other—less dry—winds imparted to the air.

Joe could understand why Rose might have pulled her blazer shut and huddled into it. This night had both the moon and the Santa Ana wind to spark a voodoo current in the spine—and a parentless boy without a name, who lived in a coffin of steel and moved invisible through a world of potential victims oblivious to him.

Are we recording?

The boy had known about the cockpit voice recorder—and he'd left a cry for help on it.

One of their names is Dr. Louis Blom. One of their names is Dr. Keith Ramlock. They're doing bad things to me. They're mean to me. Make them stop. Make them stop hurting me.

Whatever else he was—sociopathic, psychotic, homicidal—he was also a child. A beast, an abomination, a terror, but also a child. He had not asked to be born, and if he was evil, they had made him so by failing to teach him any human values, by treating him as mere ordnance, by rewarding him for murder. Beast he was, but a pitiable beast, lost and alone, wandering in a maze of misery.

Pitiable but formidable. And still out there. Waiting to be told where he could find Rose Tucker. And Nina.

This is fun.

The boy enjoyed the killing. Joe supposed it was even possible that his handlers had never instructed him to destroy everyone aboard Nationwide Flight 353, that he had done it as an act of rebellion and because he enjoyed it.

Make them stop or when I get the chance . . . when I get the chance, I'll kill everybody. Everybody. I will. I'll do it. I'll kill everybody, and I'll like it.

Recalling those words from the transcript, Joe sensed that the boy had not been referring merely to the passengers on the doomed airliner. By then he had already made the decision to kill them all. He was speaking of some act more apocalyptic than three hundred and thirty murders.

What could he accomplish if provided with photographs and the geographical coordinates of not merely a missile-tracking facility but a complex of nuclear-missile launch silos?

"Jesus," Joe whispered.

Somewhere in the night, Nina waited. In the hands of a friend of Rose's, but inadequately protected. Vulnerable.

Rose seemed to be taking a long time.

Rapping on the rest room door, Joe called her name, but she did not respond. He hesitated, knocked again, and when she weakly called "Joe," he pushed the door open.

She was perched on the edge of the toilet seat. She had taken off her navy blazer and her white blouse; the latter lay blood-soaked on the sink.

He hadn't realized she'd been bleeding. Darkness and the blazer had hidden the blood from him.

As he stepped into the rest room, he saw that she had shaped a compress of sorts from a wad of wet paper towels. She was pressing it to her left pectoral muscle, above her breast.

"That one shot on the beach," he said numbly. "You were hit."

"The bullet passed through," she said. "There's an exit wound in back. Nice and clean. I haven't even bled all that much, and the pain is tolerable. . . . So why am I getting weaker?"

"Internal bleeding," he suggested, wincing as he looked at the exit wound in her back.

"I know anatomy," she said. "I took the hit in just the right spot. Couldn't have picked it better. Shouldn't be any damage to major vessels."

"The round might have hit a bone and fragmented. The fragment maybe didn't come out, took a different track."

"I was so thirsty. Tried to drink some water from the faucet. Almost passed out when I bent over."

"This settles it," he said. His heart was racing. "We've got to get you to a doctor."

"Get me to Nina."

"Rose, damn it—"

"Nina can heal me," she said, and as she spoke, she looked guiltily away from him.

Astonished, he said, "Heal you?"

"Trust me. Nina can do what no doctor can, what no one else on earth can do."

At that moment, on some level, he knew at least one of Rose Tucker's remaining secrets, but he could not allow himself to take out that dark pearl of knowledge and examine it.

"Help me get my blouse and blazer on, and let's go. Get me into Nina's hands. Her healing hands."

Though half sick with worry, he did as she wanted. As he dressed her, he remembered how larger than life she had seemed in the cemetery Saturday morning. Now she was so small.

Through a hot clawing wind that mimicked the songs of wolves, she leaned on him all the way back to the car.

When he got her settled in the passenger's seat, she asked if he would get her something to drink.

From a vending machine in front of the station, he purchased a can of Pepsi and one of Orange Crush. She preferred the Crush, and he opened it for her.

Before she accepted the drink, she gave him two things: the Polaroid photograph of his family's graves and the folded dollar bill on which the serial number, minus the fourth digit, provided the phone number at which Mark of Infiniface could be reached in an emergency. "And before you start driving, I want to tell you how to find the cabin in Big Bear—in case I can't hold on until we get there."

"Don't be silly. You'll make it."

"Listen," she said, and again she projected the charisma that commanded attention.

He listened as she told him the way.

"And as for Infiniface," she said, "I trust them, and they *are* my natural allies—and Nina's—as Mark said. But I'm afraid they can be too easily infiltrated. That's why I wouldn't let them come with us tonight. But if we're not followed, then this car is clean, and maybe their security is good enough. If worse comes to worst and you don't know where to turn . . . they may be your best hope."

His chest tightened and his throat thickened as she spoke, and finally he said, "I don't want to hear any more of this. I'll get you to Nina in time."

Rose's right hand trembled now, and Joe was not certain that she could hold the Orange Crush. But she managed it, drinking thirstily.

As he drove back onto the San Bernardino Freeway, heading east, she said, "I've never meant to hurt you, Joe."

"You haven't."

"I've done a terrible thing, though."

He glanced at her. He didn't dare ask what she had done. He kept that shiny black pearl of knowledge tucked deep in the purse of his mind.

"Don't hate me too much."

"I don't hate you at all."

"My motives were good. They haven't always been. Certainly weren't spotless when I went to work at Project 99. But my motives were good this time, Joe."

Driving out of the lightstorm of Los Angeles and its suburbs, toward the mountain darkness where Nina dwelled, Joe waited for Rose to tell him why he should hate her.

"So . . . let me tell you," she said, "about the project's only true success. . . ."

Ascend, now, in the elevator from the little glimpse of Hell at the bottom of those six subterranean levels, leaving the boy in his containment vessel, and come all the way up to the security room where the descent began. Farther still, to the southeast corner of the ground floor, where CCY-21-21 resides.

She was conceived without passion one year after 89-58, though she was the project not of Doctors Blom and Ramlock but of Rose Tucker. She is a lovely child, delicate, fair of face, with golden hair and amethyst eyes. Although the majority of the orphans living here are of average intelligence, CCY-21-21 has an unusually high IQ, even higher perhaps than that of 89-58, and she loves to learn. She is a quiet girl, with much grace and natural charm, but for the first three years of her life, she exhibits no paranormal abilities.

Then, on a sunny May afternoon, when she is participating in a session of supervised play with other children on the orphanage lawn, she finds a sparrow with a broken wing and one torn eye. It lies in the grass beneath a tree, flopping weakly, and when she gathers it into her small hands, it becomes fearfully still. Crying, the girl hurries with the bird to the nearest handler, asking what can be done. The sparrow is now so weak and so paralyzed by fear that it can only feebly work its beak—and produces no sound whatsoever. The bird is dying, the handler sees nothing to be done, but the girl will not accept the sparrow's pending death. She sits on the ground, grips the bird gently in her left hand, and carefully strokes it with her right, singing softly to it a song about Robin Red Breast—and in but a minute the sparrow is restored. The fractures in the wing knit firm again, and the torn eye heals into a bright, clear orb. The bird sings—and flies.

CCY-21-21 becomes the center of a happy whirlwind of attention. Rose Tucker, who has been driven to the contemplation of suicide by the nightmare of Project 99, is as reborn as the bird, stepping back from the abyss into which she has been peering. For the next fifteen months, 21-21's healing power is explored. At first it is an unreliable talent, which she cannot exercise at will, but month by wondrous month she learns to summon and control her gift, until she can apply it whenever asked to do so. Those on Project 99 with medical problems are brought to a level of health they never expected to enjoy again. A select few politicians and military figures—and members of their families—suffering from life-threatening illnesses are brought secretly to the child to be healed. There are those in Project 99 who believe that 21-21 is their greatest asset—although others find 89-58, in spite of the considerable control problems that he poses, to be the most interesting and valuable property in the long run.

Now look here, come forward in time to one rainy day in August, fifteen months after the restoration of the injured sparrow. A staff geneticist named Amos has been diagnosed with pancreatic cancer, one of the deadliest forms of the disease. While healing Amos with only a soft and lingering touch, the girl detects an illness in addition to the malignancy, this one not of a physical nature but nonetheless debilitating. Perhaps because of what he has seen at Project 99, perhaps for numerous other reasons that have accumulated throughout his fifty years, Amos has decided that life is without purpose or meaning, that we have no destiny but the void, that we are only dust in the wind. This darkness in him is blacker than the cancer, and the girl heals this as well, by the simple expedient of showing Amos the light of God and the strange dimensional lattices of realms beyond our own.

Once shown these things, Amos is so overcome with joy and awe that he cycles between laughter and weeping, and to the eyes of the others in the room—a researcher named Janice, another named Vincent—he seems to be seized by an alarming hysteria. When Amos urges the girl to bring Janice into the same light that she has shown to him, she gives the gift again.

Janice, however, reacts differently from Amos. Humbled and frightened, she collapses in remorse. She claws at herself in regret for the way she has lived her life and in grief for those she has betrayed and harmed, and her anguish is frightening.

Tumult.

Rose is summoned. Janice and Amos are isolated for observation and evaluation. What has the girl done? What Amos tells them seems like the happy babbling of a harmlessly deranged man, but babbling nonetheless, and from one who was but a few minutes ago a scientist of serious—if not brooding—disposition.

Baffled and concerned by the strikingly different reactions of Amos and Janice, the girl withdraws and becomes uncommunicative. Rose works in private with 21-21 for more than two hours before she finally begins to pry the astounding explanation from her. The child cannot understand why the revelation that she's brought to Amos and

Janice would overwhelm them so completely or why Janice's reaction is a mix of euphoria and self-flagellation. Having been born with a full awareness of her place and purpose in the universe, with an understanding of the ladder of destinies that she will climb through infinity, with the certain knowledge of life everlasting carried in her genes, she cannot grasp the shattering power of this revelation when she brings it to those who have spent their lives in the mud of doubt and the dust of despair.

Expecting nothing more than that she is going to experience the psychic equivalent of a magic-lantern show, a tour of a child's sweet fantasy of God, Rose asks to be shown. And is shown. And is forever changed. Because at the touch of the child's hand, she is opened to the fullness of existence. What she experiences is beyond her powers to describe, and even as torrents of joy surge through her and wash away all the countless griefs and miseries of her life heretofore, she is flooded, as well, with terror, for she is aware not only of the promise of a bright eternity but of *expectations* that she must strive to fulfill in all the days of life ahead of her in this world and in the worlds to come, expectations that frighten her because she is unsure that she can ever meet them. Like Janice, she is acutely aware of every mean act and unkindness and lie and betrayal of which she has ever been guilty, and she recognizes that she still has the capacity for selfishness, pettiness, and cruelty; she yearns to transcend her past even as she quakes at the fortitude required to do so.

When the vision passes and she finds herself in the girl's room as before, she harbors no doubt that what she saw was real, truth in its purest form, and not merely the child's delusion transmitted through psychic power. For almost half an hour she cannot speak but sits shaking, her face buried in her hands.

Gradually, she begins to realize the implications of what has happened here. There are basically two. First: If this revelation can be brought to the world—even to as many as the girl can touch—all that is now will pass away. Once one has *seen*—not taken on faith but *seen*—that there is life beyond, even if the nature of it remains profoundly mysterious and as fearsome as it is glorious, then all that was once important seems insignificant. Avenues of wondrous possibilities abound where once there was a single alley through the darkness. The world as we know it ends. Second: There are those who will not welcome the end of the old order, who have taught themselves to thrive on power and on the pain and humiliation of others. Indeed, the world is full of them, and they will not want to receive the girl's gift. They will fear the girl and everything that she promises. And they will either sedate and isolate her in a containment vessel—or they will kill her.

She is as gifted as any messiah—but she is human. She can heal the wing of a broken bird and bring sight to its blinded eye. She can banish cancer from a disease-riddled man. But she is not an angel with a cloak of invulnerability. She is flesh and bone. Her precious power resides in the delicate tissues of her singular brain. If the magazine of a pistol is emptied into the back of her head, she will die like any other child; dead, she cannot heal herself. Although her soul will proceed into other realms, she will be lost to this troubled place that needs her. The world will not be changed, peace will not replace turmoil, and there will be no end to loneliness and despair.

Rose quickly becomes convinced that the project's directors will opt for termination. The moment that they understand what this little girl is, they will kill her.

Before nightfall, they will kill her.

Certainly before midnight, they will kill her.

They will not be willing to risk consigning her to a containment vessel. The boy possesses only the power of destruction, but 21-21 possesses the power of enlightenment, which is immeasurably the more dangerous of the two.

They will shoot her down, soak her corpse with gasoline, set her remains afire, and later scatter her charred bones.

Rose must act—and quickly. The girl must be spirited out of the orphanage and hidden before they can destroy her.

"Joe?"

Against a field of stars, as though at this moment erupting from the crust of the earth, the black mountains shouldered darkly across the horizon.

"Joe, I'm sorry." Her voice was frail. "I'm so sorry."

They were speeding north on State Highway 30, east of the city of San Bernardino, fifty miles from Big Bear.

"Joe, are you okay?"

He could not answer.

Traffic was light. The road ascended into forests. Cottonwoods and pines shook, shook, shook in the wind.

He could not answer. He could only drive.

"When you insisted on believing the little girl with me was your own Nina, I let you go on believing it."

For whatever purpose, she was still deceiving him. He could not understand why she continued to hide the truth.

She said, "After they found us at the restaurant, I needed your help. Especially after I was shot, I needed you. But you hadn't opened your heart and mind to the photograph when I gave it to you. You were so . . . fragile. I was afraid if you knew it really wasn't your Nina, you'd just . . . stop. Fall apart. God forgive me, Joe, but I needed you. And now the girl needs you."

Nina needed him. Not some girl born in a lab, with the power to transmit her curious fantasies to others and cloud the minds of the gullible. Nina needed him. *Nina*.

If he could not trust Rose Tucker, was there anyone he could trust?

He managed to shake two words from himself: "Go on."

Rose again. In 21-21's room. Feverishly considering the problem of how to spirit the girl through a security system equal to that of any prison.

The answer, when it comes, is obvious and elegant.

There are three exits from the ground floor of the orphanage. Rose and the girl walk hand in hand to the door that connects the main building to the adjoining two-story parking structure.

An armed guard views their approach with more puzzlement than suspicion. The orphans are not permitted into the garage even under supervision.

When 21-21 holds out her tiny hand and says *Shake*, the guard smiles and obliges—and receives the gift. Suddenly filled with cyclonic wonder, he sits shaking uncontrollably, weeping with joy but also with hard remorse, just as Rose had trembled and wept in the girl's room.

It is a simple matter to push the button on the guard's console to throw the electronic lock on the door and pass through.

Another guard waits on the garage side of the connecting door. He is startled by the sight of this child. She reaches for him, and his surprise at seeing her is nothing compared to the surprise that follows.

A third guard is stationed at the gated exit from the garage. Alarmed by the sight of 21-21 in Rose's car, he leans in the open window to demand an explanation—and the girl touches his face.

Two more armed men staff the gate at the highway. All barriers fall, and Virginia lies ahead.

Escape will never be as easy again. If they are apprehended, the girl's offer of a handshake will be greeted by gunfire.

The trick now is to get out of the area quickly, before project security realizes what has happened to five of its men. They will mount a pursuit, perhaps with the assistance of local, state, and federal authorities. Rose drives madly, recklessly, with a skill—born of desperation—that she has never known before.

Barely big enough to see out of the side window, 21-21 studies the passing countryside with fascination and, at last, says, *Wow, it sure is big out here.*

Rose laughs and says, *Honey, you ain't seen nothing yet.*

She realizes that she must get the word out as quickly as possible: use the media to display 21-21's healing powers and then to demonstrate the greater gift that the girl can bestow. Only the forces of ignorance and darkness benefit from secrecy. Rose believes that 21-21 will never be safe until the world knows of her, embraces her, and refuses to allow her to be taken into custody.

Her ex-bosses will expect her to go public quickly and in a big way. Their influence within the media is widespread—yet as subtle as a web of cloud shadows on the skin of a pond, which makes it all the more effective. They will try to find her as soon as possible after she surfaces and before she can bring 21-21 to the world.

She knows a reporter whom she would trust not to betray her: Lisa Peccatone, an old college friend who works at the *Post* in Los Angeles.

Rose and the girl will have to fly to Southern California—and the sooner the better. Project 99 is a joint venture of private industry, elements of the defense establishment, and other powerful forces in the government. Easier to halt an avalanche with a feather than to resist their combined might, and they will shortly begin to use every asset in their arsenal to locate Rose and the girl.

Trying to fly out of Dulles or National Airport in Washington is too dangerous. She considers Baltimore, Philadelphia, New York, and Boston. She chooses New York.

She reasons that the more county and state lines she crosses, the safer she becomes, so she drives to Hagerstown, Maryland, and from there to Harrisburg, Pennsylvania, without incident. Yet mile by mile, she is increasingly concerned that her pursuers will have put out an APB on her car and that she will be captured regardless of the distance she puts between herself and Manassas. In Harrisburg, she abandons the car, and she and the girl continue to New York City by bus.

By the time they are in the air aboard Nationwide Flight 353, Rose feels safe. Immediately on landing at LAX, she will be met by Lisa and the crew that Lisa has assembled—and the series of media eruptions will begin.

For the airline passenger manifest, Rose implied that she was married to a white man, and she identified 21-21 as her stepdaughter, choosing the name "Mary Tucker" on the spur of the moment. With the media, she intends initially to use CCY-21-21's project name because its similarity to concentration-camp inmates' names will do more than anything else to characterize Project 99 in the public mind and generate instant sympathy for the child. She realizes that eventually she will have to consult with 21-21 to pick a permanent name—which, considering the singular historical importance of this child's life, should be a name that resonates.

They are seated across the aisle from a mother and her two daughters, who are returning home to Los Angeles. Michelle, Chrissie, and Nina Carpenter.

Nina, who is approximately 21-21's age and size, is playing with a hand-held electronic game called Pigs and Princes, designed for preschoolers. From across the aisle, 21-21 becomes fascinated by the sounds and the images on the small screen. Seeing this, Nina asks "Mary" to move with her to a nearby pair of empty seats, where they can play the game together. Rose is hesitant to allow this—but she knows that 21-21 is intelligent far beyond her years and is aware of the need for discretion, so she relents. This is the first unstructured play time in 21-21's life, the first *genuine* play she has ever known. Nina is a child of enormous charm, sweet and gregarious. Although 21-21 is a genius with the reading skills of a college freshman, a healer with miraculous powers, and literally the hope of the world, she is soon enraptured by Nina, wants to *be* Nina, as totally cool as Nina, and unconsciously she begins imitating Nina's gestures and manner of speaking.

Theirs is a late flight out of New York, and after a couple of hours, Nina is fading. She hugs 21-21, and with the permission of Michelle, she gives Pigs and Princes to her new friend before returning to sit with her mother and sister, where she falls asleep.

Transported by delight, 21-21 returns to her seat beside Rose, hugging the small electronic game to her breast as though it is a treasure beyond value. Now she won't even play with it because she is afraid that she might break it, and she wants it to remain always exactly as Nina gave it to her.

■

West of the town of Running Lake, still many miles from Big Bear Lake, following ridgelines past the canyons where the wind was born, bombarded by thrashing conifers hurling cones at the pavement, Joe refused to consider the implications of Pigs and Princes. Listening to Rose tell the story, he had barely found the self-control to repress his rage. He knew that he had no reason to be furious with this woman or with the child who had a concentration-camp name, but he was livid nonetheless—perhaps because he knew how to function well in anger, as he had done throughout his youth, and not well at all in grief.

Turning the subject away from little girls at play, he said, "How does Horton Nellor fit into this—aside from owning a big chunk of Teknologik, which is deep in Project 99?"

"Just that well-connected bastards like him . . . are the wave of the future." She was holding the can of Pepsi between her knees, clawing at the pull tab with her right hand. She had barely enough strength and coordination to get it open. "The wave of the future . . . unless Nina . . . unless she changes everything."

"Big business, big government, and big media—all one beast now, united to exploit the rest of us. Is that it? Radical talk."

The aluminum can rattled against her teeth, and a trickle of Pepsi dribbled down her chin. "Nothing but power matters to them. They don't believe . . . in good and evil."

"There are only events."

Though she had just taken a long swallow of Pepsi, her throat sounded dry. Her voice cracked. "And what those events mean . . ."

" . . . depends only on what spin you put on them."

He remained blindly angry with her because of what she insisted that he believe about his Nina, but he could not bear to glance at her again and see her growing weaker. He blinked at the road ahead, where showers of pine needles stitched together billowing sheets of dust, and he eased down on the accelerator, driving as fast as he dared.

The soda can slipped out of her hand, dropped on the floor, and rolled under her seat, spilling the remainder of the Pepsi. "Losin' it, Joe."

"Not long now."

"Got to tell you how it was . . . when the plane went in."

∎

Four miles down, gathering speed all the way, engines shrieking, wings creaking, fuselage thrumming. Screaming passengers are pressed so hard into their seats by the accumulating gravities that many are unable to lift their heads—some praying, some vomiting, weeping, cursing, calling out the many names of God, calling out to loved ones present and far away. An eternity of plunging, four miles but as if from the moon—

—and then Rose is in a blueness, a silent bright blueness, as if she is a bird in flight, except that no dark earth lies below, only blueness all around. No sense of motion. Neither hot nor cool. A flawless hyacinth-blue sphere with her at the center. Suspended. Waiting. A deep breath held in her lungs. She tries to expel her stale breath but cannot, cannot, until—

—with an exhalation as loud as a shout, she finds herself in the meadow, still in her seat, stunned into immobility, 21-21 beside her. The nearby woods are on fire. On all sides, flames lick mounds of twisted debris. The meadow is an unspeakable charnel house. And the 747 is *gone*.

At the penultimate moment, the girl had transported them out of the doomed aircraft by a monumental exertion of her psychic gift, to another place, to a dimension outside space and time, and had held them in that mysterious sheltering limbo through one terrible minute of cataclysmic destruction. The effort has left 21-21 cold, shaking, and unable to speak. Her eyes, bright with reflections of the many surrounding fires, have a faraway look like those of an autistic child. Initially she cannot walk or even stand, so Rose must lift her from the seat and carry her.

Weeping for the dead scattered through the night, shuddering with horror at the carnage, wonderstruck by her survival, slammed by a *hurricane* of emotion, Rose stands with the girl cradled in her arms but is unable to take a single step. Then she recalls the flickering passenger-cabin lights and the spinning of the hands on her wristwatch, and she is certain that the pilot was the victim of a wet mission, remoted by the boy who lives in a steel capsule deep below the Virginia countryside. This realization propels her away from the crash site, around the burning trees, into the moonlit forest, wading through straggly underbrush, then along a deer trail powdered with silver light and dappled with shadow, to another meadow, to a ridge from which she sees the lights of Loose Change Ranch.

By the time they reach the ranch house, the girl is somewhat recovered but still not herself. She is able to walk now, but she is lethargic, brooding, distant.

Approaching the house, Rose tells 21-21 to remember that her name is Mary Tucker, but 21-21 says, *My name is Nina. That's who I want to be.*

Those are the last words that she will speak—perhaps forever. In the months immediately following the crash, having taken refuge with Rose's friends in Southern California, the girl sleeps twelve to fourteen hours a day. When she's awake, she shows no interest in anything. She sits for hours staring out a window or at a picture in a storybook, or at nothing in particular. She has no appetite, loses weight. She is pale and frail, and even her amethyst eyes seem to lose some of their color. Evidently the effort required to move herself and Rose into and out of the blue elsewhere, during the crash, has profoundly drained her, perhaps nearly killed her. Nina exhibits no paranormal abilities anymore, and Rose dwells in despondency.

By Christmas, however, Nina begins to show interest in the world around her. She watches television. She reads books again. As the winter passes, she sleeps less and eats more. Her skin regains its former glow, and the color of her eyes deepens. She still does not speak, but she seems increasingly *connected.* Rose encourages her to come all the way back from her self-imposed exile by speaking to her every day about the good that she can do and the hope that she can bring to others.

In a bureau drawer in the bedroom that she shares with the girl, Rose keeps a copy of the *Los Angeles Post*, the issue that devotes the entire front page, above the fold, to the fate of Nationwide Flight 353. It helps to remind her of the insane viciousness of her enemies. One day in July, eleven months after the disaster, she finds Nina sitting on the edge of the bed with this newspaper open to a page featuring photographs of some of the victims of the crash. The girl is touching the photo of Nina Carpenter, who had given her Pigs and Princes, and she is smiling.

Rose sits beside her and asks if she is feeling sad, remembering this lost friend.

The girl shakes her head *no*. Then she guides Rose's hand to the photograph, and when Rose's fingertips touch the newsprint, she falls away into a blue brightness not unlike the sanctuary into which she was transported in the instant before the plane crash, except that this is also a place *full* of motion, warmth, sensation.

Clairvoyants have long claimed to feel a residue of psychic energy on common objects, left by the people who have touched them. Sometimes they assist police in the search for a murderer by handling objects worn by the victim at the time of the assault. This energy in the *Post* photograph is similar but different—not left in passing by Nina but *imbued* in the newsprint by an act of will.

Rose feels as if she has plunged into a sea of blue light, a sea crowded with swimmers whom she cannot see but whom she feels gliding and swooping around her. Then one swimmer seems to pass *through* Rose and to linger in the passing, and she knows that she is with little Nina Carpenter, the girl with the lopsided smile, the giver of Pigs and Princes, who is dead and gone but safe, dead and gone but not lost forever, happy and alive in an elsewhere beyond this swarming blue brightness, which is not really a place itself but an interface between phases of existence.

Moved as deeply as she had been when she was first given the knowledge of the afterlife, in the room at the orphanage, Rose withdraws her hand from the photo of Nina Carpenter and sits silently for a while, humbled. Then she takes her own Nina into her arms and holds the girl tightly and rocks her, neither capable of speaking nor in need of words.

Now that this special girl's power is being reborn, Rose knows what they must do, where they must start their work. She does not want to risk going to Lisa Peccatone again. She doesn't believe that her old friend knowingly betrayed her, but she suspects that through Lisa's link to the *Post*—and through the *Post* to Horton Nellor—the people at Project 99 learned of her presence on Flight 353. While Rose and Nina are believed dead, they need to take advantage of their ghostly status to operate as long as possible without drawing the attention of their enemies. First, Rose asks the girl to give the great gift of eternal truth to each of the friends who has sheltered them during these eleven months in their emotional wilderness. Then they will contact the husbands and wives and parents and children of those who perished on Flight 353, bringing them both the received knowledge of immortality and visions of their loved ones at the blue interface. With luck, they will spread their message so widely by the time they are discovered that it cannot be contained.

Rose intends to start with Joe Carpenter, but she can't locate him. His coworkers at the *Post* have lost track of him. He has sold the house in Studio City. He has no listed phone. They say he is a broken man. He has gone away to die.

She must begin the work elsewhere.

Because the *Post* published photographs of only a fraction of the Southern California victims and because she has no easy way to gather photos of the many others, Rose decides not to use portraits, after all. Instead, she tracks down their burial places through published funeral-service notices, and she takes snapshots of their graves. It seems fitting that the imbued image should be of a headstone, that these grim memorials of bronze and granite should become doorways through which the recipients of the pictures will learn that Death is not mighty and dreadful, that beyond this bitter phase, Death himself dies.

■

High in the wind-churned mountains, with waves of moon-silvered conifers casting sprays of needles onto the roadway, still more than twenty miles from Big Bear Lake, Rose Tucker spoke so softly that she could barely be heard over the racing engine and the hum of the tires: "Joe, will you hold my hand?"

He could not look at her, would not look at her, dared not even glance at her for a second, because he was overcome by the childish superstition that she would be all right, perfectly fine, as long as he didn't visually confirm the terrible truth that he heard in her voice. But he looked. She was so small, slumped in her seat, leaning against the door, the back of her head against the window, as small to his eyes as 21-21 must have appeared to her when she had fled Virginia with the girl at her side. Even in the faint glow from the instrument panel, her huge and expressive eyes were again as compelling as they had been when he'd first met her in the graveyard, full of compassion and kindness—and a strange glimmering joy that scared him.

His voice was shakier than hers. "It's not far now."

"Too far," she whispered. "Just hold my hand."

"Oh, shit."

"It's all right, Joe."

The shoulder of the highway widened to a scenic rest area. He stopped the car before a vista of darkness: the hard night sky, the icy disk of a moon that seemed to shed cold instead of light, and a vast blackness of trees and rocks and canyons descending.

He released his seat belt, leaned across the console, and took her hand. Her grip was weak.

"She needs you, Joe."

"I'm nobody's hero, Rose. I'm nothing."

"You need to hide her . . . hide her away . . ."

"Rose—"

"Give her time . . . for her power to grow."

"I can't save anyone."

"I shouldn't have started the work so soon. The day will come when . . . when she won't be so vulnerable. Hide her away . . . let her power grow. She'll know . . . when the time has come."

She began to lose her grip on him.

He covered her hand with both of his, held it fast, would not let it slip from his grasp.

Voice raveling away, she seemed to be receding from him though she did not move: "Open . . . open your heart to her, Joe."

Her eyelids fluttered.

"Rose, please don't."

"It's all right."

"Please. Don't."

"See you later, Joe."

"Please."

"See you."

Then he was alone in the night. He held her small hand alone in the night while the wind played a hollow threnody. When at last he was able to do so, he kissed her brow.

■

The directions Rose had given him were easy to follow. The cabin was neither in the town of Big Bear Lake nor elsewhere along the lakefront, but higher on the northern slopes and nestled deep in pines and birches. The cracked and potholed blacktop led to a dirt driveway, at the end of which was a small white clapboard house with a shake-shingle roof.

A green Jeep Wagoneer stood beside the cabin. Joe parked behind the Jeep.

The cabin boasted a deep, elevated porch, on which three cane-backed rocking chairs were arranged side by side. A handsome black man, tall and athletically built, stood at the railing, his ebony skin highlighted with a brass tint cast by two bare yellow lightbulbs in the porch ceiling.

The girl waited at the head of the flight of four steps that led up from the driveway to the porch. She was blond and about six years old.

From under the driver's seat, Joe retrieved the gun that he had taken from the white-haired storyteller after the scuffle on the beach. Getting out of the car, he tucked the weapon under the waistband of his jeans.

The wind shrieked and hissed through the needled teeth of the pines.

He walked to the foot of the steps.

The child had descended two of the four treads. She stared past Joe, at the Ford. She knew what had happened.

On the porch, the black man began to cry.

The girl spoke for the first time in over a year, since the moment outside the Ealings' ranch house when she had told Rose that she wanted to be called Nina. Gazing at the car, she said only one word, in a voice soft and small: "Mother."

Her hair was the same shade as Nina's hair. She was as fine-boned as Nina. But her eyes were not gray like Nina's eyes, and no matter how hard Joe tried to see Nina's face before him, he could not deceive himself into believing that this was his daughter.

Yet again, he had been engaged in searching behavior, seeking what was lost forever.

The moon above was a thief, its glow not a radiance of its own but a weak reflection of the sun. And like the moon, this girl was a thief—not Nina but only a reflection of Nina, shining not with Nina's brilliant light but with a pale fire.

Regardless of whether she was only a lab-born mutant with strange mental powers or really the hope of the world, Joe hated her at that moment, and hated himself for hating her—but hated her nonetheless.

17

Hot wind huffed at the windows, and the cabin smelled of pine, dust, and the black char from last winter's cozy blazes, which coated the brick walls of the big fireplace.

The incoming electrical lines had sufficient slack to swing in the wind. From time to time they slapped against the house, causing the lights to throb and flicker. Each tremulous brownout reminded Joe of the pulsing lights at the Delmann house, and his skin prickled with dread.

The owner was the tall black man who had broken into tears on the porch. He was Louis Tucker, Mahalia's brother, who had divorced Rose eighteen years ago, when she proved unable to have children. She had turned to him in her darkest hour. And after all this time, though he had a wife and children whom he loved, Louis clearly still loved Rose too.

"If you really believe she's not dead, that she's only moved on," Joe said coldly, "why cry for her?"

"I'm crying for me," said Louis. "Because she's gone from here and I'll have to wait through a lot of days to see her again."

Two suitcases stood in the front room, just inside the door. They contained the belongings of the child.

She was at a window, staring out at the Ford, with sorrow pulled around her like sackcloth.

"I'm scared," Louis said. "Rose was going to stay up

here with Nina, but I don't think it's safe now. I don't want to believe it could be true—but they might've found me before I got out of the last place with Nina. Couple times, way back, I thought the same car was behind us. Then it didn't keep up."

"They don't have to. With their gadgets, they can follow from miles away."

"And then just before you pulled into the driveway, I went out onto the porch 'cause I thought I heard a helicopter. Up in these mountains in this wind—does that make sense?"

"You better get her out of here," Joe agreed.

As the wind slapped the electrical lines against the house, Louis paced to the fireplace and back, a hand pressed to his forehead as he tried to put the loss of Rose out of his mind long enough to think what to do. "I figured you and Rose . . . well, I thought the two of you were taking her. And if they're onto me, then won't she be safer with you?"

"If they're onto you," Joe said, "then none of us is safe here, now, anymore. There's no way out."

The lines slapped the house, slapped the house, and the lights pulsed, and Louis walked to the fireplace and picked up a battery-powered, long-necked butane match from the hearth.

The girl turned from the window, eyes wide, and said, "*No.*"

Louis Tucker flicked the switch on the butane match, and blue flame spurted from the nozzle. Laughing, he set his own hair on fire and then his shirt.

"Nina!" Joe cried.

The girl ran to his side.

The stink of burning hair spread through the room.

Ablaze, Louis moved to block the front door.

From the waistband of his jeans, Joe drew the pistol,

aimed—but couldn't pull the trigger. This man confronting him was not really Louis Tucker now; it was the boy-thing, reaching out three thousand miles from Virginia. And there was no chance that Louis would regain control of his body and live through this night. Yet Joe hesitated to squeeze off a shot, because the moment that Louis was dead, the boy would remote someone else.

The girl was probably untouchable, able to protect herself with her own paranormal power. So the boy would use Joe—and the gun in Joe's hand—to shoot the girl point-blank in the head.

"This is *fun*," the boy said in Louis's voice, as flames seethed off his hair, as his ears charred and crackled, as his forehead and cheeks blistered. *"Fun,"* he said, enjoying his ride inside Louis Tucker but still blocking the exit to the porch.

Maybe, at the instant of greatest jeopardy, Nina could send herself into that safe bright blueness as she had done just before the 747 plowed into the meadow. Maybe the bullets fired at her would merely pass through the empty air where she had been. But there was a chance that she was still not fully recovered, that she wasn't yet able to perform such a taxing feat, or even that she could perform it but would be mortally drained by it this time.

"Out the back!" Joe shouted. "Go, go!"

Nina raced to the door between the front room and the kitchen at the rear of the cabin.

Joe backed after her, keeping the pistol trained on the burning man, even though he didn't intend to use it.

Their only hope was that the boy's love of "fun" would give them the chance to get out of the cabin, into the open, where his ability to conduct remote viewing and to engage in mind control would be, according to Rose, severely diminished. If he gave up the toy that was Louis Tucker, he would be into Joe's head in an instant.

Tossing aside the butane match, with flames spreading along the sleeves of his shirt and down his pants, the boy-thing said, "Oh, yeah, oh, wow," and came after them.

Joe recalled too clearly the feeling of the ice-cold needle that had seemed to pierce the summit of his spine as he had barely escaped the Delmann house the previous night. That invading energy scared him more than the prospect of being embraced by the fiery arms of this shambling specter.

Frantically he retreated into the kitchen, slamming the door as he went, which was pointless because no door—no wall, no steel vault—could delay the boy if he abandoned Louis's body and went incorporeal.

Nina slipped out the back door of the cabin, and a wolf pack of wind, chuffing and puling, rushed past her and inside.

As Joe followed her into the night, he heard the living room door crash into the kitchen.

Behind the cabin was a small yard of dirt and natural bunch-grass. The air was full of wind-torn leaves, pine needles, grit. Beyond a redwood picnic table and four redwood chairs, the forest rose again.

Nina was already running for the trees, short legs pumping, sneakers slapping on the hard-packed earth. She thrashed through tall weeds at the perimeter of the woods and vanished in the gloom among the pines and birches.

Nearly as terrified of losing the girl in the wilds as he was frightened of the boy in the burning man, Joe sprinted between the trees, shouting the girl's name, one arm raised to ward off any pine boughs that might be drooping low enough to lash his eyes.

From the night behind him came Louis Tucker's voice, slurred by the damage that the spreading flames had already done to his lips but nevertheless recognizable, the chanted words of a childish challenge: "Here I come, here I come, here I come, ready or not, here I come, ready or not!"

A narrow break in the trees admitted a cascade of moonbeams, and Joe spotted the girl's cap of wind-whipped blond hair glowing with pale fire, the reflection of reflected light, to his right and only six or eight yards ahead. He stumbled over a rotting log, slipped on something slimy, kept his balance, flailed through prickly waist-high brush, and discovered that Nina had found the beaten-clear path of a deer trail.

As he caught up with the girl, the darkness around them abruptly brightened. Salamanders of orange light slithered up the trunks of the trees and whipped their tails across the glossy boughs of pines and spruces.

Joe turned and saw the possessed hulk of Louis Tucker thirty feet away, ablaze from head to foot but still standing, hitching and jerking through the woods, caroming from tree to tree, twenty feet away, barely alive, setting fire to the carpet of dry pine needles over which he shambled and to the bristling weeds and to the trees as he passed them. Now fifteen feet away. The stench of burning flesh on the wind. The boy-thing shouted gleefully, but the words were garbled and unintelligible.

Even in a two-hand grip, the pistol shook, but Joe squeezed off one, two, four, six rounds, and at least four of them hit the seething specter. It pitched backward and fell and didn't move, didn't even twitch, dead from fire and gunfire.

Louis Tucker was not a person now but a burning corpse. The body no longer harbored a mind that the boy could saddle and ride and torment.

Where?

Joe turned to Nina—and felt a familiar icy pressure at the back of his neck, an insistent probing, not as sharp as it had been when he was almost caught on the threshold of the Delmann house, perhaps blunted now because the boy's power was indeed diminishing here in the open.

But the psychic syringe was not yet blunt enough to be ineffective. It still stung. It pierced.

Joe screamed.

The girl seized his hand.

The iciness tore out its fangs and *flew* from him, as though it were a bat taking wing.

Reeling, Joe clamped a hand to the nape of his neck, certain that he would find his flesh ripped and bleeding, but he was not wounded. And his mind had not been violated, either.

Nina's touch had saved him from possession.

With a banshee shriek, a hawk exploded out of the high branches of a tree and dive-bombed the girl, striking at her head, pecking at her scalp, wings flapping, beak click-click-clicking. She screamed and covered her face with her hands, and Joe batted at the assailant with one arm. The crazed bird swooped up and away, but it wasn't an ordinary bird, of course, and it wasn't merely crazed by the wind and the churning fire that swelled rapidly through the woods behind them.

Here it came again, with a fierce *skreeeek*, the latest host for the visitant from Virginia, arrowing down through the moonlight, its rapier beak as deadly as a stiletto, too fast to be a target for the gun.

Joe let go of the pistol and dropped to his knees on the deer trail and pulled the girl protectively against him. Pressed her face against his chest. The bird would want to get at her eyes. Peck at her eyes. Jab-jab-jab through the vulnerable sockets at the precious brain beyond. Damage the brain, and her power cannot save her. Tear her specialness right out of her gray matter and leave her in spasms on the ground.

The hawk struck, sank one set of talons into the sleeve of Joe's coat, through the corduroy, piercing the skin of his forearm, planting the other set of talons in Nina's blond hair, wings drumming as it pecked her scalp, pecked, angry because her face was concealed. Pecking now at Joe's hand as he tried to knock it away, holding fast to sleeve and hair, determined not to be dislodged. Pecking, pecking at *his* face now, going for his eyes, Jesus, a flash of pain as it tore open his cheek. Seize it. Stop it. Crush it quickly. Peck, the darting head, the bloody beak, peck, and it got his brow this time, above his right eye, sure to blind him with the next thrust. He clenched his hand around it, and its talons tore at the cuff of his coat sleeve now, tore at his wrist, wings beating against his face, and it bobbed its head, the wicked beak darting at him, but he held it off, the hooked yellow point snapping an inch short of a blinding wound, the beady eyes glaring fiercely and blood-red with reflections of fire. Squeeze it, squeeze the life out of it, with its racing heart stuttering against his relentless palm. Its bones were thin and hollow, which made it light enough to fly with grace—but which also made it easier to break. Joe felt its breast crumple, and he threw it away from the girl, watched it tumble along the deer trail, disabled but still alive, wings flapping weakly but unable to lift into the night.

Joe pushed Nina's tangled hair away from her face. She was all right. Her eyes had not been hit. In fact, she was unmarked, and he was overcome by a rush of pride that he had prevented the hawk from getting at her.

Blood oozed from his slashed brow, around the curve of the socket, and into the corner of his eye, blurring his vision. Blood streamed from the wound in his cheek, dripped from his pecked and stinging hand, from his gouged wrist.

He retrieved the pistol, engaged the safety, and jammed the weapon under his waistband again.

From out of the surrounding woods issued a bleat of animal terror, which abruptly cut off, and then across the mountainside, over the howling of the wind, a sharp shriek sliced through the night. Something was coming.

Maybe the boy had gained more control of his talent during the year that Rose had been on the run, and maybe now he was more capable of remoting someone in the outdoors. Or perhaps the coalesced power of his psycho-geist was radiating away like the heat from a rock, as Rose had explained, but just wasn't dispersing fast enough to bring a quick end to this assault.

Because of the blustery wind and the express-train roar of the wildfire, Joe couldn't be certain from which direc-tion the cry had arisen, and now the boy, clothed in the flesh of his host, was coming silently.

Joe scooped the girl off the deer trail, cradling her in his arms. They needed to keep moving, and until his energy faded, he could move faster through the woods if he carried her than if he led her by the hand.

She was so small. He was scared by how small she was, nearly as breakable as the avian bones of the hawk.

She clung to him, and he tried to smile at her. In the hellish leaping light, his flaring eyes and strained grin were probably more frightening than reassuring.

The mad boy in his new incarnation was not the only threat they faced. The explosive Santa Ana wind threw bright rags, threw sheets, threw great billowing *sails* of fire across the flank of the mountain. The pines were dry from the hot rainless summer, their bark rich with turpen-tine, and they burst into flame as though they were made of gasoline-soaked rags.

Ramparts of fire at least three hundred feet across blocked the way back to the cabin. They could not get around the blaze and behind it, because it was spreading laterally faster than they could hike through the under-brush and across the rugged terrain.

At the same time, the fire was coming toward them. Fast.

Joe stood with Nina in his arms, riveted and dismayed by the sight of the towering wall of fire, and he realized that they had no choice but to abandon the car. They would have to make the trip out of the mountains entirely on foot.

With a hot *whoosh*, roiling gouts of wind-harried flames spewed through the treetops immediately overhead, like a deadly blast from a futuristic plasma weapon. The pine boughs exploded, and burning masses of needles and cones tumbled down through lower branches, igniting everything as they descended, and suddenly Joe and Nina were in a tunnel of fire.

He hurried with the girl in his arms, away from the cabin, along the narrow deer trail, remembering stories of people caught in California brushfires and unable to outrun them, sometimes not even able to *outdrive* them when the wind was particularly fierce. Maybe the flames couldn't accelerate through this density of trees as quickly as through dry brush. Or maybe the pines were even more accommodating fuel than mesquite and manzanita and grass.

Just as they escaped the tunnel of fire, more rippling flags of flames unfurled across the sky overhead, and again the treetops in front of them ignited. Burning needles swarmed down like bright bees, and Joe was afraid his hair would catch fire, Nina's hair, their clothes. The tunnel was growing in length as fast as they could run through it.

Smoke plagued him now. As the blaze rapidly intensified, it generated winds of its own, adding to the force of the Santa Anas, building toward a firestorm, and the blistering gales first blew tatters of smoke along the deer trail and then choking masses.

The cloistered path led upward, and though the degree of slope was not great, Joe became more quickly winded than he had expected. Incredible withering heat wrung oceans of sweat from him. Gasping for breath, sucking in the astringent fumes and greasy soot, choking, gagging, spitting out saliva thickened and soured by the flavor of the fire, desperately holding on to Nina, he reached a ridgeline.

The pistol under his waistband pressed painfully against his stomach as he ran. If he could have let go of Nina with one hand, he would have drawn the weapon and thrown it away. He was afraid that he was too weak to hold on to her with one arm, that he would drop her, so he endured the gouging steel.

As he crossed the narrow crest and followed the descending trail, he discovered that the wind was less furious on this side of the ridge. Even though the flames surged across the brow, the speed at which the fire line advanced now dropped enough to allow him to get out of the incendiary zone and ahead of the smoke, where the clean air was so sweet that he groaned at the cool, clear taste of it.

Joe was running on an adrenaline high, far beyond his normal level of endurance, and if not for the bolstering effect of panic, he might have collapsed before he topped the ridge. His leg muscles ached. His arms were turning to lead under the weight of the girl. They were not safe, however, so he kept going, stumbling and weaving, blinking tears of weariness out of his smoke-stung eyes, nevertheless pressing steadily forward—until the snarling coyote slammed into him from behind, biting savagely at the hollow of his back but capturing only folds of his corduroy jacket in its jaws.

The impact staggered him, eighty or ninety pounds of lupine fury. He almost fell facedown onto the trail, with Nina under him, except that the weight of the coyote, hanging on him, acted as a counterbalance, and he stayed erect.

The jacket ripped, and the coyote let go, fell away.

Joe skidded to a halt, put Nina down, spun toward the

predator, drawing the pistol from his waistband, thankful that he had not pitched it away earlier.

Backlighted by the ridgeline fire, the coyote confronted Joe. It was so like a wolf but leaner, rangier, with bigger ears and a narrower muzzle, black lips skinned back from bared fangs, scarier than a wolf might have been, especially because of the spirit of the vicious boy curled like a serpent in its skull. Its glowering eyes were luminous and yellow.

Joe pulled the trigger, but the gun didn't fire. He remembered the safety.

The coyote skittered toward him, staying low, quick but wary, snapping at his ankles, and Joe danced frantically backward to avoid being bitten, thumbing off the safety as he went.

The animal snaked around him, snarling, snapping, foam flying from its jaws. Its teeth sank into his right calf.

He cried out in pain, and twisted around, trying to get a shot at the damn thing, but it turned as he did, ferociously worrying the flesh of his calf until he thought he was going to pass out from the crackling pain that flashed like a series of electrical shocks all the way up his leg into his hip.

Abruptly the coyote let go and shrank away from Joe as if in fear and confusion.

Joe swung toward the animal, cursing it and tracking it with the pistol.

The beast was no longer in an attack mode. It whined and surveyed the surrounding night in evident perplexity.

With his finger on the trigger, Joe hesitated.

Tilting its head back, regarding the lambent moon, the coyote whined again. Then it looked toward the top of the ridge.

The fire was no more than a hundred yards away. The scorching wind suddenly accelerated, and the flames climbed gusts higher into the night.

The coyote stiffened and pricked its ears. When the fire surged once more, the coyote bolted past Joe and Nina, oblivious of them, and disappeared at a lope into the canyon below.

At last defeated by the draining vastness of these open spaces, the boy had lost his grip on the animal, and Joe sensed that nothing spectral hovered any longer in the woods.

The firestorm rolled at them again, blinding waves of flames, a cataclysmic tide breaking through the forest.

With his bitten leg, limping badly, Joe wasn't able to carry Nina any longer, but she took his hand, and they hurried as best they could toward the primeval darkness that seemed to well out of the ground and drown the ranks of conifers in the lower depths of the canyon.

He hoped they could find a road. Paved or graveled or dirt—it didn't matter. Just a way out, any sort of road at all, as long as it led away from the fire and would take them into a future where Nina would be safe.

They had gone no more than two hundred yards when a thunder rose behind them, and when he turned, fearful of another attack, Joe saw only a herd of deer galloping toward them, fleeing the flames. Ten, twenty, thirty deer, graceful and swift, parted around him and Nina with a thudding of hooves, ears pricked and alert, oil-black eyes as shiny as mirrors, spotted flanks quivering, kicking up clouds of pale dust, whickering and snorting, and then they were gone.

Heart pounding, caught up in a riot of emotions that he could not easily sort out, still holding the girl's hand, Joe started down the trail in the hoofprints of the deer. He took half a dozen steps before he realized there was no pain in his bitten calf. No pain, either, in his hawk-pecked hand or in his beak-torn face. He was no longer bleeding.

Along the way and in the tumult of the deers' passing, Nina had healed him.

18

On the second anniversary of the crash of Nationwide
Flight 353, Joe Carpenter sat on a quiet beach in Florida,
in the shade of a palm tree, watching the sea. Here, the
tides came to shore more gently than in California,
licking the sand with a tropical languor, and the ocean
seemed not at all like a machine.

He was a different man from the one who had fled the
fire in the San Bernardino Mountains. His hair was
longer now, bleached both by chemicals and by the sun.
He had grown a mustache as a simple disguise. His
physical awareness of himself was far greater than it had
been one year ago, so he was conscious of how differently he moved these days: with a new ease, with a
relaxed grace, without the tension and the coiled anger of
the past.

He possessed ID in a new name: birth certificate,
social security card, three major credit cards, a driver's
license. The forgers at Infiniface didn't actually forge
documents as much as use their computer savvy to
manipulate the system into spitting out *real* papers for
people who didn't actually exist.

He had undergone inner changes too, and he credited
those to Nina—though he continued to refuse the ulti-
mate gift that she could give him. She had changed him
not by her touch but by her example, by her sweetness

and kindness, by her trust in him, by her love of life and her love of him and her calm faith in the rightness of all things. She was only six years old but in some ways ancient, because if she was what everyone believed she was, then she was tied to the infinite by an umbilical of light.

They were staying with a commune of Infiniface members, those who wore no robes and left their heads unshaven. The big house stood back from the beach and was filled at almost any hour of the day with the soft clatter of computer keyboards. In a week or two, Joe and Nina would move on to another group, bringing them the gift that only this child could reveal, for they traveled continuously in the quiet spreading of the word. In a few years, when her maturing power made her less vulnerable, the time would arrive to tell the world.

Now, on this anniversary of loss, she came to him on the beach, under the gently swaying palm, as he had known she would, and she sat at his side. Currently her hair was brown. She was wearing pink shorts and a white top with Donald Duck winking on her chest—as ordinary in appearance as any six-year-old on the planet. She drew her knees up and encircled her legs with her arms, and for a while she said nothing.

They watched a big, long-legged sand crab move across the beach, select a nesting place, and burrow out of sight.

Finally she said, "Why won't you open your heart?"

"I will. When the time's right."

"When will the time be right?"

"When I learn not to hate."

"Who do you hate?"

"For a long time—you."

"Because I'm not your Nina."

"I don't hate you anymore."

"I know."

"I hate myself."

"Why?"

"For being so afraid."

"You're not afraid of anything," she said.

He smiled. "Scared to death of what you can show me."

"Why?"

"The world's so cruel. It's so hard. If there's a God, He tortured my father with disease and then took him young. He took Michelle, my Chrissie, my Nina. He allowed Rose to die."

"This is a passage."

"A damn vicious one."

She was silent for a while.

The sea whispered against the strand. The crab stirred, poked an eye stalk out to examine the world, and decided to move.

Nina got up and crossed to the sand crab. Ordinarily, these creatures were shy and scurried away when approached. This one did not run for cover but watched Nina as she dropped to her knees and studied it. She stroked its shell. She touched one of its claws, and the crab didn't pinch her.

Joe watched—and wondered.

Finally the girl returned and sat beside Joe, and the big crab disappeared into the sand.

She said, "If the world is cruel . . . you can help me fix it. And if that's what God wants us to do, then He's not cruel, after all."

Joe did not respond to her pitch.

The sea was an iridescent blue. The sky curved down to meet it at an invisible seam.

"Please," she said. "Please take my hand, Daddy."

She had never called him *daddy* before, and his chest tightened when he heard the word.

He met her amethyst eyes. And wished they were gray like his own. But they were not. She had come with him out of wind and fire, out of darkness and terror, and he supposed that he was as much her father as Rose Tucker had been her mother.

He took her hand.

And knew.

For a time he was not on a beach in Florida but in a bright blueness with Michelle and Chrissie and Nina. He did not see what worlds waited beyond this one, but he knew beyond all doubt that they existed, and the strangeness of them frightened him but also lifted his heart.

He understood that eternal life was not an article of faith but a law of the universe as true as any law of physics. The universe is an efficient creation: matter becomes energy; energy becomes matter; one form of energy is converted into another form; the balance is forever changing, but the universe is a closed system from which no particle of matter or wave of energy is ever lost. Nature not only loathes waste but forbids it. The human mind and spirit, at their noblest, can transform the material world for the better; we can even transform the human condition, lifting ourselves from a state of primal fear, when we dwelled in caves and shuddered at the sight of the moon, to a position from which we can contemplate eternity and hope to understand the works of God. Light cannot change itself into stone by an act of *will*, and stone cannot build itself into temples. Only the human spirit can act with volition and consciously change itself; it is the only thing in all creation that is not entirely at the mercy of forces outside itself, and it is, therefore, the most powerful and valuable form of energy in the universe. For a time, the spirit may become flesh, but when that phase of its existence is at an end, it will be transformed into a disembodied spirit once more.

When he returned from that brightness, from the blue elsewhere, he sat for a while, trembling, eyes closed, burrowed down into this revealed truth as the crab had buried itself in the sand.

In time he opened his eyes.

His daughter smiled at him. Her eyes were amethyst, not gray. Her features were not those of the other Nina whom he had loved so deeply. She was not, however, a pale fire, as she had seemed before, and he wondered how he could have allowed his anger to prevent him from seeing her as she truly was. She was a shining light, all but blinding in her brightness, as his own Nina had been—as are we all.

To contact The Compassionate Friends, a self-help organization offering friendship and understanding to bereaved parents and siblings, write or call:

The Compassionate Friends
National Office
P.O. Box 3696
Oak Brook, Illinois 60522-3696
(630) 990-0010